Shoot. Evie did not need *him* here now. But he was. She turned to find Reverend Brad standing in the tiny alcove between her and the door. Dressed in black, his thick blond hair combed back from his face, there was no missing the anger in his dark blue eyes, the impatience thinning his normally wide mouth. No telling herself he'd see this as a good thing. "What are you doing here?"

"Collecting my bride."

She tightened her grip on the bouquet of roses her mother had given her. Roses from her mother's prized bushes. The roses she'd always told Evie were going to bring her luck when she married the man she loved. "I've decided this is a bad idea."

"Your input is not required."

"I'm the bride." Nothing was going to happen without her cooperation.

Brad took a step forward. For all that he was reputed to be a man of God, there was a wild side to him. A dangerous edge lurking beneath the civilized facade he presented to the world.

PROMISES REVEAL

SARAH McCARTY

BERKLEY SENSATION, NEW YORK

THE BERKLEY PUBLISHING GROUP
Published by the Penguin Group
Penguin Group (USA) Inc.
375 Hudson Street, New York, New York 10014, USA
Penguin Group (Canada), 90 Eglinton Avenue East, Suite 700, Toronto, Ontario M4P 2Y3, Canada
(a division of Pearson Penguin Canada Inc.)
Penguin Books Ltd., 80 Strand, London WC2R 0RL, England
Penguin Group Ireland, 25 St. Stephen's Green, Dublin 2, Ireland (a division of Penguin Books Ltd.)
Penguin Group (Australia), 250 Camberwell Road, Camberwell, Victoria 3124, Australia
(a division of Pearson Australia Group Pty. Ltd.)
Penguin Books India Pvt. Ltd., 11 Community Centre, Panchsheel Park, New Delhi—110 017, India
Penguin Group (NZ), 67 Apollo Drive, Rosedale, North Shore 0632, New Zealand
(a division of Pearson New Zealand Ltd.)
Penguin Books (South Africa) (Pty.) Ltd., 24 Sturdee Avenue, Rosebank, Johannesburg 2196, South Africa

Penguin Books Ltd., Registered Offices: 80 Strand, London WC2R 0RL, England

PROMISES REVEAL

A Berkley Sensation Book / published by arrangement with the author

PRINTING HISTORY
Berkley Sensation mass-market edition / October 2008

Cover art by Aleta Rafton.
Cover design by George Long.
Interior text design by Laura K. Corless.

For information, address: The Berkley Publishing Group,
a division of Penguin Group (USA) Inc.,
375 Hudson Street, New York, New York 10014.

ISBN: 978-0-425-22419-9

BERKLEY® SENSATION
Berkley Sensation Books are published by The Berkley Publishing Group,
a division of Penguin Group (USA) Inc.,
375 Hudson Street, New York, New York 10014.
BERKLEY SENSATION and the "B" design are trademarks of Penguin Group (USA) Inc.

PRINTED IN THE UNITED STATES OF AMERICA

10 9 8 7 6 5 4 3 2 1

To Karen S., the Reverend's Lady of Ingenuity:
You always keep the torch burning bright
for your Alpha, and those who know you.
May that never change.

Promises Reveal

One

HE WAS STANDING on the wrong end of the shotgun.

Of all the ways the Reverend Brad Swanson thought he'd be trapped, this wasn't it. He'd imagined it often enough—a posse, a tree, a hanging noose. But this, well . . . he glanced behind the fat judge, who waited Bible in hand, to where Asa MacIntyre stood by the white satin-draped altar, the shotgun in his arms gleaming dully in the sun streaming through the large windows. He'd never seen this as his end. He shook his head. This was beyond imagining. Not only because he hadn't seen it coming, but because this had to be the first time a mother had ever seen him as fit husband material for her daughter.

"Don't bother trying to change your mind," Pearl warned in a voice too low to carry far.

Brad glanced toward the first pew of the full church to where Pearl Washington sat dressed up in her mother-of-the-bride best. From the glare she shot him from under the feather bobbing on the elaborate creation she called a hat, and the pat she gave the outline of the peashooter she called a gun in her reticule, she still wasn't believing his side of the story.

"I'm not changing my mind." *Just doubting the intelligence contained within.* How in hell had he let himself get trapped like this?

Pearl narrowed her eyes, packing as much menace as she could into the look. "Good."

Sugar cookies. He blamed his addiction to sugar cookies for the entire situation. If Pearl and her cohorts hadn't convinced him to slip them whiskey on a regular basis in exchange for the cookies, they might have believed his claim that he hadn't set his sights on Pearl's eccentric daughter, but apparently a minister who would supply the good women in town with the whiskey they requested for their meetings was considered capable of anything. Just another reminder that no good deed went unpunished.

In response to her threat, Brad gave Pearl a mocking smile that was guaranteed to piss her off. Her chin jerked up. The old satisfaction at getting under someone's skin perked—a minor pleasure in a day full of annoyance. He might be posing as a minister, but it was a thin veneer. Inside, he was the same outlaw he'd always been. In many ways the two-faced role of an upright preacher suited him. Kind of an ongoing joke between past and present. Between upbringing and choice. Still, considering it was saddling him with a wife, the joke just might be on him.

To his right his best man, Cougar McKinnely, cleared his throat. Cougar's half-Indian ancestry showed in the strong angles of his face and the darkness of his skin. His impatience showed in the jerk of his chin toward the back of the small church. Cougar's long, dark hair swung about his shoulder as he turned to look up the aisle. Beside him, his cousin Clint—equally big, equally dark, and with an equally disapproving expression on his face—turned with him. They were symbolically standing up for him now, but earlier, when the finger pointing in the wake of Evie's art show had worked up to its inevitable hysteria, both men—enemies turned friends—had sided with the Washingtons, putting the final nail in Brad's coffin. He didn't know why he'd expected differently, but he had. Which only went to show that faking respectability had gone and made him soft.

Over Judge Carlson's shoulder, Asa MacIntyre regarded him with the same threat as the rifle cradled in his arms. Somehow, Pearl had pressed him into her side of the dispute. Or maybe it had been Cougar or Clint. Or maybe the man just had reasons of his own. There was no telling with MacIntyre. He went his own way, made up his own mind. Brad probably should be grateful the man hadn't decided to just plug him for messing with an innocent. That's what Brad would have done.

That was what galled the most about Asa's defection, Brad decided. Brad might be a lot of things, but he didn't hurt women, and the only mercy he had for men who did was a bullet through the heart. Asa knew that, was cut from the same cloth, yet he'd taken the Washingtons' side.

Taking a slow breath, Brad ran his fingers through his hair. Hell, since when did he care if the men around him believed him? *In* him? As long as they followed orders and didn't land him on the working end of a noose during a job, he'd always been satisfied.

The organ music began, launching into the long treble that heralded the beginning of his wedding. Asa arched an eyebrow at him. Brad resisted the urge to flip him off. His minister image had lost enough of its shine, and since his best bet for survival was still to hide in plain sight, he couldn't afford to let it slip further. Even if it meant marrying a woman totally inappropriate to a man in his role.

Taking another breath, he turned and faced the music. Good people from the town filled the pews. People he'd come to know better than he'd planned. He was used to seeing smiles on their faces, but right now all he was looking at was a sea of disapproval under the illusion of gaiety provided by the sprays of wildflowers tied to the pews with streams of ribbons that blew gently in the breeze from the open windows. The organ music stopped and started again, holding the last note, prolonging the dramatic moment. Everyone looked to the back. Wood creaked, voices murmured. The bride didn't show.

"If your luck holds, Rev, the bride just might not put in an appearance."

Brad cut Cougar a glare. He knew damn well his luck had never been that good. "That would only make things worse."

"Can't see how they can get much worse than a minister taking advantage of a sweet innocent like Evie Washington," Jerome muttered from the second row. Franny, his wife of forty-some years, covered his hand.

"I've gotta admit that's a scandal, for sure." The apology in her tone didn't make up for her support of the case against him.

"The Reverend Swanson is a good man. I don't believe for a minute he took advantage of Evie." All heads turned as Jenna McKinnely stood up, looking like a Rubenesque angel with her blonde hair pulled back in a long braid and those big blue eyes looking at him with determination. Her adopted daughter, Bri, a small bundle of white, squirmed for freedom on her hip. "And neither should any of you. He's our minister. He deserves our support."

Thank God for Jenna's sweet nature and belief in the innate

goodness of people. She was the only one who didn't see this as a disaster. She was probably the only one on his side. And all because he'd answered "No" when she'd asked if he'd taken advantage of Evie. As if his word was good for anything.

"Then how do you explain the painting?" Jerome asked.

"I can't explain what I haven't seen."

Hardly anyone had seen that painting. Pearl, Evie's uncle Paul, and Doc were the only ones. A fact for which Brad was profoundly grateful.

Jerome thumped the wooden floor with his cane. "I'm thinking you don't have the right end of this particular stick, Jenna, and should just stay out of it."

Next to Brad, Clint stirred the way he always did when someone focused on Jenna, pulling up to his full six foot two inches of height, an unnatural stillness surrounding him. "Did you just call my wife a liar, Jerome?"

A pew creaked, and a boy as dark as the McKinnelys got to his feet. Gray, the McKinnelys' adopted son. Eleven years old, with the promise of size in his bones, and damn near feral—especially when it came to Jenna. He'd killed for her once, saving her life. Brad didn't doubt he'd do it again. Apparently, neither did Jenna. Jenna grabbed Gray's arm. Not a muscle in his body relaxed and not once did he take his eyes off Jerome. In the last couple of months, since he'd been with the McKinnelys, Gray had started settling into being civilized, but he was a long way from tame.

Jenna glared at her husband. "Clint, this is a wedding."

"I'm aware of that."

She glanced pointedly at Gray. "Arguing is not good manners at a wedding."

"Neither is another man giving my wife orders and calling her a liar."

"I didn't call her a liar."

Gray jerked his arm free. Jenna stumbled on her bad leg. The boy steadied her immediately. She leaned against his shoulder, holding him with emotion when strength wouldn't do it.

"For the love of Pete, Clint!" Jerome snorted, rapping his cane again. "Who would want to hurt Jenna's feelings that way?"

Clint studied Jenna's face, searching, Brad knew, for any sign that her feelings were hurt. "No one in his right mind, for sure."

Whatever Clint saw in Jenna's expression seemed to satisfy him. He relaxed. Gray didn't. Those too old eyes scanned the room, looking for more threats. The boy was a powder keg waiting to explode and there were two things guaranteed to set him off. A slight to his sister or his adoptive mother. If it wasn't for the fact that the overprotectiveness of the McKinnelys toward Jenna had spread to the townsfolk, he'd probably be behind bars for murder. The tension within the room escalated.

With almost desperate fervor, the organ again landed on the starting note, holding it until it reverberated down Brad's spine. Everyone turned to face the back. No bride appeared.

Jenna smiled encouragingly over her shoulder at Brad. "I'm sure she's just having trouble with her dress."

Only Jenna would worry that the groom's feelings were hurt at a shotgun wedding. Then again, only a McKinnely would be perverse enough to sit on the groom's side of the church because "It wasn't right that everyone jumped to conclusions" when the whole town was feeling like assembling a castration party.

And where one McKinnely went, they all went, so instead of his side of the church being a glaring testament to his outcast status, the pews were filled with McKinnelys and their friends. Cougar's wife, Mara, sat beside Cougar's aunt and uncle, Doc and Dorothy. Mara waved her fingers at Brad in open support. If Jenna was sweetness and light, Mara was pure fire. A good match for her uncompromising husband. One would think a woman Mara's size would be cowed by a look from Cougar, but all his glaring accomplished was bringing Mara's stubborn side to the fore. Their clashes of will were the stuff of town legend. Not because they ever got violent, but because both were intelligent and liked to get their way and it was never a sure thing who would win. It was for sure, however, that there'd be some laughs along the way.

If they'd start one of their infamous discussions about now, Brad would appreciate it. He could use the distraction. He was hiding in plain sight, not auditioning for a traveling show.

A baby cried in the next pew back. Elizabeth, Asa's wife, crooned to their daughter Tempest. From the primness of her dress and the perfection of her hair one would think Elizabeth a very proper woman, but a person would be better served taking their cue from the tendrils of brown hair escaping from her bun and the mischief in her green eyes when deciding her personality. Elizabeth MacIntyre was as wild as the crew that'd come through Cheyenne laying the tracks for the railroad. And as good at stirring up trouble. Beside her, Millie pulled a bottle from a basket, popped the cork, and dipped her finger in the contents before rubbing them over the baby's gums. Tempest stopped fussing and smiled. Millicent dipped her finger again.

"That'll be enough, Millicent."

Millicent, being Millicent, just snorted at Asa's order with the confidence of a woman on the back side of fifty who'd successfully made her way in a man's world and applied the brandy again. "The good Lord doesn't want this sweet thing hurting."

"He doesn't want her drunk in church either."

"She's not drunk."

That was from Elizabeth.

Asa frowned. "For sure, she's getting happy."

Millicent frowned and rubbed gently at the tiny gums. "Happy is good. You don't want her crying, do you?"

Asa grunted. "Do me a favor. At least keep her this side of sotted."

Elizabeth smiled at Asa as if the man's weakness when it came to his daughter was a good thing. "I can probably manage that."

"Good."

Brad smothered a chuckle. Asa zeroed in on the sound with the ruthlessness he hadn't shown when his daughter was being soothed with spirits. "For a man who is being stood up, while standing at the altar with a shotgun pointed at him, you've sure got a lot to say on things that don't concern you."

"I think the feeding of spirits to an infant is a concern to all righteous citizens," Judge Carlson interrupted.

Brad had had enough. "Shut up."

The arrogant bastard might be the only one available to marry him to Evie, but it didn't give him the right to inflict his views on the rest of the wedding party.

Asa shifted the rifle to a more active grip, the grey of his eyes reflecting the steel of the gun. "You stole the words from my mouth."

Carlson thumped his Bible against his thigh. "I won't be spoken to like this. I am a member—"

Growing up, Brad had had a bellyful of men like the judge.

Self-righteous prigs who used their standing to bully everyone around them. Stepping up onto the altar, he moved close enough that he could smell the man's pomade. "What you're a member of does not give you the right to come into *my* town and criticize *my* people."

Carlson sneered. "The same people sitting here in church railroading you into a marriage you don't want?"

Brad didn't flinch. He knew what he was. "The same."

"Judge, I'd shut the hell up if I were you," Cougar offered in that quiet voice that served as a warning to all sensible enough to hear it.

It didn't have any effect on Carlson. "Or what? You'll gut me?" He sniffed. "I know your reputation, breed, and I'll have you know I'm not impressed with it or the pardon the governor gave you."

An angry growl came from the pews.

"How dare you!" Jenna gasped. "Clint?"

Cocking an eyebrow at his normally gentle wife, Clint asked, "Want me to flatten him, sunshine?"

"Yes!"

"If he won't, I will," Mara bit off, working her way out of the pews, her red brown hair catching the light in flashes of fire. Behind her, Gray followed protectively, his knife gleaming against the black of his shirt. He loved his aunt as much as he loved his mother, and he worshipped his uncle—the man Carlson had just insulted.

Clint towered over the judge. "It'd be my pleasure."

Son of a bitch, his wedding was turning into a brawl. Brad caught Mara's hand as she came alongside. With a careful twist, mindful of the delicacy of her build, he removed the knife tucked into her hand. "Not today, Mara."

She didn't look away from the judge. Fury vibrated in the muscles under his grip. "Why not? He just insulted my husband."

"Because I'm reasonably sure it's bad luck to start a wedding with bloodshed."

She looked up at him, cheeks flushed with outrage, her cinnamon brown eyes narrowed. "Well, shoot."

"Will it soothe your sensibilities if he apologizes?"

"Maybe."

"Apologize, Judge."

"For speaking the truth?"

An ugly murmur went through the wedding guests. Pews creaked and floorboards groaned as men got to their feet. A baby wailed.

It was a wonder someone hadn't killed the fool long before now. Brad gritted his teeth. "We don't take kindly to strangers coming in here insulting one of our valued citizens."

"I'm not a stranger. I'm a respected judge—"

"You're going to have to trot out some proof on that 'respected' claim," Clint interrupted.

Carlson continued as if he hadn't heard, "In the circuit court of these United States—"

Brad grabbed his shoulder and hauled him around so he was staring square at the crowd. "What you're going to be is a dead man if you don't apologize and then shut up. Cougar is one of ours."

Carlson's gaze followed his. His face paled as he looked at the wedding guests. Brad couldn't blame him. They did look more like a lynch mob than a wedding party.

Carlson's "I'm sorry, McKinnely" was grudging, but at least it gave Brad something to work with. Brad cocked a brow at Mara. "Good enough for you?"

She held out her hand for the knife. "For now."

Cougar snagged the knife from Brad's hand before he could hand it back. "I wouldn't do that." With a jerk of his chin, he indicated Mara's mutinous expression. "*For now* is a rather unspecific term."

Mara stamped her foot. "Darn it, Cougar!"

The smile on Cougar's face was gentle. He stroked the back of his fingers down his wife's cheek. His skin was very dark against hers, the size of his hand emphasizing the differences between them. Where Cougar was tall and big boned, Mara was tiny and slight. "I appreciate the thought, Angel, but it's nothing I haven't heard before."

"You shouldn't have to listen to garbage like that from men like him."

"It's not important."

She opened her mouth to argue. Cougar bent his head, silencing her in the oldest way known to man, his long hair falling around them, hiding the kiss from view, but nothing could hide the passion and trust that had Mara stepping in to lean against his much bigger body. She'd come a long way from the shattered woman who'd once struggled so hard to rebuild her life.

There was a time Brad might have set his cap for the ex-prostitute, but Mara had been Cougar's since the day she'd seen him. He'd never stood a chance, and he wasn't one to fight pointless battles. Cougar raised his hand and touched the corner of Mara's mouth with his thumb. All the love in the world was in that fleeting caress. "You're all that matters to me."

There wasn't a soul in the room that didn't believe it.

She blinked. The hard line of Cougar's mouth softened as tears welled in her eyes. "Gray, take your aunt back to her seat."

Gray took Mara's arm. Brad couldn't resist. The kid was too damn young to always believe the worst. "Killing isn't always the answer."

The twitch of the boy's lips could have been a smile. He looked a lot like Cougar in that moment. "It would be better that you tell my aunt this."

"I was hoping you'd be more open to the idea."

He shrugged. Brad sighed as he watched him walk away. The kid had the world by the tail if he would open his eyes to see it.

Clint clapped his hand on his shoulder. "Thanks."

Brad shook his head. "He's packing a lot of anger."

"With reason, but he'll get through it."

"Hopefully sooner rather than later." Cougar sighed before looking up. "The rest of you take your seats, too. We've got a wedding to witness."

"Not without a bride," Jerome offered in his overly helpful way. The tension evaporated in a flurry of chuckles. Pearl frowned and called to her brother. There wasn't an answer, just a bit more commotion. Mara resumed her seat. The chuckles grew to laughter, highlighting the farce the wedding had become. But if Evie thought she'd leave him here as the laughingstock, she had another think coming. Brad nodded to the judge.

"Excuse me. I'll just go check on things."

Pearl stood as he reached her side, the reticule clutched tightly in her hand. He met her glare with one of his own. "You'll get your damn wedding."

Or hear from her own daughter's lips why it wouldn't be taking place.

Pearl rapped his hand with her fan. The feather on her hat bobbed in his face. "You can't swear in church."

Mara huffed. "Seems to me the good Lord will make excuses for a man being stood up at the altar."

"Angel," Cougar warned. "Now is not the time."

"I can't think of a better one."

Cougar shook his head. "Not now."

Mara's fingers tightened on the back of the pew. "Would you be forbidding me, Cougar?"

"Sounded like it to me," Brad offered, feeding the light of battle in Mara's eyes.

"Aren't you in enough trouble, Rev?"

No one could tuck a challenge into a smile like Cougar. Brad smiled right back. "Nah. I can always fit in a little more."

The other man nodded, his muscles taking on a certain tension that every man recognized as preparation. "That's obliging of you."

"I try."

Millie stood, garishly attractive in her bright purple dress that clashed with her equally bright red hair. "Boys, don't make me go get my spoon." Millie wielded her giant wooden spoon like other men wielded a knife—with devastating efficiency.

"No need to fetch anything. The Rev and I are just working our way to an understanding."

"I'm not going to take kindly to anyone who throws Millie off her cooking," Asa cut in.

"You're welcome to join in," Brad invited.

The judge took a step back and snapped his Bible closed. "I came to officiate a wedding, not a brawl."

"One more step, Judge, and you'll be sitting on a butt full of birdshot."

"You get blood on that satin, Asa MacIntyre, and I'm going to take it out of your hide," Dorothy warned.

Asa cut the judge a glance. "Don't bleed when I plug you." With a lift of his brow he asked, "Satisfied, Dorothy?"

"Of course she's not satisfied," Doc called, his hair, as always, standing on end. "She's never satisfied until she gets to the crying part."

"Ain't that the truth," Jerome chimed in. "My Franny's the

same way. Had to have just the right handkerchief to bring today. Even made me pack a clean one of mine as a spare."

"Ain't no one going to get to the crying if the bride don't show."

"Except maybe the Reverend," Cyrus muttered. "Heard tell the girl's uncle's got a noose waiting out back. That's got to be a better show than this."

A murmur of agreement went through the guests. Just the mention of a noose made Brad's skin crawl. "No one's getting hanged." He glared at the judge. "Stay."

"You're in no position to give me orders."

The man was a pompous ass. It was easy to see why Elizabeth despised him. "Asa?"

"What?"

"If he moves, plug him."

"Will do."

He met Carlson's alarmed gaze. "Satisfied with my position now?"

A nod was his answer.

"Good."

Another murmur went through the crowd as Brad headed down the aisle. He was probably acting out of character. Brad didn't care.

"My Evie wouldn't stand you up," Pearl called from behind him.

Pearl didn't have a clue what her Evie would do. The woman's daughter was mustang wild, chaffing under every societal dictate, to the point that her behavior was all but a plea for someone to take her in hand. If it hadn't been for the role he was playing, Brad probably already would have. A woman with a wild side that persistent was a real draw.

He headed for the heavy wooden door leading to the alcove. Footsteps sounded behind him. He'd heard them stalking him too many times to mistake to whom they belonged. "Don't say it, Asa."

"Don't say what?"

Asa had a razor-sharp wit and he wielded it with lethal skill. His hand beat Brad's to the door, holding it closed.

"Whatever irritating thing you're thinking of saying, I'm not in the mood."

"I recognize you're pissed, Rev, and for good reason, but don't be taking it out on the girl."

"Get the hell out of my way."

"This isn't her fault."

An elbow in Asa's gut drove him back a step. Brad wrenched the door open. "Then whose fault is it?"

"THIS IS MY fault." Evie sat on the hard wooden bench and plucked a petal off a rose in her bouquet.

Her uncle sighed. "No denying that, baby. If you'd only added a pair of pants to that painting, none of us would be here."

Uncle Paul was always the soul of logic, which made his going along with this wedding not make any sense. "I just don't understand how anyone could think that portrait is of the Reverend."

"It's a very detailed portrait."

"But I didn't include his face."

"Just that scar on his thigh he got last fall at the barn raising."

"That was artistic embellishment!"

"Darn familiar embellishment."

Evie didn't like the tone of his voice. Her uncle couldn't be thinking what everyone else thought. "What are you saying?"

"He's saying you were damn foolish."

There was no mistaking that voice, tight with the edge of anger.

Shoot. Evie did not need *him* here now. But he was. She turned to find the Reverend Brad standing in the tiny alcove between her and the door. Dressed in black, his thick blond hair combed back from his face, there was no missing the anger in his dark blue eyes, the impatience thinning his normally wide mouth. No telling herself he'd see this as a good thing. "What are you doing here?"

"Collecting my bride."

She tightened her grip on the bouquet of roses her mother had given her. Roses from her mother's prized bushes that she'd brought all the way from Missouri as a bride. The roses she'd always told Evie were going to bring her luck when she married the man she loved. "I've decided this is a bad idea."

"Your input is not required."

"I'm the bride." Nothing was going to happen without her cooperation.

Brad took a step forward. Her uncle stood. Uncle Paul was a good-sized man but the Reverend Brad dwarfed him, and for all that Brad was reputed to be a man of God, there was a wild side to him. A dangerous edge lurking beneath the civilized facade he presented to the world. She'd spent a year trying to capture that illusive edge on canvas and had never managed it. It just figured it would show itself now when her sketch pad was at her mother's house and there wasn't a charcoal in sight. Her luck had been on a downturn for the last six months. Hitching back in the seat until the wall was at her back, she deferred to her uncle. Sometimes propriety was useful, especially for avoiding confrontation.

"Uncle? Could you please handle this?"

"Of course."

Brad took another step forward, closing the distance between them, never taking his gaze from hers. Her chest tightened the way that it did whenever the Reverend focused his attention on her. "She's not yours to handle anymore."

That had an ominous ring to it.

"You're not married yet."

"All but, thanks to your wanting to marry her off so badly you jumped on a rumor like a June bug on a candle."

That was not a pretty analogy. Evie waited for her uncle to dispute the claim. He didn't.

"The picture spoke clearly."

"The picture barely grunted, but you let your niece run so wild you didn't know how to rein her in, so you decided marrying her off to me would restore the respectability she tossed away." Brad nodded slightly, causing his hair to fall over his forehead. "After all, who's more upright than the minister?"

The mocking twist to Brad's mouth did nothing to reduce his good looks, but it did add to the sense of danger coming off him. Evie's fingers itched to capture the angle of his brow that so expressively conveyed his displeasure. She was so busy studying his face, she didn't realize he'd grabbed her arm until his fingers wrapped around her wrist like manacles—hard and unbreakable.

Shoot. She needed to pay better attention.

The protest she expected from her uncle at Brad's high-handedness didn't come. Instead, Uncle Paul looked at her, his weary expression dosed with apology. "You do right by her."

"Or what?" Brad countered. "You'll bring me back in line the way you did her?"

That was entirely too much. Evie yanked on her wrist. "I was never out of line!"

She had Brad's full attention. His blue eyes were as cold as winter ice. "Woman, you've been running amok for years, but that's over."

She didn't want it to be over. She wanted the small freedoms from society's dictates that she'd fought for. Wanted more. Ignoring his anchoring grip, she set the bouquet carefully on the bench beside her. "I've decided I'm not going to marry you."

Brad didn't even blink. "You don't have a choice."

"Of course I do." She just needed time to talk it over with her uncle. He always gave her what she wanted. Eventually. And she did not want to marry this hard-souled, handsome-faced person who stood as a man of God, but looked in league with the devil. "Tell him, Uncle Paul. Tell him I don't have to marry him."

For the first time in as long as she could remember, her uncle avoided her gaze. A foreign sense of panic gathered in her stomach. "Uncle?"

"It's time you were settled."

Nothing in his expression moved as he said those horrible words.

"You can't mean that!"

Satin rustled a much quieter protest than what was screaming inside her as Brad's grip on her arm tightened.

"In case you haven't figured it out yet, princess, people only love you when it's convenient."

She refused to look at him, focusing all her attention on her uncle. Her ace in the hole. "That's not true."

"Then you tell me why your uncle is standing over there, giving you to me on the flimsiest of excuses?"

Her uncle jerked up straight. "It was a painting of you naked, Swanson. I think that says all that needs to be said."

"You keep telling yourself, but that doesn't make it the truth. It's not a painting of *me* naked, and you damn well know it, because I'm willing to bet your niece told you so."

Evie had, but she hadn't been that vehement, mostly because she hadn't wanted anyone to ask how she'd known what to sketch when it came to his privates. One whiff of what she'd been up to in pursuit of her art, and her uncle would have sent her back East to her maiden aunt. That woman defined bitter and was definitely a believer in the traditional. She'd even threatened her once with a chastity belt, obviously sharing the common opinion that women who painted anything but still lifes of insipid flowers were loose. "I did tell you."

"While not looking me in the eye," her uncle scoffed.

"I'll look you in the eye now."

"*Now* is too late," Brad growled. "*Now* everyone thinks I molest innocents. *Now* everyone is wondering if I live by the rules that I preach. My reputation will be ruined if we don't wed."

"People in town know you too well to believe that."

Brad snorted, pulling her away from the bench. "I think the fact that we're standing here in church with the judge waiting down the aisle says pretty clearly what this town is willing to believe."

What could she say? He was right. The good townspeople who relied on him for direction had been very eager to believe the worst of him. So eager, she hadn't really had to lie at all, just look embarrassed, and they'd run with their assumption and made it truth. She just hadn't expected them to latch onto the idea of a wedding so strongly that she couldn't talk them out of it once the initial excitement faded. "I'm sorry."

"A hell of a lot of good your sorries will do us now."

She bit her lip. "I'll tell the truth."

"The time for the truth was a month ago."

In retrospect it was. If she had ever dreamed that her uncle would want to get rid of her this badly, or that he would force her to marry a man who he had to know hadn't compromised her, she would have screamed the truth from the rooftops. Heck, she never would have showed her family the painting. She tried again. "Uncle, we need to end this."

"Some things can't be ended that easily, baby."

The endearment was much softer this time, but heavy with the love it carried. Love that would make her normally indulgent uncle do what he saw as his duty by her, leaving her caught in the trap of her own making. The bait had been her freedom. The price paid was Brad's. "It can't be this complicated."

"Trust me," Brad growled. "It hasn't even begun to be complicated."

"Now see here, Reverend," her uncle huffed. "When questions were asked, you didn't defend yourself."

"If I remember correctly, at the time two men were holding my arms while you pounded your fists into my stomach. I couldn't seem to catch my breath to answer."

Evie hadn't known that. "Uncle Paul, you didn't!"

She didn't need to hear Brad's snort to know it was the truth. That was written in her uncle's frown. She took a step back, bumping into Brad's side.

"You know I don't hold with violence."

"Quite frankly, when I found out you had been cavorting with a naked man, I didn't find myself caring that much for your idiotic suffragette preachings. Free—" His rant came to a sudden halt.

Evie didn't need him to finish. She'd heard it more times than she could count.

She yanked her arm out of Brad's hold and slapped the bouquet against her thigh. "I believe *free love* is the term you were searching for."

Uncle Paul scowled. "I'll not have you spouting such filth in the church."

"It's not filth. It's a development that's long overdue. Women should have the same freedom as men, including the right to fornicate, *if they want to*."

Uncle Paul's face turned florid, as it did every time she mentioned choice. He always got stuck on the right rather than on the desire. Truth was, it was a rare man who attracted her. And since the Reverend had come to town, he'd been the only one who'd tempted her. And maybe if he hadn't been a minister she might have explored the possibility of that attraction and the depth of her belief in the right to explore it, but he *was* a minister and the very symbol of all things proper, so she'd kept her fascination in check. She didn't do well with proper.

"It's filth and rubbish, and I regret the day your mother let you take up correspondence with *that woman*."

That woman was a famed suffragist. "Anna Dickinson is a very intelligent woman who makes excellent points regarding the inequities in our society, particularly when it comes to women."

Her uncle's jaw knotted. His hands clenched into fists. For

the first time in her life, Evie actually feared he might hit her. Brad's arm wrapped around her waist and pulled her into his side. With a warning squeeze that she assumed translated into "shut up," he shoved her behind him.

"Aren't you glad her ideas are now mine to deal with?"

Though she couldn't see him any more, her uncle's shaky breath clearly indicated the level of his struggle to hold his temper. "You still intend to marry her?"

As if she were some sort of unpleasant burden to be unloaded, not a woman with a perfectly good brain and ideas of her own. Why did that attitude continue to hurt her? "Uncle Paul—"

Brad cut her off. "We both know there's no choice. Not if I want to continue living here."

She poked him in the back. "Thanks."

His eyes glittered at her over his shoulder. "You're welcome."

Her uncle sighed. "She's a little spoiled."

"I'd say more than a little."

"It's possible Pearl and I were too lenient once my brother died. It didn't seem right to be too harsh with her once she'd lost her father."

This was ridiculous. Evie ducked under Brad's arm in time to see her uncle's shrug.

"I'm afraid we indulged her."

It sounded a lot like her uncle was apologizing to Brad for the parts of her personality she happened to like. "I'm not ashamed of who I am."

"Perhaps you should be." Uncle Paul sighed again.

"Why?" she snapped, guilt that she couldn't be what he wanted melding with frustration, giving birth to anger. "Because I don't see why I should pretend that I don't have an opinion and should spend my life as some man's chattel?"

Brad's response was a shake of his head as he pushed her through the door. She stumbled and spun around. She only had a glimpse of his face through the crack. His expression did not warm the cockles of her heart. It merely solidified her conviction that the Reverend was a hard man. Just before he closed it, he said, "Because you don't know when to be quiet."

Two

MAYBE SHE DIDN'T know when to be quiet. Ten minutes later, Evie stood with the Reverend by her side, listening to the judge saying the words that bound them together and debating the point. If she'd spoken up earlier, this might have been prevented. If she'd shut up sooner, rather than espousing her beliefs, her uncle and her mother might not have come to the decision that a good, solid husband like the Reverend was the solution to their problems. That was a whole lot of mights. There was no doubt, from a physical standpoint, that her fiancé was perfect. She was a tall woman and used to looking men in the eye with little effort, but the Reverend stood a good head taller than her five foot seven inches, and from the set of his shoulders and the square of his jaw it was easy to believe the story that he'd almost beaten a man to death.

Not that anyone had seen anything wrong with that at the time. Mark had to have been crazy to whip Jenna McKinnely, but many had still doubted the Reverend's ability to be so violent, even when morally outraged. Everyone except Evie.

Evie hadn't been surprised that the Reverend Brad was capable of such violence. There was something about the man that just seemed more outlaw than God-fearing. He was fascinating, masculine, and compelling, but he was also more than he appeared, deeper than he let on. He was a mystery, and over the last year he'd come to fascinate her. To the point that she had sketchbooks full of his portraits. And when that hadn't gotten her the answers she sought, she'd painted him. In church, out of church, and eventually, out of his clothes. And then she'd put it on display. Because she'd thought it would prove a point. She sighed. Fat lot of good that had done.

Judge Carlson interrupted her musings. "Do you, Evie Washington, take the Reverend Brad Swanson as your lawfully wedded husband?"

Did she? An illogical thrill of excitement went through her when common sense said all she should be feeling was dread. Not that she was surprised. Nothing about how she reacted to Brad made sense. She didn't like it and she didn't know what to do with any of it—the good feelings or the bad.

"That's your signal to either speak up or walk away," Asa murmured from behind the judge.

The creaking of the pews indicated the interest of everyone else. They were all waiting for her. Well, they could wait a little longer. Evie hadn't made up her mind yet.

"Shut up, MacIntyre," Brad snapped.

There it was again. That flash of unconventionality. She glanced up at Brad. Nothing in his profile gave a clue to what he wanted. Did he want her to speak up or walk away?

"There's no need to be rude at a wedding."

He turned in her direction. "I thought the shotguns were setting the rules."

"I prefer to think of them as ornamentation."

For a second there was no change in his expression. Then the corner of his mouth twitched. "You have an unconventional way of looking at things."

"It's probably from being on the shelf so long."

"You are a bit long in the tooth."

Twenty-five was not that old! "You can always throw me back."

He shrugged. "It's time I married. Might as well be you as anyone else."

That was a deliberate goad. She bared her teeth in a smile. "I'll try to live up to your low expectations."

"I think everyone's taking bets on that."

They were betting on her success as a wife?

"Who holds the bet that I brain you with the frying pan before breakfast?"

Clint leaned back and said behind Cougar's back, "That'd be me."

Clint was a handsome man, but not handsome enough for her to forgive him for the chuckle that rippled through the church. "Then I'll be sure to lambast him before dessert."

"I'd sure appreciate it if you would," a man with sun-streaked blond hair called from the first pew.

Brad muttered something under his breath. "Shut up, Jackson."

"If we're going to be influencing the outcome, I'd be grateful if you could see your way to belting him before the wedding cake," Doc called.

"You bet on a wedding?" Dorothy exclaimed.

"Heck no! I'm betting on the demise."

The truth hit Evie. They expected her to fail as a wife. No one in the town thought much of her ways, she knew that, but she'd never thought they'd actually wish her ill.

"After only a few hours?" she asked, burying the hurt.

"The Reverend is the provoking sort."

"He's a man of God!"

"With a provoking side," Doc argued.

There was no disputing that. Shifting her bouquet in her grip, Evie glanced up at her soon-to-be husband. He was staring straight ahead. Laugh lines fanned out from the corners of his eyes, as if this was all a big joke. As if maybe she was a joke.

"People don't think a whole lot of you," she told him with a great deal of satisfaction.

He cut her a glance. "You sure it's me they're doubting?"

No. "Of course."

The laugh lines deepened. "Don't think too highly of yourself, do you?"

She sighed. Being different did come with a price. Often the respect of others, but that was a small amount to pay for the pleasure of respecting herself. "Some days not as much as I should."

That got his attention. His eyes were very blue in the afternoon light. Very observant. "Why?"

"Lack of moral fortitude."

"The one thing you don't lack is fortitude."

But maybe he thought she lacked morals? She couldn't find an answer in his expression.

The judge, apparently feeling she'd debated enough, rapped out in that aggravatingly officious way of his, "Young lady, I'm waiting on an answer."

The man clearly didn't approve of her. She didn't care. "You can wait a minute more." Turning back to Brad, she asked, "Did you place any bets?"

"A man of God doesn't gamble."

If the laugh lines weren't still there, she might have taken him seriously. "A man of God doesn't land front and center at a shotgun wedding either."

"True enough."

"So?"

"I already answered."

"That was an evasion."

"Yup."

"That's all? Just 'yup'?"

"The time for discussion, young lady, was before you disrobed with this man," the judge intoned pompously.

Who was this fat prig to lecture her? She rounded on him. "Land of Goshen! If you're going to vilify me, get your facts right." She pointed to Brad. "He was the one naked!"

"Evie!" her mother gasped over a bark of laughter. From the guffaws that filled the shocked silence, everyone in the church had heard her gaffe. Evie wanted to scream at them to shut up, instead she glared at Brad.

"Now see what you did?"

His left eyebrow cocked up. "You're the one announcing to the world that you had your way with me."

"I did not."

"Sure sounded like it to me," the judge interrupted.

"That's because you look for the bad in people."

The judge drew himself to his full height, jowls jiggling. "I don't have to look far to know the shame of this situation."

She gasped. How dare he? Brad's hand circled her upper arm, holding her back.

"You want to repeat that, Carlson?"

"The girl is—"

The judge stumbled forward under the force of Asa's cuff to the back of his head. "The girl is the Reverend's affianced."

Evie had the satisfaction of seeing Carlson's face turn white as he realized the McKinnelys, along with Asa, were frowning at him. It didn't pay to annoy that bunch.

"I was just saying—"

"You weren't saying anything except 'will you take this man.' "

Brad was still talking in that quiet voice, but Evie knew she wasn't the only one who heard the threat in it. There was a murmur of approval from the guests. And a sputter of belated concern from the judge, followed by the most horrific advice.

"A woman like Miss Washington needs a strong hand applied on a daily basis."

"Bull feathers." She glared up at Brad. "You try to beat me and I'll kill you in your sleep."

"If I feel the need to beat you, your butt will be too sore to be doing any sneaking while I sleep."

She should have been shocked, scared. Maybe even intimidated. She wasn't. Mainly because those crinkles were still at the corners of his eyes. He was amused by something. "You underestimate me."

The lines deepened ever so slightly. "Not hardly."

"Young lady, I strongly suggest you listen to your husband rather than provoke him."

The suggestor was wearing on her nerves. "I suggest you hush."

He looked over her head as if she didn't exist and blessed Brad with his wisdom. "A daily reminder of her place would assuredly go a long way to smoothing the road of your marriage. It's my experience that 'spare the rod, spoil the child' is not a philosophy reserved just for children."

A beating. He was telling Brad to beat her. Fury flared. Evie kicked him in the shin. "You pompous ass, how dare you tell anyone to beat me?"

Retaliation was swift. Carlson lunged for her, his anger mottling his face in florid patches. "You bitch!"

She jumped back. Before her feet hit the ground, Brad had the judge facedown over the altar, his arm ratcheted up between his shoulder blades. "You crooked son of a bitch. Don't you ever touch my wife."

"She's not your wife yet!" the man howled as Brad jerked his arm higher.

"She will be in a minute."

"You were right about one thing," Cougar said as he came up beside Evie and folded his arms across his powerful chest. "The judge is a pompous ass."

Evie just blinked at the scene, the violence both horrifying and thrilling her. No one had ever stood up for her before.

"Aren't you going to do something?" she asked Cougar.

"Why? Looks like the Rev has it under control."

Because ministers were peace-loving men, or so she'd always thought.

The judge screamed as Brad wrenched his arm higher and whispered something in his ear. There was a potent pause. The judge nodded. Brad straightened and let the man go. The judge stumbled back, his face white and sweating. He glanced at Brad as he returned to her side, then at Cougar, Clint, and Asa. Residual red spots stood out on his face in vivid contrast to the pasty wash of fear.

"I'm sorry, Miss Washington."

His gaze flicked over the attendees behind her. She couldn't see, but from the angry murmur, she was reasonably sure they weren't looking at him any more kindly than she was. The community around Cattle Crossing was a small one, and as Cattle Crossing had grown from hellhole to town, the people had become very protective of their own. She nodded. It was all the grace she could work up for a man who'd suggested to her fiancé that he beat her daily.

"If you'll allow, I'd like to finish the ceremony."

Here was her chance. She could say no, and let the chips fall where they may. She could let the Reverend move on, away from his home and the life he'd built. Away from the contentment in his eyes that had only recently replaced the torment he'd come to town bearing. There'd be embarrassment, but she'd eventually be forgiven by those who loved her. After all, women were the weaker sex, unable to be trusted with life's decisions, incapable of comprehending a sense of honor as a man did.

For Brad, it would be different though. The stain would haunt him forever. Could she do that to him? With every heartbeat that passed, she felt the almost invisible tension within him increase. He expected her to repudiate him, probably had expected it all along, yet he hadn't hesitated to come to her defense. *Rats.* Why did he have to make her go and like him? Wasn't being fascinating enough? She sighed. He stiffened, and she knew what she was going to do.

Reaching out, she tucked her fingers into the callused roughness of Brad's palm. Though he didn't look down, she felt his twitch of surprise. She couldn't blame him. She didn't exactly have a reputation for doing the right thing, but then again, she owed him. Rather than reprimanding her for her disrespect toward the judge, he'd stood up for her, defending her when she wasn't even sure her own mother would have. She owed him better than betrayal. Heart in her throat, nerves jangling like a dinner bell, she made a decision. "Finish the ceremony."

Behind her, her mother broke into sobs. Beside her, Brad's fingers curled around hers. And squeezed.

"SO HOW DOES it feel to be a married man?"

Brad flicked his smoke into the dirt and glared at Cougar and Clint as they joined him outside the livery, which had been cleaned and decorated for the event. Evie's family had spared no expense celebrating Evie's return to respectability.

"Like the posse just caught up with me."

Strains of fiddle music drifted on the warm June air.

"Hell, Brad," Cougar grunted, "it's not that bad a match. The woman might be a little wild, but you're not exactly tame."

"Can't get much tamer than a preacher." He offered Cougar a smoke. The big man looked at it longingly, but shook his head.

"Mara still snapping at your heels about your habit?"

"Hell, she doesn't have to hound him," Clint interrupted, leaning back against the rail. "One dismayed look and the man is fair tossing his smokes away."

Cougar smiled. "I like a warm bed."

"Keep liking it to that extent and the woman will be pregnant for sure," Brad slung back.

Cougar paled. "Hell no."

"You can't stop nature, Cougar."

If looks could kill, Brad would be dead. "Mara's too small to bear children."

"You don't know that."

"Even Doc is worried."

"She's determined to be a mother," Asa interjected.

"There are plenty of kids who need homes."

"But she wants yours," Clint pointed out.

"Lord knows why," Cougar groused. "They'll all come out heathens, with my blood."

"Or hellions, with Mara's blood."

Cougar snapped around. "You insulting my wife, Asa?"

"Nope. Just pointing out that a woman with spirit isn't going to give you mild-natured children."

"There's nothing sweeter than Mara."

"I'll take your word for it."

A body could take Cougar's word for anything. The man never lied and would take a promise to the grave. If they weren't on opposite sides of the law, Brad would call him friend, but they were, and at some point, that code of honor the man held so dear was going to send his honor to war against his promise. Brad's skin prickled with a sense of impending doom and his nerves tightened.

He shot a quick glare heavenward. *How long do you intend to play this game out?*

There was no answer. There never was, but Brad didn't need one to know. God wasn't done with him yet. The sense of restlessness grew. He'd tossed the cigarette too soon; now he had nothing to do with the surge of energy that always accompanied contemplation of how this was all going to end. Truth was, he should have left town months ago. He looked at both McKinnelys. "Tell me something."

"What?"

"Why didn't either of you put an end to this before it went this far?"

Clint shrugged. "We talked about it."

"And?"

Cougar tipped his hat back. "We decided everyone deserves a second chance."

Shit. "Hell of a time to get generous."

Clint hitched his hip up on the porch rail. "We have our moments."

"So you just decided to sacrifice Evie to my second chance?"

"She did that herself."

"And her second chance will come when?"

"If you hurt her and I have to put your ass in the ground," Clint retorted.

That at least was a normal McKinnely response.

"Now I have to ask something," Cougar said, folding his arms across his powerful chest.

Brad had a feeling he knew what was coming. "What?"

"What on earth made you pose for her?"

"I didn't."

"Not many men have a thunderbolt carved on their thigh."

"I know." He really wished he hadn't thrown his smoke away. He debated taking out another, but tobacco was dear on a minister's pay. And as generous as the townsfolk were, they were pretty steadfast in the fact that he should not have vices, and tobacco was considered one. Which made the smokes he had precious. Too precious to waste on a moment of nerves.

Looking through the window into the livery, he could see Millicent and Dorothy clearly, but the only part of Evie he could see was the edge of her dark blue dress. An internal hunger surged the way it did whenever he got Evie within his sight. He always seemed to want more when it came to her, which made her a very dangerous woman. To whom he was now married. *Hell.*

Millicent stepped aside, her head tipping back as she laughed. He had a clear view of his wife. Evie's answering smile was full-blown, unfettered, free of artifice and restraint. Brad remembered how she'd snapped at that sanctimonious judge. Everything about Evie was natural and passionate. Including that temper. Not that Evie ever flaunted herself beyond the voicing of the more outrageous of her beliefs when the restrictions of society hobbled her, but passion was there in her walk, the way she approached new things, new situations. Brad had always thought Evie would make some man a hell of a wife. And now she was his, through trickery and deceit. He still didn't know how he felt about that, what he was going to do about it. "But I didn't pose for Evie."

"So you think the woman went around spying on you when you were naked?" Clint asked.

"That's a bit far-fetched," Asa cut in. "Evie's got a wild side for sure, but she's not sneaky."

Brad didn't like Asa noticing Evie's wild side any more than he liked him calling her Evie. "May I remind you, that's my wife you're talking about?"

Asa's response was a twitch of his lips and a raise of his brows. "Going to be a possessive son of a bitch?"

Yes, he was. Always had been. A man developed the tendency when he grew up with everything he valued being regularly and deliberately taken away. "I might be."

"Does Evie know that?" Clint asked, the same amusement on his face that was on Asa's.

"Doubt it." Cougar poured the punch in his cup over the side of the rail. "Seeing as I've heard Evie preach more than once about women not being chattel subject to a man's rule."

"Then she's going to have to change her mind." Because not only was he a possessive son of a bitch, he was a bossy one, too. At least when it came to the woman in his bed, and Evie was definitely going to be in his bed. If he was giving up his freedom, she was going to have to give up a bit of hers. His cock, semihard since she'd said "*I do*," completed the journey to hard.

He'd always considered Evie to be the town's treasure. Too independent for propriety, but not a wild child. More of a passionate soul looking for an outlet. He ran his gaze over her slender hips and pert breasts, the soft pink of her inviting mouth. His fingers closed on the images. He could definitely give her that.

Cougar reached up above the edge of the roof to the lip of the overhang. There was the sound of glass against wood and then he pulled out a bottle of whiskey. The contents caught the light, glowing amber with temptation. "You got a cup stashed out here somewhere, Swanson?"

Brad eyed the full bottle. "Doc know you've raided his stash of sipping whiskey?"

"Who do you think put the bottle up there?" Doc asked, coming through the open door with four of Dorothy's precious crystal punch glasses dangling from his fingers by their fragile handles.

"You make a habit of storing whiskey around and about?" Brad asked.

If Doc did, it would be worth knowing. No doubt, as a newly married man, he would benefit from running across a few of them.

Doc held out the glasses. "Nah, just on stressful occasions."

Brad took one. "I think this qualifies."

"You'd be hard put to find someone to argue with that," Asa said, taking a glass.

"You still haven't answered the question of how you think Evie got a glimpse of you naked."

"Have you seen the portrait?"

"Nope. But I've heard it's very detailed."

"A shame we never got a look at it."

Detailed didn't even begin to cover it. Unfortunately, if anybody ever got a peek at those details, Brad would never hear the end of it for however long it took to build the gallows from which to hang his sorry ass.

Cougar held up the bottle. Brad held out his glass. "And you're not ever going to."

"That's a damn miserly attitude," Cougar pointed out.

"Especially for somebody who had their picture painted by Evie Washington. Subject matter aside, I hear she's very good," Doc offered.

And that was the problem. She was too good. She just didn't know squat about a man's anatomy. Not only did the image show too much, it made him look like a freak. "That's just my mean nature coming out."

"You're a lot of things, Swanson, some that are at odds with each other, but mean without provocation isn't one of them," Clint stated quietly.

The compliment jerked his chin up.

Clint shrugged. "Don't look so surprised. You think we'd let you marry Evie if we had any doubts about your true character? You took your preacher vows, and no one makes promises like that to God without good backing them."

Brad was glad they were so confident. Truth was, he hadn't fought the marriage hard because he thought there was no way the McKinnelys—the only people who knew who he really was—would spill his secret rather than let the wedding proceed.

"That was also under duress." The beating his father had delivered him when he was sixteen had about killed him. And when the violence was done, Brad had promised to follow in his father's footsteps. Ten minutes later he had been ordained.

Cougar snorted. "Rev, the one thing everyone knows is your promises are gold."

"Not that one."

"That explains why you're not stinking rich from all your thieving," Doc interjected.

It was an uncomfortable feeling finding out his secrets weren't so secret. "Gold's worth more spent."

"How so?"

"People with a bit in their pocket tend to keep their mouths shut," Brad said.

"You didn't need to get shot stepping between that whore and her customer either," Asa drawled.

Hell, if he stood there long enough they'd make him out to be a saint. "I'd paid for her time first."

At least that's what he told everyone. Truth was, he lost perspective when a man beat up a woman. It was a weakness he couldn't afford, but one he couldn't seem to shake.

Clint sputtered on his whiskey. Asa slapped him on the back and muttered, "As if any woman ever charged Shadow Svensen."

Brad glanced around quickly. They seemed to be alone. "Shadow Svensen is dead." Transformed into the Reverend Swanson, but as disguises went, it wasn't that solid.

Asa shook his head. "Sorry, but it's still true."

"So because you think you know me you decided to play God with Evie's future?"

Asa took a philosophical sip. "The girl needed settling. She's had a few near misses. That can't be allowed to continue."

Brad was almost afraid to ask. "What kind of near misses?"

"Last month she decided to liberate the soiled doves over at the Pleasure Emporium. Big Luke took exception to her actions." Cougar took a drink of his whiskey. "If Elijah hadn't been hanging around, she would have been joining the doves working that night."

Damn! Brad knew Evie had been getting more reckless, but he hadn't known she'd gone that far. "Elijah's back in town?"

"For the moment."

"How's he look?"

"Rattlesnake mean."

That was hard to believe. Elijah had left the outlaw life for little Amy. Settled down to be a farmer. Swore he was never going back. And from the first time Brad had seen him with his wife, he'd believed him. Twenty years of hard living had just seemed to dissolve from his face. He'd been happy. If he'd gone back to outlawing after his wife and daughter's death from fever, it was the only time in his life Elijah had gone back on his word. And that was serious business.

"Anything I should know about?"

The other men stilled. Asa put their worry into words. "Any particular reason you ask?"

He felt the pull, the urge to feed the assumptions they were throwing at him. He took a drink of his whiskey. It was smooth and smoky, with a bite. A taste of the good life he'd never thought was for him. "Nope. Not a one."

"This is your chance, Swanson. Don't mess it up."

"Why? Because you'll be ready to take me apart if I do?"

Cougar smiled. It didn't lighten his expression. "Something like that."

Brad tossed back his whiskey. "Why wait?"

Cougar pointed to the window where the wedding guests were mingling. "Because your pretty bride might object to her husband coming to her bed too busted up to perform."

Brad followed the gesture, his gaze going instinctively to Evie. She was talking to old Ruth. The woman was deaf, with a tendency to long-winded tales, mostly about her deceased husband. He knew Evie was probably bored, but her smile didn't slip and her gaze didn't wander. It was one of the things he liked best about her, her ability to make the person she was talking to feel like they had her full attention. It spoke of a generosity of spirit that appealed to him. With her position in town society, her looks, her wit, she could easily be cruel, but she wasn't. At least, not to those who could be hurt. When it came to him, it was a whole different story. On him, she was more than willing to wield the sharp edge of her temper.

He smiled and tossed back the last of the whiskey. With him, she wasn't afraid. He liked that about her best. Handing Doc the glass, he nodded to the McKinnelys. "Well, if you're not going to indulge me tonight, I think I'll go rescue my bride."

Doc shook his head. "Don't hurry. Ruth's not doing so good. Last winter out on that old place of hers without Herb was hard on her."

Brad had noticed. "I don't think she'll survive another one."

And that would be a shame. Ruth was a sweet woman and the backbone of the community.

"It's going to take dynamite to get her out of there."

Or the right incentive. He handed Doc the glass. "I've got an idea brewing that might get her out and into a better situation."

"What is it?"

"Ask me next month."

"What's wrong with now?"

Glancing back toward Evie, Brad felt a thrill of anticipation he hadn't enjoyed in a long time. "I've got better things to do."

IF EVIE HAD to stand there one more minute, she was going to do one of two things: melt into a puddle or scream bloody murder.

"It's important to keep your man happy, young lady."

She nodded and mouthed a "yes." She was too hot to continue yelling and since Ruth read lips more than heard, it wasn't necessary.

"The Reverend Swanson might be a man of God, but he's still a man and he has needs."

Evie really wished the old lady's voice didn't carry. A blush rose to her cheeks. Ruth continued with her point.

"I was married to Herb for thirty years, and never turned him away when he reached for me at night." Ruth patted Evie's arm. "You welcome your husband the same way and you'll know the same happiness."

Evie really couldn't imagine that. Not just the making love part, but the welcoming. Brad was an intimidating man. She found that just standing beside him put an itch in her feet. Which is why she'd avoided him as much as possible for all that she'd made a habit of studying him. She'd still be avoiding him if it wasn't for that darn painting.

"Thank you. I appreciate the advice."

An arm slipped around her waist.

"Definitely, thank you." Brad said that loud enough that not only Ruth but the whole room heard.

The old lady blushed. The guests tittered. Evie gritted her teeth. He was embarrassing her on purpose. Revenge for her joke that had backfired so horribly? She put her hand over Brad's and sank her nails into him while dropping her eyes and gasping in her best innocent-miss voice. "Reverend!"

Her nails were drawing blood. Brad's smile didn't slip. "Just going along with sound advice, sweetheart."

Even in mockery he had a way of making the endearment as smooth as honey. If he wasn't a minister, she would have labeled him a ladies' man.

"You're embarrassing me," she hissed.

"Don't go making the girl blush, you rascal!" Ruth chastised, the smile on her face taking every bit of sting out of the reprimand.

"But she's so pretty when she blushes."

The stroke of her husband's finger down her cheek felt more like a warning. To shut up or to go along? It didn't matter. Evie was no man's pet. She bared her teeth in a smile. "He's full of those practiced sayings."

"Which would make you a lucky woman," Mara said, coming up on Evie's side, her brown eyes alight with humor.

"Only if I like hearing platitudes all day long."

"I would assume platitudes are better than curses."

"I guess that would depend on your personality."

"Trust me," Brad interrupted with another brush of his finger. This time the gesture ended at the corner of her mouth. His knuckle pressed gently. "You wouldn't like me in the mood that generates curses."

She parted her lips, opened her mouth, and set her teeth to his skin. "I'll keep that in mind."

Unbelievably, he laughed and tapped her cheek. "You'd best come dance with me before you get yourself in trouble."

"We don't have any music."

He lifted his hand. A small commotion began across the room. Chairs were pushed out of the way, tables pulled back. Cyrus pulled his fiddle from behind the door. She looked at Brad. "You can't dance at a wedding."

He took her hand as Cyrus tuned up the fiddle. "Who says?"

"God."

He cocked an eyebrow at her. His hair fell across his forehead, giving him that outlaw look that made her heart flutter. Her fingers twitched to push it back.

"I work for him, and he's never whispered that in my ear."

She tugged at her hand. "You know it's not done."

He tightened his grip, dragging her along. "Then we'll set a new tradition."

A high, sweet tune filled the room. The good citizens of town, her friends, fell to the side, making a path. She glared at Jenna, who rested back against her big husband's chest, the sadness that had haunted her eyes for years no longer visible.

"You should be protesting this."

Jenna's smile was soft. Her shrug barely contained an apology. "But I want to dance."

Everything about Jenna was soft. She was the nicest woman Evie knew, the opposite of her hard-as-nails husband, but no one worried about Jenna when she was with Clint. The man adored his wife. She glanced at Clint's dark hand, wrapped around Jenna's. And she was beginning to think they didn't need to worry about Clint anymore either. Jenna was good for him. She brought him smiles, normalcy, and family. She glanced at Gray, where he stood beside the couple, his baby sister in his arms. Neither were of Jenna's or of Clint's blood, but woe to whomever dared say they didn't belong. They'd been lost, and Jenna, who wouldn't say *boo* to a ghost, who'd known more horror in her lifetime than anyone should have to survive, had fought to the death to bring them home, given them a place, made them McKinnelys. And all four appeared content with the arrangement.

Clint bent his head to brush his lips over Jenna's smooth cheek. "Just one dance, sunshine. You've been on that leg enough for one day."

"I'm good enough for two."

"One." It was said in a tone that brooked no denial.

Jenna patted his hand. "We'll see."

This time Clint's lips brushed her hair, the fine strands shining against his dark skin. "One."

Evie bet there'd be two. Jenna truly was Clint's sunshine, bringing him back from that dark place he'd fallen into. Clint caught her staring at him. He smiled. She blinked. Clint smiling really did take some getting used to.

"Dance with your husband, Evie. You can trust him to take care of you."

Was there an underlying message in Clint's order? Or was that wishful thinking on her part?

"He thinks I tricked him into marriage. I'd be a fool to trust him."

Brad came up beside her. "But you will dance."

"It's scandalous."

"You like scandal."

She jumped. How did he know?

His grip shifted to her elbow as he steered her into the cleared space. The temperature in the room seemed to shoot up ten degrees but it was a good heat, an inviting heat. "It's not exactly a secret. And if anyone had any doubts, that art show killed them off."

"Mother was sending me back East."

"For wearing pants."

"I was trying to learn to ride."

He steered her to the center of the floor, his hand a warm weight at her waist, his thigh brushing hers. He turned her into his embrace. Their bodies fit nicely together. "You were testing your limits."

Evie could feel everyone watching. She kept her smile in place. "What do you know about anything?"

His hand shifted up to rest just above the small of her back, tucking her against him. This close she couldn't miss his scent—spicy, masculine, and very intriguing.

"Your family can't give you what you want."

His drawl, rich with innuendo, flowed above the opening strains of a waltz. Pitched just right, it smoothed along her senses, weakened her anger. A red flag went up. He wouldn't. She looked up, met his eyes, and knew he absolutely would. The Reverend Brad Swanson would seduce his wife on the dance floor in front of the whole town. The thrill from before came back twofold. Out of the corner of her eye she could see the mayor's wife, Shirley, frown. Evie fluttered her lashes and relaxed into Brad's embrace.

"And you can?"

Without missing a beat, he smiled and took the first gliding step, the subtle tension in his arm guiding her effortlessly into his rhythm. "Absolutely." He spun her in a wide turn. "You're not hard to figure out."

She blinked. "I'm not?"

A woman liked to feel she had some mystery.

"No, but you are intriguing."

"How?"

Other couples joined them. Doc led Dorothy onto the floor. As he took her in his arms, she smoothed his cowlick down. They were so comfortable with each other. Evie couldn't imagine being like that with Brad, but she'd like to be. The thought came out of nowhere.

Another spin, this one faster than the last, brought her gaze back up to her husband's.

"You're looking for someone you can't outthink or run over. Someone who can handle that wild side of yours."

That statement shot a thrill of excitement straight to her core. She lifted her chin. "And you think you're that man?"

His lips spread in a slow smile. With an easy grace he spun them into another turn, whirling them so fast she lost her balance. Her momentary panic was for nothing. Brad caught her effortlessly with the hand at her back. She waited, but he didn't pull her up, just held her gaze with the same easy sensuality with which he held her suspended there, helpless, back arched, legs entwined. It was a perfectly shocking, perfectly scandalous thing to do and she loved every second. When he pulled her up with a flex of his arm she went willingly, as hopelessly fascinated with this side of him as with all the others. Bringing her hand to his mouth, he pressed a kiss to the back, that knowing smile still curving his mouth.

"You can count on it."

Three

"IT'S TIME TO go, Evie."

Evie looked at the watch pinned to the waist of her skirt. The hand ticked toward six o'clock. As much as she wanted to grab it and keep it from progressing, she knew it wouldn't do any good. No amount of wishing moved time forward or backward. It just progressed inevitably. In another hour, it would be dark. She took a breath of the humid air and stared at the far-off mountains rising above the plains, desperation building with that forbidden sense of excitement that had enfolded her since she and Brad had danced. "So it is."

The rather forced smile on her mother's face faltered. No doubt she'd hoped Evie had resigned herself to her fate by now.

"The Reverend's a good man."

The stab of resentment that shot through Evie was an all-too-familiar sensation. "Whether he is or isn't is immaterial. I'm married to him. He can be whatever he wants to be and I believe my role is to smile and put a pleasant face on whatever the truth works out to be."

"That's a very cynical attitude."

"Then I guess that makes me a cynic."

Pearl fussed with the cuff of Evie's dress, her hand hovering an instant over Evie's before dropping back. "I want you to be happy."

"No. You want me to be happy in a life of which you approve."

One that stifled her so badly that she buried her face in her pillow at night and screamed with the frustration of it.

"You can't do the things you want to do, Evie. The things you want to be, they're just dreams. It's time to grow up and realize that."

Evie blew out a breath, her corset biting into her waist on the last of the exhale. She focused on the sting, needing something to keep her balanced. Otherwise, she'd go screaming from the wedding, embarrassing herself, her family, and the Reverend. The corset was as confining as the rules of society that fenced her in. She couldn't breathe—now, before, and probably never again.

She folded her arms across her chest, trying not to pin too much hope on that one moment of excitement on the dance floor. "Well, you can't get more respectable than a preacher's wife, so you don't need to worry anymore. You've saved me from a life of ill repute. Your job is done."

The truth burned like acid across her confidence and the small flicker of hope left by that scandalous dance.

"Then why don't I feel relaxed?"

Because it's not my choice. Because you know I'll only suffer this so long before I'll explode. Because you know when I do, you'll have to send me away and our relationship will be so much ash in the aftermath. "I have no idea."

"It's not going to be that bad, Evie."

It would just be the same hell she'd been running from for the last twenty years, etched forever into her future. Evie pushed away from the side of the building. Splinters of wood clutched at the material of her dress, pulling her up short. "Shoot."

"What?"

"Even my darn dress is determined to keep me here."

Pearl clucked her tongue. "I told you this material is very fine."

The only thing that kept Evie from yanking herself free was the love and hope her mother had sewn into this dress. It wasn't Pearl's fault that Evie wanted more from life than what society dictated she could have. The flaw was in her, not her mother.

She held still as Pearl worked the delicate lace collar free.

"There."

"Thank you."

Over her mother's shoulder and through the doorway, Evie could see the wedding guests smiling and talking in small groups. People who'd gathered to wish her well. People willing to disregard the disgrace that had brought her to this point and allow her a fresh start, sending all their good wishes with her. This was her wedding day and this was her mother, and as much as Pearl didn't understand Evie, she still wanted the best for her. That love was evident in the quantity of food and richness of the decorations. Pearl had always provided the best for Evie. Because she loved her.

Evie sighed. No doubt, when looking back on this day there would be a lot of things that she'd remember and regret, but one memory she didn't want was for this to be just another day she had argued with her mother.

Pearl was right. It was time to grow up. The life she'd hoped to lead, her dreams of going to Paris and pursuing a career as a professional artist were dead. She'd killed them when she'd agreed to marry. That wasn't anybody's fault but hers. As depressing as it was to know that when push came to shove, she'd chosen convention over freedom, it had still been her choice.

She caught her mother's hand as she would have stepped back.

"I don't want to fight."

"I don't either. It's your wedding day, baby. I want it to be a happy time."

Happiness was beyond her reach, but a smile wasn't. Fake or not, it seemed to relax Pearl. "Thank you for everything you've done."

Pearl unwrapped the cape from her arms and held it out.

Evie admired the way the satin caught the light in an iridescent shimmer, but she didn't reach for it. "It's still hot enough to cook an egg."

"You don't want to get your dress filthy before you arrive."

Arrive where? Brad hadn't mentioned where they were spending their wedding night. And up until now, she hadn't cared enough to ask, but it suddenly seemed a huge lack. "I don't necessarily want to arrive perspiring either."

Pearl's lips twitched. "I don't suppose you do."

That smile grated on Evie's nerves. "What?"

Pearl draped the cape over her arm. "We need to talk about what's going to happen tonight. I would have addressed it last night, but you were tired."

Good grief, she was not going to stand outside her reception and discuss relations between a man and a woman with her mother. "I know what goes on between a man and a woman."

That was a lie, but her mother was no better at telling when she was lying now than she had been when she was a child. Pearl only saw Evie the way she wanted her to be.

The lightest of blushes touched Pearl's cheekbones. "You do?"

Evie could feel heat rising in her own cheeks. "Most of my friends are married."

"I don't want you to be afraid."

"I'm not afraid." Another lie that went undetected. "And you just finished telling me that the Reverend is a good man. I would think the best a woman can hope for is to end up in her marriage bed with a good man."

"Experienced doesn't hurt."

Evie blinked. The resentment bubbled over the lid she'd put on it. "I'm not sure how to take that, Ma. Which is more important, a man who knows what he's doing between the sheets or a man of principle?"

"Evie, that's crude."

"I was thinking it was to the point."

Pearl took a deep breath. Evie braced herself. She hadn't inherited her sass and impatience from thin air. To her surprise, Pearl reached out. Her fingers slipped over Evie's and squeezed they way they always had in the past when Evie was afraid but determined to proceed anyway.

"Just tell your husband about your fears, and I'm sure he'll take care of them."

Evie glanced over to where Brad chatted with Doc and Dorothy. He was smiling, but there was a tension in his shoulders, slight, but there. He looked up and caught her studying him. She was used to summing up people's moods pretty quickly. It helped her get what she wanted, stay out of trouble. She couldn't read her husband. She couldn't imagine telling him anything, least of all her fears. "I think the Reverend wants to leave."

It was ludicrous to be calling her husband by that title, but she couldn't bring herself to use anything less formal. She wasn't ready to admit this was forever. Pearl caught her hands before she could turn away.

"You let him be good to you. Follow his lead."

"What if I don't like where he's taking me?"

The press of Pearl's lips was a warning. "Telling a man *no* in bed is a delicate thing."

It was the most intimate discussion they'd ever had and it had to be now, when there was so much turmoil between them. "Then I guess I'd better focus on saying *yes*. After all, that's my job now, isn't it? Saying *yes* to my husband?"

Darn, she sounded bitter when she really wasn't. She was just afraid to hope.

Pearl blew out a breath. "You might try giving convention a chance. The rules can't be all wrong. They work for millions of people."

But they might just be wrong for her. No one understood that though. Sometimes, not even herself. It wasn't that she didn't want to be like everyone else. She just . . . wasn't. "I'll be fine, Ma. I'll learn to adjust."

Or die trying.

"Just try to fit in, Evie. That's all you need to do."

Evie rolled her eyes as her mother's arms came around her waist and hugged her. A preacher's wife. Could she have locked herself more tightly in propriety if she'd tried?

THE SEND-OFF WAS raucous and full of good cheer, and no different from the end of any other wedding, except everyone knew this wasn't a love match, so such happiness was completely out of place. After one last wave, one last forced smile, Evie subsided back into the shelter of the buggy's top.

"Thank goodness that's over."

Brad turned slightly. "I thought it was a rather pleasant wedding."

"It wasn't real."

His brow rose. "Feels real enough to me."

Evie sighed. "Please. This is not a love match."

His expression didn't change. "Doesn't make it any less of a match though, and doesn't make people's well wishes any less sincere."

She supposed it didn't. Reaching up, she unpinned her hat, and stretched her arms out in front of her. "I wonder if a real bride receives so much advice."

His lips quirked and his gaze touched her mouth, swept over her throat, and lingered in the vicinity of her chest. "I guess you'll have to tell me what kind of advice you received before I can give you an answer."

It was a look meant to seduce a woman, designed to throw her off balance. Brad was going to have to do better than that. Between putting on her cape and walking out the door, Evie had decided she wasn't going to be that easy to seduce.

"Just the usual malarkey. Men are wonderful and all-knowing and I should believe everything they say implicitly."

"Well, now, that was a fair bit of advice."

A fair bit of horsefeathers. She placed her hat in her lap, not rising to his bait. "Why do you like to make me angry?"

"Why do you like to break convention?"

The buggy hit a bump. The cans tied behind jangled. She grabbed the side. "If you're implying 'because it's fun,' this is going to be a very long marriage."

He steered the buggy around a corner. "Until death do us part."

He didn't say it with the sense of doom that she felt. The heat burned through her cape. She unbuttoned the frogs at the throat. "God help us."

By the time she got to the third button, they'd passed the Reverend's residence.

"Where are we going?"

The twitch of his lips should have warned her. "Someplace where you can strip in private."

Heat that had nothing to do with the temperature burned her cheeks. She forced her fingers to keep doing what they were doing, as if she wasn't blushing like a young miss. "That's very thoughtful of you."

"I try to be accommodating."

Not that she'd noticed. And she'd noticed him a lot. From the day he'd wandered into town with the McKinnelys after their last hunt, he'd fascinated her. And not just because he was a fine-looking man with a powerful build, though that alone would have been sufficient to draw any woman's attention. But because he was a man who commanded everyone around him, and no one seemed to notice. She would love to have that ability.

She glanced up from beneath the shield of her lashes. He did have a nice set of shoulders. Broad enough that he made her feel crowded. Broad enough that parishioners felt secure. And after the disaster of their last preacher, a man who'd hated himself, God, and everyone he came in contact with, the Reverend Brad was a breath of fresh air. Enough so that people overlooked his idiosyncrasies for the embrace of his accepting nature.

But just because he smiled and nodded didn't mean he was going along. His accommodation was often just an illusion as he went around behind the scenes making things happen according to his preferences. There was a relentless energy about the man. Most of it under the surface, only noticeable if one knew to look for it.

The last frog released.

"Good." She shrugged the cape off her shoulders. The buggy continued out toward the edge of town. "And while I'm stripping, we can talk about a timely dissolution of this marriage."

Brad flicked the reins, looking straight ahead. "What makes you think I want it dissolved?"

Another glance showed the humor was gone from his expression. "The way it came about."

"I agree that wasn't the most positive, but Evie, when I make a promise, I'm not in the habit of backing down on it."

"No one can hold you to a promise made with a shotgun at your back." She didn't want a husband under coercion.

His jaw set. "I gave my word. 'Til death do us part."

"Well, I'm not so stubborn about the concept of a promise."

Again, one of those looks out of the corner of his eye that made her uncomfortable. "Good to know."

He didn't need to say it like that! "What I mean is, I'm reasonable enough to understand that circumstance—"

"That would be you."

She gripped a fold of the cape in her hands, squeezing for patience. "Circumstance conspired to put us in an awkward position."

"*You* put us in an awkward position."

"Fine." She slapped her hat against her thigh. "*I* put us in an awkward position. However, that doesn't mean we have to continue this farce until 'death do us part.' "

"What's the alternative?"

She took a hankie from the cuff of her dress and dabbed at the perspiration on her forehead. At last he was being reasonable. She yanked a bunch of her skirt out from under her hip. "We stay married for a sensible amount of time and then dissolve the marriage."

He clucked to the bay, drawing the buggy to the right, heading toward the edge of town. "There are only a couple of reasons a marriage can be dissolved, none of them ideal."

"I thought we'd go for non-consummation."

He made a strange sound in his throat.

"I looked it up and it seemed the least offensive."

He pulled the horse to an abrupt stop. "The hell you did."

She stopped tugging at her skirt and looked at him. Really looked at him. "You're angry."

"What gave you that impression?"

Nothing really. Certainly not his eyes, as they were shadowed by his short-brimmed hat. Not his mouth, which wasn't any more tense than normal, and certainly not by the tone of his voice. But a lack of signs didn't change what she knew. He was annoyed.

"It's more than an impression. You're angry."

"Because you think to make me a laughingstock again by telling all and sundry that, when faced with a beautiful woman, I can't be a man?"

"What do you mean again?"

"I know it's been a month since the last time you threw my masculinity into question."

A month? What had she done a month ago? A month ago she'd had her little show . . . She sat up straight, outrage spiking down her spine. "You thought my painting was an insult?"

"It sure as he—heck wasn't a compliment."

He hadn't liked her painting? How dare he criticize her art? "It was an excellent painting and immensely flattering."

It had also been the most exciting piece she'd ever worked on.

"So you told everyone who would listen."

He didn't sound at all pleased, which only aggravated her more. She might not be one to fit neatly into convention, and he might doubt her ability to be a properly restrained wife, but she was a wonderful artist.

"You have no taste!"

Instead of getting angrier, the tension left his shoulders and a smile tucked into the corners of his mouth. Why? The insult should have landed. He should be mad, not amused.

"Pretty much, it's all in my mouth."

"That's a shame, because I can't cook."

He didn't even flinch. "Then you'll have something to keep you busy for the next forty years."

"You think I'm so stupid, it's going to take me forty years to learn to cook?"

The half second it took him to shake his head had her chin snapping up. She wanted to hit him, to kiss him, do anything but just sit here quietly beside him and ride to their honeymoon. The man drove her crazy with contradiction.

"Don't look so indignant. For a bright woman, you've pulled some stupid stunts."

She glanced at him from beneath her lashes. There was definitely a come-play-with-me invitation in that grin. What he wanted to play, and the rules of the game, were still up for grabs, but he wanted her along. Her irritation dissipated in the wake of that knowledge, but the urge to kiss him lingered. She studied his mouth. It'd taken her a month of trying before she'd caught on paper the sensuality that was reflected in the chiseled shape. A month of sketching and wondering. And tonight, all that wondering would come to an end. She'd know the nature of his kiss. It seemed like forever until tonight. Of course, she didn't have to wait. She could always initiate a kiss.

She wondered what he'd do if she gave in to the impulse and leaned over and kissed him. Probably die of shock. She tucked the urge away with her hankie. Belatedly, she noticed he was studying her just as hard as she was studying him, but he wasn't being at all discreet about it, surveying her with the fervor of a fox perusing his next meal. A little shiver sneaked down her spine.

"I have not." None that she was confessing to anyway.

"What about the other night at the Pleasure Emporium?"

Oh shoot. "Who tattled on me this time?"

"Everyone was happy to tell me."

"Everyone's always happy to point out my mistakes."

"Now why do I get the feeling we're not talking about the harebrained plan you came up with?"

"It wasn't harebrained."

"Did it have you going within twenty feet of a whorehouse at night, unchaperoned?"

He knew darn well it did. "Yes."

"Then *harebrained* covers it."

There was only one more house before they left town behind. A pretty two-story with quaint gingerbread trim on the porch. Where on Earth was he taking her? "Those women need help."

"Those women aren't my concern. You are."

"That's all you're going to say?"

"Beyond the fact that you can put the idea of divorce out of your mind? Pretty much."

With a jerk, Brad released the brake. She clutched the cape, unease digging deep in her gut as he clucked to the horse. It sighed but didn't move. Brad tapped the reins against its flanks. It leaned into the harness with a snort. The buggy surged forward. "Where *are* we going?"

With a flick of his finger he indicated the road ahead of them. "That way."

She set her teeth. "Do you go out of your way to aggravate everyone, or is it just me?"

The corner of his mouth twitched. In humor or anger? "At the moment, I'm focusing on you, as you're currently my biggest irritation."

That was not good. She flopped back against the buggy seat. "It was just a painting."

"That you created to kick up a bit of a fuss."

"Life around here is so stifling."

"So you set out to stir it up."

He didn't have to be such a know-it-all.

"And now I'm married. The thing I never wanted to be. You might be right. *Harebrained* does cover it."

"Don't sound so despondent. Marriage might have a few pluses."

She wiped at her face again. "It's prison, with the husband as jailer."

"That's a bit extreme."

"That's how it feels to me."

"Well, then, I'll try to live down to your expectations."

"Don't bother."

"It'd be my pleasure."

That's what she was afraid of. "I don't understand you."

"I'm a pretty straightforward man."

"No, you're not."

That got his gaze off the road.

"You act like you are, but there are too many contradictions."

"Do tell."

There were some things she didn't want to reveal. "I don't think I will."

His eyebrow went up in that provoking manner. "I could order you to. As your husband and number one jailer, I have the right."

"Go right ahead."

"And see where it gets me?"

He was an intelligent man. "Yes."

The buggy bounced down the road. "Where are we going?"

"I told you—"

She cut him off. "Something more specific than 'that way.' "

Another flick of the reins. Another almost smile. "If you want something more specific, you're going to have to ask me nicely."

"You want me to beg?"

"I was thinking along the lines of *please* and *thank you*, but if you want to beg, I could probably work up the tolerance to listen."

Her bonnet crumpled under the tension of her grip. It was her favorite, too. "You are being more than a little provoking."

"I have a talent for it."

"It's not a good thing." She tried to smooth out her hat.

"Guess that depends which side of the provoking you're standing on."

No matter how much she tried, she couldn't straighten the brim. "I guess it does."

He didn't say anything more, just returned his attention to the road, which with every pass of the wheels diminished a little more to well-worn ruts. If she wanted to know where they were going, she was going to have to ask. Nicely. It wouldn't kill her.

"Could you please tell me where we're going?"

He pointed to a house just emerging into view as they cleared the rise. "There."

She shaded her eyes from the glare of the setting sun. "Elijah and Amy's old place?"

"Yup."

"Why?" The place, once pretty and full of hope, had been vacant since the death of Elijah's wife and his newborn daughter.

"Because as many eyes as have been on me for the last few weeks, I'm finding I want a bit of privacy on my wedding night."

"You thought we needed privacy?"

"We definitely need privacy."

A minister was a very public persona. One being forced to marry was subject to even more scrutiny. He could be telling the truth. He might just want peace and quiet.

The buggy pulled up in front of the house. Brad set the brake and jumped down.

He took her satchel from where it was tied to the back of the buggy before helping her down. "Why don't you take this into the house?"

She took the satchel. He caught her hand as she turned away. The way his thumb stroked across her knuckles brought the memory of his kiss alive. "If there's something see-through and provocative in the satchel, feel free to slip it on."

Or he might be looking for more.

Four

AT LEAST SHE wasn't going to have to cook. Evie set her satchel down on the floor just inside the door of the quiet house. There was a basket on the table, the dark wicker offset by a yellow-checked tablecloth beneath. Even from here she could smell the delicious aroma of Franny's special roast chicken. Someone had gone to a lot of trouble to make sure their first meal as husband and wife was not a disaster. Which it would be if she prepared it.

She quietly pulled the door closed behind her. Twilight settled over the interior, mellowing it with inviting charm. As she moved into the room, the scent of cleaning products mingled with the fragrance of dinner, but for all the scents of home, the house had a lonely feel. She looked around the space and tried to imagine it as it had been when Amy was alive. It wouldn't have felt empty, that's for sure. She imagined, for Elijah, it would have been a haven of warmth and love.

Amy had always been quiet and kind. She'd been a few years behind Evie in school, but Evie remembered that about her. Amy had always been the first person to welcome newcomers, always the one to share her lunch with those who didn't have any. When she'd found Elijah, a lot of people in town had reacted protectively and disapproved of the match, but Evie hadn't. Because the one thing that had always stood out about Amy was the joy she gave. She loved to make others happy. And while she'd made Elijah very happy, he'd also made her happy and no one had deserved happiness more than Amy. But she'd lost everything, leaving her husband as empty a shell as this house.

Looking around, Evie could see Amy's personality in the brightly colored quilt on the back of the couch. In the stained-glass art that hung in the parlor, the bright reds and yellows of both reflecting the joy Amy had found in each day. It was so hard to accept that she was gone. So hard to believe that God had needed her more than Elijah.

Evie sighed and hung her cape and bonnet on the coat hook. At least she'd been able to finish the portrait of Amy to give to Amy's parents before they'd headed back East. She'd tried to give it to Elijah, but he'd taken one look and walked away. The Greers had been more open to the gift. The death of their last surviving child, along with their grandchild, had broken them. The painting had given them some comfort. Nothing, however, could comfort Elijah. He'd disappeared for the longest time, and then one day came back thinner, harder, and so cold-eyed she'd hardly recognized him. He'd moved into the livery and then the saloon. He didn't smile, didn't laugh, and he never spoke of his wife or the child they'd lost. It was as if, when he'd lost Amy, he'd lost his will to live.

Evie wondered what it would be like to be loved like that. To love someone like that. Truth be told, it scared her to think so much of her happiness could depend on someone else. She ran her fingers over the freshly dusted and polished surface of the small pedestal table just to the right of the door. Loving someone that much made a person too vulnerable.

Footsteps sounded on the porch. Brad was coming. She was supposed to be waiting for him in something flimsy. She rolled her eyes. Not that she owned any such thing. And not that she was interested in pleasing him by wearing what he wanted, but she was reasonably sure there was some etiquette about wedding nights that did not involve standing in the foyer playing with the furniture.

As she stepped away from the table, her finger caught under the edge. It rocked on the smooth wood floor. Reaching out, she steadied it and sighed. She was fidgeting. Because she was nervous, she admitted to herself. Because of that darn dance.

You're looking for someone you can't outthink or run over. Someone who can handle that wild side of yours.

She'd been fine with the marriage when she'd been able to tuck the thought away as a necessary evil, like doing laundry, but that dance had changed everything. Changed the way she saw Brad. She hadn't had time to figure out how, but she was pretty sure she didn't like it. And she was pretty sure it was a threat to her independence. The door opened with the same creak as it had for her. She made a mental note to find some grease. Brad stopped when he saw her standing by the basket in her traveling clothes. He leaned his shoulder against the jamb and folded his arms across his chest. She had the impression of a big, hungry mountain lion stopping in to visit.

"And here I was hoping you'd be waiting in something sheer and floaty."

The sexy timbre of his drawl made her wish she had been. She brushed her hands down her skirt. She didn't know him like this. This was not the behavior of a staid preacher. "You didn't give me time."

He smiled, and it only added to the image of a big, lazy cat getting ready to pounce. "I admit, the possibilities of what you might have put on inspired me to hurry."

This, she realized, was the man she'd always sensed lurking beneath the facade of a proper minister. The one who drew her like a fly to honey. She was finally meeting him. She had the strangest sense of exhilaration—and an incredible urge to run. That urge drove her into the kitchen. "You've got a very optimistic view of tonight."

"Are you telling me you didn't pack something special for our wedding night?"

Had he really expected her to? She shrugged and glanced over her shoulder. "I didn't actually pack at all."

His eyebrow rose. "So there's hope."

She remembered Pearl's smile. "Maybe."

He came up behind her. The hairs on her arms rose as awareness flashed between them. She jumped when his fingers closed around her shoulder. He turned her slowly. "Evelyn Washington, are you fretting? Over a mere man of God?"

She had two choices. Avoid looking at him and appear a coward, or meet his gaze and hope what she felt inside didn't show. She opted for the latter. "But you're not a mere preacher, are you?"

She was glad she'd chosen the latter. Otherwise, she might have missed the betraying flicker of his lashes and fallen for his smooth reply: "I'm whatever you want me to be tonight."

"What I would like you to be is considerate."

"Meaning?"

Stepping back, she motioned to the distance between

them. "This isn't a real wedding, Brad." Before he could correct her, she placed her hand on his chest. "I mean we're not in love . . ."

He took off his hat and put it on the table behind her. It landed with a soft plop. He didn't step back. "You still dreaming of an annulment?"

The question wafted across her cheek. Against her palms, she could feel his heartbeat. "Honestly? I don't know what I'm doing."

He lifted the cloth covering the basket and inspected the contents over her shoulder. "Being married to me doesn't have to be a prison."

"You're a preacher!"

As he drew back just far enough to see her face, his too long hair fell across his forehead, giving him that rakish look that had the ladies sighing during sermons. "You keep trotting that out like it's some kind of talisman."

"I was thinking it was more along the lines of a curse."

He fingered the lace on the collar of her dress before he smoothed it flat. "A lot of things can imprison a person, Evie. A lot of them a hell of a lot worse than toeing a few lines to ease peoples' sensibilities."

"Not for a woman."

She said that like it was true. Brad dropped the cover back on the basket. A hundred examples of "worse" leapt to his tongue. Looking into Evie's eyes, he swallowed them back. She was entitled to her beliefs. And he was entitled to preserve her innocence. At least the innocence that kept her naïve of just how cruel the world could be to some.

He let his gaze wander down over the full curves of her breasts, the narrowness of her waist. The heavy skirts blocked his view of the rest but he had a fair imagination that filled in a very pleasing picture.

"Tell me, Evie. Are you a virgin?"

Her eyes narrowed. "Are you?"

Memories flashed through his head. Women he'd known, some of them in laughter, some in misery. All of them as unsatisfying as trying to get drunk on watered-down whiskey. "Not by a long shot."

"Then don't be asking me whether I am if you're not."

It was just a short trip from her shoulder to her chin. His

hand traversed the distance in the span of a breath. The silk of her dark blue dress wasn't nearly as soft as her skin. "Being your husband gives me certain rights."

Her chin jerked in his hand. "None that you aren't willing to give me."

He didn't let go. She didn't back down, just narrowed her eyes further and dared him. He'd always been a sucker for a dare.

"That sounds fair enough."

Her eyes narrowed further. "What exactly does that mean?"

She was right to be suspicious. He stroked his thumb over the tight line of her lips. By morning her lips would be soft and swollen, compliant rather than defiant. By morning he'd have her seduced into a better frame of mind. He'd done it many times before, with many women before. His thumb paused midway through the second pass. He'd never seduced a wife . . . and never his own. "That I'm agreeable to a fair exchange in the bedroom."

"That wasn't what I was talking about."

He figured that. She was too busy worrying. "Are you saying you don't want fair in the bedroom?"

"I want fair everywhere in this marriage."

"I'll keep it in mind."

"Why do you need to keep it in mind?"

"Because I'm the man, and in case you were wondering, I have every intention of wearing the pants in our relationship."

"And you think pants equate to power?"

"Well, that and a couple other things."

She stepped back, bumped the table, muttered something under her breath, and sidestepped free. "Which would be?"

"About six inches of height and about ninety pounds of muscle."

Grabbing her satchel, she headed down the hall. "I'll try to remember to be impressed."

She'd try to remember. Smiling and shaking his head, he followed. Evie was a tall woman but he was taller. Matching her angry strides was no strain. When she got to the bedroom door, he reached around and took the satchel from her hand, trapping her between the jamb and his body. Her breath caught. Nerves or interest? It was hard to tell with Evie. She was a bundle of nervous energy.

"I'll take that for you."

"I don't need you to take it for me."

"I'm your husband, Evie. It's my job to stand between you and anything unpleasant."

"Carrying my satchel is not unpleasant. It's a necessity."

He opened the door. "One I can help you with."

She didn't immediately step into the room. He supposed that might have to do with the big bed dominating the space. The bed had been an eye-catcher when he'd seen it piled on the wagon of a busted farmer heading back East. The farmer had been focused on heading home with less stress on his team; Brad had been focused on his wedding night with Evie. Both had been satisfied with the deal.

"Something wrong?"

Dragging her gaze away from the ornate posts of the canopy, she muttered, "There's only one bed."

Evie never muttered. "How many were you expecting?"

Her intricate bun brushed his chest, releasing the scent of wildflowers into the air as she looked over her shoulder.

"Two, of course."

Of course. "Well, we'll be bunking down in one."

Half turning, she frowned up at him. "Were you always a preacher?"

Dangerous territory. "What makes you ask?"

"Just curious."

Because of his phrasing. Normally he was better at covering that, but because he was thinking about the two of them in that big bed, he'd made a stupid mistake. "A preacher meets all kinds of people from a lot of different backgrounds. You pick up sayings."

"I guess you would."

She still hadn't moved into the room, and she was still staring at that big bed like it had teeth and might bite. "Is this Elijah and Amy's bedroom?"

Translated, she wanted to know if that was Elijah and Amy's bed. The one Amy had died in. The one that had put an end to Elijah's reformation. "Yeah, but I bought the bed this week."

"Good."

Her fingers on the dark wood were long and delicate, the fingernails pale pink and well shaped. He hadn't noticed her hands before. It suddenly seemed like a huge thing not to have noticed, leaving him to wonder what else he hadn't noticed about her.

"The day is not getting any longer."

Her grip on the doorjamb tightened. "I'm not sleeping with you tonight."

"Throwing down the gauntlet?"

She half turned. "I might as well start, as I mean to go on."

He slid into the space between her and the jamb, blocking her instinctive move to escape with the satchel, excitement humming under his skin at the challenge. "On that I completely agree."

The backward step she took brought her flush against the jamb. Her tongue flicked nervously over her lips. The lower one gleamed with residual moisture, inviting the brush of his mouth, promising the softness of her kiss. He stepped in, bringing them a fraction closer. The folds of her skirts wrapped around the heavy cotton of his pants. Her head tipped back and connected with the hard wood with a soft thunk. A heartbeat later her hands pressed against his chest, denying him the taste she'd offered. He didn't think so. "So now that we've agreed on that, why don't we settle who is going to be the one whose rules get followed."

"I'm not the obedient type."

Dipping his head, he inhaled her scent—woman and wildflowers—before releasing it in a gentle breath that blew across the exposed shell of her ear. "Then I guess it's up to me to educate you."

"In obedience?"

The snap in her voice was belied by the little shiver that shook her body as his lips brushed the top of her ear. She had a slight point to her ears. He smiled at the realization. "In learning to follow my lead."

"I can lead myself well enough."

"How do you know you won't like my way, too?"

"I don't, I guess." The breathless whisper shuddered over the skin of his neck.

Ah, an invitation to be seduced. He leaned in a little closer, trapping her a little better. The tender hollow beneath her ear commanded his attention. It was one of his favorite spots on a woman—so seductively available, so innocently exposed. So completely sensitive. "So maybe you should find out. I could be a heck of a lot more fun than you're expecting."

She turned her head, unwittingly giving him better access. He took full advantage, brushing airy kisses along the column of her throat, testing the chord of her neck with a swift nip of his lips.

"Maybe I don't want fun."

And maybe pigs could fly.

"Then this marriage is going to take some compromise."

"That's just occurring to you?"

This time, when she ducked under his arm, he let her. It was always better to let a woman contemplate pleasure rather than push her toward it. "Pretty much."

She folded her arms across her chest. "I don't believe you."

"It's a bit of a shock to me, too." One last breath of her scent, one last glimpse of the confusion in her blue eyes and he stepped past her into the bedroom. Feeling her consternation trailing him like a mosquito, he tossed the satchel on the bed.

"Don't do that!"

She was at his side in the space of a heartbeat, grabbing the bag off the bed.

"Do what?"

"Put that on the quilt." Her hands smoothed over the brightly colored, interconnecting circles that decorated the white background.

He hadn't noticed the quilt. He'd been too distracted by the uniqueness of her response. It wasn't something he'd purchased.

Her fingers lingered on a pink patch with white polka dots. "It's a wedding quilt."

"For us?"

She looked at him like he'd taken leave of his senses. He likely had. It was very hard to watch her stroke that quilt with a lover's touch and focus on the mundane question of where it came from.

"The patches are sewn from pieces of material from our lives and from pieces of material from our friends and families. It's supposed to bring good luck."

"My contribution must be the black." The only darkness on the bright, happy surface.

It amused him God thought he needed reminding.

It's not like you let me forget.

"Probably." She tapped the pink patch. "This is from the dress I wore to my first basket social." The heavy satchel bumped her leg as she whispered, "They must have worked on this night and day to get it done in time."

"They" would be the women of W.O.M.B. The town's secret social club, made up of the most influential, interfering, well-meaning, whiskey-drinking busybodies he'd ever met. He shook his head, a smile touching his lips. And they'd done it all without once calling on him to sneak them their liquor. That was indeed a sacrifice.

"Well, the one thing you can't say is that this marriage is starting off without a lot of well wishes."

Evie's fingers stilled on one of the black patches. "Just not a lot of hope."

Her pessimism was beginning to irk him. He took the bag from her hand. "Speak for yourself. I have a lot of hope."

"You can't be serious."

He grazed his fingertips across her cheek. "You forget. My job is believing in miracles."

Color flared in the wake of his touch, bringing back the heat to her cheeks and the brightness to her eyes. Brad had plenty of experience reading women, and Evie was a woman at the end of her rope, desperate, looking for a direction in which to jump. All he needed to do was provide her with one.

Her fingers curled to a fist over the quilt. "To the point you think you can create them?"

"I'm a confident man, sweetheart. I think I can work a miracle or two where you're concerned." At least between the sheets.

"To what end?"

"Enough to make you comfortable in this marriage."

"What makes you so sure?"

"The way you've always watched me."

"You know . . ."

That hollowing of her cheek probably meant she'd just bit her tongue. Evie might be impulsive, but she was also proud. If he left her thinking he saw her as a gawking child, he'd have the devil's own time warming her up later. He caught her chin and lifted her gaze to his, stretching her neck a little, letting the tension feed her awareness. "A man always notices when a beautiful woman takes an interest in his goings-on."

"I wasn't pining after you."

No. She'd been suspicious and hunting for clues. "Now that's a shame. A man likes to think a pretty woman has a penchant for his presence."

"Why?"

She was a cautious thing, wanting him to spell things out. He eyed her from head to toe, letting his gaze linger on her lips, her breasts, noticing how her breath caught and the ruffles on the front of her dress shimmied with her exhale. "Besides the obvious, I happen to enjoy your sense of humor. The time you painted those measles spots on Bull Braeger when he was passed out was pure genius."

Her eyes narrowed but she didn't pull away. "He deserved it. He's a mean drunk."

"Is this the part where I'm supposed to say vengeance belongs to the Lord?"

"Yes."

Bull Braeger was a problem he'd discussed with Asa and the McKinnelys just last week. What to do about him had yet to be decided but if they were lucky, the cowardly wife-beating son of a bitch would believe he had whatever Evie had concocted and die from the suggestion, saving Brad the effort of killing him.

"Well, I tend to see things a bit differently."

"I noticed."

She would. Most everyone else was inclined to believe the face he gave the public, not looking deeper, not suspecting a puzzle. Evie not only sensed the puzzle, she wanted to make the pieces fit. It was the way she looked at the world that gave her such insight. Her vision was sharpened by artistic interpretation, her intuition always filtering what her eyes saw. He found it fascinating. "Well, you'll have to go elsewhere to find criticism. As far as I'm concerned you can convince Bull he's down with plague every day of the week."

Another blink and a pause, and then, as if just realizing she stood submissively chained by his touch with awareness blossoming between them, Evie jerked free and rapidly moved to the other side of the room. "You make no sense."

"And here I thought I tended to the blunt."

No immediate answer. She was definitely off center.

A cooler breeze crept through the open windows, riding the last shafts of sunlight, rifling through the stagnant heat of the room. Ten feet away, Evie stood braced for a fight. His wife, his partner, and more than likely the person who would be hurt most when this was all over. Too good and too sheltered for the likes of him, yet they were married. As her husband, he owed her a lot of things. About the only thing he could deliver was a little fun until the showdown came, but there couldn't be any fun if she saw him as the enemy. "The only direction we have to go is forward, Evie."

The face she turned toward him was completely controlled, the only indication of her distress was the way her hands fisted at her side. "Is that what you're planning on doing? Moving forward?"

"Yes." He held out his hand. "Want to come with me?"

She stepped back, eyeing his hand as if he were the devil leading her into temptation, and ran up against the barrier of the bed. Sunlight, still struggling to maintain dominance in the small room, accepted her into its embrace. She looked like an angel with her hair shining pure gold and her eyes glowing so blue. She nervously licked her lips. His gaze dropped to the pink fullness. A very tempting angel.

"You're saying you don't want to fight," she whispered.

If he were closer he could lean down and take the fullness of her lower lip between his teeth, tease it with his tongue, catch the little expulsion of breath she'd make in his mouth, taste her pleasure in the small caress, make it his . . . "Not on my wedding night."

Her head canted to the side, feeding his imaginings. "We're going to fight eventually."

Yes they would. Passionately, he imagined. His cock throbbed at the possibility. And then they'd make up, just as passionately. For a heartbeat, he pictured it, her eyes flashing defiance and invitation as she sprawled naked on the bed, her perfect breasts flushed with desire, her legs opening in challenge—welcome—as he came over her.

"More likely than not."

That was something he was definitely looking forward to experiencing. He picked up the satchel she'd dropped. Putting it on the chair, he flipped the latch. A froth of lace spilled into the vee of the hinge. Fingering the silky nightgown, he caught her gaze. "I'd like to see you in this."

The color in her cheeks flamed to a brilliant red. She rushed through the shadows striping the room. The chair rocked on the wood floor as she snapped the satchel closed, trapping a lacy fold in the hinge. "What you want doesn't matter."

He crossed to the bureau and helped himself to the decanter there. He poured two fingers of whiskey into each of two glasses. They were both going to need something to steady their nerves. He handed her one. She eyed the contents suspiciously.

"What's this?"

"Whiskey."

Sniffing cautiously, she asked, "Why?"

"For the shock."

"I'm not in shock."

He smiled. "You're going to be when you find out what I want tonight is about all that does matter."

"You're trying to scare me."

Was he? Maybe. The way she had of charging through life as though there were no consequences scared the piss out of him. Not to mention made him incredibly hard, picturing that lack of restraint set loose in his bed. He touched his glass to hers. "To a happy marriage."

"May it be short and painless."

Shaking his head at her stubbornness, he lifted his glass to his lips. Evie followed suit. The whiskey was smooth and burned a familiar path to his stomach.

Evie took a large swallow, immediately turned red-faced, and spit half back into her glass, gasping as the rest burned down her throat. Obviously, this was her first time indulging.

He shook his head, taking another quick swallow before reaching over to pat her back. Good sipping stock did not deserve the sputter and wheeze Evie was indulging in. "That's no way to treat good whiskey."

Eyes watering, she tried to give him back the glass. "That is not good."

He took another sip of his, ignoring the glass she held out. "You'll be hard-pressed to find better."

"Really?"

Holding the glass up so the last bit of sunlight was absorbed into the pool of amber, he nodded. "Doc's finest, to be sure." He motioned with his glass. "Drink some more. It'll settle your nerves."

"I don't have nerves."

Like hell she didn't. "Humor me. Pretend you do."

Frowning, she accused, "You just want me drunk."

"Nope. Drunk you'd be no fun at all. I'm betting though that you'd be a chuckler with a couple drinks in you."

She blinked. "I can be fun without being drunk."

"I'm looking forward to seeing it." He motioned again. "Take another sip."

"It was bad enough the first time."

"The taste grows on you."

"Now, that's hard to believe."

"Want to place a little wager on it?"

She perked up. "What kind of wager?"

If Evie had a weakness, it was that she couldn't resist a dare. The tendency made her vulnerable in all sorts of ways a cad could exploit. A husband would protect her from that vulnerability—as long as that husband wasn't also a cad. "If you get to liking it, then you agree to wear that lacy bit of nothing for me."

"And if you lose?"

"Well, then, sweetheart, I'll wear it."

Her brows rose as she eyed the bit of lace escaping from the satchel. "It'll be worth another sip to see you in that."

Oh no, she wasn't getting off that easily. "It's got to be more than a sip. You've got to give yourself time to get used to the taste."

"How much time?"

"You have to finish the glass."

She contemplated the two fingers in the glass and, with a small grin that showed she had no appreciation for the potency of whiskey, said, "Agreed."

Another sip and another grimace and then, "So what do we do now?"

He could think of several things all within easy reach. Undoing the buttons on her blouse, tasting the lightly scented hollow of her throat, untying the ribbon at the top of her camisole, cradling her breast in his hand, plumping it to the pleasure of his mouth.

He looked at the innocence in her eyes. She had no idea of the thoughts running through his head. He sighed. Either Evie was a complete innocent or playing preacher had totally blunted his dangerous edge. "Well, we could stand here staring at each other."

Her lips twitched on a suppressed smile. "Or?"

"What makes you think there's an *or*?"

"I've been studying you, remember? You always have an alternative."

The room was getting dark. Taking a sulphur from the bureau top, he lifted the lid off the oil lamp, struck the match, and lit the wick. Holding it up so the flare of light played over her expressive face he noted the apprehension, the anticipation, the sheer joy of life that surged so strongly within her. No wonder Pearl couldn't control her. Evie wasn't a woman who could ever be forced into anything. She had to be coaxed.

"Well, I was thinking we could play some cards."

Five

"YOU'RE CHEATING."

Wood creaked a protest as Brad settled into the ladder-back kitchen chair with that deceptively easy way of his and eyed Evie with the same casual nonchalance. Cards snapped against the gleaming wood table as he made a bridge of his hands and the cards tumbled between, going from two piles to one with a hypnotic simplicity that spoke of long practice. "What makes you think that?"

"The way you're handling the cards, for one."

"You're calling my honor into question because I know how to shuffle cards?"

He made it sound so preposterous.

She frowned at him, taking a distracted sip of her whiskey, ignoring the taste and burn as she watched him pick up the pack.

"Nobody's that lucky. You've beat me four hands in a row."

His right eyebrow went up and a smile played about his lips. "I could just be that good."

"No one's that good at cards. Especially a minister."

"Why especially?"

As if he didn't know. "It's your job to discourage people from gambling."

"To hear you tell it, it's my job to keep people from having any kind of fun." He shuffled the cards so fast she couldn't really see much beyond a blur of motion. That could be because she wasn't wearing her glasses for up close things or because a comfortable lethargy was invading her limbs. It had been a long day. She smothered a yawn.

"Isn't it?"

"Do you want it to be?"

Sometimes. "Why do you keep answering a question with another question?"

"Probably because, as you seem to have already decided on the answers, it saves time."

She sighed as he split the deck with a smooth maneuver of his fingers that fascinated her. He was right, she did. But only because it was easier to think she'd married a dull-as-mud minister, rather than the real man she suspected lurked beneath his profession. "I do do that, don't I?"

It was his turn to look surprised. "Yeah."

Taking another sip of her whiskey, one big enough to burn all the way to the bottom of her stomach, she confessed, "I'm not a big fan of preachers."

"I noticed."

Up until the wedding, she'd thought she'd been pretty quiet on those particular views. "You did?"

"I saw the painting, remember?"

"What on Earth do you dislike so much about the painting?" She flopped back in her chair, glad the high back was there to support her spine. For some reason it felt about as substantial as dandelion fluff. "I put shadows in to give you mystery, painted it from an angle looking up to give you grandeur. I spent hours just getting the color of your hair right." Capturing the sun-streaked blonds and browns had been a real challenge. She frowned at him. "You have a very difficult hair color, but I captured it perfectly." Looking him over, she felt a spurt of satisfaction. She really had, including how his hair tended to fall over his brow, giving him a sexy, dangerous look completely out of place on a man of God. "I captured *you* perfectly."

The cards slid together with a clench of his fingers. "So you keep telling me."

Could he be that vain? Was that the problem? Did he want to look even more attractive than he was? "You know there's a limit to how much even I can do to enhance reality."

There was a pause. He started dealing with efficient moves, the cards flying across the table with a speed that could imply anger. "Uh-huh."

She decided to change the subject. "You're very adept at card handling."

"It keeps my fingers limber."

Picking up her cards, she glanced up from the dismal mismatch of a two and a king. He probably had aces in his hand. "Why do you need your fingers limber?"

There was another almost infinitesimal pause in which she had the distinct impression he was thinking fast, but then it was gone, and that easy smile was back on his lips. "In case anyone tries to take back their contribution to the collection plate. The church doesn't run on good graces alone."

"I can't imagine anyone stealing from you." She picked up the rest of her cards.

He glanced over. The blue backs of the cards deepened the blue of his eyes until they almost appeared black. "You can't?"

Rats. A three, a four, and another two. She shook her head and took another drink. A pair of twos might as well be nothing against Brad's overwhelming luck. This one didn't burn so badly. "No. The McKinnelys would kill him."

Might that have been a bit of surprise in the twitch of his eyelids? Why? He had to know the McKinnelys would protect him. They were known to be very protective of their friends, and from everything she'd seen of Brad and the McKinnelys, they were friends. "They will, you know. You don't have to worry about that."

His mouth twisted. "Good to know you think I need them to hide behind."

"They've been trained to handle trouble. They're marshals."

"Not anymore."

"It still makes them more than capable of protecting you." It occurred to her, belatedly, that he might be having an issue with her thinking he needed protecting. "Everyone in town, actually," she tacked on hastily.

He grunted and rapped the deck on the table. His "How many?" was sharp.

"Two."

She placed them on the table and bit her lip. Poker wasn't the easy game he'd painted it when he'd proposed it as an option. The element of luck was so much higher than with bridge. And she, apparently, had very bad luck.

"Holding your breath isn't going to make that straight happen."

How did he know she was trying for a straight? "It can't hurt. Nothing else seems to be working."

"It's a sucker's bet." With a motion of his hand, he indicated her discarded cards. "Sure you don't want to take it back?"

"And do what?"

"Fold."

And let him have her share of the brownies she'd anted up? She didn't think so. "I'm comfortable."

His smile reached his eyes. "There are more brownies in the basket."

"Doesn't matter." She pinched a crunchy edge off the nearest. "These are mine."

He caught her hand, bringing her fingers to his lips, catching the crumbs on the tip of his tongue, holding her gaze as he took them into his mouth. Not once did his mouth meet her hand, but the knowledge that it would take very little initiative, either on his part or, more shockingly, hers, to alter that seared deep. "Not yet they're not."

She tugged her hand. He didn't let go. Suddenly, she was very aware of the breadth of his shoulders, the latent strength behind his grip, the nearness of his lips, the solitude of the house. The fact that this was their wedding night. "You haven't won them yet."

"Neither have you."

Jerking her arm free she reached for her whiskey, an odd breathlessness making it hard to talk. "Fine."

She took the last three swallows in a rush, coughing and wheezing as the fumes burned her nostrils from the inside out.

Fanning her face, she choked, "What do you have?"

His finger brushed down her cheek in a touch as soft as the smile that ghosted his mouth. "Three aces."

There was something odd about him knowing that, but odd wasn't nearly as fascinating as the tingles that radiated outward from that brief touch. It meshed so well with the fascination he held for her on other levels. The fascination that had her admiring once again the sculpted perfection of his lips—not too thin, not too wide, but full enough to give a smile depth, thin enough to give anger emphasis. He had a very expressive mouth and if one watched it as much as she did, one soon learned to read his moods. Right now, he was amused by a joke only he understood. The way he always seemed to be. "Why am I not surprised?"

He shrugged. "I've been playing poker for a long time."

"It's a simple game."

"With a lot of strategy behind it."

A coherent thought burst through the fog as he reached for the brownies. There was no way he could have known what those three cards had been. He hadn't even turned them over. She slapped at his hand. "You forgot to mention cheating."

With those lightning reflexes that always startled her, he caught her hand on the upswing of the next swat. "I was careless?"

She was entirely too conscious of his fingers lacing between hers. "You didn't even look at your cards."

"No, I didn't."

"Yet you knew what they were."

His thumb stroked the inside of her wrist, once, twice, and then lingered, pressing lightly on the pulse. "Yes, I did."

"Because you cheated."

"I prefer to think of it as influencing fate."

"You're not supposed to influence fate."

"I like to hedge my bets."

"Preachers aren't allowed to bet."

"I do." Propping his elbow on the table, he brought her hand within inches of his mouth. A mouth she could easily imagine kissing hers. "Are you going to tell?"

Humor lightened his gaze, softened his expression, tempted her wild side, aroused her. "What will you give me if I don't?"

"A chance to get even."

"Are you going to cheat again?"

"You never know. I tend to hedge my bets every chance I get."

"That sounds like a warning."

"I'm a fair man."

"And that was fair warning?"

"Pretty much. You going to have a problem with that?"

At the moment she couldn't think of a single reason she should. Her head felt too heavy, her eyelids weighted. It felt right to lean into his hand. Right that his hand open and his broad palm cup her cheek. "Not if you teach me to cheat, too."

Even talking was hard.

"You'd be lousy at it."

She blinked. "I'm never lousy at anything I attempt."

"You care too much to lie with equanimity."

"I want to cheat, not lie."

"They go hand in hand."

"Then I'll learn."

"I'm not sure I want you to."

Forcing her eyes open, she frowned at him. "Because I have to be the perfect minister's wife. Boring!"

His chuckle wafted across her cheek. When had he gotten so close? "You might have to be a little restricted during the days, but I guarantee your nights will be anything but boring."

"Big talk."

His chair scraped back as he stood. "But I'm a big man."

Yes, he was. She craned her neck back, squinting against the blurring of his expression. "I think I need some more whiskey."

He took the glass out of her hand. "I think you've had enough."

"Being boring already?"

"Just stating the obvious."

"Says you."

The sexy smile left his lips. "Yeah. Says me."

"Why are you frowning?"

He helped her to her feet, which was good because the room started swaying as soon as she stood. "Because I overestimated your tolerance for drink."

She caught his arm and closed her eyes. "I'm past chuckler?"

"Not quite."

"Good. Because I feel rather floaty."

"That might be because I'm carrying you."

She opened her eyes. Disappointment shot through her. So he was. "Darn."

She'd been enjoying the illusion that she could float, but then again, she decided as she absorbed the fact that he was carrying her with so little effort, there were benefits to this, too. Being carried made her feel dainty and feminine. Something she'd never had the opportunity to experience. Snuggling in, she decided to enjoy it.

"Where are we going?"

"The bedroom."

There was something she was supposed to remember about that. She wrestled the memory from deep within the haze. "I'm not sleeping with you."

"Why not?"

"You'd be too much."

Of all the things Brad expected her to say, that wasn't it. "Too much?"

"You'll want to take over, and I don't want to be taken over. I want a nice, malleable husband."

That she could boss around and control. Turning sideways to get through the doorway, Brad shook his head. Evie would be miserable with a man like that. She enjoyed a challenge too much to spend her life with someone who'd let her walk all over him. That would truly bore her.

Belatedly, her arms came around his neck. He stopped beside the bed. She glanced around the room. "Why are we here?"

"In this room or this house?" He thought the room was pretty obvious so he wasn't surprised when she answered.

"This house. It has such a sad story."

It did at that. Elijah's hope had died here. "Maybe I just want to bring it a little happiness."

While she seemed to consider that, he let her feet slide to the floor.

"No. That's not it."

He steadied her while she swayed. He didn't have to tip her head back. She did it naturally, frowning at him, obviously still considering her point. He caught the point of her chin on the edge of his finger, more because he wanted to touch her than that he needed to steady her. She was tipsy, but not drunk. "Then what is it?"

"I asked you first."

"And I asked you second."

"Which means?"

"You have to answer me."

He did love the way her eyes sparkled and her voice snapped when she got annoyed. So much spirit packed into one very feminine, sweet body. Which was his. Every fiery, sexy, opinionated inch. He touched his thumb to the middle of her nose, smiling when her eyes crossed to see it. Cute, too. "I didn't want to be interrupted when I make love to you, so I decided to borrow this house tonight. Tomorrow, we'll go back to mine."

Another frown. "You don't love me."

But he liked her, was fascinated by her, and had been attracted to her from the moment he'd seen her stop a cowpoke in the middle of the street so she could sketch him against the sunset. She'd been oblivious to the man's annoyance. Brad doubted, even if she'd known that the wrangler had been more interested in whoring than art, that she would have cared. She was a little single-minded when it came to her work. "Then we'll just pretend."

She wrinkled her nose and squinted. She always did that when she got close to things. He'd wondered, though he'd never seen her in them, if she needed spectacles. "More influencing fate?"

"Just smoothing the path."

Enough so she didn't need to be scared. As if she read his mind, her head cocked to the side and she whispered, "Are you going to hurt me, Brad?"

"No, what makes you ask?"

"You've got to be mad. It's my fault we're married."

"I've got to admit, I'm a little annoyed things went as they did. No man likes to be forced."

Her fingers curled into fists. "I understand. It is pretty unforgivable."

It probably should be, and he'd thought it was at first, but over the last two weeks, his initial rage had faded to annoyance as he'd come to understand that Evie had never intended any maliciousness. He'd piqued her curiosity, and she'd responded by investigating. For Evie, that meant she followed him, drew him, studied him, and eventually, painted him. And when her family'd backed her into a corner, she'd rebelled by putting the painting she'd done of him on display. In an effort to prove . . . he wasn't sure what. "Why'd you show your mother the painting, Evie?"

Her response, though immediate, didn't make a lot of sense. "Leverage."

"That you'll have to explain."

"You know how when you apply a lever to a fulcrum, the job gets a lot easier?"

He did, but he was surprised that she did. Not that he doubted her intelligence. The woman was as smart as a whip—it was just the terminology. He should have known she would be a big reader. "I'm not following your drift."

She sighed as if he were being particularly dense, then she actually pouted. Up until that moment he would have sworn Evie didn't know how to pout. It was too passive. "My family wanted to send me back East to learn from my aunt."

"Learn what?" He leaned over the bed.

"How to be a dried-up, bitter wreck of a person, if you ask me." She let go of his neck and dropped onto the mattress. "But no one ever asks me."

She didn't seem to know what to do now that she was on the bed. He slipped his arm behind her back and under her legs and slid her around. "So the painting was to show them how much trouble you could get up to if they sent you away." He leaned her back against the headboard. "You didn't want to go back East?"

"I have more freedom here."

Maybe, maybe not. He'd learned a long time ago that while the grass on the other side of the fence might look greener, it was still the same grass, just located in a different spot. "That didn't quite work out like you planned, did it?"

She frowned at him as he straightened, her bun listing off center as she adjusted herself down against the pillows. "You weren't supposed to agree to marry me."

"Funny, I had the same thought about you."

She shoved her falling bun back upright. "It *is* kind of funny when you think about it. Everybody thinks we're so stubborn, but we ended up getting married because we weren't stubborn enough."

"I guess that means then, that neither of us has a right to be mad at the other."

She didn't look comfortable in that dress, not to mention it was getting completely wrinkled. As excuses to get a woman naked went, it was thin, but he could probably make it sound good, come morning. After all, with him being a preacher, she likely didn't even think he could get it up. He sat on the edge of the bed and reached behind her neck for the row of tiny buttons that marched in a seductive line down the center of her back. There were twenty-five of the round pearl teases. He knew because he'd counted them. Twice. The top button of the collar of her dress proved obstinate.

"No, I guess we don't." The frown on her face was evidence that she knew there was a flaw in that reasoning, but she got distracted by his fumbling and reached up, her fingers tangling with his. "What are you doing?"

"Not putting much shine on my skills as a lover, that's for sure."

"You shine there?"

There was no blaming her for the shock in her voice. Preachers who lectured weekly on morality were expected to live as shining examples of what they preached. Which meant any self-respecting one probably shouldn't have any skill whatsoever between the sheets. Lucky for Evie he didn't have trouble with a little double-sided living and had only recently become a practicing minister. Before he'd found the advantages that religion could provide him, he'd spent a long time studying up on how to please the ladies. "I'm hoping to, for you."

She blinked and that invisible tension that always held her slipped a bit more, putting a feminine softness in her posture that he recognized. Another invitation.

"That's very sweet."

Sweet. He smiled carefully. No one called him sweet. Not even the little old ladies of his—of the—congregation. He tucked his fingertip into the warm nape of her neck as he pondered the slip. He'd been making slips like that more often of late. That could be deadly. This role was only temporary, and when the time came for him to move on, the town would get a dedicated preacher. One who could actually do them good rather than just use charm to put a fine haze on things the way he'd used liquor to haze Evie's entry into marriage.

"Brad?"

The trust with which Evie looked at him was the kind a woman gave her husband. The kind that came from knowing your future was completely tied to someone else, and there was only one way to get through and that was together. He didn't deserve it. If he was any kind of decent human being, he would let her go untouched. Tuck her under those covers, and walk away. Go sleep in the other bedroom. Leave her to her dreams and illusions. If he was any kind of decent. That was a mighty big if. "I'm right here, princess."

She smiled, and he had the sudden urge to give decent a try.

Whatever the demon gives you boy, I'll be taking it. You can kill me and that fact won't change. God has declared this truth. You were born of sin, live in sin, and will die in sin.

Shit. At least the latter part of his father's dour prophecies had come true. He was pretty much steeped in sin and getting deeper with every slip of a dainty button through a narrow hole. He was about as far away from the notion of decent as his father's grave was from Cattle Crossing, and since he'd sworn to stop listening to the bastard the night his mother had died, he'd do better to focus on the here and now. And here and now was Evie, lying before him, watching him with big blue eyes that held the conviction that he was sweet. Hard to believe, but in her mind, he wasn't a shameful taint on a pristine reputation. He wasn't the most feared outlaw in the state. He wasn't anything but the stodgy reverend she'd married.

Not fair involving an innocent, God. She doesn't deserve to be hurt.

He'd have to take steps to protect her.

"What are you doing?"

"I'm unbuttoning your top."

"Why?"

To get to what's underneath. "I just thought you'd be more comfortable out of this dress."

Alcohol might have slowed her thought processes, but it hadn't halted them.

"You're going to make me your wife."

"You already are my wife. Anything that happens after this just puts a seal on the deal."

She licked her lips. "You should probably know, I'm not good with pain."

It was his turn to blink. She had strange notions. "You should probably know I'm not planning on hurting you."

"It always hurts the woman's first time. At least that's what I was told."

He didn't know. He'd never taken a virgin. There was little enough true innocence left in the world, so few people that managed to hold on to it, he'd never set himself up to be one of the ones taking it away. He cupped her cheek in his hand, absorbing the heat from her flesh.

"You were told wrong." No matter what happened, he wouldn't hurt Evie. If pain was inevitable, he'd make sure she was drowning in so much pleasure that it would pass unnoticed.

"Really?"

The look she gave him was so full of trust it weighed like lead on his shoulders. Didn't she have any instincts? She should be running, not lying there looking at him, ready to believe whatever he told her. Again the thought crossed his mind that he should walk away, but his baser side had another reaction to that innocence. He wanted her and everything she represented. Family. Loyalty. A permanent bond.

His cock throbbed with anticipation and eagerness. She was his wife for however long he managed to hold her. She had never belonged to anyone else. Part of him didn't care if there wasn't anything after tonight, only cared that Evie would be his and only his. Even if it was temporary, he wanted to know what it felt like to have someone like that.

He kissed her forehead, prolonging the moment, giving any decent part of him a chance to rear its head. After a few seconds he accepted it wouldn't. "I promise."

"Thank you."

Ah hell, now she was thanking him. If anything should have cooled his ardor, it should have been that, but he was hungrier than he'd ever been in his life. And it wasn't a lust just any woman could satisfy. It was only Evie he wanted to pleasure. Only Evie's cries he wanted to catch in his kiss, only Evie's thighs he wanted to feel wrapping around his hips, pulling him closer. Only Evie he wanted to hear whisper his name, welcoming him into her body and her heart. The last drew him up short. Son of a bitch. Did he really want her to love him? He shoved the thought away.

"Brad?" Evie's hand covered his. "What's wrong?"

"Nothing. Just a moment of deep thought."

"About us?"

"Yeah."

"It didn't look like a happy one."

He kissed the end of her nose and her lips, quick busses designed to distract as he resumed his assault on the buttons on her dress. "That's because I'm a worrier."

"About what?"

"Pleasing you."

With the trust of someone who'd never been betrayed, she swallowed that whopper whole.

"Sit up." He helped her. The way she leaned into his chest didn't indicate second thoughts, but he found he had to ask.

"Are you willing to give yourself to me, Evie? As a wife does to her husband?"

Her head canted to the side. "Why do I have to promise that?"

Because he wanted her giving; he didn't want to take. Not with her. With her he wanted this to seem real. "Because it's better that way."

"For you or for me?"

"For both of us, I hope."

Her hand came up and she curved her palm over the point of his hip bone, steadying them both with the intimate contact. Her lips slipped between her teeth.

He liked that she didn't give him an immediate answer. He liked that she took her time. It made the illusion more real. More possible, though it never would be. He knew that. She didn't. That was again unfair. The baser part of him—the part that had kept him alive since he was four, after his father discovered his mother's infidelity—didn't care.

"Yes."

He didn't realize how deeply he'd been depending on that answer until he got it. Relief went through him with almost dizzying strength. She was his now, given to him by the law he'd spent his life breaking. Given to him because people saw him as good. It was amazing, the impression a few calculated good deeds could put in people's minds. If they knew the truth, they'd drag him out to the big oak at the edge of their prosperous little town and hang him. Brad stroked his thumb across his wife's softly parted lips. The seventh and eighth buttons on her dress slipped their moorings. He guessed after tonight, they'd have the right, even by his definition of right and wrong.

The skin on her back felt like warm satin and heated at his touch. Her innocence burned bright in the blush that colored the pale skin of her neck and face. If he pulled the now-sagging lace collar down, he bet her chest would be red, too.

"Good. Then I want you to get dressed in that pretty nightgown your momma packed."

"You're leaving?"

"I'll be right back. I'm going to check on the horse and make sure it's settled."

She absorbed that with a little start. "Where do you want me to wait?"

He knew she really wasn't asking where, but how. He had an immediate image of her waiting on the big bed, right leg drawn up, nightgown pooling at her hip, giving teasing glimpses of the tender flesh beneath. That was a bit advanced for a virgin.

"However you want, as long as you're waiting for me as my wife."

"And how will you know that?"

He motioned to the frothy bit of temptation pinched between the edges of the satchel. "You'll be wearing that gown."

Six

THIS WAS A *choice?*

Evie tugged the peignoir around her in an effort to get the density of a fold strategically placed over those areas of her body she wanted covered. Which was pretty much everything. The gown that had looked so substantial with all those layers of lace when she was pulling it out of her satchel magically dissolved to nothing the second she pulled it over her head. The robe was no better. She tied the small satin bows that decorated the front from her throat to her waist, frowning at her reflection in the shaving stand mirror. Pretty much adding nothing to nothing just produced a semitransparent gown that seemed to delight in playing a game of peekaboo with every private part of her body. Something she was beginning to suspect Brad had known, which would explain one of his secret smiles.

She flicked the folds again, succeeding in creating a protective gather over her left nipple, which only resulted in exposing her right. With all the material drawn to one side, the curve of her hip became a lushly veiled enticement and the darker patch of hair between her legs showed through in an almost wanton display. What on Earth had her mother been thinking? One thing was clear—her modesty was going to be hard put to maintain its balance when Brad saw her in this. She backed up from the mirror. Good grief, Brad was going to see her in this!

The bolt of heat that shot through her at the thought was another surprise. She would have labeled it mortification if it hadn't lingered as a potent warmth she recognized. A week ago she wouldn't have known what it was. After the card game earlier this evening, she had no doubt. Desire. As much as she dreaded the moment of judgment when Brad saw her in this gown, she also welcomed it. She wanted to please him. Wanted the joy her mother said could be hers. It had just never occurred to her how naked she was going to be while obtaining it.

Footsteps sounded on the wooden porch. Not as heavy as she would have expected. For a man his size, Brad was very light on his feet. The back door squealed open and then just as noisily squealed shut. *Shoot.* She was out of time. She leapt for the bed, heart jumping a beat as she tugged the covers back and climbed in, shoving her feet down as she yanked the blankets up. The stairs creaked, marking every step of Brad's approach. Beneath the covers the gown and robe bunched around her waist.

"Darn it!"

Grabbing the hem, she wrestled them down. Naturally, the extra material had to be stuck under her elbow, and naturally Brad would enter the room just then, catching her in one of the most awkward poses ever.

"Problems?" he asked as he stood in the doorway, smiling in the most aggravating way.

She kept tugging, gritting her teeth against the waves of embarrassment breaking over her composure. Giving a little hop, she got the hem free of her elbow. "Nothing I can't handle."

Brad strolled into the room with that inherent confidence that bordered on arrogance, his smile spreading in proportion to her struggles. In his hand he held a bowl and a small box, which he put on the bed stand. The faint scent of vinegar stung her nostrils. "I'd be happy to help."

She just bet he would. "Don't push your luck."

"I wouldn't dream of it."

His gaze never left the moving lumps of her hands under the covers. A glance down showed it did look strange. She yanked them out, glaring at him as he stepped between the bed and the light. "If you laugh, I swear I'll brain you with the fireplace poker."

His shadow stretched over her as he came up beside the bed, making it harder to read his expression. "Then I'll do my best to keep a straight face."

She took a breath. He smelled intriguingly of soap, man, and the outdoors. He'd washed up before coming in. The courtesy softened her already weakening resistance.

Brad sat on the side of the bed. The mattress dipped under his weight. She had to brace her hands to keep from tumbling into him. He steadied her with a hand on her shoulder, chuckling when she squeaked.

"Scoot over."

She couldn't, for the same reason she'd almost fallen off the bed. "You're sitting on my gown."

Standing, he trailed his finger down her arm. A shiver shook her from head to toe. Goose bumps sprang up in its wake. "That gown seems to be giving you problems."

She grabbed the material and pulled it taut against her body, holding it against the drag as she slid over. "Trust me, it's nothing but trouble."

And so was he.

The mattress dipped again as Brad sat back down, creating a well she rolled naturally into until the side of his hip stopped her tumble. A quilt, a sheet, and a blanket did nothing to blunt the intimacy of the connection. The fading goose bumps rallied as the memory of their kiss shimmered between them in an invisible haze of heat.

When he reached up toward her head, she couldn't help but flinch. Her nerves were too raw, her anticipation too high. He shook his head and clucked his tongue. "You are a bundle of nerves, aren't you?"

"Just a little."

"I don't think 'little' covers it."

The hairs at her temple stirred, then a little farther back they pulled taut.

"What are you doing?"

"I'm unpinning your hair."

She bit her tongue on a "why." She'd asked enough stupid questions for one day. "It'll be all tangled in the morning."

"Will it?" He didn't look upset at the possibility. "Then I guess it will be up to me to brush it out."

He wanted to brush her hair? He started to unwind the coil. She had a lot of hair. It took some time. Hairpin after hairpin dropped onto the wooden bed stand.

"Just how long is your hair?"

It really was her one vanity. Thick, and very straight, it fell past her hips. "I can sit on it."

His eyes narrowed and the blue of his irises darkened. Catching a tendril, he slid it slowly between his fingers until he couldn't reach any farther. The tension in her scalp blended with the internal hum of desire, tightening her muscles as he moved his hand, manipulating the tension, admiring the play of light along the blonde strands. His gaze, when it dropped to hers, imbued his simple "I'll just bet you can" with a much deeper meaning. He released her hair. She jumped as the soft strands spilled across her cheek and neck, shivering as he brushed them off with short, tantalizing strokes. His hand slipped down the side of her neck. Chills rose up her spine and spread over her shoulders.

"I bet this gown is pretty on you."

"What there is of it. I'm all but naked!"

He chuckled, his finger leaving the lace to trace the line of her jaw. "You realize, I'm not seeing that as the problem you are?"

"I know." Which irritated her. She wanted to be as calm, as accepting. She just couldn't find the gumption to make it happen.

With the lightest of pressure, he tipped her face up. "I could get as naked as you, and then we'd be even."

"Good gravy, no!" She'd probably puff away in a burst of embarrassment if he did.

He grinned. "What happened to the bold-as-brass artist who not only painted me naked, but put that painting on display?"

"Would you believe she's had an attack of propriety?" It was as good an excuse as any for her uncharacteristic behavior.

"I hope not. I liked her unconventionality."

No matter how Evie searched Brad's expression, she couldn't see any hint of a lie. "You're a little unconventional yourself."

His finger left her jaw and found the chord of her neck, following it downward. Goose bumps chased the caress. "Which makes us a good match."

She was beginning to believe he might be right. The few controversial choices he'd made since coming to town did point to a certain compatibility. Like the time when Cougar had decided he was going to marry Mara, with or without her permission. The talk for days was about how Brad had gone against Cougar, offering the woman a choice, even marriage, which was unheard of. Ministers did not marry ex-prostitutes, even one who had been forced into the profession. "What would you have done if Mara had taken you up on your offer of marriage?"

"You heard about that, eh?"

"Everybody heard about that. So what would you have done?"

The quilt edged down under the pressure of his finger. "You mean after Cougar got done carving me into little pieces?"

It was impossible not to respond to his wry smile with one of her own. It was equally impossible not to grab the descending quilt. "Yes. Right after that."

"I would have stayed married to her until she was healed enough to move on."

Indignation squashed passion. "You'd give *her* an annulment, but not me?"

His eyes lifted to hers. "Her I felt sorry for."

"And me?"

She couldn't look away from the intensity of his gaze, holding her breath until he answered.

His smile took on a seductive edge. "You, I want."

It was a simple, straightforward statement from a very complex man. The dichotomy left her caught between belief and doubt. "I think that makes you crazier than me."

Cocking his eyebrow, he pointed out, "I'm not the one buried under quilts in the summer heat."

"No, you're not." He was also right. She was roasting. Holding his gaze, feeling as if she was stepping off a cliff with nothing to hold on to but the desire she saw in his expression, she said, "You should probably do something about that."

"Let go of the quilt and I will."

That was easier said than done. Being bold was a whole different animal than acting bold, and inviting Brad to her bed, husband or not, was the boldest thing she'd ever done. He waited patiently for her to release the covering, which she did, one finger at a time, until only her forefinger and thumb continued the fight.

Eyeing her grip, he asked, "You sure you're just a *little* nervous?"

His smile nudged hers into the open. "Maybe more than a little."

"Because you've never done this before?"

"Because maybe I want to enjoy my choice."

He shook his head and clucked his tongue. "Making sure you enjoy tonight, Evie darling, is my responsibility."

This time when he tugged, the covers slipped free. She suppressed the urge to snatch the quilt back as it slid down her torso, over her breasts, across her hips, down her thighs.

"What's mine?"

The humid air wafted over her body, soothing her overheated skin with a sultry stroke. The night was hot, but not as hot as Brad's gaze, which traveled the same path as the blanket, lingering on her breasts and the point where her gown slipped into the juncture of her thighs.

"You," he said, his drawl rough with desire as he studied her body, "can practice sighing with pleasure."

The blush started at her toes and rushed so fast to her face she felt light-headed. Clenching her hands into fists, she forced herself to hold still. "Fat chance that's going to happen, seeing as I'm about to drop dead of mortification."

His gaze came back up, hit the fiery red of her cheeks, dallied a bit before lifting to hers. "I'd consider it the perfect wedding gift if you'd hold off on that until morning."

How could he make her laugh in the middle of mortification? "You would?"

"Absolutely."

Her cheek twitched with conflicting messages. Smile, frown, yell . . . He had her so topsy-turvy, they all sounded good. "And if I don't?"

"Then I'll likely go mope around the saloon alongside Old Buzzard."

Old Buzzard was Henry's hound. He was a renowned mooch, but a successful one, his begging enhanced by the huge folds of sagging skin under his mournful brown eyes. Brad was not the type to mope. Nor, she decided, to beg.

"I'll try to hang on, but it would be easier if you'd turn out the light."

A whole lot easier.

"Feeling modest?"

What was his first hint? Tugging the hide-nothing gown away from her skin, she muttered, "Yes, as much as I get the impression it's not a quality you appreciate."

She had his full attention as his fingers reversed the trip up her body, skimming the outside of her thigh, her hip, the seam between her arm and her nibs, the side of her breast . . . They didn't go any farther, just rested there. Five featherlight points that seemed to gain weight, heat, and importance with every beat of her heart.

"Now there you would be wrong. Any other man gets within a hundred yards of you, I expect you to trot out all the prim and proper you can find."

She gasped as he moved his thumb, sending little sparks of pleasure shooting through her breast, sensations that gathered just under the nipple, causing it to tingle and draw up into an eager, aching point.

"You're going to be a jealous husband?" she managed to ask through her shock as his hand opened around the full curve of her breast, hesitating for just a second. A moment in which she lost all ability to think beyond the moment when that hesitation ended. What would he do then?

"Enough so you can take the question mark off the end of that sentence."

Not hesitating, she decided, watching Brad's expression as her breast swelled within his hold, seeking a firmer touch. Anticipating. He was anticipating the pleasure, just as she was. She let go of the lace.

"What should I do with my sense of propriety?"

He shrugged and gave her that devilish grin that tempted her wild side to let him take the lead and see just how far he would go. "You're welcome to stuff it under the pillow."

"That's convenient."

"I think it's going to work out perfectly." His thumb flirted with the tip of her breast, grazing the taut peak. She cried out, shocked by the skitter of heat. Catching her involuntary rise against his palm, he eased her through the discovery, cradling her breast in the aftermath as she subsided back to the mattress. Shadows hid most of his expression, but not the satisfaction in his eyes, or the sensual fullness of his lips. "The truth is, Evie, I prefer you less inhibited."

The words flowed over her awareness as she watched his mouth shape the words, flexing and contracting with the syllables, moving in a parody of a kiss. She licked her lips, unconsciously searching for a remnant of his taste. "How uninhibited?"

Was that husky rasp of sound her voice?

"Are you asking me what the rules are?"

Yes. She was. "I've waited a long time to be seduced. I don't want to step wrong and mess it up."

"There's no way to mess it up."

Brad braced his weight on his palm by her hip. She blinked as lamplight fell across her face. This time, when she shifted with the mattress, she fell against his forearm. The pull on her breast joined the foreign tension low in her stomach, coiling it tighter.

"We're husband and wife. Any way we want to love each other is right."

A restlessness entered her limbs, heat blossomed between her thighs, and through it all Brad watched her as a predator watched its prey, learning its habits, manipulating its responses. If he wasn't her husband she'd be afraid. But he was her husband, and the experience with which he handled her body boded well for her wedding night, if Pearl was to be believed.

"My mother said the marriage bed could be a place of joy if I'd just allow it."

At last she'd succeeded in shocking him. His fingers bit into the softness. "Are you planning on allowing it?"

Another pass of his thumb over her nipple. This time she was better prepared for the pleasure, accepting it, not resisting, finding it was even better the second time around.

She met his gaze squarely. "Can you deliver?"

Brad looked at his hand cradling the delicate softness of Evie's breast, his tanned skin dark against the white, sinfully provocative gown, his thumb hovering just above the turgid tip. Evie didn't have the experience to know how explosive the passion between them was, but he did. With complete confidence, he gave her the truth. "I'll make you scream."

"And in the morning?"

In the morning she'd be hot, tight, and perfect. He'd take her so gently, easing her into awareness the way he couldn't ease her into their union. "You'll wake coming around my cock."

She gasped and choked. Color flooded her cheeks in a hot rush. Her torso arched into his hand. His fingers closed reflexively, bringing another gasp to her lips. She had very sensitive breasts.

"Shh." Lowering his weight to his forearm, Brad brushed his lips across Evie's hot cheeks, soothing her panic. Her lashes tickled the side of his nose. First the left, and then the right. When she caught her breath, he asked wryly, "Not the answer you were looking for?"

Her "Ask me come morning" was choked. He admired her pluck almost as much as her honesty.

Because she liked it so much and because he enjoyed the way passion softened her lips and hazed her eyes, he milked her breast with gentle movements, drawing gently upward from the base until he reached the plump nipple, rubbing the rougher lace across the sensitive tip, priming her for further intimacies—the heat of his lips, the draw of his mouth, the kiss of his cock. "Planning on testing my word?"

"Maybe."

"What do I have to do to change that 'maybe' to a 'yes'?"

"Tell me exactly what's right and what's wrong so I have a prayer of staying inside the boundaries."

It was a revelation to see how much Evie actually did care about being accepted. It was a weapon he could—should—use if he wanted to save himself from her natural curiosity. All he had to do was infer, with one little lie, an impossible standard and Evie would spend the rest of their time together striving to meet it. And with each failure, her attention would become more focused on that than on him. Which was what he needed, so why was he hesitating? It wasn't as if he hadn't taken advantage of misplaced trust in the past. The role of husband should be just another act to play out, but looking into Evie's big blue eyes, a remnant of decency he'd thought extinct raised its head.

No matter how hard he tried to shove it back, it stubbornly stood between him and common sense, tying his hands by making him aware of how vulnerable Evie would be if he fed her the lie, how badly she could be hurt. *Well, shit.* Who the hell would have thought it? In the role of Reverend Swanson, Shadow Svensen really did have a conscience. And it wasn't the least bit convenient.

Brushing the hair off her face, he asked, "Are you talking about mechanics?"

"I know the mechanics," she muttered, catching his hand in hers and holding on tightly. "It's the social niceties I'm not clear on."

"Niceties?" He choked back a laugh. "I don't think I've ever heard it put quite that way."

Her nails dug in as she struggled up to her elbows. He had no complaints with the more aggressive pose as he now had a prime view of the valley between her breasts. As soon as she caught the gist of his attention, her hand slapped over the gap. "If you dare laugh . . ."

He kissed the tip of her nose. "You'll what?"

She collapsed back into the pillows, closed her eyes, and released the truth on a long sigh. "I actually think I might cry."

That was shocking. "You?"

"It's been a very long day and my delicate constitution can't take the strain."

Despite the lightness of the delivery, there was no denying the truth. Evie had reached the end of her resilience. That scrap of decency stirred again.

"Then why don't you let me handle the niceties from here on out?"

She licked her lips and nodded. "Maybe . . . just for tonight." She cracked her right eyelid. "And you're right. That does sound silly."

He stroked his thumb across the ridge of her knuckles. "So you forgive me for the chuckle?"

"I'm considering it."

"But only if I don't laugh again?"

Opening her other eye, she studied him. "If you promise not to mention I used the word *niceties* in reference to relations, maybe."

Ah, she was getting her confidence back. Good. Shy didn't suit her. "That's a tough choice."

He placed her hand on his shoulder. It just lay there. Waiting. For direction?

"Why?"

"I figured on getting at least six months of teasing out of that."

Working his hand between the softness of the pillow and the silk of her hair, he cupped her skull in his palm, felt the nervous hitch in her breath. A subtle tension gathered in her muscles.

Another breath, and then she said, "That would be a stretch."

"You don't think I could find ways to work *niceties* into the conversation frequently over the next six months?"

"Not and continue to be original."

He lifted her slightly, just enough so he could massage the tension from her neck. "That sounds distinctly like a challenge."

"How can you take something like that as a challenge?"

"My male pride has been attacked."

"That is so much rubbish."

Running his finger down the bridge of her nose, he smiled when her eyes crossed. Sass, fun, and cute. He really did like her. "Ah, but it made you smile."

"And that's what you wanted?"

Yeah, he realized, it was. "I've always liked your smile."

"You have?"

"Evie, there are more sides to me than the one that preaches on Sunday."

"I knew it!"

What did she think he was going to confess? "One of them is that I appreciate a beautiful woman."

"Even an unconventional one?"

Now she was fishing. Fishing was good. A woman didn't fish unless, in her mind, she'd already surrendered. He tapped the end of her nose. "Especially an unconventional one." Grazing his fingers down her neck, he asked, "How about you? You've been studying hard on me. Did you like what you saw?"

Indecision hovered in her eyes as she weighed the benefits of honesty versus those of a lie. He let her take her time, amusing himself by stroking his fingertips beneath the neckline of her gown, finding the slant of her collarbone, following it down to the hollow of her throat, teasing the nerve endings to life with brief, skimming touches, judging how much pressure to apply by the catch in her breath, the flicker of her eyelashes. Evie was definitely in the mood to be seduced. Finally, she swallowed and nodded.

"Good." He inched his hand lower, over the top curve of her breast, holding her gaze. Stopping just short of the soft peak, he felt the blush heat her skin, the rise of goose bumps, the subtle swelling that indicated softening elsewhere. "Then you have to know there's more than enough wildness in me to welcome all the wildness you can throw at it."

He got to see a spark of that wildness right then. Her grip tightened on his shoulder and her head cocked to the side as she pulled him down. "Is that a dare?"

"I'm sure as heck hoping you'll take it as one."

Seven

SHE MADE IT to the fourth button before she lost momentum.

"Something wrong?" Brad asked, easing the ribbons of her peignoir free with a leisurely draw. Women were miracles of softness meant to be savored. Evie, with her soft skin, soft heart, and impulsive spirit, more so than most.

"You're just so much more compelling up close." Her hands slipped between the lapels of his shirt and tangled in the wiry hair on his chest. "Seeing you from afar is just not the same."

The next ribbon slid from the eyelets in the lace without a whipser of protest, revealing more of that beautiful skin and the first hint of cleavage. The white satin, no more delicate than her flesh, trailed between her breasts in a shimmering stream. He folded the ribbon back on itself. A silky *X* to mark his spot. "As touching me, you mean?"

Her lip slipped between her teeth. "Yes. The texture is so wonderful."

The statement wasn't what he'd been expecting. Then again, Evie rarely did what he expected.

"Remind me to talk to you about your technique."

"My technique is just fine. It's just that you're magnificent."

Another burst of laughter escaped. She was always making him laugh at moments he never thought he should. There was a certain clinical precision in the placement of her palms, the press of her fingers . . . "You wouldn't be thinking about sculpting me, would you?"

Her gaze flicked to his guiltily. "How did you know?"

Leaning down, he brushed his mouth over hers, dawdling when her lips parted, accepting the invitation to repeat the caress. "You always get a certain look in your eyes when you're contemplating immortalizing something."

She didn't seem to get his hint, just kept alternating between petting and memorizing his torso, her fingers coming close to his nipples but never connecting. Promising, teasing, tormenting his chest, his abdomen, his chest again.

"I've never sculpted anyone before." Pushing him back, she worked her other hand inside the front of his shirt, that expression of intense concentration coming over her face again as her palms learned the shape of his right pectoral. "But you make me want to."

He wished he had an ounce of artistic talent, because if he did he'd preserve the way she looked right now, eagerness clashing with innocence, passion overriding reserve. "What else do I make you want?"

"You make me want to be wild." Her lashes touched her cheeks in a moment of shyness, before lifting to reveal the desire deepening the blue of her eyes. "Very, very wild . . ."

He made her feel wild? That little huskiness in her voice as she confessed was like the most vivid of rasps over his desire, sensitizing it to the tune of her voice, the scent of her skin. She took a deep breath. The twist of ribbon shimmered. Satin on satin. A gateway to heaven . . . He touched the fold with his finger, spread the tight circle until it encased his finger in a snug little hug. "Good thing I have a penchant for wild, then."

It came out more growl than drawl. Her tongue touched her lower lip in a flash of pink, leaving a hint of moisture. Brad licked his own lip, imagining it was hers. His cock throbbed as she did it again, indulging in a few imaginings of its own. Dropping his gaze, he could easily discern the pout of her nipples pressing up through the sheer gown. Sweet little nubs shining the same pink as the ribbon. He could already imagine how they'd melt against his tongue, tighten beneath his kiss, flush with her passion, beg for the graze of his teeth.

"Yes, "she sighed, her index finger tracing the flat outline of his areola. With a glance up, she caught the direction of his interest. He expected her blush, but the seductive little twist that slid the gown to the left, almost but not quite baring her breast, that was a complete surprise. "It is."

A nudge sent the gown the rest of the way. "Playing for

keeps?" he asked, pressing the engorged nubbin into the fullness of her breast.

"Yes."

It came out a high-pitched squeak, inspiring another smile. When he pulled his hand away, her breast sprang back to its natural shape, quivering just a little. Just enough to coax the cup of his hand. The nipple was harder, redder. Pinching the ribbon between his thumb and forefinger, he wrapped it around the base, pulling it tight. Her gasp whispered over his fingers. His cock jerked and stretched. She'd been watching him wrap her nipple.

"There, pretty as a picture."

Despite the blush flooding her torso, she grinned and cocked her head to the side. "Don't you want to unwrap your present?"

Shit, maybe wishing away her shyness hadn't been the best plan. Evie in the throes of exploration was as tempting as a hot summer day after a bitter cold winter. As seductive as the first moment of peace after a bloody battle. As potent as good whiskey on an empty stomach. And like the latter, she had a tendency to knock the sense right from his head. If she didn't finish getting his shirt open soon, he was going to do something drastic—like rip it off.

"Maybe I just want to wrap it tighter."

"Why would you want to do that?"

"Because you'll like it."

And she did. The proof was in the way her cheeks flushed a brighter pink, the way her lip slipped between her teeth, and especially the way the sweet perfume of her arousal scented the air. Her nails curled into his chest, still not delivering the hard caress he needed. He tied off the knot, leaving her imprisoned by the erotic little ache.

"Unbutton my shirt." Her nails grazed his skin as she battled with the stubborn fastenings, teasing, tormenting with little touches when he needed full contact. Burning through his passion until he couldn't stand it anymore. Three tugs and buttons flew across the room, plunking off the wood floor. Evie stared at him in surprise, eyes wide, mouth open. With a growl, he dragged her hand against his chest. "Touch me right, damn it."

"I don't know what that is!"

With his hand over hers, he showed her. It didn't take her long to pick up what he wanted. Her nail raked his nipple. Lightning shot from his chest to his cock, tearing a hole through every barrier he'd built. His teeth clenched on a snarl as she jerked her hand away, depriving him of what he needed. Capturing it, he brought it back, pressing her palm to his skin, holding it there as the heat seeped beneath the surface. And she let him, not moving, not fighting, not giving. Just letting him while she watched him with big blue eyes.

Shit. Tipping his head back, Brad took a steadying breath. He was supposed to be seducing his wife, not scaring her. "Sorry."

"For what?"

Losing control. Something he never did. "You don't have to worry that I'll be like that when it matters."

"Doesn't it all matter?"

"Yeah." He shifted his position until he was over her. Her breasts with their hard little nipples pressed into his skin, the left a little harder than the right. Working his knee between her thighs, he made a place for himself. "It all matters."

He'd do well to remember that. For all her curiosity, Evie was a virgin and if he didn't get his reactions to her under control this would be the only time he'd get near her lithe body. And that would be a crime, because once was never going to be enough for him to sate the lust she inspired in him. Had always inspired in him. He realized now that there was no longer a reason to keep his distance. He might have never approached her if things had stayed as they were, but they hadn't, and now she was his, about to *become* his.

He fingered the ribbon binding her nipple. "When I take this off, you're going to be very sensitive."

A twist of her torso put tension on the satin. She gasped, "I already am."

He pulled it just that much tighter, knowing from her frown that she'd crossed that line where pain and pleasure met. And she wasn't backing off. Shit. It was his turn to groan. She was going to burn him alive. "Good."

His cock brushed the inside of her thigh. Even through the layers of cloth, the contact seared.

Sprinkling kisses down her cheek, the side of her neck, along the line of her collarbone before working back inward, he gentled her into the thought of his mouth on her chest. The collar of her gown got in his way. "You've got too many clothes on."

"I was going to say the same thing about you."

"Not planning on being shy?"

She shook her head, her fingers linking behind his neck. "I'm twenty-five years old. I've spent a year painting you in parts. I think I've earned the full effect, don't you?"

He remembered the painting. "The full effect might be more than you bargained for."

Her smile was as soft as her touch. "I can feel you against me, Brad. I've got a pretty good idea of what you disliked about that painting."

She might have an idea, but the reality was bound to startle, and he didn't want Evie startled. He wanted her like this. Strong, curious, and passionate. "And here I thought the reality was going to come as a shock."

"Oh, it'll likely be a shock, but not a completely unexpected one. Most things in nature are in proportion."

He cocked an eyebrow at her. "But you didn't paint me in proportion."

She shrugged. "I was hesitant to guess."

"So you did what?"

"I transferred the . . . appendage from my friend's baby."

Parts. Bits and pieces. She'd created him from fragments. He dropped his forehead to hers. No wonder she had suspicions about who he really was. She'd never really seen the carefully constructed image he'd presented. "You could have given me pants."

"That wouldn't have accomplished my goal."

"Shocking your family?"

"Convincing them I couldn't be trusted out of their sight."

She brushed her thumbs over his nipples, her gaze narrowing when he jerked and his breath hissed in.

"That feels good?"

"Damn good."

She did it again, her eyes dark with curiosity and her own budding passion. "Like what?"

Shit, he hadn't even kissed her breasts and she had him almost to the point of no return. The next pass brought a growl of pleasure to his throat. Reaching down, he gathered up the skirt of the gown. There were volumes of material. Yards of fabric that tested his patience. "Give me a second and I'll show you."

"Don't hurry on my account." Her head cocked to the side as she used the side of her nail against the hard nub. "I like this."

If she thought she was in control, she had another think coming.

"And I like this." This was the hard ridge of his cock against her softest flesh. This was his mouth on hers, catching her gasp, giving it back in a soft "yes" as her lips relaxed, parted, and then welcomed the thrust of his tongue, lying passively as she learned the movements and then shifted beneath him. Her nails bit into his pectorals. He pulled the gown up, flicking her bound nipple with the side of his thumb. She arched and cried out.

"That's it." He nipped her lower lip, gathering up her gown. "That's what I want." Another flick, another pleasured cry. "Just give me that."

And she did, copying every move he made, reflecting back to him the desire in which he wanted to drown, luring him into deepening the kiss, challenging his control with the creative side of her nature. When she caught his tongue between her lips and sucked, he swore and tore his mouth away.

"Witch." He finally reached the end of the fabric. "Lift up."

With only the slightest hesitation, she did, clinging to his shoulders like he was all that she trusted, whispering as the gown floated to the floor, "You like me naked."

He suppressed his grin. "What makes you so sure?"

"I felt your . . . cock twitch."

Just the word on her perfect lips was enough to bring him to the edge. "Where the hell did you hear that word?"

Eyes crinkling in amusement, she trailed her fingers up over his nape to twine in his hair. "I'm twenty-five, Brad, and men aren't as careful as they could be when it comes to their speech. Yourself included."

"I'll be careful tonight." Very careful not to scare her. Careful not to forget himself, but it was going to be damn hard with her looking the way she did right now, all pink and white, her breasts hard tipped with passion, the left bound to his will.

"Not too careful. I hope. I want to have fun."

So did he. Every bit he could wrestle from this night. Evie

was like no one he'd ever known before. Indulging himself with her wasn't safe, wasn't sensible, but when she drew her foot up his calf under his pant leg, her expression absorbed as she memorized the feel of his skin, the changing pressure of his cock, he didn't care. No matter what the price for this time with Evie, he'd pay it, because this was different, unique, and he'd be damned if he'd throw it away. "Then you might want to hold back a bit on the words you use."

"Why?" Adjusting the angle of her hips until the ridge of his cock was intimately nestled, she gave a luxurious sigh and pressed up. "I think you like it when I use that word."

Like it? He dropped his forehead to hers, laughter rippling from him in a soft wash of amusement. "Evie darling, I'm so far past 'like,' it's a wonder I can still talk."

"It's almost over?"

If he'd taken her chocolate away, she couldn't have sounded more disappointed. "Not by a long shot. I have a lot of advice to work through."

"Advice?"

He inched lower. "According to what I've been told, virgins are shy, timid creatures who fear the pleasure of a man's touch."

"You thought because I was a virgin, I'd be stupid?"

He laughed again at her indignation. "Prospective grooms are treated to a lot of advice."

"And you listened?"

"A smart man always listens."

"So what was the advice?"

"Keep the lights off."

Her palms cherished the planes of his chest. Her fingertips discovered the curve of muscle, the rough edges of bullet wounds, and the longer, narrow slashes of the whip, scars that would later bring questions but right now did nothing more than cause a slight pause. Her "Absolutely not" made him smile.

"Go fast or slow, touch or don't touch. Feed alcohol—"

She gave him the bite of her nails. "That you tried."

He kissed his way down to the valley between her breasts, nerve endings snapping to attention as her nails dragged up to his shoulders in a sensual tease.

He couldn't resist giving the ribbon a little tug. "Feed chocolate."

"Oh, lands!" She caught her breath. "I would have liked that."

The spot two inches down from her breastbone was sensitive. He lingered there, sucking at the taut flesh, absorbing the resulting shiver against his open mouth before stroking his tongue over the rise of goose bumps. Her high-pitched little sigh drove him crazy. Pressing into her heat, he did it again, feeling cheated when this time she only caught her breath. He wanted that sigh, that proof of her submission. He wanted the barrier of his pants gone from between them. "I'll keep that in mind."

Moving down her body, gritting his teeth when it required he leave the intimate hug of her groin, he continued with his litany. "I'm also supposed to ignore your protests."

Her fingers wove through his hair. "At your peril."

He smiled. "Encourage your wildness."

"That you've done."

The well of her navel drew his attention. "Not enough."

Her abdominal muscles rippled at the graze of his teeth, sucked in at the probe of his tongue. Her hands fisted in his hair as he continued his journey. He made it another inch before her fingers tugged. "What are you doing?"

Looking up between her pert breasts, he stated the obvious. "Kissing you."

"My mouth is up here."

Those weren't the lips he was interested in right now. "And I'll get back to them in just a bit."

"I'm not sure . . ."

He was. He nibbled his way lower, sliding his hand up her thigh, pressing outward. "Trust me, Evie darling. You want this."

With a breathless hesitancy she asked, "How do you know?"

Her legs parted. He pressed a kiss to the top of her mound, the dark blonde hairs beneath tickling his chin, calling him to come play. Nuzzling his way down, he accepted the invite, pressing a kiss on the silken folds, steadying her through the shock with the press of his palm. "Because I'm going to drive you wild."

"Oh, dear."

She might be shocked, but she was interested. With a leisurely pass of his tongue, he took the indecision out of her hands.

"Sweet, Evie."

"I can't believe you did that."

He couldn't believe he'd waited this long. "Brace yourself. I'm going to do it again." He suited action to words. "And again."

She gasped. The sheets rustled as she arched her hips up.

"That's it." He smoothed his thumb across the swelling nub of her clit. "Make it easy for me."

She did, pulling his mouth closer, chasing that whisper of pleasure with everything in her.

"Just like that." With his thumb and forefinger he separated the outer lips, revealing the bundle of nerves within. Taking advantage of the position, he slipped his hands under her buttocks, sinking his fingertips into the lush curves as he held her to the tenderness of his kiss, the lash of his tongue, that first surge of heady passion.

"Brad!"

"Right here."

"It's—"

He stole the words from her throat with the stroke of his tongue, that sexy high-pitched sigh he sought, his reward. "Good."

"Yes." She shifted into the experience, rocking with the rhythm he set. "Very, very good."

He sped things up, applying a bit more pressure, giving her a bit more friction, steadily driving her higher, listening for that one sound that signaled he'd found the perfect pressure, lingering when he got it, focusing his passion on her. Needing this for her, for him. Needing to give this one time so maybe when he took later, the scales would balance. She whimpered and gasped. He growled and nipped. Another cry, another sigh. She was almost there.

Reaching over, he grabbed the sponge from the small bowl on the bed stand. The scent of vinegar overrode the scent of desire. For a second he held the bit of sponge, debating. It would be so easy to forgo this step. So easy to fall into the role and to hell with the consequences. He imagined Evie round with child, allowed himself one small moment of joy, and then he squashed both the image and the emotion, his father's mocking laughter ringing in his ears. With practiced efficiency, he eased the sponge into her tight sheath, irrationally resenting the scent, the act.

"What are you doing?" she gasped.

He pushed the sponge high, holding it while the muscles of

her channel clenched around his finger. She was so damn tight. So perfect. "Protecting you."

"I don't understand."

He didn't want her to. Brushing her hands aside, he nuzzled back in, distracting her with a series of kisses that expanded to a gentle suction, testing her readiness with another finger when her hips lifted in invitation.

"Oh, dear heavens."

"Easy," he murmured as she twisted away. She needed to be easy and let him make her ready.

"You be easy!"

Her heels dug into the mattress and she bucked as she fought the building climax, but she took all he offered with a hard clench and release that had him gritting his teeth. He couldn't wait to be in her.

"It's going to be good, Evie."

"It scares me."

The whispered confession cut to his heart. Shit. Of course it scared her. She was new to this. To him. And he was supposed to be making it good for her. Containing the wild lust pounding through him, Brad backed his finger from her tight sheath, gentling his touch, his expression, as he came over her. At least he hoped to hell what he managed was gentle.

"There's nothing to be afraid of."

She didn't move as he cradled her, just stared at him, big eyes wide and measuring the veracity in his words. He couldn't blame her for the doubt. Brushing his lips over her temple, he mentally kicked his ass. A man didn't come at a virgin crazy with lust. "You're not going to be in control when it happens, Evie, but you don't have to worry. I will be. I'll keep you safe."

"You promise?"

"Yes."

Her lip slipped between her teeth. "What if you forget?"

To stay in control?

The devil's loose in you boy. I can see it.

He never forgot. His life, as far back as he could remember, depended on remembering. "I won't. Ever."

There was a long pause that stretched finer than his control and then her lids dropped and she eyed him from behind the screen of her lashes. "Good." She pushed his shirt off his shoulders and smiled as he shook first one and then the other arm free. "Because I believe I mentioned I've spent a long time waiting for this moment?"

That smile shot past his control and wrapped around his heart, squeezing tightly. In the golden flicker of the lamp, her skin took on a creamy luminescence, her eyes a seductive shadowing, but what held him enthralled was the sheer vibrancy of her personality, which she was letting free tonight. With him. For no other reason than because she believed a promise *he'd* made kept her safe. Brad touched the tips of his fingers to the edge of her cheekbone. And maybe it did. It was hard to fathom, but Evie really did bring out the decent in him.

"I think we both have."

I THINK WE both have.

Evie slowed her frantic tugging. The cotton shirttail wrapped around her fingers as she studied Brad's expression. She had the impression of seriousness, a hint of surprise, definitely wry acceptance, and something soft. That touch on her cheek was incredibly tender. Special to her in the possibilities it presented. She'd accepted that she had Brad's passion and was prepared to enjoy it, but passion, she'd observed, could be a fleeting thing for a man, something he only held dear until the newness wore off. But tenderness was bigger than passion. Stronger. Tenderness was the first step toward a bond on which she could build. She wrapped her fingers around his wrists, feeling solidness of bone and muscle and a ridge of scar tissue. Tenderness was a beginning.

"Make love to me, Brad."

If she'd taken a whip to his flesh he couldn't have reacted more strongly. His eyes narrowed and his nostrils flared as he took a deep breath. Tracing her hand back up his arm, she worked it between their bodies, skating down the rigid plane of his stomach. "Please."

His lips brushed her ear as his big body shifted down. "You don't have to beg, Evie darling."

No, she realized. She didn't. And neither did he. That moment of tenderness had given her something to hold on to when that searing, scary, overwhelming passion came back. And it would come back. Brad did not have the look of a man who intended to settle for half measures.

"Promise me something."

He lifted his head from where he was nibbling on her neck. She missed the press of his mouth. "What?"

"Don't get mad if I get nervous."

"Promise me something back."

His eyes were so dark with passion beneath the rakish fall of his hair that she couldn't see the blue. He looked like a bandit, an outlaw, a predator, and she was the only game for miles. Having that much desire focused on her should have been unnerving. Instead, she found it exhilerating. "What?"

Tucking his fingers between her neck and the pillows, he pressed gently, arching her mouth up to the descent of his. "Promise me that when you get scared, instead of running away, you'll sink those pretty little nails into me and hold on tight."

It was remarkably easy to give that promise. "I can do that."

His lips touched the right side of her mouth and then the left, featherlight brushes that tormented more than satisfied. "Good."

He kissed her hard and deep, parting her lips with a gentle nip on her bottom lip, taking possession with a firm swipe of his tongue. After that, all she could do was hold tight as joy, desire, and anticipation spilled through her. He tasted of man, whiskey, sex, and pleasure. He tasted of him and faintly of her. It was shocking. It was heady. She wanted more.

Against her stomach, his cock throbbed. It felt harder than before. Bigger. She worked her hand between them, under the waistband of his pants. The sharp contraction of his stomach muscles eased her way. Her fingertips brushed smooth, hard flesh.

With a shake of his head he broke the kiss. "No."

"But I want to know."

"And I want this to last."

She made note of the want. So much want just waiting to be unleashed. "What can I do?"

"I already told you, practice your sighs of pleasure."

His hand cupped her breast. The pressure was divine. The ribbon slid against the side in a sultry caress. With two tugs, he freed her nipple from the intimate bondage. At first there was nothing, but then sensation came back, starting with small tingles that soon turned to darts of fire that flickered over her skin, stealing her breath. "Oh."

Against her stomach his cock throbbed. Above her his chuckle drifted. "That will do, too."

Languor chased the fire through her body. While her emotions pulled into a knot of eager expectation, her muscles relaxed in preparation. Hooking her ankles over the back of his calves, she squinted through the shadows concealing his chest. Was that a scar? She wished she was wearing her spectacles. She touched the faint depression two inches above and to the right of his nipple. It felt like a scar—thin and long, with an ultrasmooth center. Above it was another; this one was round with puckered edges. As she swept her palms over his broad shoulders and down his back, she felt more rough places that disappeared to smooth. More scars. How had he gotten so many? The wet heat of his mouth closed over her ultrasentative nipple, searing the question from her mind. Dear heavens, that was so good. How had she not known this was going to be so good? Bliss snapped her up into the pleasure, the suction . . .

A high-pitched sigh whispered around them—hers. She switched her grip to Brad's shoulder, holding his mouth to her, wanting more, needing more. Prepared to fight for it, if necessary.

It wasn't necessary. With a growled "Yes" Brad responded to her demand, milking her breast in a smooth rhythm that matched the suction of his mouth, drawing the taut flesh deeper in, coaxing the pleasure from her, yet somehow replacing it with an aching hunger that rippled over her body in a flash of heat before sinking deep to her center. The desire that had so scared her before surged again. Her pussy throbbed in counterpoint to the beat of her heart. Sharp and piercing, it demanded appeasement.

"Brad . . ."

The whisper of his name was all she could manage. For a second she thought he misunderstood the need housed in the broken syllable because he lifted his body away from her, depriving her of his weight. His hand worked between them, touching her thigh in odd movements and then with a grunt, he gave his weight back, coming over her with a smooth flow of muscle, casting them in the intimacy of shadow. Between her legs something broad and hot tucked into the receptive well of her vagina. Pressed . . .

Fear swept through her, passion cooling in a rush. His cock. And from the feel, it was nowhere near the sensible size she had guessed. Digging the heels of her hands into his shoulders, she shoved. "You said you were proportional."

She might as well have tried to move a rock wall. Brad was all big bones and heavy muscle.

"How do you know I'm not?"

If he laughed she would brain him with the lamp. His cock was still tucked tightly against her. And despite the fear in her mind, her body issued an invitation by softening and conforming to his shape. "Because there's no way you'll fit."

Switching his grip so his finger and thumb captured her nipple he accepted the unconscious invitation, parting her with that broad cock head that felt impossibly big. "I'll fit."

Fear, pain, and pleasure. They all blended together. She bit her lip.

"Slowly, just a little bit at a time," he explained in a drawl hoarse with strain as he pressed forward. "In an easy, sweet hug of pleasure."

It wasn't possible. She closed her eyes against the enormity of the moment. Something brushed her temple, her cheek. His lips delivering more of that tenderness she so needed. She held on to it, held on to him.

"Please don't laugh."

"I'm not laughing, Evie darling." His fingers skimmed down her thigh, making her vividly aware of her nakedness, her vulnerability, her total lack of control. She stiffened. His mouth brushed hers once, twice. His thumb grazed the top of her cleft, worked between, found that spot of flesh that so hungered for the pressure. "I'm pleasuring you."

And he was, too much. She remembered her promise.

"You'll keep me safe?" she gasped as desire drove through her in a devastating spike, thrusting her deeper into the maelstrom.

"Always." The promise flowed into her with her next breath, weaving through the chaos. "Just hold on to me."

She did—was—with everything she had as his thumb swirled around her clit, creating a haven of pleasure from the burn as his cock spread her.

"You're in me."

"Almost." The guttural response forced her eyes open. His face was honed by passion into a primitive beauty. His eyes glittered down at her. As her gaze met his, his cock jumped within her. It was too intimate.

"No, don't look away."

She couldn't, seeing his pupils dilate as he stretched her farther. For an instant his thumb didn't move and she felt the inevitability of his complete possession.

"You're mine, Evie."

The answer stuck in her throat. Her inner muscles rippled a protest as Brad held himself still, depriving her of the joy he'd promised as he waited. For her, for her consent. Did she dare? The answer came in an airy whisper, "Yes."

He surged against her, slow and steady, emphasizing his claim with the inexorable penetration that was so much more than sex. So much more important than pleasure. Eyes locked with his, she couldn't evade the moment, the connection. His thumb swirled as he went deeper than he had before. There was a sharp pain. She bit her lip.

"Your virginity."

"Then why are you stopping?"

"This is your last chance."

For what? To go back to a life full of tension, devoid of magic? "I don't want chances. I want you."

The circling of his thumb was constant now, creating such sweet havoc that it was almost pain, but a sweet pain that hungered for an explosion that was just out of her reach.

"No matter what, there'll be no going back after this."

She cupped his face in her hands, her body as taut as a bowstring under his as she gave him some tenderness of her own.

"No matter what."

"Shit."

His fingers closed on her clit, milking it strongly as his hips pressed down. Her orgasm crashed over her as his cock tore through the shield of her virginity. She screamed as her muscles clenched around the incredible sense of fullness. Brad caught the cry in his mouth, muffling the sound, pressing her into the mattress, his harsh curse burned forever into her mind as he wrapped his arms around her and pumped into her with hard thrusts that tossed her higher into the storm before he drove into her one last time, holding himself high inside her as he filled her with his seed.

"Mine."

She didn't argue, couldn't, not when every pulse of his cock caught on the ripples of her climax, spiking it to new, higher peaks. Not when he held her through it all with a sheltering tightness, so tightly she'd have bruises. Not when she'd cherish those because they stemmed from that tenderness she was beginning to understand he held only for her.

As he mated his mouth to hers, she had the strangest thought. Maybe this marriage wouldn't be so bad after all.

THE KNOCK AT the door woke him up. Brad glanced over to the moonlit face of the clock. Nothing good happened at four A.M. He eased his arm from beneath Evie's cheek. She whimpered a protest, but slept on, exhaustion and alcohol taking their toll. He touched the faint love bruise on her neck. He hadn't meant to be so demanding, but once he'd gotten within her snug little body he'd been almost possessed in his need to mark her emotionally, physically, permanently. As if by doing so it would keep her with him. He shook his head. A woman like Evie wasn't for him. All he'd have with her was all he'd ever had with anyone. Stolen moments until the inevitable occurred. He'd do well to remember that.

The knock came again. He slipped over to the window, instinctively avoiding the floorboard halfway across that had a tendency to creak. Below, at the bottom of the porch steps, a woman stood looking up, impatience in every line of her posture, her identity hidden by darkness, a blanket covering her head. He could only think of one woman who would interrupt his honeymoon, and only one reason.

Glancing back to make sure Evie slept on, he leaned out the window. "I'll be right down."

Nidia nodded. He wasn't fooled. He wouldn't have long. The madam did not have an ounce of patience in her voluptuous body. He gathered his clothes and dropped them by the chair. He pulled the covers down Evie's body. She rolled onto her back, legs splayed. Between them, he could easily make out the swollen folds of her pussy. More proof that when it came to her he had no control. She was going to be raw and sore for a few days. With a hand on her mound he kept her still as he slipped his fingers inside and withdrew the sponge. She frowned and moaned, but didn't wake. Very sore. He tossed the sponge in the small waste can before wetting the washcloth and cleansing her with the same gentleness. Dropping the cloth back in the bowl, he pressed a kiss on the top of her cleft.

"I'm sorry."

For a lot of things, but mostly for being bastard enough to steal a bit of the normal others took for granted. Pulling the covers over her well-loved body, he memorized the moment before turning on his heel and leaving it behind. He was an outlaw. Hiding out as a preacher might extend his life, but eventually the hangman would find him, and when that happened, there would be no avoiding his fate.

Nidia was pacing when he reached the porch. She was also alone.

"Where's Elijah?"

"He is having one of his moods."

Which meant his demons had gotten to be too much and he'd headed off to ride them out. "You shouldn't be out here alone."

Her laugh was mocking. "I am the madam of the local whorehouse. What could happen to me that anyone would say I didn't already deserve?"

A lot, but there was no talking to Nidia when she got in this mood. "Elijah's not going to like it."

"Elijah is not my boss."

Maybe, but Elijah took Nidia's safety pretty seriously.

"Besides," Nidia continued, "if you would not drop your problems at my doorstep, I could still be sleeping."

"My problems?"

Nidia shrugged. "She heard you married."

Brad took a deep breath. Immediately, he was inundated with the scent of roses. Beside the porch, a lone rosebush thrived, one of the blooms just opening. He imagined trailing it down between Evie's breasts, waking her with the kiss of the bloom against her lips. Evie would like that rose.

"Shit."

"Brenda's words were harsher."

He just bet.

"She is disturbing my women. You must handle this."

"It's my wedding night."

"That is not my concern."

With a sigh, he tore his gaze away from the rose and settled his hat on his head. "Then I guess that makes it mine."

Eight

BIRDS WERE SINGING. Humid morning air wafted through the window, bringing with it the subtle fragrance of roses. Without even opening her eyes, Evie knew it was going to be a beautiful day. She eased onto her back. Memories of the night drifted through her mind with the same sweet, lazy flow of the breeze. Desire resurrected in a hard clench as she remembered the rasp of Brad's tongue, the way her body opened to accept the thrust of his cock, the delicious havoc of making love on her sensitive inner muscles, her senses, her emotions. Her mother had definitely been right. An experienced husband between the sheets was nothing to shake a stick at. Rolling over, Evie reached out, expecting to encounter warm muscle. Instead, all she found were cool sheets.

Through the divide in the curtains, she could see the sun was just clearing the horizon. It was early. What could he be doing? She listened, straining to detect any sound of Brad's presence within the house. There was no aroma of coffee brewing. No sound of movement, just that particular sense of emptiness that told a body they were alone. Grabbing Brad's pillow, Evie hugged it to her chest, dread pursuing satisfaction. This wasn't good. Common sense dictated that a satisfied man didn't sneak out of his wedding bed before the crack of dawn. He'd reached for her four times, and she'd thought that meant he was pleased, but maybe he'd just been hoping she'd improve?

The more Evie thought on it, the more the latter seemed likely. A well-pleased man did not sneak out of bed like a thief in the night. Remembering the things she'd whispered, the way she'd responded to his touch . . . She buried her face in the pillow. Had she really been that wild? Done all that? No wonder Brad wasn't here. He was probably horrified.

She heaved the pillow at the door. The soft thud it made as it hit the wood was not the least bit satisfying. Neither was the subsequent plop when it hit the floor. Both were too soft, too delicate for the violence seething inside. Even if Brad found her lacking in that area of marriage, she deserved better than being left to figure it out for herself. And before her morning coffee, no less.

She kicked the covers back, threw her legs over the side of the bed, and hopped out. Outside the birds still sang, but her smile was long gone. Brad had no right to do this. Dipping a clean cloth into the pitcher, she took a quick bath, her anger mounting with every minute that passed. Even if she'd been the biggest disappointment in the world, he owed her better than this. Opening her satchel she took out a clean blouse and skirt. As her nightgown drifted to the floor, she kicked it. It wasn't enough. The dang thing had gotten her into so much trouble. Making her believe that this marriage just might be a place for someone as unconventional as her. But despite all Brad's big talk, she must have done something to upset him, something to convince him she wasn't the wife he wanted. He just hadn't had the guts to let her know, the coward. He'd just run out. And when he came back, he'd probably have a perfectly logical explanation for why he'd left like a thief in the night, leaving her to wonder and come up with her own reasons, which were probably much closer to the mark than the drivel he'd present.

Wadding the nightgown and robe into a ball, she walked over to the little stove used to heat the room in winter. She opened the metal door. It clanked against the other side as she shoved the garments into the grate. Grabbing the sulphurs off the top, she struck one and tossed it in. For a moment the sulphur flared and the material around it darkened, but then the flame sputtered, dwindled. Failed.

Like hell. She grabbed the whiskey decanter off the dresser, grunting in disgust at the sparkling play of light through its amber depths. It hadn't just been Brad's charm and the nightgown that had done her in. The whiskey had done its part. For a vile-tasting concoction, it had a sneaky way of working its way under a woman's inhibitions and shaking them loose. Dumping the contents on the nightgown, she gave it a second to soak in.

This time when she tossed in the match, the response was much more satisfying. Flames sprang up with a whoosh, filling the interior before flashing outward. She jumped back then watched the hungry fire devour the expensive gown. In a very short time the nightgown and everything it had represented were nothing more than a bit of ash. *Good.*

It only took a minute to dress, roll on her thin wool stockings, and stomp into her shoes. Another to stuff yesterday's clothes in the satchel. She'd pay for the careless stuffing later with a good hour of ironing, but maybe she'd just burn them, too. Maybe she'd burn everything that made her remember the fiasco of this wedding. As she laced up her shoes, she knew it wasn't going to be that simple. She had her pride, and Brad had ground it into the dust—with her permission. Darn, that's what stung the most. She'd done this to herself. Brad had given her a bunch of sweet talk and she'd fallen for it.

Grabbing up her satchel, she headed to the kitchen. The stove was cold. She poked at the coffeepot sitting on top. It slid across the burner. Empty. So much for her mother's caution to contain her normal morning grumpiness so she wouldn't upset Brad. According to her mother, the way Brad treated her after the wedding night and the consideration she showed in kind would set the tone for the marriage. She recentered the pot on the burner. From the looks of things, the next fifty years were going to be war.

The silence of the house pressed in on her. Looking around the kitchen, she couldn't help but wonder if everything was as Amy had left it before she'd gotten sick. It was cleaned up, but had it changed? In the hutch beside the door opposite the stove sat the bright, cheery dishes with their yellow rose pattern that Elijah had worked so hard to get for Amy. He'd worked a second job for months to buy those dishes for her as a wedding present. From the day Amy had wistfully remarked on their beauty in the mercantile, nothing would do for Elijah but that she have them. It had been a wonderful gesture, complicated by the fact that because it was a secret, Amy had begun to suspect Elijah had another woman who made demands on his time. It had been quite the summer social when that situation exploded. Before that day, no one had even suspected Amy had a temper.

Smiling at the memory, Evie opened the hutch door and

touched the pretty yellow rose on a delicate cup. Elijah's love had not been one-sided. Everything in the house had been decorated around that one special gift. The yellow-checked tablecloth draped over the large table was the exact color of the rose. The theme was picked up in yellow curtains with white lace trim. All the chairs around the table bore bright yellow cushions. She turned slowly, just absorbing the depth of love and hope that had gone into this home. There had been a lot. With a sigh, she closed the hutch door. She didn't know what she'd been thinking. If fate wouldn't allow Amy and Elijah to have a life together, what in heaven made her think she and Brad had a chance?

The silence grew heavier, her anger sharper, and that deep inner pain stronger. Tears burned the back of her eyes. She blinked them away. She would not cry about this. This might be the reality of her life, the consequence of her choice, but it wasn't going to break her. She glanced around the cheerful, hope-filled interior. The honeymoon was over.

Grabbing up her satchel, she headed out the back door. Dew beaded the grass and hung in the air in a thick mist. The day had all the makings of a scorcher. Her destination stood one hundred feet behind the house. The small barn reflected the same care as the house. To the right of the double doors rested her wedding buggy, still decorated with bottles, cans, white ribbons. Hope. The painted wooden sign with the words "A bright future, here we come" hung perfectly aligned on the back. There was no way she was riding back into town with that monstrosity, making her a laughingstock because of her situation. She also wasn't walking back into town lugging her satchel like a beggar. Brad might have ground her pride in the dust, but she didn't need to announce it to the world.

Dropping the satchel she spun around and marched back into the kitchen and picked out the biggest knife she could find. Ignoring the heat and the blinding sunshine, she marched to the buggy and started hacking. It was a very satisfying half hour, cutting the geegaws and good wishes from that buggy. As she sawed on the thick rope holding the sign to the buggy back, she heard a footstep behind her.

"I take it the honeymoon's over?"

Evie spun around. Jackson Burchett leaned against the side of the barn, idly twirling his dark brown hat in his hand, his long blond hair blowing about his shoulders. On another man hair that long and that color should have looked feminine, but on Jackson it just gave the aura of a Viking warrior, accentuating the strong line of his jaw and the amusement in his blue eyes. Five years ahead of her in school, she didn't know him as well as she knew his sister Lori, who was a couple years younger than her, but she knew him well enough to know she was not in the mood this morning for the swipe of Jackson's wit. She pointed the knife at him. "Don't start with me, Jackson."

He held up his hands. "I never start with anyone before coffee."

"Good. That philosophy could keep you alive."

"Doesn't sound like you've had your morning coffee either."

She hadn't had a lot of things she should have. "No, I haven't."

"Want me to make some?"

And give him an excuse to linger? "Not particularly."

His eyebrows lifted. She ignored the invitation to confide. Instead, she went back to work on the darn rope that held the sign. No matter how hard or how fast she sawed, the strands refused to separate. She was acutely aware of Jackson watching, the thoughts that must be going through his mind, the pity she'd likely find in his gaze if she were stupid enough to look up. Damn it. She wiped the sweat from her brow with her sleeve. Why wouldn't the darn rope cut?

Jackson's hand covered hers. A wicked-looking hunting knife flashed in her field of vision. The rope she'd been futilely sawing split like butter under a hot knife. A mental picture of how easily that knife could glide through human flesh filled her imagination. She blinked away the image. That wasn't a portrait she wanted to paint.

Jackson slid the knife back into its sheath on his belt. He held out his hand. With a sigh she placed hers in it. His touch didn't contain that ripple of shock that Brad's did. And when she stood before him, she didn't feel small and delicate. Which was just as well. For all his easy humor, she'd never gotten the sense that Jackson was safe, and she definitely didn't need to hop from the frying pan into the fire. Brushing off her skirts, she asked, "So, why are you here?"

"Brad sent me over. He had an emergency he had to tend to. He said to go on and have breakfast. He'd be back likely before you were done."

She just bet. "How considerate of him. And what does he expect me to eat?"

Jackson picked up a dark wicker basket and lifted the lid. "Millicent sent this over."

The scents of bacon and ham rose to fill the space between them.

"Millicent said there's pancake batter already mixed up to go with the ham and bacon. She also included some fresh-picked blueberries, if you're interested."

Evie loved blueberry pancakes, but she wasn't going to sit here like a pet dog waiting for Brad. And she wasn't going to explain herself to Jackson. She turned back to the wagon. Switching the knife to her left hand, she flexed the fingers on the right, releasing the cramping muscles. There was one bottle still hanging off the cart.

"Could you put that in the kitchen please?"

Jackson eyed her as if he knew she had no intention of waiting for Brad. "He really couldn't help leaving, Evie. It was important."

"Maybe I want to be important, too. At least important enough to warrant a good-bye when left alone on my wedding night."

Well, shoot. She hadn't meant to say that. Jackson didn't have an immediate response to that, which was probably good, because she might have poked him with the knife, she was so furious. He dropped the lid on the basket and straightened. She went to work on that bottle.

"To be fair, Rev's not used to being married."

He couldn't be serious. She sawed harder. The bottle rattled against the wooden side. Her breath came in an uneven rhythm. "Well, neither am I." The bottle thudded to the ground. She tossed the knife beside it, coming to a decision. "But I can tell you right now, I won't be for much longer."

TWO HOURS LATER, she was still married, her temper was still frayed, and she was no closer to having someone to take it out on than she had been when she woke up that morning, but if Herschel Wallinger, the local lawyer, kept treating her like a pet dog who'd momentarily lost her senses, she might move him up the list. The man was unbearably pompous.

"The best thing you can do, Mrs. Swanson, is to go home and wait for your husband."

No man that short, spindly, and especially that annoying should ever take that tone with an irritated woman. Evie tightened her grip on her bonnet, struggling for control. "Pardon me, but for a lawyer, you don't seem to know much."

The solid wooden chair groaned as Herschel leaned back and steepled his hands in front of his chest. "I know enough that you won't be getting a divorce if the Reverend doesn't want one."

The urge to smack the smile off his face grew overwhelming. Evie might be a woman, but she wasn't stupid. The only thing that was guaranteed in the law was the fact that there was always a loophole. "I realize it might be difficult to get a divorce without the Reverend's approval, but certainly there must be some exceptions to that rule."

"No."

She didn't believe him. The man was as white as the underbelly of a fish. She'd thought at first that it was a good sign. Surely a man who spent all his time locked up in this gloomy office, surrounded by books, would have the information she wanted, but she might have been wrong. Herschel might actually be hiding in his books. "There's no way the rules can be bent?"

"I suppose, if you have enough money and enough influence in the right places, concessions could be made." His gaze traveled from her hastily pinned-up hair down over her torso, no doubt taking note of the serviceable material of her blouse and the dust clinging to the cuff of the sleeve. "Do you have money and influence?"

He knew darn well she didn't. He just wanted to hammer home the point that she hadn't considered the ramifications when she'd entered his office, wanted to play omnipotent male to her helpless female. And if the laws of the country weren't laid out so he could, she'd argue him into the ground. Herschel knew the law, but he wasn't particularly agile mentally.

"No."

Herschel sighed and smoothed the waxed end of his heavy moustache. "A marriage is always easier when a woman accepts the natural order."

"Thank you for your advice."

"I'm sure the Reverend will be a most considerate husband if you strive to please him. If you don't mind me saying so, I think a man of God is ideally suited to provide the discipline you need."

"So I've been told."

By her mother. By her uncle. She'd even heard it whispered on the street as she marched to Herschel's office. And now Herschel himself, a virtual stranger, felt obligated to point it out and seemed to feel she'd be grateful for the information. Evie stood clutching her satchel to her chest as if her last hope rested within it and let her lips tremble slightly as she held out her hand to the officious prig, dressed in his perfectly white, perfectly starched shirt with his perfectly waxed moustache that overwhelmed his narrow face. "Thank you so much for your time."

He took her hand. Instead of just grazing her fingertips with his, he held it, keeping her put. The utter rudeness of the presumption froze her in place. The sweaty dampness of his hand repulsed her.

"If you confide your fears to your husband, I'm sure you'll find he's a reasonable man."

"Like you?"

It was the smugness in his "yes" that snapped the hold she had on her temper. She let the satchel slip. It dropped onto the open inkwell, toppling the black liquid all over the papers, the blotter, and the light oak grain of the equally pretentious desk.

Herschel leapt to his feet. "Oh my God! You did that on purpose!"

She gave him her sweetest smile. "Try being reasonable about it."

"Reasonable?!" he sputtered, diving for the inkwell, thought better of it as his shirt brushed a clean part of the blotter, and jumped back, eyes glued to the horror of spreading ink. "You're crazy."

No, but she was angry.

A hand closed around her upper arm from behind. She jumped and swung a wild fist. Brad caught it easily, not looking at her, all his attention on Herschel, a pleasant smile on his face. How had he avoided making the door squeak? "My wife has a different definition of *reasonable* than most people."

"She needs a firm hand."

"So I've heard."

Brad's grip was just short of painful. A glance out of the corner of her eye revealed the set angle of his chin. He was angry. Well, so was she.

"I don't need anything except to be left alone."

The look Brad sent her clearly said, "Shut up."

She gave an experimental tug. There was no breaking his grip.

"We'll be discussing what you need when I get you home."

Herschel collected his dignity from whatever corner he'd stashed it in, straightened his vest, and pulled himself to his unimpressive height. "Good morning, Reverend."

"Morning yourself, Herschel. Thanks for taking the time to answer my wife's questions. What do I owe you?"

"Not a thing." Herschel came halfway around the desk. He had delicate hands, almost feminine. They trailed along the wood surface. "New brides are often subject to fits of nerves."

Herschel lived with his mother, had never been looked upon with favor by any of the women in town, despite the stability of his financial position, yet he stood there on the other side of that desk talking as if he were an authority on wives and women? Evie wished she'd dumped the ink on his head.

Evie jerked her arm. She might as well have been tugging against iron. "I'm not hysterical."

Brad, darn his hide, just kept smiling that same pleasant smile he'd been wearing since he walked in the door. "I'll keep that in mind." He still didn't look at her. "And, Herschel?"

"What?"

"You touch my wife again and I'll kill you."

For a moment Herschel and Evie had something in common. Utter shock. Herschel recovered quicker.

"I was only—"

Brad cut him off, still talking in that easy drawl. "I'm aware a man can fool himself sometimes with the 'onlys.' That's why I gave you the warning." He tipped his hat. "Have a good day."

While Evie gaped, Brad spun her toward the door so fast, her satchel flew outward. She relaxed her muscles, letting centrifugal force propel it into the tall, overloaded bookcase on the adjacent wall. It hit and snagged. The bookcase teetered, groaned. Brad glanced back before yanking her forward two steps. The heavy piece came down where she had been standing. Hershel swore. Brad pushed her out onto the wooden sidewalk. Evie blinked against the brightness of sunlight. Behind them Herschel yelled. Beside her Brad sighed.

"Guess we'll have a long ride to the next lawyer if we have the need."

"He's an idiot."

"You didn't behave much better."

"You didn't give me a choice."

"Only because I knew you were on the verge of getting hysterical."

"I've never had a hysterical day in my life." His much longer legs ate up distance faster than hers. She had to skip to keep up. "And what were the threats all about?"

For the first time, Brad looked at her. His blue eyes were icy. Anger etched the lines bracketing the sides of his mouth. A chill went down her spine.

"I don't make threats."

She stopped tugging on her arm. The man was furious. "Preachers don't kill people."

"No one touches you."

It was probably completely wrong to find that statement arousing, but she did. To the point that more of her own anger slid aside. No man was that possessive over a disappointment. "Not even you?"

His nostrils flared and he came to a stop. People turned and stared. Evie didn't care. For once, she was seeing the real Brad, the one who kept emerging in her paintings. Deeply elemental, primitively masculine. Exciting. She shivered in a purely feminine reaction. Brad's gaze narrowed as he followed the betraying gesture. He pulled her up onto her toes against the solid strength of his body. "You, Evie darling, are going to wear my brand all over that sweet little body."

Her knees gave out. "Oh."

The right corner of his gorgeous mouth tipped up. "Anything else you want to know?"

She shook her head.

"Good." Stepping down into the street, he switched his grip to her waist and swung her down beside him. There wasn't a thing improper about the way he did it, but everything in her snapped to vibrant, yearning attention. She couldn't take her eyes off his mouth. "Where are we going?"

His arm came around her waist. "Home, so I can deal with your hysteria."

She planted her feet so hard dust rose up. "I am *not* hysterical."

"Trust me, you want me stewing on the fact you're hysterical rather than the fact that you have just, for the third time in twenty-four hours, humiliated me."

His arm tightened and he propelled her forward. The satchel bumped awkwardly against her knee. "Me? Humiliate you? You're the one who took off in the middle of the night."

"For a damn good reason." He steered around Homer and Brian where they sat outside the now quiet saloon. "Morning, gentlemen."

"Morning, preacher." The only greeting they gave her was a reproving glare.

She glared right back. "For your information, he's the one in the wrong."

Homer spat tobacco juice to the side. "You don't say? The preacher?"

Brad didn't slow down for the conversation, forcing her to yell over her shoulder, "Yes!"

"I don't think they believe you," Brad grunted, as he waited for her to step back onto the high wooden walk. "Must be your reputation is worse than mine after all."

That stung. The church loomed before them. She blinked rapidly to keep the tears out of her eyes, not wanting him to see. One got past her control. She rubbed at it with her shoulder. Brad would choose precisely that moment to look down.

"Shit."

He reached for the doorknob of the church door. She braced her feet. With a simple heft, he popped her off the ground. In the space of a heartbeat, they were inside. The dark interior was cool compared to the heat outdoors, the sudden dimness blinding. Evie only had a second to register the place was empty before Brad hefted her up onto the small table just inside the door. With a push of his hand he tumbled her back. There was barely enough time to catch her weight on her elbows before her skirts flew up over her face. As she fought to push the material aside, Brad's hands smoothed up the inside of her thighs. Her breath lodged in her throat. With a frantic look at the door, she gasped, "What are you doing?"

His drawl was as deep as his touch was potent. Last night had trained her in many things, including what that low rumble meant. His fingers flirted with the slit in her drawers. Inner muscles contracted in delight before relaxing in anticipation. "Curing your hysterics."

She shoved the skirt down, managing a swat at his head before she had to brace herself again. The table rattled. Brad chuckled. "For the last time, I'm *not* hysterical."

His "I disagree" was muffled under the folds of material. The rasp of his morning beard against her inner thighs stole her argument. The instant his tongue touched her flesh, hot and moist, fire licked across her nerve endings, racing up her spine, spreading to her breasts, raising goose bumps, anticipation, before plunging back down to gather in her core. Her nails scraped across the polished wood as he dragged her forward. The satchel hit the floor with a loud thud.

Another pass, another gasp. "This is the cure for hysteria?"

She was sore, but he was tender, laving her gently, finding those spots he'd trained to respond to him last night, stimulating them, her. His shoulders wedged beneath her thighs. "Only one known for the female variety."

It was only natural that her legs draped over his shoulders, that her ankles crossed, that her knees spread wider. Natural that she gave him greater access. Even more natural that he took complete advantage of it.

Cotton tore again as he made room for the press of his mouth. The church door rattled under the breeze. She almost jumped out of her skin. From the corner of her eye the cross over the altar loomed.

"We're going to hell for this."

His tongue slipped between her folds in a leisurely pass. "It'll be a fun trip."

"You're angry at me."

"Getting less annoyed by the minute." His tongue laved, lips kissed, teeth nipped.

She gasped under the searing bolt of lightning that shot deep. "Someone could come in."

"Then you'd better pay attention and get over your hysteria fast, because I'm not stopping until you do."

The door shifted again. Dust motes drifted in the thin beam of light. She knew how they felt. Ever since she'd met Brad she'd been floating along, subject to forces she didn't understand. Still was, because despite the fact that she just knew somebody would come in that door and catch her with her legs spread and her husband kneeling between them, desire outgrew caution. "Someone will see. It'll be humiliating."

The cool silk of his hair slid up her right thigh as his mouth pressed against her left. There was a slight suction and then a sharp stab of pleasure, which left her gasping and clutching his head to her long after he ended that particular kiss. "No more humiliating than my friends thinking I've got a penis the size of a smidge or the whole town thinking my wife wants a divorce because I didn't satisfy her in bed."

"No one thinks that!"

"The hell they don't." He didn't sound angry. Why didn't he sound angry? Working his hands under her buttocks, he lifted her to his mouth, each word a heady invitation to the joy only he offered. "Now, I want you to concentrate on coming for me."

"I can't," she gasped, her eyes locked on the door.

His tongue flicked over that high point at the top of her mound that held all the sensation in the world. Desire shot through her again like lightning across the summer sky, flashing and flickering.

He rubbed his chin against the flesh he'd so recently kissed. Lightning turned to fireworks at the delicate scrape. "Then I guess I'm going to have myself a long, leisurely lunch."

Another breath-stealing pass of his tongue. "Oh God."

"God's not going to help you here, Evie. I'm all you've got to hold on to, so give me what I want. Give me those sweet little cries as you come."

She didn't have a choice. Where before he had been gentle, now he was voracious, a predator intent on devouring his prey, stalking her response, tracking every catch in her breath, herding her desire into a tight ball that pulsed and expanded with each lap, each nip, adding the rasp of his beard, the edge of his teeth, until she was twisting on the table, pulling him closer with her legs, trying to get the pressure where she needed it, craved it. "Brad!"

"Right here." His fingers slipped inside the aching emptiness of her pussy, first one and then another. "Come, now."

She did, reality splintering away on the next thrust, hurtling her out of herself into the wildness beyond.

It could have been seconds or minutes later that she became aware of her surroundings again and blinked. She was face-down over the table. The weight of her skirts were piled on her back and her legs dangled off the edge, her toes just touching the floor. The table creaked as Brad's hand came down beside her cheek. As the palm flattened on the smooth surface, his cock pressed intimately. Her muscles clenched. With her passion satisfied, she was once again aware of the precariousness of their location. She closed her legs, trapping the hard ridge of his cock between.

"Brad . . ."

A hot sting spread through her right buttock in a burning heat. "Open for me."

She reared up. Her hair fell over her face as she tried to look over her shoulder. "Did you just spank me?"

A foot kicked hers apart and she lost her leverage, falling forward over the table. "Yup. And if you play your cards right, I'll do it again."

She didn't know if she wanted him to do it again. "We can't do this."

"Too late." The small, sweet sting came again, but this time the heat went deeper, lingered in her womb before spreading to her clit, and she had her answer. Again was shockingly good. "This is already happening."

And it was. In a slow steady glide, his cock parted her swollen tissues. The burn was delicious, the mixture of pain and pleasure almost too much for her mind to absorb. Her muscles clamped down. Brad grunted. This time he didn't stop at one spank. There were two, three, four, and with every spank came the pulse of pleasure, the mesmerizing prelude that melted her resistance until she couldn't remember why she'd been fighting.

She pushed back. "Oh heavens."

The next spank came hard and hot on the heels of the previous, ripping through her resistance as the force of the following thrust shot her forward again. The table hit the wall. His thighs hit her buttocks, his cock a depth she didn't know was possible. Her shriek was little more than a tangle of sounds. He didn't back off, just held himself there, as his big body came over hers. His hand tangled in her hair, pulling her head back. His lips grazed her cheek, the corner of her mouth, the line of her jaw. "More?"

Oh God, she couldn't take more. He was so deep. She shook her head.

He growled. "Yes." His mouth closed over the chord of her neck, sucking hard. "All of me, Evie."

Everything in her responded to the primitive declaration, rose to the challenge. The tendons in her neck strained to improve the angle of his kiss, the muscles in her thighs struggled to push her hips higher, her pussy ached to stretch wider, to take that last inch . . .

A knock came at the door. "Evie?"

Oh dear heavens. Her mother! She tried to twist away.

Brad held her firm. The door rattled, hit something. "No."

His foot, she realized. He was holding the door shut with his foot. She tried to remember how big his feet were. He pulled out, the thick length of his shaft caressing every nerve along the way, and she gave up. They had to be big enough. He forged inexorably back in, the force dragging her clit across the edge of the table. She bit her lip on a small cry.

"Yes," he muttered, tilting her head back a fraction more, watching her expression as her muscles rippled around him. "Take me just like that.

"My mother—"

"Will have to wait."

The knock at the door came again. Pearl called, "Are you all right?"

Oh God, she didn't know. She couldn't do anything but sprawl passively on the smooth table while Brad rode her hard and fast, forced to accept her pleasure as he chose to give it, able to do nothing, each entry a jolt to her senses, every withdrawal a mournful loss. The table flicked her clit like a hard finger, the burgeoning ache building to unbearable heights. His hand left her hair. She collapsed forward. His forearm cushioned her fall.

Brad's next thrust was so hard she bit down on his arm and screamed—so close, so close.

"Son of a bitch."

The curse was little more than a hiss of breath. His weight left her back. His hand fumbled between them and then something thick tested the point of their joining. His thumb?

"Tell your mother 'just a minute.' "

She shook her head. There was no way she could manage speech.

"You don't tell me no, Evie." For once she didn't want to argue. All she wanted—needed—was for Brad to give her just a little more.

"Just a minute, Ma."

"Are you all right?"

Brad's thrusts grew shallower, faster.

"Yes. Just give me a—" His thumb swirled, slid higher, pressed. Another scream built as a dark pleasure swirled through her. She held it back and choked out, "A minute."

Above her, Brad commanded, "Now, Evie."

Her world ruptured. Brad swore and pulled out. The door rattled. Hot liquid splashed on her buttocks, spilled between.

His seed, she realized with an erotic shock. She rubbed her hips in counterpoint to his shallow thrusts. His mouth brushed her ear. His thumb pierced her that first tiny bit. "Next time, I'll take you here."

She couldn't help herself, she pushed back into the sensual tease. "Yes."

Brad swore. Stepping back, he pulled her up. Her skirts fell about her legs. Catching her face between his hands, he kissed her hard, before growling, "Let your mother in."

She could only blink uncomprehendingly as he turned on his heel and strode away.

Nine

SHE WAS GOING to kill him. She was going to learn to shoot a gun, and she was going to kill him. One bullet at a time until the darn thing was empty, Evie decided as she watched her husband stride, with his usual arrogance, down the narrow aisle to the back of the church. The door vibrated against her foot as her mother pounded with more urgency. Brad skirted the shadowed altar, his black clothes rendering him all but invisible as he moved from light to shadow. There was an ease to the blending that fed her irritation. He was entirely too good at disappearing.

The door swung inward. Evie braced her feet, using her weight to push it back, understanding why Brad had placed her here, but if he thought giving her the opportunity to control when her mother gained entrance was going to make up for anything, he had another think coming. She still had to face her mother with the last remnants of her orgasm pulsing through her. And somehow she had to look normal. *Damn him.*

This time the door hit her back hard enough to bruise. "Evie, open this door right now."

Evie had grown up with that tone. There was an end to Pearl's patience and she'd just reached it. One touch was all it took to verify that her hair was past repairing. Before stepping back, she checked her skirts. At least they seemed to be in place, likely wrinkled in the back, but at least the front was not too horrible. She took one breath, two, reached for her hair and jumped back.

"Come in, Ma."

The door swung open hard enough to hit the wall. Bright

sunlight streamed into the dark interior. Her mother's silhouette—tall, plump, still curvaceous—stood framed by the doorway. "Are you all right?"

"Of course." Flipping the disaster of her hair over her shoulder, she brushed her hands down her skirt. Sometimes a brave front carried a woman past the embarrassment of the obvious. From the back of the church there came the sound of a door closing. Brad had left, the coward.

Pearl took one look at her and clucked her tongue. "I told you, you can't go aggravating a husband like you aggravate everyone else."

"I wanted to see for myself."

"And now look at you. You're a mess." With a motion of her hand, Pearl indicated Evie should turn around. "And did you get what you wanted or did you simply lose your temper?"

"The latter."

Her mother sniffed and gathered up Evie's hair. "That's what I thought."

"Are you sick or was that disapproval?"

"Just fighting off a cold. I got caught in that downpour last week."

Finalizing plans for her wedding. Evie sighed. Sometimes it felt like guilt was going to be her constant companion. She glanced back. "I'm sorry."

"Don't be." Pearl started braiding with familiar efficiency. "I'm going to give it to Millicent, and after that I'll be fine."

Evie glanced over her shoulder, struggling with a smile. "What did Millicent do this time?"

Pearl snorted with disgust. "She's been practicing her recipes."

Practicing recipes meant interest in a man. Millicent and her mother might be friends but when it came to men, they were also rivals. "The new blacksmith?"

"Don't you get smart with me, young woman."

"What? He's a fine-looking man. Those white streaks at his temples make him look very distinguished."

Pearl grunted and slapped a ribbon into Evie's hand. "He can't be that distinguished if he's blinded by a fancy dessert."

"You're a beautiful woman, Ma. If you want him, go after him."

"Don't underestimate the value of good food to a man."

Evie turned as best she could, struggling to see her mother's face. "I also wouldn't be overestimating it."

Pearl gave Evie's braid a tug. "Hold still or everyone is going to be thinking you've been cavorting in church, and that you won't live down."

Evie was suddenly, vividly aware of all the evidence that said she had done just that. Her thighs touching through the tear in her pantaloons, her swollen lips, the stinging spot on her neck where Brad had nipped her as he'd ordered her to hold still for the thrust of his cock, the faint scent of lovemaking permeating the warm interior . . . Thank goodness for her mother's cold. Clearing her throat, she agreed, "We wouldn't want that."

Pearl took the ribbon from her hand. "Even if it is true."

The heavy weight of the braid struck her back. Evie spun around, appalled. "How did you know?"

That got her a pitying shake of the head. "Your lips are swollen, your hair is mussed, and you don't have the look of a beaten woman."

Evie could only gape.

Pearl shrugged and pulled another ribbon from the seemingly endless supply she always had in her pocket. "I wasn't born forty-three, Evie. There were times your father and I kept someone cooling their heels while he stole a kiss."

A kiss. Her mother thought Brad had only kissed her. Some of Evie's mortification died back, but not much. "You're not upset with me?"

"I could wish you didn't enjoy provoking your husband so much, but I'm glad he's the type to stake his claim with a kiss rather than a fist."

They really didn't know Brad at all. The man was too thorough to settle anything with just a kiss.

Flicking the pink ribbon, Pearl said, "Lift your chin."

"Why?"

"To cover that love bruise your husband put on your neck."

You, Evie darling, are going to wear my brand all over that sweet little body.

Brad hadn't been joking. Evie covered the sting with her hand. "He marked me?"

With a quick flick of the ribbon that showed her many years

as a seamstress, Pearl wrapped it around Evie's neck. "Quite thoroughly."

Holding up her chin, Evie asked, "How badly?"

"Bad enough men will be smiling smugly and women will be sighing with envy. You can check it when you get home. You won't even need your spectacles."

She'd be checking the spot that stung on the inside of her thigh, too. "He probably did it on purpose."

Tilting her head to the side, Pearl chuckled as she finished tying the ribbon at Evie's throat. "Probably. I wouldn't have figured the Reverend for a possessive man, but still waters do run deep, and I guess the collar doesn't make him less a man."

You touch my wife again and I'll kill you.

She shivered. "No. It definitely doesn't."

Pearl rested her hands on Eve's shoulders. "Are you happy, baby?"

Startled, Evie realized she had to look down to meet her mother's gaze. When had that happened? It had to have happened years ago, but how could she not have realized? She licked her lips, tasting the remnant of Brad's kiss, reliving in a flash of memory the torrent of emotion he brought to life. "I think I could be."

As soon as the words left her mouth, the panic started. She wasn't good at keeping a man's love. And to think about making any part of her happiness dependent on a man, even one whose reasons for marrying her she understood, was terrifying. She licked her lips again, tasting nothing this time but her own fear. "If I asked my husband to let me go to Paris and paint, do you think he'd let me do that?"

To her credit, Pearl didn't miss a beat at the sudden change of subject. "Probably not if you ask him out of the blue like that."

"I would approach the subject more delicately."

"Good, because the man is not the monster you seem to want him to be."

He also wasn't the saint her mother wanted him to be.

"I don't want him to be a monster."

"Funny, no one could tell that from your actions."

"What actions?"

"It's all over town that he left that house before dawn."

"Am I the only subject anyone has to discuss around here?"

"Right now, you're the most exciting."

"Maybe the sheriff was a little hasty running that medicine show out of town," she muttered.

Pearl didn't bite. "So, what'd you do to make him leave you last night?"

Followed his lead, as Pearl had told her to do. "What makes you think I did anything?"

"Sweetheart, I've known you your whole life, and when told to push, you're more likely to pull."

"Maybe Brad doesn't want me to conform."

"He's a minister. A certain level of conformity is required."

He might be a man of the cloth, but Evie was beginning to think he wasn't that proper. A proper man of God didn't pleasure his wife on a table just inside the front door of the church. Especially when anyone could come in. A proper minister didn't keep making love to his wife after her mother knocked on the door. A proper man of God wouldn't recognize the wild side of her the way Brad did.

"I'll work on it."

Just maybe not that hard.

Pearl rolled her eyes, obviously hearing the total lack of conviction behind the declaration. Stepping back, she examined Evie's appearance from heard to toe. "At least you're presentable."

"And no one's going to notice that my hair, which was up, is now down?"

"The one good thing about your unconventional ways is that I can answer that—no."

"And you thought those years of constantly losing my shoes and hair ties were all a waste."

"I never thought it was a waste, baby. I just worried that your need to make your mark in a different way would get in the way of your life."

That was her mother's worry? "I never had any intention of allowing that to happen."

Pearl brushed her hands down her skirt, checking her pockets to make sure the geegaws she carried as necessary to her profession of seamstress were properly tucked away. It was a familiar gesture, one Evie had seen many times. This was the first time she realized it was a nervous gesture.

"Good, then you might want to get on home and prepare your husband's lunch. Word is he didn't get a bit of that breakfast Millicent sent over."

Did no one in this town have anything better to do than poke their noses into her life? "Who's the gossip this time?"

Pearl shrugged. "Jackson has a weakness for sugar cookies, too, and according to him, Brad took one look around the house, saw you weren't there, and stormed back out again before he could even say a word."

"And you know all this because . . . ?"

"Jackson was concerned. He came looking for me when Brad stormed out."

"He didn't have faith in a man of God?"

"I think he had more faith in your ability to push a man past his limits."

"A great opinion you have of me."

"You do like to tweak people."

"Not to that degree."

"So what did happen?"

"I got annoyed and decided I wasn't going to wait around like a fool for him to show up from wherever he'd disappeared to."

"You went to the lawyer. That's more like waving a red cape in front of a bull."

In hindsight, it might have been. "I needed to know my options."

Pearl sighed. "I can't fault you for what I taught you. A woman should always know her options, but did you have to go in full view of the town?"

"That might have been a mistake, but—"

"You were angry," Pearl sighed, finishing the sentence for her. "That temper of yours will be the death of you one day."

"I remember Pa saying that a time or two."

"You do?" As always the mention of her father immediately softened Pearl's demeanor. "I'm glad you remember that."

"I remember he used to tell you I had spirit."

"He did." Pearl's tone grew wry. "And all it took to bring out that spirit was to tell you no. You were never good with that word."

Evie shrugged. "It doesn't fit with my philosophy." She bit her lip. They didn't often talk about her father, mostly because it made Pearl sad. Even now, nineteen years after his death, there were tears in her eyes and her arms were wrapped around her torso as if to hug the memories close.

"You loved him very much, didn't you?"

"Very much."

"Did he love me?"

"Evie! What kind of question is that?"

"The kind that's been bothering me for years."

Shadows haunted Pearl's eyes. "Every man loves his daughter."

Which wasn't the same thing as saying he loved her.

"You've been answering me that way for ten years. This time, I'd like the truth."

"He fell in love with you the day you were born."

Evie had heard the story a hundred times, how the midwife hadn't been able to come and it'd just been poor Ed Washington there with his laboring wife. It was a favorite part of the Washington family legend. The romantic part was how Ed had delivered his daughter and taken one look into her blue eyes and fallen in love with his little girl. She remembered the love enough to miss it, but she didn't remember why it had been taken away. Just that it had left long before her father's death.

She didn't want her mother to lie. Didn't want her to smooth over the truth. "I remember that he didn't seem to come home much after a while. That he'd look at me and get a funny expression on his face and then walk away."

Without asking for the hug he'd always demanded before.

Pearl shook her head. "We had a misunderstanding. You got caught up in it, but he loved you."

The urge to press for the nature of the misunderstanding built like a cough cutting off her air. She wanted to know. She didn't want to know. "Was it because I was a difficult child?"

Pearl's mouth opened. Closed. Lines of strain appeared around her eyes as her complexion paled. Fear welled in a black swirl, threatening to take Evie under. Like it had that snowy night so long ago when Uncle Paul had come and given them the news. Her father was dead. He wasn't coming home ever again. Whatever Pearl was hiding, Evie suddenly knew she didn't want to hear it.

"Never mind. I think I know the answer to that."

Pearl caught her hand. "He loved you, Evie. More than anything."

"There was just a reason he stopped showing it?"

Devastated, tortured, unsure—all described Pearl's expression. Her blue eyes, so much like her own, filled with tears. "Marriage is complicated. Things happen. Sometimes life interferes before there's time for a resolution."

Such as how a father felt about his child.

Pearl licked her lips. "You'll find that out for yourself."

"I suppose I will." Or the knowledge would go the way her father's love had gone. Somewhere else, with no explanation other than she had to have done something, because for sure, Ed Washington hadn't stopped loving her mother. Evie remembered that, too.

It took a few seconds, but Evie mustered a small smile. Her father was dead. Her mother wasn't, and it was way past time for a change of subject. "Before I learn that, there's something else I need to figure out."

Her mother, her indomitable mother, actually took a step back.

She forced her smile bigger, hurting for her mother, hurting for the secret they couldn't share, longing for the rapport they'd just left, wanting it back. "What in the world am I going to feed Brad for lunch?"

Two heartbeats later, Pearl relaxed into the safety of the subject. "Well, one thing is for sure, you're not going to cook, because if you do, the next one to be visiting the lawyer will be Brad, and likely he'll get whatever he wants."

"My cooking's not that bad."

"Fool yourself about a lot of things, honey, but don't kid yourself there. The man could likely get a divorce based on your stew alone."

She would bring that up. "People burn meals all the time."

"But they don't wrap them up in a ribboned basket and bring them to a box social."

"You told me to show up, and not to come empty-handed."

Pearl rolled her eyes. "Don't try that on me, young lady. You wanted to drive off Peter Simmons."

"He was a pest and a pig."

"So we all figured when he came charging out of the woods wearing that blackened mess."

He'd not only run out of the woods; he'd run screaming she'd tried to poison him. Peter Simmons's continual rantings over the next few months that only through the grace of God and a spilled pot had he avoided death had kept the gossip mill churning. Evie folded her arms across her chest. The Simmonses were not the brightest pigs in the poke. Neither were the townsfolk if they believed those claims. She was an intelligent woman. If she'd wanted to kill him, she would have been a lot more efficient. "He also tried to take liberties."

"Which is why your uncle had a talk with him, but since we don't want your husband thinking you're trying to poison him, too, a few of my friends have agreed to . . . support you for the first few weeks."

At last some good news.

"I'd do it all," Pearl continued, "but you know I'm leaving next week."

Her mother's yearly buying trips back East for fabric and supplies were planned far in advance and carefully scheduled for good weather.

"Uncle Paul's still going with you?"

"Of course. I couldn't travel all that way alone. It would be too dangerous."

"Very. And thank you for arranging for me to have help."

Evie would put up with anything if she didn't have to cook. Even her mother's friends poking their noses into her business.

Tugging her gloves up on her wrist, Pearl nodded, sending the fake bluebird on her hat bobbing. "Only for the first few weeks though."

"A few weeks would be wonderful—"

"During which time," Pearl continued, cutting her enthusiasm off, "you will help Millicent over at her restaurant and learn to cook properly. "By the time I get back from my buying trip, you'll be competent in the kitchen."

Considering how bad Evie was at cooking, competent was probably optimistic. "I will?"

Pearl gave her that hard look that brooked no resistance. "You will. The Reverend's a good man. A good preacher. We can't afford to lose him."

They expected her to move into that huge mausoleum of a parsonage today and just become the perfect wife? "So keeping him here is all on me?"

Pearl turned and adjusted her hat before heading toward the door. "You married him."

Evie couldn't resist retorting. "Not by choice."

With a wave of her fingers, Pearl got in the last word. "Doesn't make him any less yours."

She guessed it didn't. And surprisingly, while the thought of living in the parsonage was going to take some getting used to, she kind of liked the thought of owning Brad.

BRAD ENTERED THE saloon, blinking against the sudden dimness after the morning sunshine. He couldn't count the number of times he'd made the same transition. Couldn't count how many times the stench of stale beer and smoke had wrapped around him, drawn him in with the promise of forgetfulness. He needed it today. Pushing his hat back, he surveyed the near-empty interior.

"Morning, Rev."

The greeting came from the rear of the saloon. Squinting through the dimness of the interior, Brad saw Cougar sitting, back against the wall, watching the door. In front of him sat a bottle and a series of shot glasses neatly arranged.

"Morning, Cougar."

Nodding to Mark, the bartender, Brad wandered over, the hollow thud of his footsteps as he crossed the uneven floor settling the chaos inside him. Sometimes a man had to get back to what was familiar to keep perspective. Cougar kicked out a chair with his foot. "Have a seat."

A quick glance told Brad that Cougar had been here for a bit. The whiskey bottle was only half full and all the glasses were used.

"Must be a hell of a day for you to be drinking before noon."

Had to be a hell of a day anyway. Cougar wasn't a man to indulge often or much. He valued control too much. Cougar didn't straighten, just took another pull on his whiskey.

"Pretty much over, as far as I'm concerned."

He poured whiskey into one of the empty glasses and shoved it toward Brad. "Seeing as you're here before lunch, yours can't be going much better."

Brad spun the chair around and straddled it. "You could say that."

"Heard tell your wife went to the lawyer."

"Her impulses lean toward provoking."

Cougar still didn't look up. "How provoking?"

"Enough."

At that, Cougar looked up, his expression guarded. "You hurt her?"

"Maybe her pride." Tossing back his whiskey Brad asked, "How 'bout you?"

"I did hurt her."

He had to be talking about Mara, which left only one response: "Bullshit."

Cougar drained the last of his glass. "Now, is that any way for a preacher to talk?"

"Some situations call for the plain facts."

"Uh-huh." The glass clicked on the table. "Mark, I'm running out of glasses."

"And I'm sick of cleaning them. Reuse what you've got."

Cougar reached down and pulled the big knife out of his belt. The one that had earned him the nickname Gut'm McKinnely. He set it on the table. "Now, that is a shame."

A soft curse from Mark. "More glasses coming up."

Brad eyed the knife and what he could see of Cougar's expression under the brim of his hat. It wasn't like Cougar to threaten pointlessly.

"I don't think you need another glass."

"Mind your own damn business."

Light swung into the dim interior with the opening of the door. Backlit from the sun, the only clues to the newcomer's identity were the shocks of hair standing up on top of his head.

"Morning, Doc," Brad called.

Doc strolled over. The shadows faded, revealing his exasperation as he got closer. "Thought I'd find you two here."

Cougar grabbed the bottle. "Mara tattle?"

"You know darn well that woman wouldn't say a word against you." He looked at the near-empty bottle. "Mark, bring us over another."

"You're drinking, too?"

"Might as well. Doesn't look like the day's going to get any better." Doc dragged a chair from another table. He gave Brad his attention. "Heard tell you made a fool of yourself on your wedding night."

"Not hardly."

"That's not what I heard this morning."

Brad rolled his eyes. There really was no getting around

everyone knowing your business in a small town. "She'll get over it."

Cougar rumbled. "Or else you'll find your bags packed and sitting in the street."

The thought of Evie leaving him sent a dark mood swinging over Brad's complacency. He took a drink, letting the burn feed his discontent. "That's not going to happen."

"Might be possible, if Pearl gets her teeth into the subject," Doc interjected.

"Why the hell would Pearl want that?"

"Pearl isn't the complacent sort, any more than Evie," Doc explained. "She's just a bit more devious about making her point."

"What does that mean?" Brad growled.

"I think it means you'd better have another drink."

"So should you."

Cougar poured the alcohol. "Why?"

"I just got done dropping Dorothy off at your place."

Which explained Doc's bad mood. Dorothy refused to ride a horse and Doc hated to ride in the wagon. Claimed it shook his bones up.

"What kind of mood is Dorothy in?"

"Well, she's madder than a wet hen at you for upsetting Mara, and pleased as punch she's going to have a baby to spoil."

Cougar shook his head and tossed back the last of his drink.

Mark put another bottle on the table, along with a tray of glasses. "Congratulations, Cougar."

Cougar took the bottle out of his hand and flipped a glass over. Despite the amount of liquor he must have consumed, the glass landed precisely where he wanted it and his speech was perfectly clear. "I'd rather have my wife."

Doc held out a glass. "It's not an either-or thing, son."

Cougar ignored the request. "You said she wasn't a good candidate to bear children."

"I'm just a country doctor, what the hell do I know?"

"Enough to save Mara when she miscarried."

The truth of that lay heavy in the silence.

Doc grabbed the bottle out of his hand. "Lots of women as small as her have babies without problems."

"She's already had a problem."

With a lift of his grizzled eyebrow, Doc held the bottle over

Brad's near-empty glass. What the hell. Brad nodded. There were worse things a man could do on a Saturday morning. One of them being all but raping his wife in a church where anyone could walk in.

Doc poured the whiskey and then picked up the conversation. "She had a miscarriage, that's not the same thing."

"Feels like it to me."

"I always thought it'd be an outlaw that took me down." The glance Cougar cast Brad was heavy with irony.

Lord knows in his day Brad had given it a try. The only lawmen he'd never been able to shake off his trail had been the McKinnelys. They'd been like deadly blood hounds, riding his tail so close by the end of a year they were almost like a reflection of himself, so when they'd been bushwhacked, he'd given in to the impulse and saved their lives. Occasionally, it was an impulse he regretted. He gave Cougar his most taunting smile. "I could go back to trying."

Cougar arched a brow. "Missing that price on your head?"

"Sometimes."

Cougar cracked his knuckles. "Say the word and we can reinstate it."

"I don't want it reinstated." He shoved his glass toward Cougar. "I simply want the option of tearing up the place when I get pissed."

"Hell, so would I." Cougar tipped the whiskey bottle. The glass filled in three splashes.

"Next time you decide to show your gratitude by giving me a new start, make it something less confining."

Cougar shrugged. "Like it or not, Rev, you've got preacher ways."

"What the hell does that mean?"

"It means it's been good for everyone since you went straight," Doc interrupted.

Brad remembered how he'd left Evie—panting, her face having that shell-shocked expression he'd seen on the faces of men after the war. And her mother beating down the door. "Not everyone."

"See," Cougar pointed to the table. "That's a man's downfall."

Brad looked at his hand, seeing nothing but the faint scars and his wedding ring. "What is?"

"A woman. A tiny little slip of a woman."

Since Brad wouldn't call Evie tiny, Cougar must be back to talking about Mara. He couldn't imagine how scared Cougar must be right now. His wife was in danger, in his mind he'd put her there, and worse, there was nothing he could do to mitigate it. "Mara will be fine, Cougar."

The other man looked up, his dark eyes haunted. "I never should have touched her."

"Don't be an ass," Doc snorted. "It's bad enough we've got the Reverend making a spectacle of his wife by dragging her all about town. We don't need Mara kidnapping you again."

Cougar smiled with remembered pleasure. "That part was fun."

Doc shook his head and growled in his gravelly voice, "Hell, it's a wonder the two of you survived long enough to get out of knee pants. With the mess you've both made, it's a sure thing Dorothy is going to be in a foul mood tonight."

"So?"

"So it's Saturday, and I've got a long-standing date with my wife."

Brad spewed whiskey across the table. Cougar choked. "Shit, Doc, we don't need to be hearing that kind of stuff."

"Oh yeah, I forgot how lily-white pure you two are."

Brad was with Cougar. "Hell, Doc, I like you and Dorothy both well enough, but I sure as shit don't want to be imagining you between the sheets."

"Well, who in hell invited you to? I merely pointed out I don't appreciate you giving my wife something else to think about."

"There's nothing for her to think about."

"You don't think Evie and Mara are going to talk to Dorothy, do you?"

"Hell, Cougar, use your head. Everyone talks to Dorothy. The woman has a knack for making people spill their guts."

An uncontrollable heat spread up the back of Brad's neck. There were some things he wasn't comfortable with anyone else knowing, including the fact his wife drove him so crazy he'd dragged her into the church and made love to her, unable to stop even when her mother stood just on the other side of the door. "I'm sure there are some things even Dorothy can't pry free."

Doc scoffed. "Don't kid yourself."

Cougar swore again and looked as uncomfortable as Brad felt. "Hell."

"Or shit." Doc shrugged. "Spit out whatever curse takes your fancy. By now, Dorothy probably knows exactly how Mara got pregnant and"—he pointed at Brad—"what you did to your wife once you got her alone in the church."

Which likely meant Brad would never get close to Evie again. That was unacceptable. He took a bigger sip of his whiskey.

"So, since you seem to know everything, what in hell do you think we should do?"

"Well, gentlemen," Doc picked up the bottle and poured another round. Waiting until they picked up their glasses, he lifted his in a mock salute. "Considering the mess you've made of your marriages and how the resulting mess is going to impact mine, I think the best thing we can do is sit back and finish this bottle."

Brad raised his glass. "Amen."

Ten

THE KITCHEN DOOR of the parsonage squeaked a warning. Brad was home. Evie hastily smoothed her braid and settled the basket Gray had dropped off from Dorothy onto the kitchen table. Her nerves skipped like a leaf in a windstorm, images of the morning racing right behind.

"Looks like I got here just in time."

Out of the corner of her eye she could see Brad standing in the doorway. However, she couldn't turn her head to save her life. A blush scalded her cheeks. "If you want a prayer of lunch, yes."

"That mean you're as hungry as I am?"

There was absolutely nothing suggestive in the statement, and yet the heat in her cheeks intensified. "Yes."

Still out of the corner of her eye, she saw Brad take off his hat and hang it by the door. A stray beam of sunlight caught the blue of his eyes and the top of his shoulders, while the shadows hugged his hips and thighs. The combination emphasized the perfection of his build. He was impossibly handsome, obviously virile. Very appealing. Scenes from this morning in the church wouldn't go away. There had been nothing saintly about the man then. There was little saintly about him now. He was all aggressive male. All pure masculinity. All . . . perfect.

She took a step back as he came forward, folding her arms across her chest. Her gaze fell to the open neck of his shirt. His skin was deeply tanned, almost as dark as any cowboy's. It was a gorgeous brown color, as rich as coffee, and set off the bright blond of his hair. Beneath the smooth tan of his skin, she could see his pulse. She counted the beats. One, two, three. Her fingers tingled. If she touched him, he'd be warm and smell like leather, man, and tobacco. He ran his fingers through his hair, ruffling the thick mass into waves. She couldn't help but remember how those same strands had felt like the coolest silk in her fingers as she'd held him to her. He peeked into the basket, releasing the scents of rosemary and fresh-baked bread.

"Now, that smells good. You cook it?"

He knew she hadn't.

It was hard to get the words to form in her suddenly dry mouth. "Aren't you afraid I'll poison you?"

He pulled the towel back farther. "Hmm, it's a possibility, according to the Simmonses."

This close it was impossible to miss the new scents clinging to his clothes that hadn't been there this morning—smoke and alcohol. Only one place drenched a man in those odors. "And getting stronger by the minute."

Glancing at her from under his lashes he asked, "Are you warning me or testing me?"

She had the incredible urge to push his hair off his forehead. "Maybe a little of both."

He pulled out a chair. "In the testing department, are you hoping I'll pass or fail?"

She started pulling items from the basket. It was either that or succumb to the inappropriate urges that were prodding her. There was fragrant baked chicken, crusty sourdough bread, mayonnaise, butter, fresh whipped cream, biscuits, and juicy fresh strawberries. "I haven't decided yet."

He picked up his napkin. "Then why don't we call a truce until after lunch? I'm starving."

So was she, but she also had to know. "You've been drinking."

"Can't deny that."

It wasn't even noon. "At the saloon?"

"Yeah."

Loose women were at the saloon. Her thumb broke through the crust of the loaf. Had he gone to a prostitute after leaving her in the church? Against her will, she remembered the warmth of his seed on her back. Did he come in the woman at the saloon? Give a prostitute what he wouldn't give her?

"Alone?"

"Cougar and Doc kept me company."

"Cougar was in the saloon?"

Ever since the night Mara had kidnapped Cougar, he'd avoided the place.

"Half-lit when I found him."

"So you went there to keep him company?" It was all she could do to keep the hope out of the question.

"I went there to get drunk."

She grabbed up the knife. "From the red rimming your eyes, I'd say you succeeded."

He paused in reaching for the bread. "You think I'm drunk?"

The smile edging his lips grated on her nerves. He had nothing to be amused about. "Aren't you?"

"Not for lack of trying, but that Cougar can be a selfish bastard when he's determined to go on a bender. Doc and I barely got a sip. Mostly, I'm just tired."

That was his own fault. She pulled out her chair at the other end of the rectangular table. Beyond a lift of his eyebrow, he didn't comment on her choice of seating. Part of her was grateful. The other part was annoyed. He could at least care enough to notice. "Maybe you'll have time to catch a nap later."

"Is that an invitation?"

"For what?" The question popped out before she could censor it. His brow arched higher, and he grinned, damn him. Grinned that grin that made him more sinner than saint. The one that had every sore inch of her perking up in interest.

"I must be doing something wrong if you need me to spell that out."

"You don't need to spell anything out. It's bad enough everyone knows what you did in the church this morning."

"*I* did?"

"Yes, you."

"You weren't there coming so hard I had to cover your mouth to muffle your screams?"

How could he just say things like that? "You led me astray."

Brad tugged the platter of chicken toward him. "Interesting."

She couldn't help noticing how dark his skin looked against the white platter, couldn't help remembering how good those hands felt on her body. How skilled they'd been. "Everybody in town thinks I'm loose because of you!"

"First off"—he picked up the carving knife she'd set out earlier—"a woman can't be too loose with her husband."

"Says who?"

"Says me, your local spiritual voice." He glanced up. "Do you prefer white or dark meat?"

"White. What's secondly?"

Brad severed the joint with one cut. He was awfully good with knives. "What makes you think there's a 'secondly'?"

"If there weren't, there wouldn't be a 'first off.' "

With deft grace, he settled the leg beside the breast. "Good point."

She licked her lips and pulled the cutting board with the loaf of bread toward her. She needed something to take her mind off the pure sexuality of the man. "So what is it?" she asked, cutting into the loaf.

"The only way anyone would know what happened in the church would be if you colored berry bright—like you're doing right now, incidentally—when they asked you about it."

Her hand jerked. The knife angled off to the side. The first piece of bread fell off halfway down.

"You can't blame me for that."

"I don't blame you for anything. I rather like the reputation that blush gets me. Offsets the rather staid image of a minister."

She reset the knife on top of the loaf, keeping all her focus on the bread as she cut down. "I thought your staid image was everything."

"The blush works fine for me."

The knife slipped and skidded off the edge of the wooden board.

"Whoa now." Brad caught her wrist, keeping the knife from demolishing the butter crock as it skidded across the table.

"Thank you."

He didn't let go of her wrist. Out of the corner of her eye, she could see his thumb. Such an innocuous appendage. At least on anyone's hand but Brad's. Long, elegant, with neatly trimmed nails and thick calluses, it was a workingman's hand. Her lover's hand. And not more than three hours ago, it had had her screaming his name as joy crashed over her. In church. Oh God. He probably thought no more of her than anyone else.

"Evie, look at me."

"I've got to finish cutting the bread."

"The bread can wait."

No, it couldn't. Not if she didn't want him to see how flustered she was. "I thought you were hungry."

He sighed. "My hunger can wait."

She tugged her hand again. "No it can't."

"Why not?"

"Because, no doubt, every woman in this town is trying to peek in the windows to reassure themselves I'm taking care of you correctly."

He let go of her wrist. "It's a little hard on you, being married to me, isn't it?"

"I'm sure it's harder on you."

He stole the piece of crust she'd originally cut off. Scooping some butter from the crock with his spoon, he spread it on the slice. "Nah, pretty much, I've got free license to do whatever I need to do to get you in line, including and up to beating you."

She snapped the knife down. The serrated edges bit into the hardwood of the cutting board. Yanking it up, she angled it at him. "You beat me, and you won't be waking up in the morning."

He snagged the handle of the breadboard and spun it toward him. In a move so quick her fingers were still closing on air after the knife was gone, he took it from her grip. As if he hadn't done the most extraordinary thing, he put the blade to the bread. "I stand advised."

He didn't look advised. He looked completely in control and unconcerned. While she, looking at him and then at her hand that still bore the sensory impression of the knife, was stunned. How had he done that? With smooth efficiency, he cut four slices.

"I could finish cutting that."

A full smile tugged his lips. "I have a policy of taking over the cutting when anyone starts threatening to gut me."

Evie sat down because there didn't seem to be anything more for her to do. Brad had taken over cutting the bread, his lunch . . . her life. All with the same lazy never-saw-it-coming competence.

"Do people often threaten to gut you?"

"You'd be surprised by how often preaching the good word gets people's dander up."

She couldn't resist. "It might not be the good word, but the way you preach it that gets them riled."

His smile turned completely charming, disarming if one

didn't look beneath the surface. "You just don't have it in you to be cautious, do you?"

There was no sense lying. "Probably not."

He started spreading mayonnaise on the bread. "At least you're honest."

"Sometimes."

As he layered the white meat on top of the bread, he asked, "And is this one of those times?"

Surprisingly. "Yes."

"Good." Sprinkling salt over the top, he asked, "What the hell were you doing in that lawyer's office?"

She poured lemonade from a pitcher into two glasses. "Finding out what my options were."

He put another slice of bread on top, put it on the plate, and pushed it over to her. "Because you woke up alone this morning?"

It wasn't a question. "It certainly didn't make me happy." She licked her lips. "Where did you go?"

There was the barest hesitation before he started on a second sandwich. "An old friend needed help."

The only reason a man would hesitate to tell his wife about an "old friend" was if that old friend was female. "Is she your lover?"

Another look from under his lashes. "I'm a married man."

He didn't deny the person was female. "That doesn't answer my question."

"It sure as hell should." He slammed the top piece of bread down on the sandwich, smashing it flat. He was upset.

She didn't really care. "But it doesn't. Is she your lover?"

"It's as good an answer as you're going to get."

"So, when you think I'm getting too close to another man, you can drag me around in some archaic display of male strength, but when I have the same concern, I have to take it on faith?"

"Pretty much." He caught the glass she shoved at him. Lemonade sloshed over the top. "However, I don't see any need for me to drag you anywhere." Holding her gaze, he leisurely lapped the liquid from his hand. Heat that had nothing to do with embarrassment poured through her. She took a hasty drink. The flush that had just left her cheeks came back. "Not when there's a perfectly good table right here."

The swallow, caught halfway down her throat, turned into a hacking cough. Standing, she wheezed for breath. Brad stood and slapped her back. She pitched forward against the table in almost the same position in which he had taken her before. His fingers lingered, tracing her spine, from between her shoulder, past her waist, to the top of her buttocks. "Would that be an invitation, darling?"

The breath she'd managed to suck in exploded out as that wicked hand came around her front, opened over her stomach, and pulled her back into the strength of his chest, the hardness of his thighs. Even through the layers of her skirt and petticoat, she could feel the thrust of his cock. Between her legs, the flesh throbbed a welcome.

"You can't possibly want to make love again! I'm still wet from last time."

She only realized what she'd said when Brad froze and his fingers curled into her stomach. His chin tucked into the curve of her shoulder and neck. His mouth brushed her ear as he whispered, "If you're trying to discourage me, darling, you're going about it all wrong. Reminding me that my seed is still nestled between those sweet thighs is only going to make me want to give you more."

"That's crude."

"That's honest. Nothing a man enjoys more than marking his woman."

She touched her neck. "You are beginning to sound as if you're a dog instead of a man!"

Steady pressure turned her around, despite her efforts. She rose up on her toes, resisting, but all that did was make it easier for Brad to arch her over his arm, capturing her between the strength of his chest and the hardness of the table. His expression was very serious as he said, "The most important part of that sentence is the word *man*."

He shifted his grip, knocking her off balance. She grabbed for his shoulders. His hand brushed her hip, then her thigh before hefting her skirt with two tosses.

"What are you doing?" And why wasn't she resisting?

"Checking for myself how wet you are."

His callused fingers skimmed up the inside of her thighs, slipping into the slit in her new drawers, finding her as wet as she'd implied—but not with his seed. Her desire was what he found. She closed her eyes, mortification rising faster than a fresh blush.

"Damn."

"It's your fault."

His fingers swirled gently against her opening. "Sweetheart, there isn't a man alive who would mind taking the blame for this."

Another swirl of his fingers emphasized the dampness she couldn't seem to help. As he had before, he probed lightly with one finger, inserting it just a little. It caught on her raw flesh. She bit her lip to fight back a cry, but when he inserted a second one, she couldn't help but flinch.

His palm flattened over her vulva. "Sore?"

He was always so matter-of-fact about these things. She didn't know how he did it or why it excited her so, but it was almost a relief when he straightened, taking her with him, holding her close. Her skirt fell about her thighs, gathered in the middle, hugging his arm.

"Are you sure you're a man of God?"

Another hesitation. "Are you asking because I have a man's appreciation for your body?"

"I'm asking because you have an understanding of my body that even I don't have."

A burst of laughter reverberated down her spine, mocking her. She shoved at his arm and elbowed him in the stomach. He let her go as far as she could, which wasn't very, considering she was still trapped between him and the table.

His hand came up. "Look at me."

She batted it away. "I know where that's been."

"That was my other hand." Inexorably, he tipped her chin up. "I owe you an apology."

"For forcing me to marry you?"

"No, that doesn't need an apology."

"Then what does?"

"I lost my temper earlier. I had no right to humiliate you."

He was apologizing for their interlude? How dare he? "No, you didn't. Anyone could have come in that church. My mother almost caught us."

That devil smile was back on his lips. He stroked the back of his fingers down her cheek. "That wasn't humiliation, sweetheart. That was fun."

This conversation was getting her nowhere. "If you weren't apologizing for that, what were you apologizing for?"

"Dragging you through the streets."

"I think a hundred residents cheered."

He grimaced. "And that was wrong."

"Are you saying you're never going to get mad at me again?"

Another stroke down her cheek. "Heck no. I imagine you'll get my dander up four or five times a week."

"But?"

"How we resolve that will be just between us."

"You're sparing my pride?"

"I like your pride. I don't like seeing it ground into the dust."

She noticed his knuckles. They were bruised.

"You got into a fight?"

"I had a bit of a discussion with someone."

She also noticed the blood spots on the right knuckle. He hadn't fought last night.

I like your pride. I don't like seeing it ground into the dust.

Anger left her in a rush. She touched her fingers to the darkest bruise.

"Someone made fun of me, didn't they?"

He took a step back so fast that she had to catch herself against the table. "He won't make that mistake again."

"You're a minister."

"You keep harping on that."

"Ministers don't fight."

With a shrug, he said, "So I'm a bit Old Testament."

No, he wasn't. He was the most understanding preacher their town had ever had. Sunday sermons were full, and people who hadn't gone to church in years showed up to bend his ear. Cattle Crossing had become a town rather than a mud pit solely through his popularity.

And he'd fought for her. When he'd been right and she'd been wrong, simply because . . . She didn't know why. She caught his hand before he got back to his seat.

"Why?"

He looked surprised, as if she should know the answer ahead of time. "You're my wife."

The elation fled. It was his pride he'd been protecting, not hers. She should have known.

"You've got my support, always."

She blinked. Not his pride. The tears came out of nowhere, burning her eyes, clogging her throat. Oh shoot, now she was going to make a fool of herself?

"Are you crying?"

"No."

He sighed. "You are."

"Well, what do you expect?" She took a swing at him. "You fought for me."

He caught her fist. Tears blurred her eyes, blocking his image. "You'd rather I let some yahoo drag your name through the dirt?"

"I'm trying to hate you, darn it."

"Evie, that doesn't even make sense. I'm your husband."

"Who I was planning to divorce."

He pulled her against his chest. The shake of his head vibrated against her cheek. It was natural to bury her face in his shirt, to breathe in the comfort of his scent.

"How can I hate you when you do something like that?"

"Give it time. I'm sure I'll give you cause."

"No, you won't. You're a saint."

"I'm about as far as a body can get from sainthood."

"Not in my eyes."

He tipped her chin up. She didn't even know with which hand. What's more, she didn't care. "Give me time, I'll likely do something to horrify you."

"Then I guess we're pretty much suited to each other, because I'm sure I'll horrify you, too."

"You tend to make me smile."

She liked the thought of that. Her stomach rumbled. His immediately answered with a rumble of its own. "And if we don't get something to eat soon, the congregation will find us propped against this table, dead of starvation."

"We can't have that."

She searched his gaze, seeing nothing but the truth in the darkened depths.

"Never doubt that I'm proud of you, Evie."

His hand slid down over her neck, opening over her chest before contracting around her breast. "So, how sore are you?"

Sore, but when she thought of how he'd defended her, something no one had ever done, of the sense of loyalty that had him doing that despite the fact that her behavior had to have embarrassed him, she took a step closer and snuggled his cock into her stomach. "Not that sore."

His smile was soft, tender, hot. "Good. Because I thought we'd try something different."

"Really?"

His fingers threaded through her hair, tugging softly, sending erotic pings of awareness through her body. "I wouldn't want you to get bored."

Eleven

IT WASN'T UNTIL three days later that she realized he'd never answered her original question. And she might not have realized it then if Nidia hadn't come into Millicent's restaurant. Not as big as her first restaurant in Cheyenne, Millie's II had the same garish exterior, the same bursting-at-the-seams clientele, and the same mix of proper with improper. Millie's determination to make a buck and the banishment of anyone who complained were the definitive levelers of most social conflicts.

But Millie's was a place of equal opportunity for everyone, and Nidia did walk through the door, looking stunning as always in her smart navy dress that showed off her curvaceous figure and snapping brown eyes. Her hair glowed a glossy black in the bright light and her lips glistened, a full pouting red.

The woman fascinated Evie to nearly the same extent that Brad did, and for the same reasons. Nidia owned the Pleasure Emporium, the whorehouse that operated above the saloon. She was a woman who should be hard, and *was* by all accounts hard, but whenever Evie painted her, another image appeared. Like it did with Brad, her artist's eye saw Nidia as other than what she pretended to be. Something softer, more vulnerable. Another puzzle to be shifted through.

"Hey there, Nidia," Millicent called, coming out of the kitchen, plates of steaming food stacked up her capable arms, "don't often see you here twice in one week."

At Millicent's call, every male head in the room turned. If Evie hadn't been watching Nidia so closely, she would have missed the other woman's stiffening. In anyone but a notorious madam, she would have called the shiver that took her . . . distaste.

Head up, shoulders back, a look as haughty as that of any queen on her face, Nidia moved farther into the room. "I have a wish to speak to you."

A few of the men stood as she approached. Off-colored comments followed. Millie bonked the man closest to her on the head with her big wooden spoon. "Find some respect."

"What the hell for? She's just a goddamn wh—"

This time Millie's spoon smacked across his face. "To keep some teeth in your head."

"Darn, Chuck, watch your mouth." The speaker—Chuck's tablemate—cuffed Chuck on the back of the head. "I don't want to get banned from the best eats in miles because you don't have the sense God gave a goose." He looked up at Millie, his face all but obscured by facial hair and his hat. "Chuck's real sorry, Millie. It won't happen again."

Millie huffed and folded her arms across her ample chest. Everything about Millie was . . . ample. Her personality, her taste in clothes, her build. Her generosity. "I don't like the look of him."

Chuck looked up, wiping his mouth, "I'm sure not that fond of the look—"

The wrangler on the other side of Chuck, the one shoveling food into his mouth as if he hadn't seen it before, elbowed him in the side hard enough to knock the wind out of him.

The door jangled again. A mean-faced man with his hat pulled down low over his sandy brown hair came in to stand behind Nidia. In the last year Elijah had become Nidia's champion for reasons Evie didn't understand.

All it took to have men sitting back down and the risqué murmurs ending was one glance from his dark green eyes. Sometimes it was very hard for Evie to remember Elijah as the gentle man who'd loved Amy so much and worked their farm with such peaceful enjoyment.

It almost seemed like that was the illusion, and this hard-faced, deadly shell of a man, just looking for an excuse to release the rage inside him, was the real thing. It was almost as if Amy's death had ripped the mask from his soul.

The door slammed behind Elijah as another patron came in, startling her. Evie dropped the glass she'd been using to cut the biscuits. It rolled across the counter. Elijah caught it before it could roll off. His eyes met hers. "Careful."

The banked anger in his gaze made her shiver. "Thank you."

Millie rapped her spoon on the counter. "Everyone, this here's the Reverend's new bride, Mrs. Swanson. She's here to learn how to cook. I don't have to remind everyone how good things have been since we got Reverend Swanson to come here—"

"The preacher don't make no never mind to me," a man called from the packed doorway.

Millie slammed her hands on her hips. "You just never learn when to shut that yap of yours, do you, Red?"

"I came to eat, not socialize."

"That's as plain as the hair on your face."

Red was a bear of a man with a big handlebar moustache, which was the only kept-up thing about his otherwise sweat-stained, smelly appearance.

"Seems to me you should have learned that lesson a year or so back when Cougar knocked your front teeth down your throat."

This was the man Cougar McKinnely had kicked through the window of Millie's last summer? The man who'd called Mara a whore? Obviously, he was short on brains as well as teeth, because everyone knew better than to touch, with word or hand, what belonged to a McKinnely. They were a very proud family and fiercely protective of their women. That also explained the strange enunciation of his words.

"I'm not eating with a fucking whore."

"That tears it!"

Millie came around the table, spoon raised. As big as Millie was, and she was a big woman in both height and girth, she was no match for Red, who was large enough to make her look small. But Millie didn't seemed to grasp that. She just bore down on the man as if through sheer force of will, she'd eject him. "You get the hell out of my establishment."

Red's chin came up. "I'm not going anywhere without my dinner. I've been waiting fifteen minutes for a seat."

Evie grabbed the stone rolling pin and quickly moved behind Millie. A hand on her arm stopped her. Elijah met her gaze and shook his head. She yanked her arm free. She wasn't leaving Millie to fight this unequal battle by herself. Another hand, much smaller, caught her wrist. *Nidia.* The shock of the woman touching her froze her in place.

"I could be persuaded to escort Red out for a piece of strawberry-rhubarb pie."

The drawl cut across the tense silence. Millie snapped around, scanning the waiting crowd beyond the door. "That you, Jackson?"

"Yup."

Men and women stepped aside. It had become fashionable on Saturday afternoon to take lunch at Millie's II, the wait for a table a time to socialize. Jackson strolled forward, the easy smile he was known for on his handsome face. He pushed his hat back. "Lunch sure smells good, Millie."

"When did you get here?"

"About two pies ago and I've got to admit I'm a bit worried you'll sell out before a place opens up for me."

The one thing Millie never ran out of was food.

"Hrrmph!"

Evie noticed, for all the casualness implied by his pushed-back hat and nonchalance, there was tension in Jackson's body as he came up beside Red. "For a piece I'll move this one along."

"You aren't going to do shit, pip-squeak," Red snarled, his temper obviously fraying.

While not huge like Red, Jackson was hardly a pip-squeak. He was easily six feet, with a lean musculature that promised strength. Half turning, Red shifted into Jackson's space. "Now get."

Evie tightened her hand on the rolling pin. Jackson just smiled casually at the bigger man. "I'd do a hell of a lot for strawberry-rhubarb pie, including removing that one ball Cougar left you last summer." He glanced at the ladies as Red's jaw worked. "My apologies for the language."

The acceptance was automatic. Most of the ladies were enthralled with the drama unfolding, Evie included. Despite all her efforts, she'd been pretty sheltered from encounters like this. She always heard about them secondhand, but now she was in the middle of one. She shifted her grip on the rolling pin, excitement sweeping through her blood. She met Elijah's gaze with a lift of her chin. He snorted and shook his head, stepping between her and the confrontation, to the point he blocked her view. Men were so exasperating.

"Putting a gun in my privates isn't fair."

"I'm not interested in fair. I'm interested in pie, and if shooting off what's left of your manhood will get that for me, I'm easy about it."

The statement was delivered with the lightness of a joke, but leaning around Elijah provided Evie with a different view of the situation. Jackson did have a gun barrel wedged in the other man's privates and a glance at his face was enough to convince her he meant every word. If Red pushed this, Jackson would shoot him.

"Heck, Jackson, either shoot or get out of the way," a man called from beyond the door. "You're not the only one who wants pie."

The order was picked up by the other patrons. There seemed to be more calls for shooting than anything else. Red was not popular.

After another tense silence, during which Evie couldn't see a thing, thanks to Elijah shoving her back behind him again, there was the unmistakable sound of an angry stomp down the walk.

"Show's over, folks," Millie called. "Get back to eating. If you let my food get cold, I'll take it personally."

Elijah stepped aside in time for Evie to see Millie turn around. The older woman's gaze fell on the rolling pin in her hand. "Now what in the world were you going to do with that?"

The way Millie said it made Evie feel ridiculous. "Knock some sense into whomever needed it."

Millie's bright red eyebrows shot up in her garishly painted, yet strangely attractive face. "Didn't you just hear me get done telling everyone that we want the Reverend happy?"

"So?"

She plucked the rolling pin from her hand. "He's not going to be happy if his wife is hurt in a brawl."

"Elijah would not let that happen," Nidia murmured.

Millie glanced at the man as if just noticing his presence. Her glance cut to Nidia and then back to him. "Still playing the fool, I see."

Elijah didn't respond, just held her gaze for as long as Millie chose to extend the confrontation. Nidia was the one to break up the stare down. To Evie's surprise, a hint of color touched the madam's face as she snapped, "You will not speak to him this way."

"Little lady, you'll have to grow some inches and some muscle before you can tell me what to do."

"Nonetheless—"

Millicent cut her off. "I don't have time for this nonsense.

Bellies are going empty. Elijah, sit yourself at that table yonder and I'll get you some pie, too."

"Dang it, Millie," Jackson protested. "He didn't do anything, and you're giving him my pie!"

"No. I'm giving him his own pie. Now hush and find a seat."

Elijah looked at Nidia. Though the woman made no visible response by word or expression, he said, "I'll take my pie to go."

"There are more appreciative women you could tie your loyalty to, wrangler."

"More decent ones, too," one of the women muttered.

Nidia did not even acknowledge she heard the insults. Neither did Elijah, but Evie thought he moved a little closer to the small woman. Then again, it might have been the press of the crowd.

"I came to ask if you had more of that rice pudding you sent over the other night," Nidia said.

"Liked that, did you?"

"It was very good."

"I told the Reverend it'd do the trick."

Nidia jumped and cast Evie a startled glance. "Thank you."

That look put Evie's nerves on edge.

"I don't have any right now"—Millie grabbed a plate—"but come back in an hour and I'll have it ready."

Nidia glanced around at the ogling men and the disapproving frowns of the ladies. Once again Evie thought she saw something vulnerable in her gaze, and then it was gone. Her chin came up. "I will be back."

"I can—"

She glared at Elijah. "I have said I will pick it up."

Elijah's lips tightened. "I told the Reverend—"

This time it was Evie's turn to grab Nidia. "You were with Brad two nights ago?"

"I had need of him."

Brad had left her bed on their wedding night to go to this woman? "He won't be coming to you again."

Of that she was sure. Even if she had to castrate him to assure it.

It was a toothless statement. She had no control over Brad's comings and goings. The pitying smile Nidia gave her said she knew it.

"If I call him, he will come."

With sick acceptance, Evie didn't doubt her.

Elijah gabbed Nidia's arm. "Enough."

"I merely responded."

"Lashing out is not a response." He pushed her through the crowd. "And you're a better person than that."

"I'm a whore."

Elijah propelled Nidia through the door. Evie never got to hear his response. She didn't care to. Her mind was still stuck on the confidence with which Nidia had said Brad would come when she called. Only one thing gave a woman that much confidence—the certainty of her claim.

"It's probably not safe for you to have that any longer," Millie muttered.

Pain in her fingers alerted Evie to the fact that she clutched the rolling pin so tightly her knuckles were white. "What did she mean?"

Evie wished the words back as soon as she uttered them. The last thing she needed was a public discussion of where her husband had spent their wedding night.

The rolling pin was pried from her fingers. "She was likely just trying to get your goat. Occasionally, Nidia gets a need to lash out." Millie slapped the rolling pin down on the counter. "She hasn't had an easy life, you know."

Evie didn't suppose she had, but that didn't give her the right to make comments about her husband.

Millie shoved a pie plate into her hand. "Take this on over to Jackson. He's waiting."

"I thought he wagered for a piece of pie."

"The boy bought himself a peck of trouble, taking on Red like that. He gets the whole thing."

Evie was beginning to understand that Millie coddled those she loved through food. She weaved her way through the tables, avoiding the groping hands of a tipsy cowboy and arriving at Jackson's small table unscathed. He was frowning back over her shoulder at the wrangler who'd now broken into song. "I don't think it's a good idea, your working here."

"I'm not working. I'm learning."

He reached for the pie. "I'll have a talk with the Reverend."

Being here was the most excitement she'd had in months. "Don't you dare!"

"You giving me orders?"

She snatched the pie back. "Yes, I am. If you want the whole pie, then you can't talk to Brad."

"The whole pie is already mine."

She shook her head. "You only wagered for a piece."

"I could take it from you."

She held it way back, off her shoulder. "I'll throw it to the floor."

He blinked. "You're that serious?"

"I'm that serious."

His chair came down on four legs, and in a move so fast she didn't have time to react, he snatched the pie from her hands.

"Then I guess I'll keep my mouth shut."

"Because I threatened you?"

"Well, that was amusing." He cut into the pie with the side of his fork. "But also because I think it's going to be darn entertaining seeing the Reverend's face when he finds out what you've gotten into."

She rolled her eyes. Men, they were all alike.

IT WAS PAST supper time before her learning was done. Beyond cutting out biscuits she hadn't learned much about cooking, but next to painting, today was the most fun Evie'd had all year outside of Brad's arms. She found she experienced a whole new side to the town from the inside of the restaurant. People weren't so circumspect with those who served food, often forgetting that the person was even there. If she were a gossip, she'd already have a lot to tell. Number one being the new blacksmith was sweet on Millie, who didn't seem inclined to give him the time of day, except when it came time to give him pie. Millie had refused to give him that dessert. Taking a personal interest in his meal, she'd finished off her efforts with a beautiful strawberry shortcake just for him. When Evie had cast the older woman a questioning glance, Millie had blushed and grumbled she'd give pie to whomever she wanted and shortcake to those she preferred.

Evie thought it had more to do with the fact that the blacksmith was a fine-looking man for any age. She could picture him standing like the god Thor in the midst of a lightning storm, his long auburn hair blowing in the wind, the distinct white streaks at the temple just adding to the impression of power and competence. The laugh lines by his mouth and eyes added the draw of humor to the whole impressive image. Maybe she could get him to sit for her. Especially if she persuaded Millie to put him in a good mood with some good food before she asked.

Wiping the sweat from her brow with her sleeve, Evie untied her apron and sighed wearily. Fun or not, working at the restaurant was harder than anything she'd ever done before. She was ready to go home, to her husband and the trouble waiting there.

"Here."

She turned, finding Millie standing behind the counter, a large basket almost obscuring her from view.

"What's that?"

"Dinner."

She barely kept from wrinkling her nose. After smelling the food all day, she had no desire to eat it. Still, she wouldn't upset Millie by rejecting it. Suppressing a sigh, she took the basket. "Thank you."

"Be careful how you hold it. If you spill the gravy, you won't have any for your dumplings."

"Dumplings?"

"You always order chicken paprika when you come in."

So Millie had made it for her. "I didn't think you'd noticed."

"It's dinner, not a declaration of love."

"Oh."

Millie snapped a towel over her shoulder and dried her fingers on the ends. "When you serve it up tonight, you tell that husband of yours I was thinking about him special-like, when I made it."

Evie hefted the basket off the counter, staggering a bit under its weight, a blush rising. Of course Millie had made it for Brad. "I'll pass the message along."

"You do that." Her head cocked to the side. "You coming back tomorrow?"

"Wild horses couldn't keep me away."

"Good. I'll teach you to make pancakes."

Lovely. "I'll see you then."

With a grunt, Millie turned and headed back into her precious kitchen. Evie hauled the basket around the nearest table and headed for the door. All she wanted to do was go to bed.

She was even too tired to work on that wildflower in her latest painting. Too tired to eat. Too tired to fight with her husband about his nocturnal visits to Nidia.

She opened the door, catching it with her hip so she could slip through. Hopefully, Brad would have had a full day, too, and not be inclined toward conversation. She wasn't in the mood to chat, make nice, or be kind. Especially after finding out he'd spent their wedding night with Nidia.

If I call him, he will come.

She let the door slam. *Like hell, he would.* If they were married for better or worse, that held for him, too. There wouldn't be any other woman who could crook her finger and summon him to her side.

She stepped down into the street, waiting for a wagon to pass before heading over to the other side. It was only three blocks to the house, but with the awkward weight of the basket dragging at her, she had to rest. She stopped at the first alley and set the basket on the edge of the walk.

"You shouldn't be here."

Well, that was an intriguing start to an eavesdropping. She peaked around the corner. Gray stood talking to someone she couldn't see.

"I was looking for you."

A girl, young if the voice could be judged. Evie racked her brain, trying to recall any young woman in whom Gray had shown an interest.

"Why?"

He certainly wasn't going to make a good impression with that.

There was the scuff of a foot on dirt.

"You said I could . . . if I needed to."

A very young woman, Evie decided.

"What's wrong?" Gray sounded much older than his years.

"Nothing. I just wanted company."

"It's late."

"Just for a few minutes."

"Is anyone home at your place, little one?"

"I'm not little."

That statement, delivered in such a petulant voice, pulled Evie into the alley. The girl was very young and maybe in trouble.

"Gray?"

He turned, blocking her view of the child. Whether by accident or design, she didn't know. "Do you need help?"

His chin set in that stubborn way he had. "No."

She shifted to the right. He shifted right along with her. So it was deliberate. Gray was protective of the girl. There was a scurry of feet behind the boxes. She had a view of one small foot, a pale, skinny calf, and then the girl was gone.

This could turn out so badly if anyone found out an Indian boy was close to a young white girl. Clint and Cougar had earned the town's respect and were at least half white. Gray was all Indian, with no history to soften his violations of the rules. "Oh, Gray, you'll have to be careful."

His lip curled. "Worried I'm going to sully some pretty white girl with my touch?"

She was in no mood for this. "I'm worried you'll get hurt because someone else will take offense at your friendship."

He folded his arms across his chest. "Yeah, I'm the one you're worried about."

God, he looked so like the McKinnelys then. "Whether you believe it or not, I am."

"I don't need your help."

"What about your friend?"

"She doesn't need your help either."

"It sounded like she needed someone's help."

"She's just afraid to be alone."

"Nighttime can be scary."

His lip curled. "What would you know about being afraid?"

The kid was beginning to annoy her. "Apparently not as much as you feel I should."

Gray looked over her shoulder as someone approached. His expression became carefully blank.

"Whatever you know is more than enough for me."

She glanced over her shoulder. Her heart skipped a happy beat. Brad. It was silly to feel so safe as his hand came around her waist, but she did. "What are you doing here?"

His eyebrow cocked up. "I was coming over to walk you home."

"Afraid I'd run away?"

He looked between her and Gray, his gaze assessing. Despite

the quickness of the glance, she was sure he'd memorized every nuance of the encounter. "Nah. I just missed you."

That was the one thing she hadn't expected him to say. She didn't know how to respond. Thankfully, Gray was just belligerent enough to keep her from having to do so.

"I will leave you now."

He made it two steps before Brad called out, "Gray?"

The boy turned. "What?"

Brad pulled her into his side. It was a very a possessive gesture for such an easygoing man. "You know where I live if you need me."

For a moment, man and boy stared at each other. Gray nodded sharply, and then sprinted in the direction his companion had gone.

Looking down, Brad asked, "Want to tell me what that was all about?"

"Not really." Staring after Gray, she couldn't shake the feeling that that moment between them had been private. A secret not to be shared, not even with her husband. Brad turned her within his embrace until they were facing. His thighs pressed her skirts against her hips as his fingertips brushed down her cheek.

"Is whatever the boy's involved in dangerous?"

"Not from what I've seen." Gray was smart enough to make sure his friendship didn't turn into a danger.

Brad's grip tightened. "You wouldn't lie to me?"

"Not about something like that."

"But about other things, you would?"

"Well, if you wanted me to clean and I wanted to paint, I might hedge the truth about how much time I spent on both."

"That's fair enough."

His head shifted just the barest bit to the right. The setting sun cut across his face in an aggressive slash, catching on the shadow of his beard, highlighting the blue of his eyes, the faint lines at the edges, turning his eyes from dark to brilliant. Beautiful. He was so beautiful, and so . . . wild-looking. The severe black of his suit only emphasized the strength it struggled to cloak. Her fingers curled around his wrist as she memorized every shadow, every aspect, committing it to memory before the moment passed. "I'd love to paint you just like this."

He stilled, and then the right corner of his lip quirked. "Standing in the middle of the street?"

The scene flashed in her mind, Brad standing at the end of the street, the spreading oak to the left of his shoulder, sunlight filtering through the leaves, slanting across his silhouette, his hat sheltering all of his face except the chiseled shape of his mouth as he drew his gun . . . She blinked. A minister with a gun? She was definitely getting fanciful. And he was still waiting for an answer.

"Yes, in the street."

"You're a strange woman, Evie."

"So I'm told."

Twelve

SHE WAS A strange woman. Brad rubbed his thumb over Evie's mouth, luxuriating in the damp cling of the soft flesh. Bold as brass at times, innocent and sweet at others. A strange mix of fancy and courage. And when she looked at him as she did right now, he got the feeling she saw more than the facade he presented. And that was not good.

"Well, if you ever get the urge, do me a favor and keep my pants on."

She blinked and then frowned. "I can't believe you're still harping on that."

"That" being the painting she'd done of him. "Trust me, sweetheart, no man wants to have his privates so . . . minimized."

She rolled her eyes and jerked her chin off the shelf of his hand. With a brisk swat at imaginary dust, she took a step back. "Well, maybe I prefer the world to see you that way."

Interesting argument. "Now, why would you want to be setting yourself up for pitying glances?"

Her mouth worked and he could actually see her sense of caution battle with her sense of outrage. It was a sucker's bet as to which would win. Evie was not a cautious woman. Her hands planted on her hips and her chin came up. Her gaze locked firmly on his, aggression and challenge blazing out at him. Desire leapt to life. Nope. Not a lick of caution.

"So maybe you would be tempted to stay home at night."

Ah, he'd wondered when she'd get back to that subject. He headed over to where she'd left the basket. "There's a saying, Evie. A woman can catch more flies with honey than vinegar."

She followed. "There's another saying that is equally popular. 'Hell hath no fury like a woman scorned.' "

He picked up the basket. She almost bumped into him. Taking advantage of her subsequent stumble, he pulled her into his side. "That is the truth." He still bore the knife scar from one scorned woman, and the teeth marks from another. Women who'd wanted to tie him down and who'd gotten a bit hostile when he hadn't shared their enthusiasm for the idea. "But I haven't scorned you."

"You went to Nidia on our wedding night!"

Damn. He'd been hoping to have a little more time before she found that out. "I went to help a parishioner in need."

"You went to a prostitute." The point of her elbow dug into his side.

He shifted so that it slid harmlessly behind. Across the street he saw Millie watching. Restraining Evie so her struggles were little more than twitches, he nodded. Evie took advantage of his distraction to bite his side. Her teeth were no match for the thickness of his suit coat. Damn, if that temper of hers didn't set his fuse to sizzling. He waved to Millie, who waved back, a too friendly smile on her face.

He didn't have time to speculate on Millie's amusement. He had his hands full with Evie.

"Let me go."

And have her pitch a fit right there? He didn't think so. He'd worked too hard to be quietly in the background to let Evie throw them any farther front and center than their need to wed already had. Across the way, lace curtains drew back from an open window. "Unless you want to give the folks watching a hell of a lot more gossip for their gristmill, I'd suggest settling down."

"You're afraid of gossip?"

She not only looked, but sounded, shocked.

"Yes."

A glance around and her struggles ceased. "Then you shouldn't behave in such a way that inspires it."

"Probably not." But Evie wasn't the only one who chafed under the restraints of expectations.

She cut him a suspicious glare. "Then why do you do it?"

"It keeps people on their toes."

That bit of truth stilled her struggles as no order could. Taking advantage of her distraction, he steered her down the street, remembering to shorten his steps to hers when she skipped a couple of times. "Sorry. I forgot you're just a little bit."

"I'm tall for a woman."

"Uh-huh." She was still a little bit compared to him.

"I'm taller than Nidia."

He sighed. "You do have a burr under your saddle when it comes to her, don't you?"

"I have a burr under my saddle only in regard to you leaving my bed for hers."

"Son of a bitch."

He shoved her into the next alley, glancing around quickly to make sure they didn't have any spectators. Her eyes were big in the shadows. The basket hit the ground with a clatter. She jumped, her eyes darting to it before coming back to his face. If she had any sense at all, that catch in her breath would be fear.

Pinning her to the side of the building by her shoulders, Brad growled, "I'm getting damn tired of you painting me with the morals of a tomcat."

Those incredible eyes of hers narrowed. "Then maybe you shouldn't act like one."

"Damn it, woman!"

He wanted to shake her. He wanted to kiss her. She was so reckless, so willing to challenge his dominion over her when there shouldn't be any doubt. "You're my wife."

"And you're my husband. When you remember that"—her finger poked into his chest—"I might remember that I'm your wife."

Sliding his hand behind her neck, he pulled her into a kiss, growling, "I've never forgotten."

The next puff of air exploded into his mouth. She smelled of strawberries, tasted of coffee and womanly defiance. The latter drove him crazy. She was his wife—his claim wasn't something she could pick up and discard as she wanted. It was permanent and she was going to acknowledge it whether she wanted to or not.

He probed her lips with the tip of his tongue. She smashed them flat, denying him entrance. Giving her a little shake, he ordered, "Open your mouth."

Her eyes narrowed further. "No."

The barest parting of her lips was all it took to get the word out. She might as well have shouted. The syllable hit his dominant side with the power of a sledgehammer.

The urge to shake her harder grew. "You don't tell me *no*."

"I just did."

He closed his eyes against the urge to teach her who wore the pants in this relationship. God-fearing Reverend Swanson was an easygoing man, not inclined to need his wife's submission. The problem was, the Reverend was a sham, but Shadow Svensen wasn't, and Shadow Svensen found just about everything about Evie Washington an intriguing challenge. Including the thought of coaxing her around to submission.

Was that part of your plan? That I would fall for her before you took her away?

As always, God let him supply the answer for himself. Yes.

The heck of it was, he didn't care. He wanted to experience at least the illusion of love.

He dropped his mouth to the curve between her shoulder and neck. "Don't push me on this, Evie."

She gasped and turned her face away. Defiance or invitation?

"Don't tell me what to do."

Ah hell. "You just had to push me, didn't you?"

Her gaze searched his, too late finding whatever it was that it took to spark a sense of caution in her bones. "No. I was just—"

"Pushing me," he finished for her. "Well, sweetheart, you just found my limits."

With his thumb on the side of her jaw, he tipped her face to the angle he wanted. This close, he could see her pupils dilate, the expanded black bringing out the dark grey flecks in her eyes until they reminded him of pale blue violets in spring. Fragile-looking flowers that flourished in the most unexpected of places. That little pink tongue touched her bottom lip, tempting him. As soon as she noticed his focus, she tucked it in and pressed her lips back into that flat line.

He leaned in, letting his chuckle be the prelude to the lesson he was about to instill. Her lips pressed tighter and her frown grew deeper while his determination just grew stronger. Slipping his thigh between her legs, he leaned his torso into hers. The plumpness of her breasts nestled into his chest, teasing him with each rapid breath.

"You can fight me anywhere you want, Evie, but not here. Not when you're in my arms. Here, we're honest with each other."

"Meaning?"

"This."

He pressed a butterfly kiss on the corner of her mouth, not giving her time to realize that he wasn't forcing her before he touched another to the opposite corner, lingering a little longer there, repeating the caress until he felt the tiniest of quivers.

"Open your mouth."

She shook her head again, but the gesture lacked the vehemence of before, and against his chest, he could feel the poke of her nipples.

She was being unreasonably stubborn. Bringing his mouth back to hers, he slid the back of his fingers down her arms, applying just enough pressure to stimulate. The prod of her nipples grew stronger and a shiver took her from head to toe.

"You liked that, huh?"

"No."

Very stubborn. Her wrists were narrow. He circled them with his fingers, using his greater weight to keep her pinned, while he drew her hands up to either side of her head, increasing her sense of restraint. "I think you're lying, Evie. I think you liked it so much, you've got goose bumps. I think you liked it so much, you felt that little shiver all the way to your core."

She shook her head again. More telling than her denial was the curl of her fingertips into her palms.

"No lies, Evie."

"I'm not lying."

He hitched his knee until it pressed with intimate precision between her thighs. At the same time, he switched his grip from her wrist to her hands. Her palms were only half the size of his. The way her fingers immediately laced between his was a betrayal.

He let her turn her head away, but only because it exposed the sensitive side of her neck and the tempting lobe of her ear to the brush of his lips, the flick of his tongue, the graze of his teeth.

Her fingers threaded through his.

"That's right"—he nipped her lobe before soothing the sting with his tongue—"hold on."

She did, with a jerk and gasp. He pressed up with his knee, rocking it gently against her as he murmured in her ear, "If the shadows were just a little deeper out here, Mrs. Swanson, do you know what I'd be doing?"

She swallowed hard. "I don't want to know."

Yes, she did. He knew she did, from the hard swallow, and utter stillness with which she waited. "I'm keeping track of these lies, you know."

"Why?"

"To know how much discipline you'll require later."

"I'm not a child."

"No, you're not. You're a very hot, very eager woman who's too stubborn for her own good."

"Just because I'm not falling at your feet—"

"You'd be a puddle on the ground if you weren't riding my knee."

Her cheeks flared from pink to red. "Just because I'm not falling at your feet," she continued, "doesn't make me wrong."

He brushed his lips over the heat of her blush. The spikes of her lashes tickled his lips as he kissed her eyes closed. "Are you so worried about being right that you really don't want to know what I'd do if these shadows were just a bit deeper?"

It might have been his threat or her natural sense of curiosity, but whatever the reason, she opened her eyes. Her whispered "What?" shot to the heart of his desire and detonated it into a full explosion. Shit, she was a hot little thing.

"I'd pull up these skirts, slip my hands between your thighs, and make that pretty pussy of yours sing."

Her respirations picked up. "Where anyone could see?"

He nodded. "We'd be in the shadows, but you'd have to be very quiet."

This time, when he kissed the corner of her mouth, her lips were relaxed. Nibbling on the lower, he waited until her lips parted on a soft sigh. "You wouldn't be able to moan when I dipped my fingers in that sweet cream." Her hips bucked on his thigh. "You couldn't cry out as I rubbed your little clit."

He teased the inner lining of her mouth as her nails bit into the backs of his hands. "You'd just have to stand there and hold all those hot cries inside and let each wave of pleasure wash over you."

"Oh God." She was very close, her hips rocking on his thigh, her lips biting at his.

He raised her hands higher, letting the tension in her arms spread down her body, angling her hips so she received maximum sensation where she needed it.

"Open your mouth, Evie."

This time she did, with the desperate desire of a woman who only needed a little bit more to reach satisfaction. He kissed her hard and deep, letting her feel the full force of his passion before breaking off the kiss, teasing himself with the depth of her response before he stepped back, letting her slide down his leg, keeping her suspended in his grip one heartbeat. He admired the dazed look in her eyes, the rise and fall of her breasts, her swollen lips, berry red from his nips and kisses, the faint scent of her arousal. Damn, he'd like her naked like this. Before the strain could tell in her arms, he released her hands. She started at him uncomprehendingly, hands still above her head, still leaning back against the wall as he grabbed up the basket. It just about killed him to put the necessary nonchalance in his voice as he turned away. His cock ached so bad he didn't need an interpreter to translate the message. If it could have wielded a blade it would have slit his throat for walking away right then.

"We'd better get going. Supper's getting cold."

SHE STORMED INTO the house about five minutes after he did.

"You did that on purpose."

He leaned back in the chair. "I told you, you don't tell me no."

She stopped dead. "That was punishment?"

"No. If I punish you, you'll know it. That was more of a reminder."

The glint in her eye as she shoved back the hair that had come loose from her braid did not bode well for his longevity. "A reminder of what a great lover you are?"

"Shoot, why didn't you ask me that earlier? That would have been a better lesson."

She eyed the legs of the chair as though she'd like to kick them out from under him. "Maybe because I didn't need a lesson at all."

"Yeah. You did."

"In what?"

He brought the chair down on four legs and started unloading the basket. "In what's real."

She grabbed for the handle. He was faster. "Sit down."

"I don't want to."

It was easy to guess what had her feathers in a ruffle. "That was more of a request than an order."

"How was I supposed to tell?"

She had him there. It might be time to soften his edge a bit with his wife. "I thought I'd serve you tonight, seeing as you've been on your feet all day."

She blinked, the statement clearly giving her nowhere to go with her anger. He sighed, motioning again to the chair. "Please."

Eyeing him suspiciously, she did.

As he opened the lid, the smell of Millie's chicken paprika got stronger. Looks like Evie would have her revenge anyway. He hated chicken paprika. "Did you make this?"

She shook her head. "Millie made it for you. She told me she made it especially for you."

Shit. No guessing where Evie heard about Nidia. Had to be at Millicent's. Millie wouldn't be pleased about him leaving Evie on her wedding night. She thought of Evie as her daughter and she'd been very specific in her expectations that he make her happy.

The pot was still hot. He quickly dropped it on a towel on the wood cutting board on the end of the table. "Did she pack us anything for dessert? Maybe strawberry shortcake?"

Maybe Millicent wasn't that mad and she'd left him dessert. "Oatmeal cookies I think."

He sighed and pulled out the cloth-wrapped bundle. Setting it on the table, he didn't bother to open it.

"With raisins."

If she was hoping to raise his enthusiasm, she was barking up the wrong tree. Ladling the stew into a bowl, he asked, "I'm guessing there was gossip at the restaurant today?"

She took the bowl he handed her and shook out her napkin. The move was too careful and too precise to be as casual as she wanted him to believe. She stabbed her fork into the bowl so hard, it clanked on the bottom. "Nidia stopped by."

Of course she did. Another sign that his luck, thin to begin with, was wearing out. "And?"

There had to be an and.

Evie poked her fork around in her bowl a couple more times before looking up. "She seems to be under the impression that all she has to do is call and you'll come running."

Shit again. "I'm the town's minister. I pretty much come running when anyone calls."

"That's not what she implied."

"Then someone must have ticked her off."

"I'm sorry?"

"Nidia has a habit of reacting when she's hurt."

"Then maybe she should change jobs."

"You're smarter than that, Evie. There aren't many jobs for women like Nidia."

She had the grace to blush.

"Nidia's a good person under all that bluster. There are several charities that wouldn't have gotten off the ground without her."

"I don't like her."

"Because you think I went from your bed to hers."

She shoved her bowl away. "You did."

It pissed him off that she saw him that way. "You know I didn't."

"What makes you think that?"

"Because I wouldn't have gotten a sigh out of you in that alley if you did. You're a proud woman."

"Then why did you grind my pride in the dust?"

The answer, when it came to him, was shocking enough that he actually took a bite of the stew. Because he wanted her to think badly of him, so when she found out the truth, she wouldn't be hurt. Hell, on top of everything else, was he developing a conscience? "I didn't. You jumped to conclusions."

He took a drink of cool water. He would have preferred whiskey. Evie glared at him. "You didn't give me any other choice."

"There's always a choice. You could have believed in me."

Pushing her chair back, she stood. "Then maybe you should give me something to believe in."

He watched her leave the room, ignoring the strange sense of unease. Taking advantage of a woman's soft heart was an old game he'd been indulging in for years. Pull them in and then push them away. It kept women off balance, gave him an edge as they struggled to fix what was wrong. And when he was ready to leave, he just pushed them that one time too many and the relationship ended. On his terms. So why didn't it feel right this time?

Evie stomped up the stairs. She was pissed. He'd succeeded, so where was the sense of accomplishment? Dinner sat before him, getting colder by the second. Upstairs his wife was following suit, stewing in the juices he'd provided. A step farther away than she'd been this afternoon. Ten feet farther than she'd been on their wedding day. It was all going as he'd planned, following a course he'd perfected over the last fifteen years. The spare bedroom door slammed.

He washed the taste of stew out of his mouth with another sip of water. The ensuing silence stretched ominously. A soft breeze blew through the windows, sending the curtains fluttering in time with the slow chirp of crickets. Above it all, he heard the distinct sound of a sob. Crying. Evie was up there crying. He told himself it didn't matter. Told himself he didn't care. It was even to be expected. The sound came again. Another sob? Shit.

He pushed his chair back. He didn't fucking need this. The bottle of whiskey sat on the ornate sidebar in the parlor. He poured a hefty amount into one of the crystal glasses that matched the decanter, a gift from a grateful traveler after Brad had found his daughter, who'd run away with a cowhand. It hadn't been that hard to bring her back. The girl had already been having second thoughts, but there'd been no telling the traveler that. In his mind, Brad had worked a miracle. Brad tossed back the whiskey. The crystal set, the most expensive thing the man owned, had been his reward for being a hero.

Another sob drifted down through the air vents, the muffled sound flaying him with unexpected force. He'd had the guilt beaten out of him before he'd sprouted his first chest hair, so he damn well knew what bothered him wasn't that. Three more sobs and another couple shots and he'd had enough. Pouring two glasses this time, Brad swore and headed upstairs, not clear where he was heading until he got in front of their bedroom door. The bedroom where Evie wasn't, but should be. Curled up soft and warm in their bed, waiting for him to tuck her against him so she could sleep.

No more sobs came down the hall. She'd either fallen asleep or heard him come upstairs. The thought of her behind the door holding on to her pride bothered him more than the thought of her crying herself to sleep, but not by much. He turned too fast.

Liquid splashed over his hands. He glanced down, not understanding the wetness at first and then he remembered. He'd brought Evie and himself a drink. Being careful not to spill any more of Doc's best, he walked the ten steps it took to get to the bedroom door. He debated knocking. If he just walked in, she might be more offended, but she sure couldn't turn him away. The deciding factor was that his hands were full. He knocked with the toe of his boot. Once. No answer. Twice. No answer. He didn't bother with a third, just kicked hard. The door bounced against the wall. Evie screamed and sat up.

"Shh, you'll wake up the neighbors."

Glaring pointedly at the door while she scrubbed at the tearstains on her cheeks, she asked, "You think they're asleep?"

The scrubbing was a waste of time. Her eyes were swollen and her face was splotchy. Even if he hadn't heard her, there was no way he could miss the evidence that she'd been crying.

"What are you doing in here?"

He handed her a glass. "I brought you a drink."

She took it, her gaze bouncing between him and the glass. He put the other on the bed stand and started unbuttoning his shirt.

"Now what are you doing?"

"Getting ready for bed."

"I'm mad at you."

"I know. I heard you crying."

"I had a hard day."

Shucking his shirt, he started on his boots. "And I didn't help."

She blinked and sniffed. "No, you didn't."

She was holding the drink like it was poison.

"If you sip your whiskey, you'll feel better."

"No, I won't."

The second boot was more stubborn than the first. "Are you arguing with me again?"

"Yes, and you can't sleep here."

"Husbands and wives sleep together." His thoughts might be a bit unclear due to the amount of whiskey he'd drunk on an empty stomach, but he was sure on that fact.

"No, they don't."

"I swear, woman, you'd argue the color of the sky if you got in a mood."

"I'm not in a mood, I'm indisposed!"

That snapped his head up. "You're sick?"

Illness could be another reason for the splotchy face.

"No." She clenched her teeth. "I'm indisposed."

He stopped unbuttoning his pants. "I'll get Doc."

"No!" She took a hefty swig of her whiskey, wheezing and sputtering, her face getting so red he thought it might catch fire. Just when he thought she'd get her wind back, she clutched her stomach and bent double. He caught the whiskey before it hit the floor.

"Just go away."

Alarm sharpened his senses. Placing her whiskey beside his on the bed stand, he squatted in front of her, lifting her chin so he could see her face.

"Now's not the time for modesty."

Just last month Clancy almost lost his wife when she wouldn't tell Doc her stomach hurt because she was worried he'd want to see the location. It'd taken a hell of a lot of sweet talking on Brad's part, but eventually, Doc had not only seen her stomach, he'd removed the appendix that was threatening to kill her. Damn, could that be happening to Evie, too? "Tell me what's wrong."

Her expression a mixture of pain, misery, and embarrassment, she repeated herself, the emphasis on each syllable imparting a meaning her narrow-eyed glare said she clearly expected him to get.

"I'm in–dis–posed."

"I don't know what the hell that means."

"It's my time of the month!"

The last was yelled loudly enough to be heard the next block over. Over the sound of crickets came the sound of male laughter.

"Oh God." Tears filled her eyes as she turned her face away. "Just go away."

And leave her like this? He didn't think so. Processing what she'd told him and what he could see, he asked, "Your belly hurts?"

She bit her lip and nodded, clearly in too much pain to worry about mortification anymore. He shucked his pants.

"I can't—"

"Don't worry. I've already figured out you're not going to be much fun tonight."

While she sputtered her indignation, he walked around the bed and slid in on the other side. The mattress dipped under his weight. Taking advantage of the moment, he worked his arm behind her and pulled her into his shoulder as he leaned against the headboard. "Drink the rest of your whiskey."

She shook her head. Her hair rubbed his cheek. The soft scent of wildflowers surrounded him.

"It'll relax you."

Beneath the covers, his hand found her abdomen. The muscles were rock hard beneath the silken skin. With a nudge, he pushed her hand away and laid his much bigger hand over the area, letting the heat seep in. After a minute she relaxed into his shoulder, turning more fully into the warmth of his hand.

"I'm still mad at you." It was a very soft, determined declaration.

"I know you are." He brushed his lips over her hair, his insides tied in knots. He didn't like seeing her like this. "Drink your whiskey."

She reached for the glass, taking a cautious sip. He felt the relaxing of her muscles that signaled the end of the cramp. Turning her a little more into his arms so he was half supporting her, he started to massage the affected area lightly through the thin cotton nightgown.

"Oh."

"Feel good?"

The only answer he got was a nod. "How long does this last?"

"A week."

"You suffer like this for a week?" If that was the case, he didn't care what she said. She was going to see Doc.

"I only hurt for a day or two."

A day or two? "Drink faster."

"Are you trying to get me drunk?"

"Just trying to catch you up."

"You're drunk?"

"Working on it. Whiskey hits hard on an empty stomach."

"You didn't eat your dinner."

"Millie knows I hate chicken paprika."

For some reason her whole face lit up. "I love it."

"Want me to get you a plate?"

She took another sip of her whiskey. "I think I'd rather just get drunk."

"Are you a happy drunk?"

"Is there any other kind?"

"Oh yeah."

"I'll try to be happy."

The way she gulped the next swallow told him the pain was coming back. He tucked her just a little closer, easing his other hand around so he could work at the tension in her back. "Don't tense up."

"What do you know about it?"

"Not much." He'd never been close enough to a woman to know her cycle and the problems that came along with it. "I'll talk to Doc tomorrow though and get informed."

"You will not!"

He held her when she would have pushed away. "I'm not having you in pain."

"It's normal."

Not for his wife. "I'm talking to Doc."

"You'll embarrass me." A tear dampened his chest as she moaned and pulled her knees up.

"I'll be discreet."

She shook her head. "You don't know the meaning of the word."

"You don't know the first thing about me."

"I know you're more than what you seem."

Shit. Now was the time to be mean, to throw her off, but she was small and hurting and curled up in his arms, letting him comfort her. He brushed another kiss across the top of her head. "Trust me, it's all good."

There was a tense silence and then, "Tell me you didn't make love to Nidia the other night."

Ah hell. "I didn't make love to Nidia or any other woman. I didn't have sex with her or any other woman. What's more, I didn't want to."

"Why?"

He could lie, should lie, should do something to keep her at a distance, but what came out was the truth. "Because she wasn't you."

For a minute she didn't say anything. He couldn't tell if she was thinking or just in so much pain she didn't care what he'd said, but then she turned just a little more into his embrace and sighed.

"We argue."

"Passionate people often do."

Another silence as she mulled on that. "You don't hurt when you argue."

"I'm not a bully." The one thing he swore he'd never be is a man like his father, a man who used his size and his position to abuse those who had no protection. A man who guided through terror.

Her fingers curled around his nape—the action was soft, sweet, and trusting. Making him feel ten times the heel he was. He didn't deserve her trust.

"No, you're not."

The admission flicked his conscience with whiplike precision. He was an outlaw and a bastard, a man who'd walked so far from God there could be no return. Some would say a real son of a bitch. Yet Evie saw him as good.

The door to forgiveness is always open. All you have to do is walk through.

Brad tipped the glass toward Evie's mouth, ignoring the refrain that had been tempting him of late, growing in frequency right along with his commitment to the town and its people. There was no undoing the past.

"Drink."

"This doesn't change anything." She took another large sip before repeating, "I'm still mad at you."

That made him smile. "You worried that you're going to forget?"

"Yes."

This time, when he kissed her, he didn't pull back, just kept his lips on her hair, holding her, an odd sense of rightness invading him as he provided her comfort. "Then I promise to do something to remind you."

"But not now?" she sighed into his kiss.

"No, not now." Now he just wanted to hold her and pretend that Shadow Svensen had never existed, that he was the man Evie thought him to be, and that this life he'd always dreamed of as a boy too stupid to know better really could be his. "Now we'll just pretend everything is perfect."

She stirred and grumbled. "Perfect is boring."

Only to someone who'd never known hell. "Then for tonight, let's be boring. No pain, no past, no pressure, just us."

She broke the kiss to meet his gaze. More than what he wanted must have shown in his expression, because she relaxed against him and her hug cradled him the same way he cradled her, protectively.

"That would be nice."

He nestled her closer. Yeah. It would.

Thirteen

"I DIDN'T JUST demand everyone be here today because I was feeling underappreciated."

Brad's words filtered through the bustle of the congregation as they gathered their belongings, preparing to leave. Evie, for whom the hour had passed in an agony of faking serenity while her belly cramped, was as surprised as everyone else.

"You didn't?" Doc asked. "Then why in hades are we packed in here tighter than pigs in a poke?"

Brad didn't immediately answer, his blue eyes slightly narrowed as his gaze swept over the congregation with an expectancy that had people shifting uncomfortably. Evie shifted right along with them. It wasn't Brad's normal pattern to start another sermon after he'd just finished one. Had seeing her so indisposed last night made him rethink his insistence on the marriage being real? Was he going to announce he wanted a divorce? She hunched down in her pew.

"Because I wanted to talk to you."

The sick feeling didn't leave Evie's gut, and it had nothing to do with the agony of her monthly and everything to do with fear that her marriage was about to end.

"Heck, Rev, you just spent thirty minutes jawing our ears off."

His smile didn't give anyone comfort. "That was just to soften you up for what I really want."

"And what is that?"

"To talk to you about the need to follow our beliefs as strongly as we voice our opinions."

Total silence descended upon the church. A baby wailed. Pews creaked as people looked at each other. Evie pressed her hand to her stomach and looked at her mother, who sat in the third row. Pearl just shrugged. She didn't have any idea either.

I like your pride.

Evie sat up as Brad's words came back to her. Whatever this was it had nothing to do with her marriage. Any issues Brad had with that, he'd handle in private.

"A year ago Cattle Crossing was a cesspool of ill repute. Bandits hid out here, raiding the surrounding area, believing they were safe from retribution because of the fear that held the citizens paralyzed. Some of our beloved citizens were abused, some were held against their wills and forced into lives they never would have chosen for themselves."

Everyone turned to face Mara and nodded. Cougar growled.

"You damn well—"

"Cougar," Mara gasped, "you can't swear in church."

"Then the Rev best find another way to make his point."

"The truth is never an insult," Brad continued. "And the truth is, while the McKinnelys did a good job of routing the bandits, the rest of us haven't done our job."

Cougar settled back down, his gaze speculative. Evie relaxed further. This definitely did not sound like the start to an I've-decided-I-don't-want-my-wife-anymore speech.

"We've turned a blind eye to the problems still in our community, letting the weak be abused and exploited while telling ourselves there's nothing we can do. We've made this choice time and time again, and I'm sick of it."

"Could you get to the point, Rev? I've got a whiskey with my name on it waiting at the saloon," a wrangler standing among his three friends in the back shouted.

Brad smiled that cold smile that didn't reach his eyes. "I'd be happy to. You all know me." He glanced pointedly at the drunken quartet in the back. "I'm a tolerant man when it comes to some things, coming to church on Sunday with the effects of Saturday night clinging to you being one of them, but there are things going on in this community that turn my stomach, things that we excuse because the law says it's fine to turn a blind eye, and societal rules make it even more convenient."

"What kind of things, Rev?" Clint asked in his deep voice.

"There are still women trapped in a life they don't want, abused, their children's stomachs cramping with hunger, their little bodies sporting bruises that shame us all. Because we look the other way."

The congregation shifted again, looking toward Bull Braeger's small family.

"What the hell are you all looking at?" Bull snarled.

The congregation shifted again, no one wanting to face that much muscle.

Everyone except Brad. He met Bull's gaze directly, stepping down from the pulpit. When Bull stood, displaying his massive size and muscle, Brad didn't even pause, just headed down the center aisle.

"They're looking at a problem that needs to be solved."

"My family is my business."

"Not anymore."

Bull's hands fisted and his face flushed while Brad, apparently oblivius to the warning signs, just kept walking with that smooth, measured glide that Evie recognized as signaling he meant business. Oh shoot! Searching the church for a weapon, she considered the freestanding candelabra to her right. It was heavy enough to put a dent in even Bull's thick skull.

"The hell you say," Bull snapped.

"Yes. I do."

On the aisle opposite Bull's family, Patrick, the new blacksmith, rose to his feet and watched Brad's progress with a calm Evie wished she felt. Bull made two of most men.

"This morning, Erica Braeger came to me in tears, desperate, asking for help." Brad casually nodded to Millicent as he passed. "And I've decided to give it to her."

"Thank God."

That came from Jenna.

After a hard glare at his wife, Erica, that had her cringing, Bull spat, "You ain't got no call to come between a man and his wife."

Brad was even with the Braeger family. "Your wife and your children are members of this congregation, same as you."

He held out his hand to the oldest girl. She was about seven. Her too small dress was spotless, her complexion ghostly pale. The girl shook, glanced at her father, her mother. Erica's nod was infinitesimal.

"It's okay, darling," Brad murmured in that voice that all women, no matter what age, responded to. Because it made them feel safe, Evie realized as the girl placed her palm in Brad's. "I promise, you're going to be fine from here on out."

"Don't you move, Hannah Lynn!" Bull bellowed.

The child froze, shaking as if she had the ague, trapped between the threat of her father and the promise of safety that Brad held out.

Brad's mouth tightened. With a suddenness that shocked, the normally mousy Erica jumped to her feet and thrust herself physically between Bull and her children, shoving the two-year-old who had been in her lap into her five-year-old girl's arms, desperation in every line of her slender body. "Go! Oh God, go!"

Bull hauled Erica back, all but throwing her down in the pew while the children shuffled toward Brad, terror making their movements more awkward than did the lack of space. The congregation gasped at the crude splint now visible on the baby's arm. Once in the aisle, the kids didn't know what to do. With a sweep of his massive arms, Patrick herded them across the small space to the row of seats behind him before planting himself solidly at the end. They crowded in next to Millicent—shaking, eyes glued to their father and mother, harsh, terrified sobs ripping from their throats.

"Momma?" the oldest asked in a thin thread of sound that broke Evie's heart.

Brad held out his hand again, not a lick of fear in his stance. Evie could have smacked him. His profession wasn't going to save him from Bull's muscle.

"You come, too, Erica."

Erica shook her head, not looking at Brad, Bull, or anyone. She stared at the floor as if it held the secrets of the universe. "I can't."

"Yes, you can."

Erica cast Bull a fearful glance from beneath her lashes. "He won't let me, and the law says—"

A muscle jumped in Brad's jaw. "The law says a whole lot of things that I don't care about."

Tension rippled through the congregation. Evie stood.

"Go, Erica," Jenna whispered from where she stood two pews down, leaning against Clint's arm, her face as white as the children's. "This is what you've prayed for."

Erica's mouth worked. "He'll let the children go."

Evie caught Clint's eye. "Do something!"

"Do what? It's the Rev's show."

She didn't know what. Maybe trade places with him. He was an ex-marshal and ex–bounty hunter, for heaven's sake, while Brad was just a preacher. The only show that was going to occur was the one in which he got pulverized.

"Let her go, Bull."

"The hell I will," Bull snapped.

"The hell you won't," Brad countered, walking around the packed line of pews, heading to the back. "This is my congregation, these are my people, and no one"—his hand slapped against wood as he cleared the rear pew. Everyone jumped—"husband or not, is going to abuse one of them."

Bull hauled Erica up against him with a grip so tight it would leave bruises. Not a sound passed her lips, but she jerked with terror. Shoving his bearded face in hers, he growled, "You filthy whore. This is who you've been screwing? The goddamned preacher?"

The uneasy rumble in the congregation grew. Evie looked around frantically. Why wasn't someone, anyone besides Brad, doing something?

"Let her go, you no-account son of a bitch or I'll break your arm, the same as you broke that baby's when she took that biscuit to fill her little belly."

Women gasped, men swore, and congregation members slowly came to their feet, propelled by outrage and the tension Brad was fueling.

"Big talk for a preacher," Bull snarled.

"You would think."

"Not big talk for me, I'm thinking," Patrick said in his thick brogue. "For me, I'm thinking ridding the world of your stench would be a fine way to start me Sunday."

"I don't need your help, O'Shaunessy," Brad snapped, as he came down the outer aisle, his gaze locked on Bull, one step flowing into the next with predatory grace.

"Now there I'd be seeing things from a mighty different view, Reverend, seeing as how I'm a member of this congregation and as rightly offended as you at these goings-on."

"Momma!" the baby cried. Blocking their view of what was happening directly across the aisle with his huge body, Patrick kept the children in the pew.

Brad spared him one glance. "This is my fight, Patrick."

"It's all right, babies," Erica called to her sobbing children, leaning away from Bull as she stared at him with the terror one usually reserved for a striking rattler. "Just stay there. It's going to be all right."

Evie couldn't blame the kids for crying. She didn't believe Erica either.

"You claiming the Braeger women and children, Rev?" Cougar asked in that calm way of his that made one think of an approaching storm.

"Absolutely."

Evie covered her mouth as understanding hit her. Brad wasn't just challenging Bull; he fully intended to fight him. Good grief, was he insane? Reverends didn't fight. Especially not against veritable mountains pretending to be men.

"Need help?" Clint asked in the same conversational tone as Cougar.

"Nope."

"A pity," Asa added.

Bull sneered, "You'd better take the help, Reverend."

Brad smiled and leapt sideways up onto a pew before balancing on the back of the next like a mountain lion moving in for a kill. The whole time his gaze never left Bull. "Thanks for the advice."

Brad leapt, hitting Bull high, knocking him backward. Erica jerked free with a scream as Bull grabbed for him. The two men crashed to the outer aisle. Patrick took a few steps forward, reached over, and gently pulled Erica away.

"Here now, you don't want to be near that tussle."

Erica gaped at him. As if she wasn't looking at him like he had two heads, Patrick calmly tucked her into the pew with her children and Millicent.

"You have to help him." Erica sobbed the words that were caught in Evie's throat. "Bull will kill him."

"I'm thinking the Rev has the look of a scrapper about him."

Who the hell cared what he looked like? Bull was huge! "Leave him alone, you brute!" Evie yelled, snatching up the candelabra and dashing up the aisle.

Asa caught the candelabra in one hand, pulling her up short. "If the Rev needs help, he'll get it."

"And how the hell do you know?"

"Evie!" her mother gasped.

Yanking at the candelabra, she snapped, "Well, excuse me for swearing. My husband is getting beaten to a pulp while his congregation looks on. I'm just a little upset."

Clint, who'd put himself between Jenna and the fight, motioned to the men as they crashed into the wall. "Doesn't appear to me that the Rev's getting the short end of this deal."

Evie blinked in astonishment. No. It didn't. Brad had Bull's face smashed into the wall and was holding him there with a hand at the base of his skull while the other wrenched Bull's arm up behind his back.

"Knew he had the look of a scrapper," Patrick said, arms folding across his massive chest.

"Heard over in Cheyenne that the Rev was a bit Old Testament," a wrangler offered from the back.

Leaning in, saying something only Bull could hear, Brad shoved hard on Bull's arm. There was a god-awful *snap* and Bull screamed.

"Appears he's got a real fondness for the eye-for-an-eye part, at least," another wrangler agreed over Bull's swearing.

"Got to admire that."

"Bastard deserved it," someone else muttered.

"Stop swearing in my church," Brad ordered, still holding the now-writhing Bull against the wall. He could have been talking to Bull or the cowboys. Both shut up, though only the wranglers looked abashed.

"Sorry, Rev."

"About time someone put Bull in his place," Jerome said.

"It's a shame what those children have gone through," a woman fussed.

"Poor little darling," another muttered. "She was just hungry."

No matter how she listened, Evie couldn't hear any disapproval in the rumbling among the congregation. That was, until Brad made his next pronouncement.

"As soon as we're done here, Herschel's going to draw up divorce papers, and you, Bull, are going to sign them."

"I'm not paying for a goddamn divorce."

"Now, this is where you get to think of today as your lucky day. Herschel's going to do it for free."

Herschel, on his feet like everyone else, gasped. "A divorce is complicated. It could take years."

Clearly he was thinking of the cost. Brad didn't take his attention from Bull. "That's why I wouldn't trust anyone but you to oversee it, Herschel. Can't be too careful when it comes to the law. We certainly wouldn't trust one of our own to an outsider."

"No, we wouldn't," Millicent chimed in. "We don't need no snake oil salesman posing as a lawyer taking advantage of Erica. If Herschel does this, we know it will be done right."

The congregation stirred with approval.

"Darn straight."

"Herschel knows his law."

"Learned it back East at that fancy school."

"Don't have no idea what he's saying when he goes to talking all legal, but it sure is impressive to listen to," Jerome tossed in.

"So how about it, Herschel?" Brad asked, the strain of holding Bull telling in his voice. "You going to help the Braegers out?"

Herschel, looking a little dazed by the outpouring of confidence from the community that normally took him for granted, nodded to Erica. "It'd be my privilege."

The woman, looking just as dazed, whispered a "thank you." Evie couldn't blame her. It had been a rather rapid, not to mention violent, switch in her situation.

"Well, now that that's settled, why don't Clint and I escort Bull to your office, Herschel?" Cougar offered, heading over. "You can meet us when the Rev finishes up his preaching for the day."

"Shoot," a wrangler interjected, settling back against the wall with an aura of anticipation. "The Rev's got more up his sleeve?"

"It would appear so," one of his friends said when Brad nodded and stepped back as Clint and Cougar converged on Bull. "Though I think it's going to be hard to top this."

Asa let go of the candelabra and settled his hat on his head. "I'll keep an eye on the Braeger women while they get settled."

Brad looked over, saw Evie with her makeshift weapon, and shook his head as Cougar and Clint, none too gently, shoved Bull toward the door.

"I'd appreciate it."

"I could just shoot him," Elizabeth offered. Evie saw she

had a small derringer in her hand. Asa glanced over his shoulder at Elizabeth as he passed Brad. "Not today, darlin'."

"It would save everyone a lot of trouble."

Unfazed by the sight of his wife brandishing a gun in church, Asa smiled. "That it would but seeing as it's bad luck to murder a man on Sunday, we might want to do this the Rev's way."

Brad took the candelabra from Evie. "Maybe next time, Elizabeth."

"Heck, let her shoot him, Rev."

The smile Brad gave Evie as he set the candelabra aside was incredibly soft. "We don't need bad luck chasing us, Cyrus."

Brad slid his arm around her waist, his touch as soft as his smile. The church and the congregation faded away. There was nothing but his eyes and the tender way he was looking at her. "This isn't where I left you."

"I thought you might need help."

"I'd rather you'd stayed where I left you."

Pressing her hands into her stomach, she tried to still her shaking. "I would rather you didn't try to commit suicide by attacking men as big as mountains."

He escorted her back to the front of the church, continuing as if she hadn't interrupted, "So I don't have to worry about you."

There was blood on his face, his suit was torn, and there was no telling how much damage Bull had done during the scuffle, and he was worried about her? Evie placed her arm around his waist, wincing as a cramp bit into her abdomen, supporting him the best she could.

He must have felt her flinch. "You still hurting?"

"I'm fine."

His fingers rubbed her waist.

"I told you to stay home."

She surreptitiously checked his chest, his ribs, looking for signs of pain. Unlike her, he didn't flinch under her probing.

"And miss all the excitement?"

He stopped at her seat, watching her with concern as she sat. She gave him her best smile. All she got back was a frown. In a now familiar gesture, he ran the backs of his fingers down her cheek.

"Well, it's not done yet."

"You've got more of the same?"

"Yeah, so why are you smiling?"

"Because I think what you said before was pretty wonderful."

His thumb pressed at the corner of her mouth, as tender as a kiss. "You realize it means I'm likely out of a job."

"Who cares?"

"You are one strange woman."

"Good thing you like strange."

He didn't respond for a second, then, "Yeah, it is."

With another brush of his thumb, he turned and stepped up to the pulpit.

"Sorry about the disturbance, folks."

"You planning on putting on a show like this every Sunday, Rev?"

Brad honestly didn't know. All he knew was that the rage that had been building for as long as he could remember—the rage that had gotten worse and worse since he'd been a kid, swallowing his father's curses like they were gospel, growing with every injustice—had this morning with Erica's desperate plea for help just reached . . . enough. "It depends."

"On what?" Dorothy asked.

"On whether we're going to stand up as a town and do what's right."

"You can't change the world."

"This might make me as selfish as everyone else, but I don't care about the world. I'm just concerned with what's happening here and now. In Cattle Crossing." He slapped the pulpit. "Here, I want change."

"What kind of change?" Ruth asked.

"I'm tired of watching our weakest citizens get hurt."

"The law ties our hands."

"I'm willing to chance a run-in with the sheriff if it means a little girl not getting her arm broken."

"Well, all I got to say is, it's about time this town had a man with balls enough to take a stand."

"Ruth!"

"Oh, hush up, Shirley. There are times when the Lord understands the need for a good curse word, right, Reverend?"

"I'm not sure I'm in his good graces right now."

"You're closer than our last Preacher ever got." Ruth stomped her cane. "Worse thing that ever happened to this territory was the arrival of the law. Back in my day, a man took to beating his wife and kids, family took care of it, and failing that, the community took care of it. Now, everyone sits on their hands, claiming they're tied. It's a disgrace and a shame."

"You've got to have law," Homer cut in.

"Maybe, and maybe not, but I'm with the Reverend. When the law doesn't help, we've got to help ourselves."

"Sounds dangerously like vigilantism to me."

"You going to sit here, Dan, and tell me you think it's right for a man to break a little girl's arm and feel safe doing it while decent folk just sit about and listen to her screams?"

"Heck no."

The cane hit the floor again. "Then shut up and let Reverend Swanson speak."

There didn't seem much for Brad to do but go along.

"Thanks, Ruth."

"Glad to be of help."

Doc leaned over the pew and helped the older woman sit. When she was settled, everyone just stared at Brad, expecting him to lead them. Really lead them, not just meddle here or there. He only knew one way to do it. And it wasn't going to be popular.

A small black-clad figure stepped out from the alcove in back. And about to get even more unpopular. *Nidia.* The woman was determined to be the bane of his existence. She lowered the mantilla covering her hair to her shoulders. "This protection for the weak, does it extend to all citizens? Even prostitutes?"

As he'd thought, she was forcing his hand. Pews creaked as the congregation turned from Nidia to look at him.

"Not now, Nidia."

"I'd like to hear the answer to that," Mara called.

"So would I," Shirley chimed in.

Mara would be in favor but Shirley was the other side of the coin. She had strict views on what was proper. And as the mayor's wife, she had the influence to enforce those views.

"I hadn't planned on getting into this so soon, but . . ."

"But what?" Jerome groused. Brad didn't fool himself that it was because he cared about the subject matter. It was more likely that his stomach was telling him it was getting on toward lunch. "Just spit it out. Ain't like Shirley's going to like it none the better for the delay."

Evie wasn't going to like it either. "Yes."

"You're not planning on driving off business, are you, Rev?" called Mark.

Brad waited for a lull in the commotion and then went for broke. It wasn't like it mattered. Once the truth was out, he'd be out, but in the interim maybe he could plant some good.

"No, but those that want out, should have a way out, whether it's from a bad marriage or a bad life."

"And we have to provide it?"

Brad met Red's gaze squarely. "Yes."

"Hell, Rev, once a whore, always a whore."

"And once an ass, always an ass," Mara shot back.

Brad held his temper. "I doubt there's one of us here who hasn't been forced by circumstance to do what we didn't like to survive at one time or another. Options are just fewer for women."

Jenna's "amen" was heartfelt.

The rumbling didn't cease. He didn't expect it to. His terms were pretty radical by anyone's measure.

Brad raised his voce to be heard above the ruckus, keeping his eye on Evie. He couldn't tell if the white line around her lips was from pain or anger. "You might as well know up front that I feel strongly about this, but I also understand your hesitation. I realize my stand on this may necessitate your requesting another minister."

"This is a lot to spring on us willy-nilly," Doc interjected.

Brad nodded. "I realize that, too. You can give me your decision in a month."

"And until then?" Shirley asked, stopping him before he could descend.

"We can either go on as we have or you can make do without."

"Hell, preacher, that ain't rightly fair, giving ultimatums."

"Life isn't fair, Dan. Now if you'll excuse me, my wife is feeling poorly, and I'd like to get her home."

He made it halfway around the pulpit before Gray stood, his dark face intent. "The McKinnelys do not need time."

Shit. The first time Gray stood as a McKinnely and it had to be over this, backing him. "Still, you might want to take it," he cautioned.

Gray's shoulders squared, his chin leveled. "I do not need time."

Probably not. Gray's real mother had been beaten to death by an insane customer. The same man who'd later kidnapped Jenna and Mara.

"Your words are good. The McKinnelys stand with the Reverend Swanson."

"A wet-behind-the-ears boy doesn't talk for the McKinnelys," Dan sneered. Evie came to Brad's side. He glanced down as her hand slipped into his, small and warm. She gave his fingers a comforting squeeze.

"Did you forget what happened the last time you denied Gray his standing?" she asked.

Clint had kicked the shit out of the man because of Gray but also because of the boot print on Jenna's shoulder.

"I haven't forgotten anything."

Jenna, patting a fussing Brianna, stood beside Gray, pride in her gaze as she turned and swept it across the congregation. "You heard my son."

Mara stood, too, though it was hard to tell. The woman had sure been shortchanged on height, but she repeated Gray's claim. "The McKinnelys stand with the Reverend."

"Well, I for one don't appreciate being railroaded. I have a daughter to consider."

Evie bristled. Brad squeezed her hand, warning her to be quiet. "I understand, Shirley, and I'd be the last one ever to want her to be in a position of no choice, so you take your time." He nodded to Millicent. "Can Erica and the girls stay with you?"

"Absolutely."

"Thank you."

As he passed the McKinnelys' pew, Brad stopped. "That's quite a son you and Clint have there, Jenna."

She smiled, ruffling Gray's hair with the love of a mother who didn't take into consideration the boy's fragile sense of consequence. He ducked away, but his scowl wasn't nearly as dark as normal. "We're so lucky he chose us."

Truth was, Gray hadn't stood a chance once Jenna had decided to love him, but that was Jenna. Always loving without condition, always giving. Clint's sunshine. Gray's and Brianna's salvation.

Evie smiled. "He's definitely done you proud today."

Brad was probably the only one who heard the tightness of pain in her voice.

"Yes, he has. And your husband has done us all proud."

Evie's hand squeezed his. "Yes, he has."

The praise sat uncomfortably on Brad's shoulders. He was an outlaw. Fighting came as naturally as breathing. It wasn't anything special. When he met Jenna's gaze, he grew even more uncomfortable. There was knowledge in her big blue eyes. *Damn. Clint wouldn't have told her . . .*

"It's not every town that's fortunate to get a man with the Reverend Brad's experience."

Shit, Clint had.

"We can't afford to lose him," Jenna continued, not letting go of his gaze.

They couldn't afford to keep him. If she knew who he was, Jenna had to know that, too. As if the truth didn't matter, Jenna continued, "And I for one, intent to do everything in my power to make sure he stays."

"Sometimes a man doesn't have a choice."

"And sometimes he does."

She was spinning fairy tales, but there was no arguing with Jenna when she got her mind set. "Thank you for the vote of confidence."

Jenna nodded as if she wasn't holding him to an impossible goal.

Uncomfortable with her expectations and worse with the longing that sprang up inside him as he contemplated them, he slipped his hand to the small of Evie's back, urging her forward, away from the pointless tease of possibility. "Now, if you'll excuse me, I've got to get Evie home."

IT WAS RAINING outside; the streets were filling with mud. Lightning flashed in the sky. In another two minutes, it'd be a deluge.

"Looks like we'll have to make a run for it."

Beside him, Evie groaned and grabbed her middle. "You go ahead."

"Shit." She *was* hurting. Scooping her up in his arms, suppressing a groan of his own as his ribs let him know they didn't appreciate the strain, Brad dashed across the wide street, mud splashing up his pants legs, Evie clinging to his neck. When he set her down on the stoop, there was mud on her skirt.

He brushed at the smears. "Well, so much for my attempt at a good deed."

She didn't even glance at her skirt. "I think what you did today is enough to last a lifetime."

"It's not hard to take a swing at Bull. The man's an ass."

"But it took a lot to stand up for Erica and her family. It could cost you your job."

The job that really wasn't his to begin with. He'd long since lost touch with God. Brad opened the door, feeling her muscles tense under his hand as he guided her in. "There's right and there's wrong."

It was a wonder a lightning bolt didn't strike him dead as soon as he finished the statement. Instead, Evie blessed him with the gentlest of smiles. "I'll cook you lunch."

"That's my reward?"

The door closed with a quiet click. The darkness of the house closed around them.

"If you'll settle for pancakes. I'm pretty good at pancakes. I only burn every other one."

"Do you burn the first or second?"

"First."

"I'll take the second then."

"What, no chivalry?"

"I used up my quota with Bull."

She turned, hands pressed to her stomach, eyes shining, looking so beautifully feminine it made him ache inside for what might have been. "I could love you for that."

"Don't be tossing your love away so cheaply."

Her head cocked to the side. "I'm stuck with you forever, what's so cheap about that?"

The next wince happened around her eyes. Pulling her into his arms, he kissed the top of her head, guilt clawing at him. "Not a damn thing." Another kiss and he picked her up. "Let's get you up to bed."

"It's barely noon."

"I have it on good faith from Doc that a dose of laudanum, a hot water bottle, and your husband's attentions will go a long way to making you feel yourself."

"I don't like laudanum."

"I'll put it in sweet tea."

His ribs were screaming by the time they got to the top of the stairs.

"I hate tea."

"How about coffee?"

She wrinkled her nose.

He set her beside the bed. "Then I'll just have to wing it."

He started unbuttoning her dress. Swatting at his hands, she said, "I can undress myself."

"But I enjoy it more."

"Why?"

"Because it's like opening my own private, very special present."

How did he always manage to find the sweetest things to say? Admiring the breadth of his shoulders and the leanness of his hips, knowing the beauty those clothes hid, she sighed with disappointment. "An indisposed present."

"You sound sad."

"I am." She caught his hand and kissed the back. "I like sleeping with you."

The shock of the confession ripped through Brad in a torrent of right. Other women had said that to him. He was an excellent lover, it was to be expected, but hearing the words from Evie who guarded her vulnerability so closely hit him hard on the same dream spot Jenna had tenderized with her conviction. A wife who believed in him, a congregation that relied on him.

He glanced heavenward.

Can't you leave it alone? I am what I am.

Evie's lower lip slipped between her teeth at his hesitation. "That's good, right?"

Apparently not. He silently sighed and tipped Evie's chin up. He hated seeing her hurt or uncertain. Hated knowing he was the one who was going to eventually hurt her.

Resentment surged right along with the hunger. *Did you think of that when you laid this out?*

"It's so good sometimes it's scary," he said.

"I find it hard to believe a man who would take on Bull Braeger would be afraid of anything."

"Then you'd be wrong." He set to work on the buttons at the collar of her Sunday dress. Severity didn't suit her. Evie was a wildflower, completely unconventional, totally beautiful, and surprisingly tough. "You scare me, Evie."

She tipped her head back into the crook of his shoulder. Her natural trust that he would take her weight settled on the void that lurked inside, filling it a bit more. "Why?"

"Because with you I want a whole lot of things I have no business wanting."

She blinked and then grinned with only a hint of uncertainty. "Wild sexual things, I hope."

He smiled back, the ease of her acceptance encased in amusement, as always, chasing away the blackness of his conviction. "That, too."

Her grin twisted and she hugged her stomach. "Ugh, I'm sorry I can't be more fun."

"I don't always need fun, Evie. Caring for you is good, too."

And the truth of that scared him more than anything else. He wanted to be the only one to care for Evie when she was sick, sad, happy . . . His hand slid to her stomach. Pregnant.

Shit. He yanked his hand back. What the hell was he thinking? He couldn't get her pregnant. As Evie rested against him, he made short work of her blouse, her corset, and her camisole, sliding the latter off her shoulders. He expected her to hunch over and hide; she didn't. Just lifted that chin and let him look his fill. Until a cramp hit particularly hard. Grabbing her stomach, she doubled over.

"I'll make lunch for you tomorrow," she groaned.

"I'll look forward to it." Of all the lies he'd told in his life, that was probably the kindest. Evie really couldn't cook. "Lie down now."

"I'm sorry."

"There's nothing to be sorry for."

"You must be hungry."

"I'm not."

He tugged on the skirt, and she lifted her hips. The skirt came off. He draped it over the chair. Handing her the extra pillow, which she immediately clutched to her stomach, he said, "I'll be right back."

"You don't have to."

"I know." But he wanted to.

By the time he got back upstairs with the water bottle and

the laudanum disguised in a cup of hot chocolate, Evie was curled in a ball on the bed. It was hot and stuffy in the room.

"Bad?"

She nodded. Outside, lightning flashed and the house shook under a blast of wind. Lifting the sheet he tucked the water bottle against her stomach. She moaned and hugged it to her as she leaned against the headboard. He brushed the hair off her sweaty cheek. "How about we let the storm in?"

"I don't care."

The window stuck. He had to hit the sash three times to get it open. The storm blew in with a gust of damp air. The curtains billowed around him as he repeated the procedure on the second window. The scent of summer rain swept through the room on a gust. "That's better."

Evie didn't reply, just reached for the hot chocolate. Brad only debated a minute before shucking his clothes and sliding into bed beside her. "Scoot up."

"Don't you have something to do?"

Lightning flashed again. "Nothing more important than you."

As he settled behind her, she whispered, "I hate this house. It's so big, so formal, so . . . perfect."

"It came with the job."

Thunder rumbled. "I'll try to be grateful."

He tucked her into his chest. "Don't bother on my account."

"I thought you were going to remind me to be angry at you," she murmured as she leaned back against him with a trust she wouldn't have shown him just days before. A trust he didn't deserve.

"I'll get around to it eventually."

Putting his arm around her, he accepted her weight, cradling her breast as the damp wind blew around them.

Her head dropped back onto his shoulder as she took a sip of the hot chocolate. "What are you doing?"

Gazing down into the blue of her eyes, seeing that spirit shining in her gaze, he saw the future he might have had, had things gone differently all those years ago when he'd had a choice.

"Stealing a bit of heaven."

Fourteen

LAST NIGHT HAD been a revelation. Another piece to add to the puzzle that was her husband. Evie smiled as she dried the last glass from the breakfast dishes before setting it on the washboard. She didn't think he had even got any sleep. She'd never seen Brad unsure before, but she had the distinct impression that the last two nights had been the first time he'd comforted a woman. He'd been good at it though. Every time the pain had come, he'd been there, holding her through it with a rather endearing determination, as if through sheer force of will he could vanquish it. Her damp fingers drifted to her stomach, where the sensation of his touch lingered. It was the first time she hadn't minded monthly cramps.

The knock at the front door was a welcome distraction from the dishes. Tossing the towel down, she headed through the house, the echo of her footsteps in the big dining room sounding overly loud to her ears. She really didn't know if she could ever adjust to this house being her home. She much preferred the warmth of Amy and Elijah's old house. It was cozy and warm and inviting. And every room had great light.

Through the glass panels at the sides of the door, she could see a man standing, something bulky in his hands.

"Who is it?"

"It's me, pumpkin."

She opened the door. "Uncle Paul!"

Throwing her arms around him she gave him a hug.

"Whoa! I haven't been greeted that enthusiastically since the day I bought you that special red paint you liked."

She stepped back. "Ochre. It was ochre."

"Does this mean you've forgiven me?"

She thought of the way Brad had taken care of her, of how he'd stood up for Erica and her children, for her, and of the way he made her feel in bed. "Yes."

"Good. Then I can give you your wedding present." He hefted the large, paper-wrapped package.

She took it. "The painting?"

"The painting. I didn't think the Rev would want it loose. And I didn't want to leave it around before your mother and I headed East tomorrow."

No. That wouldn't be good. "Thank you."

She set it inside the door. "Do you want to come in for coffee?"

"I don't have time. I've got an appointment in five minutes. I just wanted to check on you."

"I'm fine." Maybe even more than fine.

"The marriage working out?"

"More than that, it's even beginning to feel real."

He chucked her chin the way he had since her earliest memory, a happy connection between past and present. "Good. I brought you something else."

Turning, he headed back to his buggy. From the bed he pulled out a familiar box. After putting the painting inside the door, Evie hurried down after him.

"My paints!"

"Brad sent a note asking for Pearl to send them over. She wasn't in favor of the idea, seeing as you get all wrapped up in what you're doing when you paint, but Brad insisted."

Evie could take that two ways. She preferred to think Brad knew how much painting meant to her and wanted her to be happy. "As well he should."

Uncle Paul handed her the box and gathered up the canvases. "You going to do a new painting of him?"

"There's nothing wrong with the one I did."

Her uncle chuckled, following her up the steps. "You mean besides the fact that he's unimpressively naked?"

She sighed. "Except for that."

"He'd probably appreciate a more flattering version."

"Maybe I'll save it for his birthday."

"Didn't he just have one?"

His twenty-ninth. "The wait will do him good."

"You're a hard woman, Evie Swanson."

She put the paints on the dark mahogany table. "I'm just giving him something to look forward to."

He put the rolled-up canvases beside the box. "Of course."

Grabbing a canvas before it could roll off, she smiled at him, her fingers tingling with the urge to touch the paints, check that they were all there. "Thanks for bringing these over."

He gave her a quick hug. "Just don't get to painting and forget you have a husband."

The laughter welled from within. "I don't think that's possible."

THE HOUSE WAS quiet in the wake of her uncle's departure. The dark interior, elegant and refined, seemed to close in on her. She wanted to take her paints to a sunlit field and paint the wildflowers, feel the sun on her skin, the joy of creating, just feel like she had room to smile. But that wouldn't get the dishes done, or teach her how to cook. More's the pity.

Casting one longing look to the sunshine outside, she headed back toward the kitchen. Her foot caught on the edge of the painting. Paper tore.

Darn it. There was a gaping rip across the bottom and up the middle. Through it she could see the flesh of Brad's abdomen. Curiosity drove her to tear it the rest of the way. Now that she'd had time to study up, just how accurate had she been?

The paper tore with a louder rip, exposing the hard muscles of Brad's chest. She hadn't gotten that quite right; his pectorals were bigger, more delineated. And the scars. She touched the first spot below his left pectoral. The canvas was rough against her fingertips, but if she closed her eyes, she could easily summon the heat of his flesh, the firmness of muscle, the ripple of response, the ridge of scar. She sighed and released the breath she didn't realize she'd been holding. She'd missed a few of them.

Brad had a lot more scars than any man had a right to own, let alone a preacher. After yesterday, it wasn't hard to see how he'd gotten them, but he didn't need any more. Just the thought of him getting more scared her in ways she didn't want to define.

Another knock came at the door. Through the sheers covering the glass that bracketed the heavy wooden panel, she could see a small, slight silhouette.

"Evie?"

Mara. Oh shoot, she couldn't let her see the painting. Brad would be mortified. He was senstive about how she'd painted him. A man's pride was a delicate thing. And apparently his pride in his manhood the most delicate of all. "Just a minute."

Before she could even lift the painting, the door swung open and Mara darted in.

"I don't have a minute." Turning so fast her skirts twisted around her legs, Mara closed the door behind her. Pulling the curtain back, she peeked outside.

"What's wrong?"

Straightening, she turned around, a gamine grin on her beautiful features. "I've run away."

"From Cougar?"

"Of course from Cougar." She rolled her eyes. "The man missed his calling as a prison guard."

Evie positioned herself between Mara and the exposed painting, hoping her skirts were a sufficient width to work as a shield. "You're supposed to be somewhere you're not?"

"To hear Cougar tell it, in bed wrapped in cotton wool for the next seven months."

Seven months. She looked at Mara again, seeing nothing but a very slender woman with copper hair and cinnamon brown eyes. Of course, at two months, there wouldn't be a sign. "You're with child?"

"Yup. And Cougar's about fit to be tied."

"He worries about you. Ever since . . ."

She bit her tongue. Mara didn't need to be reminded of that.

Mara sighed. "Since I miscarried, you mean. Don't you start spinning there, too. It's bad enough that Cougar can't get past it."

"With reason. You're a very small woman."

"And he's a very big man," Mara finished for her, stepping farther into the room, "but it's not going to make a difference this time. This baby will be healthy."

What could Evie say to that? "So where does Cougar think you are?"

"At home. I figure I've got the whole day to myself since he's out helping the Reverend . . ." Her gaze dropped to the painting and her voice trailed off. "Holy smokes! You painted that? It's gorgeous."

Evie braced herself for criticism or laughter. "Yes."

Mara cocked her head to the side. "You really are talented when it comes to capturing the real spirit of the man. I've always seen him as sort of an outlaw at heart . . ." Her voice trailed off. Evie had the urge to throw the tablecloth over Brad's image. "He's almost as beautiful as my Cougar."

Cougar was a beautiful man, but in the way a wildcat was beautiful for the sheer lethal killing grace rippling beneath the skin. Brad was beautiful in a different way. His power was less overt, she realized as she looked at the painting, but there.

"That would be your opinion."

"Of course," Mara continued, the tightness of suppressed laughter in her voice. "There are some differences." She pursed her lips in an effort to contain her smile, and met Evie's gaze. "One thing's for sure, either you were a virgin on your wedding night or you were one disappointed bride."

It was hopeless to try to appear nonchalant, but Evie gave it a stab anyway. Ignoring the blush burning up her cheeks like wildfire, she cleared her throat and pulled the torn edges of paper over Brad's image. "Not everything was in proportion."

Mara's brows arched. "Bet you were glad to discover that."

A shiver shimmered down her spine as she remembered the slow push of his body into hers. "Yes."

Mara waggled her eyebrows. "If you offer me a cup of tea, I'll let you tell me all about it."

"What if I don't want to?"

"Well, then, I'll let you bribe me with a cup of tea not to pester you."

It was easy to see why Cougar found Mara both frustrating and totally irresistible. The spirit inside her shone so brightly. Evie would love to capture it on canvas. She led the way into the kitchen.

"I can probably manage a cup of tea."

"Thank goodness. We're out, and Cougar tried to convince me coffee was just as good. Made me sicker than a dog."

"I won't offer you coffee then."

"Thank you."

Eve slid some sticks under the burner and put on the kettle before mentioning in the most causal way she knew, "I'd like to paint you sometime."

"I might be open to the possibility."

She turned, hearing the "but." "What?"

"You have to give me breasts." Mara stood beside the big farmer's table and held her hands out a foot in front of her chest. "Big impressive breasts, like Jenna has."

"Would Cougar like that?"

Mara tossed her head, sending her thick hair swinging. "It's not about what he likes. It's about what I want, and for once I'd like to look at an image of myself and see something that looks womanly."

"I keep telling you, Angel, you've got to start seeing yourself through my eyes."

Evie gasped and spun around. Cougar stood in the kitchen doorway, dominating it with his size, his personality.

"And there isn't a prettier woman this side of anywhere."

Mara squared her shoulders and sat down at the kitchen table. "I thought you were gone."

"Obviously, since you're not where I put you."

Apparently Brad wasn't the only one stuck on that "stay" rule.

He took a step into the room. And just as when Brad did, it immediately felt too small. Evie took an involuntary step back, drawing Cougar's gaze. For an instant she felt the whip of his personality and then he was back to stalking Mara.

"I believe I told you to stay in bed."

"I'll go crazy if I stay in bed."

Cougar frowned, his eyes glittering under the brim of his hat. He looked as mean as all get-out with his black hair falling around his high cheekbones, until Evie looked into his eyes again. If Evie wanted to paint Mara because of her spirit, she wanted to paint Cougar like this. Devastatingly human in his love for his wife. Almost vulnerable. Her fingers positively itched.

"You were sick this morning."

"I'm better now."

"It might come back."

"Not if I eat, and Evie's making me some tea."

Cougar cut her a glance. "Seems to me she's doodling."

She was—on the counter, with her fingernail. Evie yanked her hand back. "I'm just waiting to see if Mara is staying."

"Of course I'm staying."

"Mara . . ." Another step and Cougar was within reaching distance. Mara caught his hand and pulled him closer, tugging until he bent and she could place his hand on her stomach. His hair fell around them, obscuring her face from view, leaving only the poignant silhouette of the big man cradling the hope of life with both fear and love.

His "You take too damn many chances" escaped the confines of the intimate moment.

Evie grabbed the pencil by the stove. There was nothing to sketch on. She opted for the pale wood of the countertop, working quickly, struggling to capture the emotion before it disappeared.

"Never with what's important," Evie heard Mara murmur.

"I want you home."

"I'm as safe here as I am at home. Here Evie can keep track of me."

Cougar looked up; his gaze went from the pencil to her face. Immediately, Evie felt like confessing.

"I—" She stopped right there. Cougar just wasn't a man to whom she was comfortable saying, "You were too beautiful not to sketch." People generally didn't understand the compulsion to sketch that took her. Cougar looked less likely than others. She tried again. "It was just . . ."

Mara came to her rescue. "You're a beautiful man, Cougar. She couldn't help herself."

"Shit."

Evie didn't know if that was good or bad. The McKinnely men kept their emotions close to their chests, and that made them hard to read, except, she realized, when they looked at their wives, as Cougar was looking at Mara now. Then, there was the barest hint of a schism that allowed outsiders to glimpse the depth of emotion that lurked behind the masks. She looked down at the drawing, the emotion captured in the few lines. Jealousy flared through her. She'd give anything to be loved like that, accepted like that.

"Please, Cougar," Mara coaxed.

He muttered something under his breath.

"Evie will watch me like a hawk."

"You won't let her do anything?" he asked, cocking his eyebrow.

"Strenuous," Mara hastened to tack on.

"Anything," Cougar growled.

"I'll watch her." As much as anyone could.

Cougar grunted and spared her a glance. "I heard you're sick yourself. Brad said your woman's time is bad."

"Brad told you . . ." It came out a strangled squeak. If a hole had opened up in the floor right then, she would have gladly fallen through it. "I'm better now."

Cougar didn't share her embarrassment. "Doc can probably help you with that."

Evie's "thank you" was a strangled rasp.

Mara groaned and shoved at Cougar. "Don't you need to go somewhere and save someone?"

"As a matter of fact, I do." Skimming his fingers down Mara's cheek, he brushed her lips with his thumb. "You, I'll see tonight."

It sounded like a threat to Evie. Mara just smiled and kissed his palm. "I'll be waiting."

Cougar chuckled and headed out the door. He stopped on the threshold and pinned Evie with a glance that she imagined would have outlaws shaking in their shoes. "Take care of her."

He didn't have to say "or else." It was implied.

As soon as the door swung closed behind him, Evie blinked. "I think I was just threatened."

Mara shook her head and came over to the counter. "At best, warned. Cougar has trouble delegating responsibility and he sees me as his biggest challenge."

She touched the simple sketch, her fingers lingering on the lines that made up the longing in Cougar's touch before shifting to his face. When she looked up, her eyes were moist. "You really do see people, don't you?"

Evie shrugged. "Sometimes."

Mara touched the pencil marks that had captured the stern line of her husband's mouth along with the hint of vulnerability at the corner. "No one ever sees that he can be hurt."

"He's a very intimidating man."

"He's a very good man."

"Who doesn't want me to paint you with watermelon breasts," Evie pointed out.

Mara's smile was very soft. "No, he doesn't." She tapped the sketch on the counter. "Will you finish this?"

There wasn't a prayer that Evie had any choice. There was so much emotion in that moment that her fingers ached to complete it. A prospective father sheltering his wife and child in the love and hope he held for them. "Yes."

"Now?"

She shrugged. "If you want."

Mara smiled and reached for the cups. "I definitely want. And when it's done, you can name your price."

THE NOTE HAD said to come alone.

Brad pulled up just outside the clearing a mile shy from where he was supposed to be meeting Casey. He wasn't alone, and if the hairs on the back of his neck were to be believed, his company had a gun sited on him. Shit.

If it was Casey, there was a fifty-fifty chance he'd pull the trigger before he got around to stating what he wanted. Casey could be unpredictable that way. Ambitious and aggressive, with an unstable temperament that couldn't be trusted, the outlaw was a wild card. And he held Brad's future in his hands. Shit again.

Is this a test? Because I'm getting sick of your tests. There was no answer. Just the squawk of a blue jay.

Brad pulled out his makings and waited. There was only so much foolishness a man could indulge in a lifetime, and he'd about used his up while playing preacher. A twig snapped behind him.

"I told you to meet me at the creek ten minutes ago."

Brad didn't turn to confront the speaker. Striking his sulphur, he shrugged. "I figured this was a pretty spot for a smoke."

"Since when do you think you have a choice in anything?"

"Since I kicked your ass six ways to Sunday three years ago."

"A lot's changed in the last three years."

That was the truth. Including who held the cards in this little confrontation. Brad took a draw on the smoke, relishing the simple pleasure, as a man did when it might be his last. "Not that much."

"I was in town yesterday."

So that had been Casey's paint tied up outside the saloon. "A pity you didn't stop by the church and say hello." He'd have slit his throat and they wouldn't be going through this dance right now.

"Heard tell you've got yourself a pretty new wife."

"Been snooping?"

"It always pays to get the lay of the land before looking up old friends."

"We've never been friends." More like uneasy cohorts in crime. Casey had been the leader of the first gang he'd joined. He'd taught Brad a lot. Mostly how a man shouldn't behave.

"Does she know who you are?" Casey asked around the unlit cigar in his mouth. The gun in his hand wasn't a surprise. Neither were the new lines etched across his forehead and around his eyes. The outlaw life wasn't conducive to longevity.

"I didn't see any need to tell her."

"Just planned on leaving everything in the past?"

Brad flicked the ash off the end of his cigarette. "Pretty much."

"Even your friends."

"I think we already covered that. We're not friends."

"Well, I'm still feeling a bit of camaraderie." The hammer clicked back on the gun. "Especially when I consider you've got my wife and daughter."

Shit. Casey always was good at lucky guesses. "I have them?"

"It has to be you. You're the only one she'd run to."

Only after the son of a bitch threatened his own daughter. Although Brenda was terrified of leaving Casey's dubious protection, she loved her daughter more. Fear for Brenna was the only thing that had made Brenda go out in the world again. "Well, you must have missed someone else, because I don't have her."

"She took the train to Cheyenne."

Brad shrugged, covertly studying the ridgeline for signs of Cougar. Had he followed Casey? "Maybe she kept on going."

"Not hardly." The muzzle centered on his chest. "I want my family back."

"I don't blame you."

Casey smiled around the unlit cigar. "Good, then you'll understand why you're going to get them for me."

Belle shifted and snorted, uneasy with the tension in the air. Brad patted her neck. "I'm not a bounty hunter."

"But you do have something to hide."

"I've got to be straight with you, Casey. If Brenda did find the courage to run, I'm not particularly moved to fetch her back."

"Then I might not be too inspired to keep your identity a secret."

Brad eased his hand down the reins. "Well, in that case, I'll just have to put aside nostalgia and put you out of my misery."

Casey grinned, his teeth surprisingly white for a man of his bad habits. "I'm the one with the gun."

"And I'm the one with Gut'm McKinnely covering his ass."

Casey's smile disappeared. Brad's grew. When all else failed, bluff.

"You look disappointed."

"Not at all."

Because he hadn't intended to kill him today, Brad realized. The same way Brad hadn't intended to kill Casey. Not yet at least. Not until he knew what Casey knew and who he'd told about Brad's "rebirth."

"So tell me, how'd you know I was here?"

"Word gets around."

Years of playing poker with a man came in handy. It familiarized the opponent with the other's tells. When Casey flipped that cigar to the other side of his mouth, it was a sure sign that he was lying. At least the fact that Shadow Svensen was alive and living as the Reverend Brad Swanson wasn't common knowledge.

"I've heard a few things about you, too."

"Such as?"

"You've moved up from stagecoaches to trains."

"Can't hold a man's ambition against him."

"A woman was killed in that last robbery."

"You always were squeamish about women."

"So you've told me a time or two. What happened?"

Casey shrugged. The gun didn't drop. "She got in the way after Bill shot her husband when he objected to donating to our cause."

"It never pays to play the hero."

"No," Casey agreed, "it doesn't, so why don't you toss me that peashooter you've got tucked up your sleeve?"

"I'm a minister. I don't carry weapons."

"Those fools in town might buy your game. I don't. Hand it over."

Turning slowly, Brad raised his hands and shucked his cuffs. There was no holster. No gun. With Cougar as backup, who the hell needed them?

"Well, son of a bitch, you've become a preacher just like your daddy."

He hated being compared to his father. Casey knew it. "Keep pushing me, Casey, and you'll find that I haven't forgotten everything."

"Neither have I."

Shit. Brad knew that look. He dropped back, grabbing the rifle as he fell, rolling under Belle's belly. Two bullets peppered the ground beyond. Leaping to his feet, he whipped the rifle up. Belle squealed and pranced, but Asa MacIntyre had trained her and she held her ground through her terror, providing him with a shield. This close, Casey couldn't get off a shot, but Brad knew Casey wouldn't hesitate to kill the horse. Belle tossed her head, the whites of her eyes showing, looking to him for guidance. Ah hell.

Taking a chance on Cougar being on the ridge, he ducked to the right, away from Belle, bringing up the rifle as he did. Cougar's shot didn't come, but Casey's did. There was a bright flash and a bullet slammed into his side. Brad gritted his teeth, holding his stand through sheer determination. The rifle fired. Once, twice. Repeaters were a wonderful invention, allowing a lot of shots in a short amount of time. Enough to send Casey riding for cover. Enough to buy him time.

Brad whistled in two short blasts. Belle came over immediately, sidestepping and tossing her head, her tail swishing nervously, but she came. There was no pain, but Brad knew from his tight respirations that it was just a matter of time. Pressing his hand to his side, he reached for the horse. Belle snorted at the smell of fresh blood and shied away. "Easy girl."

He could hear Casey riding away. He didn't hear Cougar approaching. Which only meant one thing. Cougar hadn't found

Casey before he'd moved the meet, and while he was likely tracking the shots right now, until he arrived Brad was on his own.

"C'mere, Belle. We need to get home."

Back to Evie and a whole host of explanations that would require more lies than he could likely spin about the shape he'd be in when he got there. He looked at his hand, covered in blood. Especially if he kept bleeding like this.

The pain hit just as he was swinging up into the saddle, exploding through him with the same power of the shot. Then came the dizziness, and black spots filled his vision, blocking the green of the grass and the blue of the sky. He blinked. Blue sky? Shit, he was slipping.

Closing his eyes, he forced himself up and over, his midsection slamming into the saddle. Blinding pain clawed at his gut. Nausea hit just as hard as the next wave of agony. He retched, hoping like hell he missed the saddle. Gut shot. The horror of it was almost enough to have him letting go right there.

Hell of a way to end things. I expected more of a show.

"Get me home, Belle."

She started walking. He looped the reins around the saddle horn. Blood soaked his pants. His skin felt cold and clammy and sweat burned his eyes. Even if he hadn't seen Casey leave the meeting place, Cougar would have heard the shot. He'd be here soon. Unless Casey or one of his cohorts had gotten the drop on him. Hard to believe: Cougar was good. Casey wasn't exactly a slackard, however, and a few of the men who rode with him were rats in disguise. The thought gnawed at him. He couldn't go back to town without knowing. A man owed his friend better. Brad turned Belle up the ridge. "Let's go find Cougar, darling."

Any help would be appreciated. Cougar doesn't deserve to die out here.

There wasn't an answer. Then again, he wasn't expecting one. It was just him and Belle and a whole lot of wilderness to cover. Perfect.

FIVE MINUTES LATER he was barely conscious, and he couldn't find any evidence of Cougar, or even that he'd been in the vicinity. Brad turned Belle down toward the valley. With every step he was thrown forward. Pain, so familiar as to be almost family, ground on his awareness, becoming the sum of his existence. Leaning back would have eased the motion. Leaning back would upset the tenuous grip he had on the saddle. Leaning back wasn't an option.

Brad unwound the rope from the side of the saddle. He wasn't going to make it back under his own power, and he wanted to make it. Not only to get revenge on Casey, but also to see Evie one more time. She was the only responsibility he'd ever had. And truth was, he wasn't ready to be shed of her yet.

You gave her to me, so you can just keep me alive until I get back to her.

He tied himself to the saddle. Come hell or high water he would make it home. Casey might have planned for him to die out here, but he wasn't in a mood to oblige. Patting Belle on the shoulder, no longer fighting the pain and weakness, just letting it roll over him, Brad closed his eyes. "Get us home, Belle."

He didn't know how long he rode like that. One minute slowed to the next as hot liquid filled his boot and drained his strength. He built a picture of Evie in his mind, eyes flashing, mouth set, temper flaring, and held on to it. As a talisman, he couldn't find better. Evie had the tenacity of a badger.

"Rev!"

The shout didn't register at first. After the third shout, he lifted his head, able to make out the shadowy form of a rider coming hard. He titled his rifle and hooked his finger on the trigger.

The weapon was yanked out of his hand.

"Son of a bitch."

Cougar. "You're a little late to the party," he rasped.

"It would've helped if you hadn't moved the damn thing." Steel flashed in his field of vision. The rope binding his hands around the horn snapped. "How bad is it?"

"Think I'm gut shot."

"Only think?" Cougar's deep drawl was deceptively calm.

"I wasn't going to strip down in the middle of battle to check."

There was the sound of material parting under a metal blade. Air streamed into the wound like acid.

"Goddamn!" He found his breath. "How's it look?"

Very carefully the material settled back over the wound. "Like we need to get you to Doc."

Brad grunted as his horse changed direction and speed. As soon as he found the rhythm, he glanced over at Cougar.

"Do me a favor and save your funeral voice for when I actually have one."

Not a muscle twitched in the other man's expression. "Done."

Shit. That was no comfort.

Fifteen

"HE WAS DEPENDING on you, wasn't he?" Evie asked Cougar.

Cougar didn't move, just stood there in the foyer, head up, shoulders back. "Yes."

She wished he'd prevaricated, hedged, defended himself, provided her with an outlet for the cauldron of emotion boiling inside her. Brad was upstairs in bed, unconscious, feverish from his wound and there wasn't anything she could do but wait and see if he woke up. She clutched the pile of dirty sheets to her chest. "You were supposed to protect him."

"I know."

"He could die."

"Doc said he should be fine."

"If he doesn't get an infection." It was a very big if, much bigger than the innocuous-looking hole in his stomach that had caused so much trouble.

"The Rev's a tough man. No bullet's going to take him down."

It scared her witless that she didn't know if Brad was tough enough to survive this, but she did want to know who had hurt him. Her nails bit into her arms, the stinging pain centering her control. "Who was the coward? Who shot him?"

Cougar shifted his hat in his hand. His mouth flattened to a thin line. "I didn't get there in time to see."

"Get to where?"

"To where they had moved the meeting."

"A meeting implies that he knew who he was meeting."

"He did."

"But you didn't."

Cougar didn't look away, just kept her gaze with that impassive expression that gave her nothing to play off. "Pretty much."

Her nails cut deeper. "How could you agree to that?"

He spun his hat in a half circle. The first break in his calm that she'd seen since he'd walked in the door fifteen minutes before. "Your husband has a mind of his own."

Cougar wasn't a man to go into anything blind. Only one thing could make him do something so unorthodox. "He called in a favor, didn't he?"

Cougar didn't answer. Evie didn't press. Mainly because it wouldn't do any good. Cougar's sense of honor went bone deep. He wouldn't betray Brad's confidence. Period.

"So until he regains consciousness, we won't even know who did this to him?"

Cougar settled his black hat back on his head, angling the brim down over his eyes. And that fast, civilization seemed to leave him.

"We'll know."

"How?"

After a quick knock, the front door opened. Clint stepped halfway into the room. "You about ready, Cougar?"

"Just about." Cougar reached out. The breadth of his palm took up the entirety of her peripheral vision. The tips of his fingers touched her temple before grazing down her cheek. Inside, the wall she'd built against the fear that Brad would die groaned beneath the understanding contained in his touch. "You stay strong."

Swallowing hard, she ducked his gaze. Not breaking down to a blubbering mess of emotion was taking the little bit of her strength left over from caring for Brad. "I will."

"Asa and Jackson are going to be watching the house. Nothing can get past those two, so don't be worrying about anything." She nodded. His middle finger glided along the underside of her jaw. When it reached the point of her chin, he pressed up. Evie had no choice but to meet Cougar's gaze, to see the understanding and purpose there.

"I promise you, the man who did this will not walk away from the repercussions."

She knew she should tell Cougar that it wasn't necessary. She knew she should keep him home, away from danger, so he could live to see his child born, but she wasn't that good. All that filled her mind was the knowledge that whoever had done this to Brad was still out there. And that was intolerable. "Thank you."

She glanced over at Clint, thinking of Jenna, Gray, and Bri. "Promise me you'll be careful."

"It's my middle name."

Cougar dropped his hand to the hilt of his knife. She stared at his lean fingers wrapped around the wooden handle and remembered how that same hand had cradled the prospect of his child so tenderly. Dear God, what would Mara do without her Cougar? "You, too."

There was too much anticipation in Cougar's smile to ease her nerves. "Never intended to be anything but." He called over to Clint "You got that package, Clint?"

"Right here."

He tossed it. Cougar caught it before passing it to her.

It was surprisingly heavy. "What's this?"

"A wedding present."

Putting it on the foyer table, she watched him stroll through the door as if he wasn't going on a manhunt, facing killing, facing death. She shuddered. When she'd wished for excitement in her life, this wasn't the kind she'd been hoping for. Before the door closed, she caught a glimpse of Asa leaning against the house, rifle draped across his arm. He tipped his hat. She managed a shaky smile. The door clicked shut.

She became aware of a dampness against her chest. Pulling the sheets way, she saw the bright smear of blood across the pale yellow of her bodice. The one she'd worn in case Brad woke up because she thought the color would cheer him. Without thinking, she touched the spot. Her hand came away stained with the same red. A streak discolored the gold of her wedding band. She closed her hand over the stain. She was going to have to do laundry. Almost everything they had was blood-soaked.

EVIE SAT BY the bed, the hard edges of the ladder-back chair she'd dragged up from the kitchen cutting into her thigh. There were more comfortable chairs already in the room, big overstuffed things that encouraged a body to curl up and relax—the one thing she couldn't do. Doc had said Brad should wake tonight. She needed to be there when he did, needed to see awareness in his eyes.

Moonlight cast the room in a pale glow. Brad lay in the middle of the bed, his skin leached of its natural vitality by blood loss.

He was so white, his breathing so shallow. Evie had the overwhelming feeling that the only thing keeping him breathing was the amount of effort she put into willing it. It didn't matter what Doc said, that the laudanum he'd given him for pain caused the shallow breaths. Didn't matter that Cougar had meant to be there for Brad. She wasn't interested in efforts. She wanted results.

Brad frowned and shifted on the bed. His eyelids fluttered, his hand slid up over the covers toward his hip. Leaning forward she caught his hand. His flesh was hot and dry. "Shh, don't move."

His frown deepened. "Brenda?"

Who was Brenda?

"No. It's Evie." She squeezed once, probably holding on too tightly. She just wanted him to open his eyes. "You were shot."

"Father found us?"

Good heavens, he thought his father would shoot him? "No. Someone else."

His hand turned in hers, squeezing hard. "He's coming."

His voice sounded so young. Was he reliving his past?

"Where?" she asked, taking advantage of the moment.

"Where he can't find you."

As an experiment, she asked, "Where's that?"

"To the woods by the river, there's a cave. He won't find you there."

"He's a reverend. A man of God."

He shook his head, grimacing. "Hurry!"

Brad was breathing hard, his heart beating fast. Dear heavens, what had gone on in his home? Stroking her fingers across his brow, she pushed his hair off his face, giving him what he obviously needed to hear. "I'm hurrying."

His eyes opened as his grip on her hand changed, pushing rather than pulling. "Get in."

Delirium ruled his mind. She placed her palm on his shoulder. He was burning up. Swallowing back her terror at all the fever implied, she whispered, "I'm in."

The frown cleared from his face. "Good. Safe."

His breathing changed, his muscles tightened. She clutched his hand before he could let go. She didn't want him to hurt, but she had to know. Just had to know that it all turned out right.

That he'd been safe, too. Kissing the back of his hand, she asked, "What about you? Are you safe now?"

There was a pause. He frowned. For an instant she thought he was awake. She wanted him to be awake but then his body jerked three times in a row. Breath hissed through his teeth and he snarled, "Touch her, and I'll kill you."

Touch who? Brenda? Kill who? His father?

He jerked again, his hands slamming into the mattress above his head while his body bucked under blows she couldn't block. Pressing his shoulders into the mattress, she tried to keep him still. It was impossible. He was trapped in a nightmare she couldn't stop. If he continued, he'd rip out his stitches. "Brad, please, you have to stop fighting."

He fought even harder, forcing her to throw her weight over him. His groan tore her heart out, but he didn't stop fighting. If anything, his struggles intensified with a desperation that drove through her heart like a spike. No one should have memories so painful, so vivid.

"Never. Whip me all you want. Have your congregation pray when you do it. I won't be praying ever again. She's dead, you bastard."

Those scars she'd imagined were from an act of heroism had actually been put there by his father? Stretching her middle finger, she touched the faint mark that curled over his shoulder and imagined the pain he'd endured as a child. The humiliation. "No one's going to whip you."

His eyes found hers, seemed to focus. In a surprisingly lucid voice, he said, "She's dead, you know."

"Who?"

"Mom. I killed her."

The only one who was dying here was her. This glimpse into his past was devastating. "How?"

"He told me if I prayed hard enough she'd live. But she didn't."

What kind of monster told a child that? Kissing his cheek, her heart bleeding, she whispered, "He lied, Brad."

He blinked, suddenly looking totally adult, completely male as his mouth twisted with wry amusement. "God does that a lot."

At least he wasn't tossing about. "What?"

"Lie."

He couldn't believe that. "No, he doesn't."

She was talking to herself. Brad slumped back into the pillows, all the vitality she associated with him snuffed out. And that scared her more than anything else.

Grabbing his shoulders, she leaned over so she could whisper in his ear, "Don't you dare die on me, Brad Swanson. Unless you want me chaining your spirit to this Earth with the most off-kilter wailing and burnt dinner offerings you or any other ghost has ever seen, you'd better not die."

It might have been her imagination, but she thought he smiled.

THREE HOURS LATER there was another change. Brad went very still. Even his breathing stopped. She rushed to the bed. His eyes opened. For a minute, his gaze was vague, but then it focused. "Evie?"

The tears she'd been battling for the last day welled. He recognized her. "Who else did you expect to find beside your bed?"

He blinked. His "hurt?" was a dry rasp.

"You were shot," she explained.

He closed his eyes and licked his lips, clearly trying to remember. "Casey."

Well, at least she had a name. "Casey shot you?"

He nodded. "Cougar?"

"He's fine."

He grunted. "Couldn't find him."

"You searched for him?"

He cleared his throat. "Thought Casey might have picked him off."

So that explained why he'd been up on the ridge bleeding all over the place. She wanted to slap him for being so damn loyal.

"He's fine, so you don't have to worry anymore."

Brad relaxed. "Good."

She filled the glass with water from the pitcher on the bed stand. "You must be thirsty."

Immediately, he started to get up.

"No, don't move." He was so weak, just her hand in the center of his chest kept him put. His skin was warm, but not too warm. That, at least, was a positive. "You can't afford to lose any more blood."

Beneath her palm, a subtle tension entered his muscles. His right hand curled into a fist. "How bad?"

She wanted to cry at the careful question. Clearly, he remembered the wound's location. She brushed his hair off his forehead, hoping he didn't notice the tremble in her fingers. "The bullet missed everything important." Slipping her arm behind his head, she angled him up toward the glass. "Doc said it was a miracle," she whispered, savoring the texture of his skin against hers, the flex of his muscles as he drank, mentally encouraging him to take more, her hand shaking so badly she spilled some. "Sorry."

The tears pressed harder, needing an escape. She fought them back.

"Never thought the good Lord would waste one of those on me."

Emotions churned inside, built, exploded outward. "Shut up."

She was too close to snapping to hear such nonsense. The order came out harsher than she'd intended, betrayed more than she wanted.

Brad pushed the glass away. "Hell."

If her voice sounded bad, his sounded worse. Scratchy and hoarse.

He patted the bed. "Come here."

"No." She tipped the glass back to his lips. Water spilled as he turned his head away. "Now look what you made me do."

He didn't make a sound as she eased him down on the bed, and the reason became apparent as soon as she tried to straighten. He'd been lying in wait. His fingers curved around the back of her neck, holding her in place. She didn't dare put any strain on his muscles.

"You're scared."

"I was terrified."

His eyes narrowed. "You still are."

"You see too much."

"You're just not very good at hiding."

"From you." And that was true.

"I like it that way . . . now come here."

There was nowhere to go. Any dipping of the mattress would cause him pain and she couldn't do that, but the hand behind her head was surprisingly strong.

"The laudanum is making you feel better than you are."

"The laudanum is wearing off." His eyes narrowed. "You've been crying."

"No, I haven't." Not yet. She hadn't broken down yet.

"Then you're about to."

"Not if you let me go." If he let her go, she had a prayer of holding on to her composure.

"I don't want to let you go. After spending what seemed like an eternity in hell imagining I was holding on to you, I find I'm a little hungry for the real thing."

"I'll bawl like a baby."

The hand behind her neck didn't budge. His jaw set. Clearly he was prepared for the worst. "You need to be held."

She needed the last eighteen hours rewritten. "I'm not going to fall apart."

"Maybe I am."

She blinked. She couldn't imagine that. "Why?"

"I wanted to see you again."

She took his hand from behind her neck. She meant to put it back on the bed, but somehow found herself holding it, unable to put it down, memorizing the creases in the back of the knuckles, the tiny nicks of scars, the shape of his nails, memorizing everything. "Why?"

The grin he shot her was a pale imitation of his normally devastating one. She shouldn't have found it sexy, but she did. "I've never had a woman to come home to before."

The tears broke free, spilling over her cheeks, dripping onto her chest and his arm. "You almost didn't."

"Ah, sweetheart." His fingers threaded through her hair. "Don't."

The stupid tears wouldn't stop. "I can't help it."

"Then you're going to have to let me hold you."

"I can't, without hurting you."

"Anyone ever tell you you're stubborn?"

"No."

"Now that's a lie."

"If you knew the answer, why'd you ask?"

He struggled up on his elbows.

"What are you doing?"

"If you won't come here, I'll come there."

Oh God, he couldn't do that. She slid to her knees. "How about if I sit here beside the bed?"

His arm came around her shoulder, a heavy masculine weight she cherished. It made her so angry he'd put himself in danger. She swatted his arm. "If you ever take a risk like you did yesterday, you won't have to worry about someone killing you. I'll do it myself."

"I was bushwhacked, Evie. It's a hard thing to predict."

"You should have waited for Cougar."

"I don't need a keeper."

She ignored his scowl, glaring at him through the flood of tears that just wouldn't stop. "That argument would hold more water if you weren't on the verge of death."

"Stop arguing with me, sweetheart, I'm wounded."

"It's your own fault."

"You still have to deal with it, and unless you come here, it's just going to get tougher."

"How could it be tougher?"

"I'll start fussing."

"As if you aren't now?"

"This is nothing compared to how bad I can get."

Even through her tears, she could see his determination. For some reason it was important to him to hold her and he wasn't going to settle until he got it. He looked so tired, so pale, that she was afraid to indulge him. Afraid not to. What if he tried to get up again?

With a grunt, she pushed to her feet, her body feeling eighty, her soul feeling ninety. "You are entirely too used to getting your own way."

A bit of his usual humor was in his "Not that I've noticed."

It comforted her.

BRAD WAITED, THAT restless determination that had been holding him upright through the agony of the long ride surging beneath the pain as Evie stood. There were times when a man had to give in to weakness, and for him this was it. He needed to hold Evie more than he needed to take his next breath.

As soon as she settled in beside him, the sense of rightness increased and the tension eased. He bit back a groan as the mattress shifted, knowing she'd leap away the second she knew he was in pain. For a woman used to risking everything for the satisfaction she got at the moment, she was amazingly stingy when it came to him enjoying his moments.

"Are you all right?"

He cupped her buttock in his hand and forced a smile. "Getting better by the minute."

Hair tumbled out of her braid, softening the sternness of her glare. "Would you tell me the truth if you weren't?"

"I'm a man of God."

"A fact you only trot out when it's convenient."

"Want to hear me spout scripture?"

"Not particularly."

"It might help you feel more comfortable with my job."

"It would put me to sleep," she grumbled as she settled against him.

A slap on her rear got her attention. "I believe that's blasphemy."

"Huh. More like self-preservation." She snuggled a little closer. He held her a little tighter. "You can be long-winded when you want something."

"And what do you think I want from you?"

That pulled her up short. "I don't really know."

That made two of them. "Well, for right now, I'd like to feel you lying against me, close enough that I can feel your breath. How's that sound to you?"

Those tears were still coming so he shouldn't have been surprised when she said, "I want to feel you breathing, too."

He made a note. Evie had the tendency to surrender at the oddest times. "Then stop fooling around and come here."

As soon as she rested full length against him, he could breathe. "Move on up a bit." She did—gingerly, carefully.

Torture wasn't this tough. "Sweetheart, put your head on my shoulder. I won't break."

"I'll hurt you."

"No, you won't."

When her head rested on his shoulder, her arm carefully settled across his chest. He released the breath he didn't know he'd been holding.

This was right.

He could feel her eyes upon him, searching his expression. Tears soaked his skin. "Got to admit, this is good."

"My crying?"

"No, just you here with me." The shudder that rippled through her started high and ended at her toes. Brushing his lips across her hair, he whispered, "I'm sorry you were scared."

Her hand fisted on his chest. "I'm sorry you were hurt."

"I'm glad you cared."

"I'm your wife."

"I'm glad for that, too."

He hadn't meant to say that. Must be some of the laudanum was still in his blood. He was sure of it when she kissed his chest and sighed almost too softly to be separated from her breath. "So am I."

All his senses focused on the impression of her kiss while his mind wrestled with the implications. He was falling in love with his wife. Who the hell would have thought it? "Told you I'd grow on you."

"Just like a wart."

Balancing the weight of her braid in his hand, he smiled. "Right under your skin."

The puff of her laughter blew over his throat. For a few minutes, Evie didn't say anything and neither did he. The ache of his wound, the weakness of his body, they were all secondary to the sweetness of just lying here listening to the birds sing beyond the open window. It all seemed so peaceful, safe. But it wasn't.

He didn't kid himself that Casey would just pack up his toys and go away. It wasn't his nature. Casey saw the world as a series of interconnected injustices that built on each other. Each one designed to test his mettle, each one surmounted as proof of his right to take what he wanted. And what he wanted was Brenda. To Casey, Brenda was like a big, shiny gold nugget. A prize beyond price. He'd do anything to possess her, and kill anyone who got in his way. And right now, he was thinking Brad was standing in his way. That was going to be a problem. He kissed the top of Evie's head. For all of them.

"Did Cougar post guards?"

"Asa and Jackson."

There wasn't better. Asa could be rattlesnake mean when the mood took him and second to none with a gun. Jackson wasn't far behind. The only one better was Elijah, but there was no figuring where he stood these days.

"Right before they went after whoever shot you."

"Shit." They should have waited for him to talk to them. Warn them.

"They'll be all right, won't they?"

He had to believe they would. They were marshals, had years of experience behind them. Casey wouldn't be the first snake in the grass they came up against. "Yes."

Some of his doubt must have bled through. "I didn't try to stop them."

"When?"

"When they said they were going. I wanted them to find who hurt you and I wanted them to kill him."

"Wanted?"

"Lying here with you, I'm worried about what could happen, and what that would cost Jenna and Mara. I think maybe I should have convinced them to let the shooter go."

She'd have had as much luck teaching pigs to fly. "There's nothing you could have said to stop them. Some things a man can't let go."

"Maybe I could have gotten them to wait."

He tipped her chin up, meeting her gaze and holding it. He had enough guilt for both of them. She didn't need to be taking on any. "No, you couldn't."

And Casey knew that. He would have done his research before he set up his little attack, finding out who was offering Brad protection; therefore he would be expecting the McKinnelys. It was the code. Bushwhack a man and his friends would come calling. Considering Casey had to know the repercussions of his actions, Brad had to wonder if that had been Casey's plan all along. To lure the McKinnelys away from their homes. Away from town, because for sure he wouldn't leave the area until he'd retrieved Brenda. Shit.

Evie shifted and her braid fell over his arm. He wrapped it around his wrist. "I don't want you leaving the house without someone going along."

"Why?"

"Because I don't know that the man gunning for me won't include you in his anger."

"This Casey?"

"Yes."

"Why does he hate you so?"

"He thinks I stole his woman."

Her fingers curled into his chest, the nails digging into his skin. "Did you?"

That she'd asked should've anger him. But it didn't. "No."

For a moment there was silence, and he couldn't tell whether she believed him. Then she nodded. "Do you think he'll try again?"

"Yes." Casey didn't have many limits. Evie had to be protected against all costs.

"Then we'd better get ready."

She slipped away from him, ducking under the restriction of his arm.

"Evie?"

"I'll be back in a minute."

She was as good as her word, but when she came back into the room, she was packing a revolver and a box. The gun looked so out of place in her small hand. Settling on the bed beside him, she held out the weapon. "Show me how to load this."

His instinct was to say "no." He didn't want his past touching her, but the reality was that it already had. It was now a threat. She was right—she needed to be ready.

He met her gaze and held out his hand. "You don't pick up a gun without being willing to pull the trigger."

Placing the gun in his hand, she said with cold calm, "I'll pull the trigger."

Maybe she would. Holding the gun up, he checked it over. "Where'd you get this?"

"Cougar gave it to me."

"It's a good choice." He checked the hammer and the action. "This has got a strong pull." He closed the chamber, cocked the hammer, and pulled the trigger. The hammer came down with a sharp click. Evie jumped.

He looked over at her. "It's only a weapon if it has bullets."

She frowned. "I know that."

"Good, because if you jump like that when you fire, you're going to be taking the shots rather than giving them."

She hitched her knee up to see better. "I'll keep that in mind."

"Also keep in mind that the gun has a kick and you have to

prepare for it." He pointed the gun at the ceiling, surprised at how hard it was to coordinate the effort, how tiring it was to hold the position. "Lock your elbows like this. Take a breath like this, release half"—he took a breath, steadying himself into the pull and pulled the trigger—"then fire."

The hammer clicked down. This time Evie only winced. Shit, he hoped she never had cause to use it. "And you can relax. This gun has a strong pull. It's not going to go off accidentally."

"Thank God for that."

At this point he'd thank God for any help. This whole situation was going to hell in a handbasket—fast.

You got her into this. Now you need to protect her.

"That pull means you're going to have to pull that trigger like you mean it and you're going to have to allow that extra split second that it's going to take you to pull the trigger when you're planning your shot."

"You're saying I shouldn't plan on any quick-draw contests?"

"Don't even think about it."

"I was only joking."

He couldn't joke about this. "This is serious, Evie. If you feel you're in a position where you have to point this weapon, I don't want you to hesitate. I don't want you worrying about right and wrong; trust your gut and shoot. Don't give them a chance to fire first. There's no playing fair in a gunfight. It all boils down to who has the guts to take the shot."

"How do you know so much about it?"

"I wasn't always a minister."

"What were you before?"

"Young and foolish."

She blinked. "I find that hard to believe."

So did he, when he sat here living a life that could have been his if he hadn't let his father twist him into believing there was no other path than the one he took. "Doesn't change the truth."

She gave him a strange look. "No, I guess it doesn't."

He held out the gun. "Think hard before you take this."

She licked her lips. "I have."

"Unless you're sure you can pull the trigger, don't even pick this up."

"I know." She took it from his hand. He couldn't believe he was lying in bed—shot, so weak that just lifting a revolver had worn him out—teaching his wife how to fire a weapon. He sighed, looked out the window, heard the townspeople going about their business beyond. "This isn't how I saw our marriage going."

She raised an eyebrow at him. "Were you under the impression that this is how *I* wanted it to go? Trust me, it isn't. But it's what we have, so we'll deal with it."

Yeah, he guessed they would.

"How do you know this woman that this Casey thinks you stole?"

He wasn't sure how much to reveal.

"I grew up with her in a town real similar to Cattle Crossing."

She cautiously pulled back the hammer. Too carefully. "Did you love her?"

He eased the muzzle away. "Not like your tone implies. Brenda had a hard life. I just got used to protecting her and she got used to depending on me."

"And she still does?"

"Brenda's fragile."

"And you care about her."

He didn't like that bite in her tone. "Like I would care about a sister if I had one."

"And that caring is why Casey is determined to kill you?"

"He's got a mean temper and he likes to exercise it on his wife. I've stepped in a few times. Apparently, Brenda finally ran away, and he's convinced it was to me."

"Because she loves you?"

"No. She loves him."

"Even though he beats her?"

He shook his head. He'd never understood it, no matter how many times he'd seen it. All Casey had to do was put on that hangdog "I'm sorry" face, and Brenda forgot all about her bruises and started making apologies of her own. He'd thought, when little Brenna came along, things would change, but they hadn't. It'd just given Casey one more thing to own and Brenda one more thing to worry about. "There's no accounting for people's feelings."

Her gaze snapped up. "You feel guilty."

He shrugged, weariness, old and new, dragging at his bones. "It's hard not to."

"You're a minister, not a miracle worker."

"Thank you for that."

Easing the hammer down, she tilted her head to the side and studied him with those discerning artist's eyes.

"She's why you feel so strongly about helping Erica, isn't she?"

"Partly. And there's also the fact that the law is just wrong in the choice it leaves."

"Yes, it is." She held up the gun. "Show me how to load this."

Sixteen

THE KNOCK CAME again. Harder, breaking into her concentration.

"Go away."

There was no chance whoever was pounding on the door heard her muttered order, any more than she was going to be able to utilize the last few minutes of good light this stingy house allowed her with which to paint. The reflection of the sunrise on the church's window was going to have to wait. Downstairs, the front door latch clicked.

"Evie?"

Asa. She dropped the paintbrush into the tin of turpentine and wiped her hand on a rag. She practically flew down the stairs, stopping halfway when she saw him standing inside the door. Her skirts swung about her legs as she asked, "What's wrong?"

Asa looked up from where he was hanging his hat on the hat rack. "Not a darn thing. I'm heading home to catch a few minutes with the family, and was wondering if maybe Brad was up and feeling like company."

If he wasn't, he would be. The man needed a distraction from the fact he was stuck in bed. "Of course!"

Asa raked through his hair, smiling and looking up at her from under his forearm. "That's a lot of enthusiasm. Brad that bad of a patient?"

"The absolute worst I've ever taken care of."

"How many would that be?" he asked, following her up the stairs.

"He is my first, and definitely my last."

"Let me guess—he won't stay in bed."

She turned at the top of the stairs and looked at him. "To the point I've now started making threats."

Asa laughed, coming up alongside. "I bet that was effective."

She knocked on the bedroom door before walking in. "Actually, it's been quite effective."

Brad sat propped up against the headboard, papers spread on the sheet in front of him. Beside him on the table was the breakfast she'd cooked. Untouched. The frown on his face said that not only had he been listening, he wasn't amused.

He put the papers carefully on the bed beside him, the control in the act belied by the darkness of his glare. "You'd do well to remember I'm not going to be in this bed forever, Evie."

"Lord, I hope not." She'd probably bash him on the head with a bedpan if he were. She motioned Asa in. "See if you can lighten his mood, would you?"

Asa smiled, stepping aside so she could pass through the door. "I'll do my best."

Brad waited until Evie's footsteps faded before asking, "You wouldn't happen to have a cigarette on you, would you?"

He could use both a cigarette and a stiff drink. Brad wasn't used to being weak, didn't tolerate it well, especially when his wife was in danger. Relying on others to protect her went against the grain and made him distinctly uneasy.

Asa laughed and grabbed the chair, dragged it closer to the bed before dropping into it. "Evie riding you that hard?"

Brad sighed. "That would be a no?"

Asa nodded. "That would be a no." He jerked his thumb at the plate on the bed stand beside him. "What in hell is that?"

Brad sighed again, his stomach clenching on nothingness. "My breakfast."

With a poke to the side of the dish, Asa asked, "What was it before you gave it last rites?"

"I think scrambled eggs."

"Damn!" Sitting back in the chair, he shook his head. "Maybe she really was aiming to poison the Simmons kid."

"Nah. She's just that bad at cooking."

"How can a woman that creative with a paintbrush be that cursed in the kitchen?"

Brad wished the hell he knew. "No clue, but I'm thinking that hoping she'll develop some skill is a lost cause."

"So what are you going to do?"

"Either find someone to take over the job, or learn to do it myself."

"Shadow Svensen playing wife? I know a lot of men who'd pay to see that."

Cutting a glance at the door, he hissed, "Watch what you say."

"You haven't told her yet?"

"There's no *yet* about it. She's not ever going to know."

"That's a tough game, especially with Casey playing fast and lose with revelation."

"I'll handle Casey."

"And if you can't?"

"Then I'll handle the consequences."

"If Evie's not prepared, it could cost you everything."

"No shit." What had started as a game had turned into something serious, but while he might want to change the rules now, the game was set, the ending preordained. And when it was over, the one place Evie would not be standing was by his side. What he didn't need was Asa reminding him of it. "Shouldn't you be home doting on your daughter and spoiling your wife?"

"Shouldn't you be making a daughter of your own?"

A little girl with Evie's spirit? Big eyes? The thought filled him with dread, and a wrenching longing. "No."

"A shame." Asa hooked his ankle over his knee. "I think you'd make a good father."

"Because my own father was such a stellar example?"

"Because of who *you* are."

Damn, he'd love to believe that. "It's not going to happen."

Asa sighed. "You are so stubborn on the way you see things."

"It's my nature."

"Want me to change the subject?"

"Yes."

"Want to talk about the current betting frenzy going on in town?"

"Not if I'm the subject."

Asa leaned back in the chair, the corner of his lip lifting in a provoking half smile that raised the hairs on the back of Brad's neck. "Then you pick a topic."

"What the hell did you do?"

Asa rested his head against the back of the overstuffed chair. "I didn't have to do a darn thing."

With Asa, one always had to watch the phrasing. "If you didn't have to do anything, then someone else did. What's up?"

"There might be a few bets going 'round."

"Bets on what?"

"On how long it's going to take you to piss off your wife to the point she starts showing that picture of you all over town."

He closed his eyes. Damn. When he opened them, Asa's smile had grown. "They heard the argument this morning?"

"Pretty much everyone in town heard her declare that if you didn't settle into being a better patient, she would take that painting and hang it on the front porch."

"That will never happen."

"You might not have a say in it. There are a few souls with a vested interest in the relationship between you now. Quite a few who are damn curious about that painting."

Shit. "Who?"

Asa cracked his lids. "Well, Doc has a bet placed. I believe Millie and Patrick both took a piece of it. Of course, once Cyrus got word of the hoopla, he placed a bet."

"Not that his wife knows." Cyrus's wife, Gertie, was notoriously tightfisted with money.

"Nope. Though there are some side bets on how soon he'll be riding into town for a pound of that candy to sweeten her temper once she finds out."

"I'm afraid you're all in for a disappointment." Because no way in hell would anybody see that picture.

"Uh-huh. I guess we'll have to wait for time to tell that." With the motion of his hand, he indicated Brad's wound. "How are you feeling?"

"I should be good enough to help y'all look for Casey in a few days."

Evie's voice carried clearly through the door. "I heard that."

"Good," he hollered back, "then that will save an argument when I ride out."

Asa shook his head. "You want some advice?"

"What?"

"You don't challenge a woman like Evie that way. Unless"—the door opened a crack, and there was the slide of wood across wood—"you want to suffer the consequences," Asa finished on a bark of laughter as the door closed, leaving the naked painting of Brad leaning against the wall.

"Son of a bitch!" Brad lurched up. Pain knifed through his side. He grabbed it, bellowing, "Evie!"

Asa kept laughing. Brad threw a pillow at him. "Stop looking at the damn thing."

"Kind of hard to look away."

"Find a reason to."

Sweet as pie, Evie called back, "You get out of bed, Brad Swanson, and it's going on the front porch."

That just set Asa into fresh guffaws.

"When I get out of this bed, Evie, you're going to get your ass paddled."

Just imagining that had him hard with anticipation, forcing him to draw up his leg to hide the reaction.

"I'll worry about that when it happens."

Asa just laughed harder. "Good to see you've taught the little woman who's boss."

"Like you taught Elizabeth?"

"Hell, man, I never even tried. I like her wild. Keeps me on my toes."

Truth was, Brad liked Evie wild, too. He just hated that painting. "Do me a favor and bring that painting over here, would you?"

"I don't think so."

There was only one reason he would refuse. "You placed a goddamn bet, too."

The man didn't even have the grace to fake guilt. "I got caught up in the excitement."

"Like hell." Asa never did anything without a plan. "You keep laughing, you irritating son of a bitch, and I'll wipe your brain clean with a bullet."

Running his hand down his face in a token attempt to hide his laughter, Asa asked, "You mean the one in the revolver downstairs?"

The anger inside coalesced into a tight ball. Laid up without even a revolver within reach did not put a smile on his mood. "Meant to talk to you about that."

"There was the risk of delirium. We didn't want you shooting up the place."

He bared his teeth in a smile. "I'm not delirious now."

"Now you're pissed, so I think we'll just leave the thing where it is until you calm down."

Brad cracked his knuckles. "You're running up quite a tab."

"Consider it payback."

"For what?"

"For being so aggravating."

No one was more aggravating than Asa. "Isn't that the pot calling the kettle black?"

The door opened. Cougar stood in the doorway. "Which one of you is the kettle and which one is the pot?"

Brad gritted his teeth. "Evie let you in?"

"Even invited us for coffee."

"Us?"

"If Cougar would stop hogging all the space, you'd see I'm here, too," Clint called from behind.

Asa got to his feet, still grinning ear to ear. "That wife of yours sure has a mean streak. If I were you, I'd stay on her good side. At least until you heal."

"You heading out, Asa?" Cougar asked.

"Yep. I thought I'd catch some breakfast with Elizabeth and Tempest before hitting the sack."

It struck Brad then how much Asa was sacrificing to protect him and his family. How much they all were. He knew why Cougar and Clint were helping him out. Saving a man's life put him in another's debt, but Asa didn't owe him anything that he could recall. "Hey, Asa."

"What?"

"Thanks."

The man turned back and actually looked surprised. "No problem."

Driven by that inner voice that said safety lay in keeping accounts even, Brad called, "I owe you."

Finally, Asa stopped grinning. "You can fucking try."

As he passed through the door, only Brad noticed the sleight of hand that had the as-yet-unnoticed painting traveling discreetly with him. The inner voice quieted under the press of guilt. Hard to fathom, but he got the impression he'd hurt the gunslinger's feelings.

Cougar's "You sure can be thick" only increased his unease.

Brad stared at where the painting had been. Asa had no reason to take the painting with him. No reason at all as it would have been a hell of a lot more fun to share the joke with Cougar and Clint.

"Hell, you know friends don't owe each other," Clint growled.

Yes, he did. He just hadn't thought the rule applied to him, because he hadn't realized there'd been a shift. That pretend had become reality.

"You'll owe him an apology," Cougar tacked on, sitting in the chair. "Asa can be touchy that way."

"And if you don't want him reminding you of it for the rest of your life at the most inconvenient, not to mention, the most embarrassing moments," Clint drawled, "do it soon."

Brad blinked. They were right. He'd been living in the shadows so long, never depending on anyone, glossing over offers of friendship, just passing through life, that he hadn't noticed the change when it had occurred. But it had, and whether he'd planned it or not, he had friends. And apparently a life. The revelation was a shock.

What else do you have in store for me? He was afraid to find out.

THE MAN RODE too darn fast. Evie pulled the buckboard up at the fork in the trail and searched the fields of grass for signs of Asa. Her plan had been to follow him home and make her request there, but she hadn't allowed for the man's penchant for speed. Her plump little mare couldn't hope to keep up, especially pulling the buggy, which now meant she had no idea whether to ride left or right. She only had a vague idea of where the Rocking C was located. While it had seemed like such a good idea to follow Asa out into the countryside at the crack of dawn, now that she was sitting in the middle of the vast stretch of rolling grassland spreading toward the dramatic rise of the mountains, she could see there might be a few flaws in her plan. Like her ability to keep up. The potential for getting lost. Her relative vulnerability. She curved her hand around the hard outline of the pistol, taking comfort from its presence. "Any ideas, Betsy?"

Betsy whickered. Her ears pricked up and she looked down the path to the right. The horse had a better sense of hearing, and they had been following Asa since he left town. "All right. To the right it is."

All it took to get Betsy in motion was releasing the reins. A half mile farther the path dipped down and then up. At the tip of the next rise she spotted a large sign with the words *Rocking C* emblazoned in the wood with a well-worn path cutting beneath.

"Good job, Betsy."

Betsy snorted and picked up her pace. That could only mean one thing: a barn ahead. Betsy was notoriously lazy except when in pursuit of grain. At the top of the next rise, she whinnied a greeting. Evie couldn't blame her. The Rocking C was quite a spread with two barns, four corals, and what looked like two bunkhouses. To her, it screamed success. To Betsy it had to scream comfort.

Nestled at the foot of the mountains, the ranch bustled with activity, even at this early hour. In her heart of hearts, Evie had always wondered what could have driven Elizabeth to propose to the hard-eyed Asa two years ago. A ruthless gunslinger, whom she knew only by his reputation. A stranger to her. She now had her answer. The Rocking C wasn't just a home. This was a dream, a future in the making. The kind of thing a woman fought for the same way Evie had fought for her freedom. Elizabeth's path had been clearer to her goal, while Evie's had taken an unexpected turn, but both goals were good. Clucking her tongue, she sent the eager Betsy down the hill. She just hadn't achieved hers yet.

As soon as she got to the edge of the ranch buildings, Old Sam limped out of the barn and waved, his smile, beneath the low brim of his hat, putting more creases in his face than were in his faded blue-checked shirt.

"Morning, Evie. Asa says you're to go on up to the back door. Breakfast will be waiting."

She set the brake. "Asa told you . . . ?"

Sam came up alongside and offered her his hand. "Said you'd be along in a bit."

Asa had known she was following. Taking Sam's gnarled hand, she stepped down. "Thank you."

"You go on up now." Sam moved up toward the mare's head, patting her softly as he did. "I'll take care of this sweet girl."

"Her name's Betsy," she called after him.

Taking a breath, inhaling the scents of horses, hay, summer, and hope, she headed toward the house. Since the MacIntyres were expecting her, she opted for the kitchen door. At her knock, Asa called, "Come in."

Elizabeth smiled over her shoulder from where she stood at the stove as Evie entered. "Breakfast will be ready in a minute."

From the wonderful aroma, they were having bacon and eggs. "Thank you."

Evie glared at Asa, who held Tempest in his lap. The little girl was alternately standing and sitting, chortling every time she stood, grunting every time she sat. Asa was laughing with her, obviously enthralled by his daughter's enthusiasm for the simple game.

"If you knew I was following you, why didn't you stop?"

Asa didn't spare her a glance. "You seemed to be having so much fun with your sneaking, it didn't seem worth spoiling your game."

"I almost got lost."

That did have him looking at her. "Almost doesn't count for much."

"It scared me."

"Good."

"Asa," Elizabeth sighed, taking Tempest from him. Tempest fussed but then shoved her fist in her mouth and started chomping. "You didn't stop?"

He shrugged, making a face at his daughter that had her staring. With her blonde hair wisping all over her head, she looked like a startled elf. "The woman's so bound and determined to be foolish, I figured she needed the excitement."

Evie wanted to smack him. "I just wanted privacy to talk to you."

"What about?" Elizabeth asked, settling Tempest in her high chair before heading back to the stove.

Evie took the gun out of her pocket and placed it on the table before Asa. Giving it a little shove, she said, "I want your husband to teach me to shoot."

"He can certainly do that."

Asa wasn't so accommodating. He stared at her with those too discerning eyes, only the barest shift in his smile indicating the change in his mood. "Brad that irritating?"

She blinked, gathered her thoughts, and found her sense of humor. "My last nerve is feeling the strain."

"I've always found the Reverend to be very easygoing."

Asa glanced over at his wife. "The eggs are burning, Elizabeth."

Her hands came down on her hips. "If you don't want my input, just say so."

"I want your opinion, but considering my stomach is gnawing on my backbone, I'm interested in breakfast."

"Well, shoot." She turned back to the stove. "Then talk louder, so I don't miss out."

Reaching for his coffee, he winked. "Remember to speak up."

A little of Evie's tension slipped. It was getting easier and easier to see why Elizabeth adored the man. He might have lived a hard life, and killed more than his share of outlaws, but he had an easy way about him with the people he liked, and he clearly adored his family. "I'll do my best."

"Now . . ." He took a sip of his coffee. "Any particular reason you chose me?"

"You're the best there is with a gun."

"That's flattering."

"It was meant to be practical."

Asa glanced toward Elizabeth, his smile soft. "Well, now. I'm right fond of practical."

The frying pan clattered as Elizabeth moved it aside, a small grin on her lips.

"What does Brad say?"

"He's too busy keeping secrets to be sensible. Besides, he can't get out of bed, let alone teach me to shoot."

"It's not my nature to step between a husband and wife."

Elizabeth snorted as she set plates of food before Asa and Evie, keeping a third for herself. "Since when?"

That hint of a smile grew as he drew the gun toward him. "Since about the time you taught me how much trouble women can get into."

Elizabeth shook her head and spooned a bit of egg into Tempest's mouth. "We're not the ones who cause the trouble, are we, Evie?"

"In my experience, it's always the male of the species with the propensity to complicate things."

Asa picked up the gun. "On that, I'm going to disagree. As the preacher says, 'Women are the root of all evil.'"

"Brad doesn't say that!"

Sighting down the barrel, Asa smiled. "I don't recall saying he did." Sunlight flashed off the revolver as he bounced it in his grip. "This isn't one of Brad's."

How did he know that? "Cougar gave it to me."

"Hmm." He put it back on the table. Motioning with his fork, he ordered, "Eat."

Forcing down her impatience, she took a bite of the eggs. They were light and fluffy and seasoned with a sweet spice. Nothing like the disaster she'd created for Brad. "These are very good, Elizabeth."

"Thank you, but they're just scrambled eggs."

"You wouldn't say 'just' if you'd tasted the ones I made. I think even Dan's pigs turned up their noses."

Tempest, gumming the tiny nibble of egg Elizabeth had given her, reached for the plate. Elizabeth pulled it out of her reach. "Greedy girl. Finish what's in your mouth first."

Tempest grinned from ear to ear, showing everyone her pink gums, the egg in her mouth, and the natural charm that was hers. A charm for which Asa had obviously fallen, because he smiled right back, his whole expression softening to the point that it was hard to remember she had come here for lessons because he was the most notorious gunslinger in the state.

"She's not greedy, darling, she just knows what she wants and goes after it. Like you."

A fact of which her father clearly approved. Elizabeth pulled the plate farther out of reach when Tempest half climbed on the table, her brow creased with determination. "You won't be saying that when she sets her sights on her first beau."

"She can set her sights all she wants," Asa drawled. "No overeager boy is getting near my daughter."

Brows arched, Elizabeth exchanged a look with Evie and returned Tempest to her seat. "The same way no woman was getting near you?"

Still smiling, Asa trailed his fingertips down Elizabeth's arm, lingering at the pulse on the inside of her wrist before curling around and tucking her hand into his. "No woman did. Only my wife."

The look the couple shared burned jealousy deep into Evie's heart. She wanted Brad to look at her like that. Most of all, she wanted to be comfortable enough with him to give him the same in return.

Asa picked up his coffee cup and turned his attention back

to her. With a lift of his cup he indicated the gun. "So how'd you and your friend get out of the house?"

"Cougar and Clint are keeping Brad distracted."

"Meaning you slipped out."

"Pretty much."

He leaned back in his chair. "So you're here on borrowed time?"

She nodded. "Which is why I don't have time to chat."

Scooping up more of the egg, Elizabeth fed it to Tempest. "I'll send one of the boys into town with word of where you are, that way you can take all the time you need."

"I haven't said I'll do it, Elizabeth."

Elizabeth stood. "Of course you will. There's no reasonable benefit to anyone for Evie to remain helpless."

"I'm not exactly helpless."

No one paid her any attention.

"Brad won't thank me for her jumping into a gunfight."

"She's not going to jump into anything, are you?" Elizabeth didn't even wait for Evie to finish her "no." "She just doesn't want to be a sitting duck."

"She might be better off as a protected one."

Evie's "No, I won't" coincided with Elizabeth's "You know better than that."

Asa sighed and sat forward. "I'll think on it over breakfast."

Impatience bit at Evie's control. Elizabeth shook her head when she opened her mouth. Grabbing the coffeepot by its towel-wrapped handle, she topped off Evie's cup murmuring, "He'll teach you to shoot."

"How do you know?"

"Because he let you follow him out here. Asa never does anything without a purpose."

Asa looked up, catching Evie's gaze, laughter in the depths of his. "There was a time when people feared me."

Remembering her initial reaction to the assessment when he'd turned his attention on her, she shook her head. "They still do."

The laughter in Asa's gaze spread to his lips. "Good to know. When do you want to get started?"

She grabbed the bacon off her plate. She could eat it on the run. "Now would be good."

"Then now it is." His chair scraped across the wood floor. "I've got a little place set up where I'm teaching Gray."

THE LITTLE PLACE was about a half mile from the house, back in the woods. A series of stumps and rocks poked up in front of a grass-covered hill. Broken glass and cans littered the area around the stumps and rocks. Asa grabbed a few bottles and put them on the nearest stump. Then he walked back twenty feet waving her closer. "Come on up."

"Shouldn't I shoot from here? That's too close to be challenging."

He pushed his hat back. "Once you start hitting them from here, we'll back it up."

Though it seemed a waste of time to walk up there, take one shot, and then walk back, she could tell from the set of Asa's jaw that he wasn't budging from his plan.

"There's no way I can miss from here."

He took the gun from her. "It's always a mystery how that happens." He checked the chambers and shook his head. "You came all this way with the gun in your pocket like this?"

"It won't do me any good empty."

"It's not much good to you if it puts a hole in you accidentally either." Handing her the gun, he advised, "Always leave the first chamber empty. That way if the gun misfires you're still in one piece."

She swallowed, taking it gingerly. "They misfire?"

"All the time."

"I didn't know that."

"Now, you do." He adjusted her grip on the handle. "Now, this here's a nice little gun. A little big for a lady but it rarely misfires, loads easily, and doesn't have much of a kick." He looked at her. "The thing about revolvers is, they're not real accurate far away. You don't want to be taking potshots at people from over the ridge. The bullet's going to just fly off aimlessly somewhere in between, and you'll have given away your position. Not good."

She nodded. "Got it. Distance isn't good."

"Neither is giving away your position."

She nodded again because he seemed to expect it.

"Now let's go over some safety rules."

He went over them twice, making her repeat them before he was satisfied, then loaded and unloaded the gun properly. She thought she'd scream when he emptied the bullets out of the gun one last time.

"I understand the rules."

That earned her another shake of his head. "You're as bad as Gray, always wanting to cut to the chase with little regard to how you're going to get there."

"I just don't have much time."

"Elizabeth sent word."

"Brad won't care."

"Doesn't like you out of his sight, huh?"

"No." And she didn't him like being out of hers. Though she knew he was fine, that Jackson was watching the house, and Cougar and Clint were keeping him busy, she worried he'd insist on following her, reopen his wound, and generally undo all her hard work. "And if he gets too impatient, he could decide to fetch me back and undo all my hard work."

"And then you'll have to shoot him?"

There couldn't be a woman alive who was immune to Asa's smile when he turned on the charm. Even married, she felt its impact. "Probably." She took back the gun. "He's a lousy patient."

"All right then, show me how you load it and we'll get started."

She did.

"Remember to leave the first chamber empty."

"Even now?"

"Good habits can be learned just as well as bad."

"Good to know."

"There are a lot of things that are good to know."

She put the last bullet in the chamber. "Including the truth about my husband?"

It was a shot in the dark. Not by a flicker of an eyelash did Asa let on that it had hit its mark.

"The Rev's a good man. What do you need to know beyond that?"

She didn't know, but it was driving her crazy, thinking that she should. "I don't like surprises."

"Then take up your concerns with your husband."

Another dead end. "There's such a thing as too much loyalty."

"I'll keep it in mind."

No, he wouldn't. He was Brad's friend, not hers. It was good, but it was also frustrating.

"Now stand, hold the gun out, and lock your arms. If there's a stump or rock around, don't be too proud to use it as a brace to steady your aim. Sight down the barrel here and pull the trigger. There's going to be a—"

Squinting against the glare of the sun bouncing off the bottle on the right, Evie pulled the trigger. The only thing that kept the gun from kicking up in her face was Asa's hand.

His fingers clamped down on the gun. Behind her, she felt the sigh expand his chest. "Just like Gray, you've got no patience."

"I didn't know—"

"My point exactly. You didn't know, and the worse thing you can do when you don't know is rush in with assumptions."

"Are we still talking about guns?"

"Maybe." Again that deceptively lazy smile. "Now, next time wait until I finish giving the instructions."

At her nod, he continued, "As I was saying, keep your arms stiff. There's going to be some recoil and if you aren't prepared for it you could be eating the revolver and your next smile could have some gaps."

That was an image she could do without. "Thanks for the warning."

"Now, try it again. Aim for the bottle on the right."

She sighted down the barrel in the direction of the blurry bottle, locked her arms, and pulled the trigger. The recoil was manageable. There was a *ping* and the can went flying off.

"I hit it!"

"So you did." His tone was entirely too dry.

"What?"

"You were aiming at the bottle."

"True, but I hit the can."

She was inordinately glad to have hit something. Asa didn't seem to share her enthusiasm.

"And if it doesn't matter who you drop, friend or foe, I guess that will do."

"Spoilsport."

Between one blink and the next, his smile disappeared. "A gun's not a toy. You miss, and the wrong people can get killed."

He was right. "Let me try again."

She leveled the gun.

"Remember to—"

"Lock my arms," she finished for him. She fired and missed. This wasn't as easy as it seemed.

They practiced for an hour. She hit exactly one bottle at twenty feet. Ten at thirty feet. She was dead accurate at fifty.

Asa shook his head and pushed his hat back when she paused to reload. "I've never seen the like. Most people get worse the farther they get away."

After checking to make sure it was empty, she set the gun on the nearby rock, and shook out her hands. "I don't see well up close."

"Well, that explains a lot, including the portrait you did of the Rev."

No amount of will could bury her blush. It rose in a steady flood of heat. "When are you people going to forget about that portrait?"

"Not anytime soon, that's for sure."

Shoot. "Why not?"

"You might have been a bit loud this morning with your threats."

This morning . . . What had she said this morning? Oh dear heavens, she'd threatened to hang it off the front porch if Brad annoyed her anymore. "Oh heck."

"I would have used a stronger term, but that will do."

Now, everyone would be waiting for the day Brad annoyed her and they finally got to see the infamous painting. She didn't know whether to laugh or cry. "Couldn't you have done something?"

"I tried knocking, but you were on a tear."

Yes, she had been. Living in fear was not having a positive effect on her nerves. Looking at the gun, she would say it was even making her rebellious. "Then I guess we'll just have to live with it."

"I'm looking forward to it."

"Are we almost done?"

"There's just one more thing I want to show you." He took his revolver out of its holster and handed it to her. She grabbed it like he'd taught her. It was heavier than she'd expected, slipping out of her grasp, the chamber spinning a couple clicks. She made a grab for it with her other hand. Her finger brushed the trigger. It fired in a horrible explosion of sound. The recoil was ten times the impact of her little revolver. It flew back past her ears. She screamed and released it to its fate, covering her ears, waiting for the explosion of pain that said she'd blown off her toes.

Asa caught it with the lightning reflexes that made him a legend. She could only stare at him, shaking, feeling so weak she thought she was going to faint. Holstering the revolver, he caught her arm, steadying her, his gaze just as uncompromising. "Lesson number two: Like men, not all guns are the same. Don't assume if you know one you know them all."

Clearing her throat, she found her voice. "Neither are all women, and just so you understand the difference, I'm putting you on notice. If there's a lesson three, the town will have something new to gape at."

"Going to paint my picture?"

Picking up her gun, she met his mocking grin with one of her own. "Bigger than life, smack-dab on the side of the livery so all can see."

"Da—Darn, you fight dirty."

"You probably shouldn't forget it."

Seventeen

IT WAS ALMOST dark. The town was coming to life in a slow pulse the way it did every Monday night with wranglers straggling in off the trail. Not the usual time for a woman to go out alone, but Evie was only going out for a moment and she desperately needed the touch of normalcy after the last two weeks since Brad had regained consiousness. Staying holed up in that house with Brad kept her focused on the danger and if she didn't get just a minute of a normal routine, she would scream. She liked excitement, but worrying someone was going to bust down the door and start shooting was not the kind with which she did well. This trip to Millie's to let her know she'd be coming back for her lessons might be a small excursion, but she desperately needed it.

Ahead, a cowboy flew out the door of the saloon and landed in the dirt. Laughter trailed out behind him. He struggled to his hands and knees, reaching for his hat before pitching face forward in the filth. Piano music, smoke, and laughter continued to drift into the night, snaking in an ominous thread through the beautiful evening. Despite the weight of the pistol swinging from her wrist, the shadows took on a more sinister edge. She bit her lip. This might be a good time to cross the street, something she'd been delaying doing because of all the unsavory deposits that blended with the clumps of dirt. Deposits made by horses, pigs, cattle, and men. Deposits she couldn't see in the twilight without her spectacles. Another glance at the saloon convinced her she didn't really have a choice. With a near miss a time or two, she made it to the opposite side with clean shoes.

By the time she came even with the alley below the saloon, the cowboy hadn't moved, but others—his friends she hoped—came stumbling out of the saloon. Another dirty wrangler with too much to drink knelt in the dirt beside him. He poked his friend. She didn't think he was going to have much luck getting him to move. The man was clearly unconscious.

A board creaked under her foot. The friend glanced up and gave her a lopsided smile. "Hi, pretty lady, why don't you come join us?"

In the middle of the dirt and refuse? She shuddered and turned her face away. It didn't stop his comments from following. How in heaven's name could Nidia's ladies bear to entertain men like that, night after night?

A glance over her shoulder revealed he wasn't following. That was a relief. Still, she'd feel a lot safer once she got past the alley on the opposite side of the saloon. Movement in the shadows to the right caught her eye. It only took a second to make out who it was. Gray, and he was watching the wrangler. Obviously he'd been prepared to intercede if necessary. She shook her head. The boy took too many chances for his age, took on too many responsibilities. His gaze, when it met hers, was stern—shades of his father and his uncle. She sighed. Shades of the man he would one day be.

She ignored the implied order to go home and hurried on. The streets at night really weren't safe for a woman alone. It wasn't any more safe for Gray. Looking over her shoulder again, she expected to see Gray heading toward his horse and his own home. Instead, he ducked into the dark alley she'd just passed, carrying something wrapped in linen. An eleven-year-old boy should be nowhere near an alley beside a saloon at any time, no matter how much he thought he could take care of himself. Casting a longing glance down the street toward the warm glow of lights from the homes comprising the better end of town, she sighed and turned back to the harsh reality of Cattle Crossing in full celebration. She couldn't leave Gray alone to do whatever he was doing. She'd never be able to face Jenna if anything happened to the boy.

This time when she crossed the street she wasn't as lucky as before. A squish and a foul odor alerted her to the fact that what she'd thought was the up end of a rut in the street was actually a pile of horse dung. *Ugh!* She scuffed her shoe along the dirt, watching the alley in case Gray came out. That boy officially owed her now. If not the cost of new shoes, at least a bit more caution in his behavior.

The alley was little more than a narrow slit between the saloon and the undertaker's next door. The juxtaposition of the two buildings had always amused her; now it just seemed particularly ominous. The stench of urine and chemicals mixed to form a noxious odor. She put her forearm against her nose. Ahead she could see Gray standing with his back to her. There was an unnatural stillness about him that alerted her to the fact that he wasn't alone. Ducking back into the shadows, she watched.

"You shouldn't be out here."

"It's quiet here."

Only if *quiet* was a relative term, Evie thought.

"It's not safe."

"It's as safe as anywhere else. Besides, I knew you were coming."

The voice was female and very young. Maybe the girl Gray had been talking to before?

"No, you didn't."

There was the sound of a huge sigh. "You always come."

"So?" That belligerent response sounded like an eleven-year-old boy.

"So I knew you would come tonight, too."

"I won't come tomorrow."

"Oh."

It was a very disappointed "oh." Even Evie felt for her, and she didn't even know the girl. "It's probably good. My mother's new friend gets angry when I talk to other people."

Gray seemed to tense. "Brenna, what did you do?"

"I haven't done anything."

"Well, don't. You're just a little girl."

Around Gray's side, Evie could make out the jut of an elbow at about midthigh. A very skinny elbow that had to be attached to a small child. It wasn't hard to imagine a little girl with her hands on her hips, glaring at Gray. Eventually Gray drove everyone to glare at him. He knew too much for a boy his age and tended to deliver that knowledge with an arrogance that grated.

"I'm not just anything."

"Are you just a little hungry?"

"Oh yes."

"Good. I brought you some supper."

"Biscuits?" It was a very hopeful question.

"Yeah, but I can't bring you biscuits tomorrow. Jenna will get suspicious if I keep asking for them."

"No, she won't. She'll just be happy that you give her something to do for you. She loves you."

"Uh-huh. She loves everybody."

"She doesn't love me."

Evie got her first glimpse of the little girl as she hopped up on top of a crate. It was more of a shadow than a real view, but it was enough to determine she was even more slender and small than Evie had imagined. It was easy to see why Gray felt protective of her. Evie didn't even know her, and she felt protective.

"She would if she met you." Gray handed her the packet. She shook her head as she opened it, her pigtails flopping around her face, glints of red catching the faint light from the upstairs windows.

"That wouldn't be safe. My father doesn't like people to love me." Holding up the small pile of food, she asked, "Do you want some?"

"You eat it. You need it more."

She sighed. "You think I'm too skinny."

"I think you need someone to take better care of you."

"When you're older, you can."

"If I were older, they wouldn't let me."

Brenna paused, the biscuit halfway to her mouth. "Why not?"

"Because you're white."

"That's silly."

With a sigh of his own, Gray motioned with his hand. "Just eat."

She took a bite. "Ouch."

Gray immediately stepped forward. "What's wrong?"

"Nothing important."

"Don't lie to me."

"I never lie."

Evie lost sight of the girl as Gray stepped between them. "You have a bruise."

"Just a little one. It's not important."

The single-minded intensity was back in Gray's voice. "Who hit you?"

"I told you he gets mean."

"Your mother's friend?"

She shrugged. "I talk too much. It hurts his head."

Gray's hand went to the hilt of the big knife Cougar had given him over Jenna's objections. "You do not talk too much."

There was a cold flatness to the statement that sent a shiver down Evie's spine. He sounded just as Cougar had when he'd said he was going hunting for Brad's attackers. It had sounded natural on Cougar. The scary thing was it sounded equally natural on Gray.

"I'm fine, Gray. You don't need to be mad."

He tipped her small face up. From here, Evie couldn't see any sign of a bruise, but the touch of Gray's thumb to the little girl's cheek was eloquent. "The bastard."

"You're not supposed to use words like that around me."

Gray dropped his hand. "I'm sorry."

Evie smiled at the reprimand and Gray's response. Whomever the precocious little girl was, she was special to Gray.

Brenna patted the crate beside her as she took a bite of the biscuit. "You can sit with me."

Gray looked around. Evie hugged the wall so he wouldn't see her. "I'd better not."

Brenna's feet stopped swinging and the hand holding the biscuit dropped into her lap. "Oh."

"Oh what?"

"You think I'm ugly, too."

Evie couldn't prevent her gasp. Fortunately, Gray's curse covered the betraying sound.

"That was a very bad word," Brenna reproached, not looking at him.

"Sorry." He sat beside her. "Who told you that you were ugly?"

"The other kids, when they wouldn't let me play." Kicking her foot Brenna muttered almost too low for Evie to hear. "They called me an 'ugly, freckled whore's get.' "

The brats! The light was getting dimmer. Evie had to strain to see, but it looked as though Gray put his arm around his friend's shoulders.

"I like your freckles."

"I tried to get rid of them, but they won't come off."

Evie's heart clenched in her chest. Brenna couldn't be more than five or six. Too young to be called such names, too young to have to feel the pain of being ostracized.

"Don't try anymore."

"But if I didn't have freckles, kids wouldn't think I was ugly and they'd play with me."

For an awful moment, Evie thought Gray was going to explain the real reason the other kids wouldn't play with her. When he didn't, she breathed a sigh of relief.

"What are those creatures your God sends down to help people?" he asked.

Brenna took another bite of biscuit and thought on it. "You mean angels?"

"Yeah. Angels. I think of your freckles like the kisses of angels over your face."

The tattoo of the little girl's shoes against the crate took up a happier beat. "That's pretty."

"So are you."

Brenna and Gray fell silent. The muted sounds of merriment from the saloon underscored the rap of Brenna's heels. The two children sat in companionable silence as Brenna finished the last of her meal, wiping her mouth with the napkin. Sometime in the child's life someone had instilled manners.

Folding the napkin, she handed it back to Gray. "I suppose you have to go now."

Gray nodded. "It would be bad for you if someone saw me here."

"Because your skin isn't white?"

"Yeah."

"I don't care." Her small hand covered his, pale and tiny, barely visible in the dim light, emphasizing the difference between them even as it communicated the similarities, the bond. "I think you're beautiful, too."

"Oh, darn." The exclamation just popped out. Gray's head whipped in Evie's direction. She didn't know if he saw her. The saloon door opened. Light spilled into the alley as someone came out, capturing Gray with his arm around Brenna for whomever stood in the doorway to see.

"What in hell is going on here?"

Gray leapt to his feet. Brenna shrieked. Evie was frozen in place as a big bear of a man stepped into the tiny alley. Bull. And from the way he slurred the word *hell*, he was inebriated.

"Get away from that Indian, girl."

Gray grabbed Brenna and shoved her behind him, standing tall in a foolish display of courage, because the man was easily a foot taller and over a hundred pounds heavier.

"Don't you touch him," Brenna screamed, trying to get around Gray.

"I'll do more than touch him." Bull cracked his knuckles.

"Stay behind me!" Gray ordered, blocking her jump forward with his arm.

"No! He'll hurt you."

"Damn straight I'm going to hurt him. He's got no right even looking at a white girl, let alone touching her."

"And you have no right to touch her," Gray snarled back.

Bull smiled. "I've got a hell of a lot more right than you."

It was such an evil smile. Evie dug in her reticule for the gun as Gray's deadly quiet "No longer" reached her in a chilling prelude to violence. The bullets clanked against the metal. She snagged two. Damn Asa and his lessons. If he hadn't scared her so, the gun would be loaded and she wouldn't be fumbling in the dark.

In the split second it took to get the gun clear of the reticule, Brenna darted around Gray, kicking at Bull's legs for all she was worth. Bull grabbed her, yanked her off her feet, and tossed her behind him. She went flying through the air like a doll, mouth open in a silent cry. Her scream broke as her head hit the wood. She crumpled to the ground. Gray lunged with a snarl, his knife flashing in a lethal arc. Evie held her breath, fearing the worst. What if he killed him? What if he didn't?

Even inebriated, Bull was more than a match for the boy and knocked his arm aside. Instead of a lethal blow, the blade carved a path through Bull's thigh with a nauseating, whispering swish.

Bull should have gone down. It didn't make sense that he didn't, but he stood, blood gushing from his thigh, and knocked Gray aside with the same devastating strength with which he'd tossed Brenna. The boy hit the ground hard and then rolled, springing to his feet, his long black hair flying about his face, the bloody knife clenched in his hand, his lips drawn back from his teeth. The word he spat when he saw Bull crouched in an equally aggressive posture between him and Brenna needed no translation.

Dear God, Evie had to do something and she had to do it

now. Throwing the reticule and bullets to the side she hurried forward, empty gun brandished as if she meant business. Which she did.

Brenna moaned and sat up. Bull took a step back. Gray took two forward.

"Get away from her."

Bull wiped the blood from his hand on his shirt. "Not killing me was a mistake, injun."

"One I will not make again."

Brenna stood. Her face, with its multitude of freckles and big green eyes, was starkly pale and strangely expressionless as she swayed. "I'll go in now, Mr. Braeger."

"You will come to me, Brenna."

The little girl took one small step and then another, away from Gray. The acceptance in her voice hurt Evie's heart. "He'll hurt you, and I'll have to go anyway."

"You've got that right."

Gray's response was another of those words she didn't need an interpreter to understand, but he didn't look away from Brenna. "I will keep you safe."

Her next step was smaller than the previous two, but it still took her a bit farther from Gray. "You promise?"

"Yes."

It was a big promise for a boy to make, but Evie didn't doubt he meant it, just as she knew he was going to need help keeping it.

With a small cry, Brenna ran for him. He caught her hand. Bull caught the other. Neither let go, leaving the child stretched between them.

"Get back here, brat."

"Leave her alone," Evie ordered.

As if she wasn't standing there with a gun leveled at his heart, Bull ignored her. It wasn't a surprise. Never a big thinker, Bull lost all sense when his temper ignited. Evie took another step forward, angling in so she was between Bull and the children. "You are a very rude man, Bull Braeger."

"Fuck you."

"With a very filthy mouth."

Gray lunged forward as Bull yanked on Brenna, riding the momentum like a game of whiplash, stabbing downward when he drew even with Bull, laughing when the man hollered and let go, blood gushing from his arm this time. Scooping up Brenna, Gray ran toward Evie.

"Where did you come from?" he gasped as he ducked behind her.

She kept her eyes on Bull. "I was curious as to what you were up to."

"Uh-huh." He reached for the gun. "The Reverend won't be happy."

She jerked the revolver out of his reach. "If you don't tell him, he'll never know."

"He'll know." That long-suffering truth came from Brenna. "They always know when you're bad."

It was very hard to imagine the sweet-looking child who reminded her of a fairy as bad. "Well, we can at least try." She turned back to Bull. "Don't move another step."

His fleshy face florid, his eyes narrowed as beads of sweat dripped down from his hairline, he reminded Evie more of a pig than a bull.

"Then pull the trigger."

She would have pulled the trigger long before now if there were bullets in the gun. "Don't push me."

"Shoot!" Gray ordered.

"Shut up," she hissed at him. "You take one more step, Bull, and I swear, I'll pull this trigger."

The threat didn't have the desired effect. Bull just tossed her a mocking smile. "The Reverend's little wife threatening to commit murder?"

"Yes."

"Aren't you afraid of burning in hell?"

"I'm more afraid of you right now." That was the truth.

"You oughta be."

With a blink, she realized Bull had a revolver of his own, bigger than hers, and it was pointed right at her chest. When had Bull pulled the gun? The round opening in the muzzle seemed cannon sized, and getting bigger every second that she stared at it.

He took one step, two, a sneer twisting his features when the shaking inside spread to her hands. The pistol wobbled. Gray swore again in some language she didn't understand and yanked the gun from her hand, knocking her aside.

"No!"

He pulled the trigger. The hammer clinked uselessly. Bull's laughter froze, and then when he realized what had happened, he sneered. "Ought to make sure your weapon's loaded, boy."

Gray didn't move as Bull leveled his own weapon, just stood where he was, drawing the fire to himself, Evie realized. Inside a scream built. Brad's name. Dear God. They needed help.

The saloon door opened again. A much smaller figure stepped into the alley. Nidia's gaze narrowed as she took in the scene and then her expression dissolved into a sultry pout and she gingerly stepped into the alley.

"*Querido*, what do you do out here in this smelly place?"

Evie didn't know whether to laugh or cry as the madam sashayed forward, her full hips swinging, her red lips pursed in a pout. "I wait inside for you, I turn many men away, and still I sit alone until others laugh and say I cannot hold my man."

"I'll be back inside shortly."

Nidia's dark eyes darted between the gun, the children, and Evie. Disdain flickered across her beautiful, sensual face before she slid her small hands around Bull's beefy forearm. The one holding the gun. "You need to come in now."

"I said, get your ass back inside."

Nidia leaned her full breasts against his arm. "Surely this silly woman and these children do not hold any appeal for a man such as you?"

The move caused her breasts to billow so far out of their confines, Evie wanted to slap her hands over Gray's eyes.

"Gray, come here."

He ignored her order, watching Bull and Nidia carefully, still using his body as a shield. Gray would be quite a man someday, but right now he was a child and he needed protection. This time, when she reached for him, she didn't take no for an answer, just grabbed his arm and yanked with all her might. "Get back now."

"He is drunk."

"And I'm annoyed, which probably puts us on equal footing for doing something stupid. That being the case, there's no reason for you to be hogging all the glory for yourself. Now, get back."

He hesitated. Lowering her voice, Evie whispered, "If push comes to shove and we need to move fast, I'm not strong enough to carry Brenna."

His gaze flicked to Brenna who was standing, fists clenched at her sides, tears pouring down her pale face. With a sharp nod of his head, which caused his long hair to slide over his shoulders, he stepped back, putting his arm around Brenna's waist. One problem down, one more to go.

Bull was staring down into the depths of the cleavage Nidia so predominantly displayed.

Please God, let him want that more.

"I'm going to take the children home now," she said with more bluster than true courage. "I'm sorry for the inconvenience."

Bull jerked upright. "The boy stays. He and I have something to settle."

Nidia pouted harder. "*Querido* . . ."

Bull shook her off. "Shut up, whore."

Nidia shut up. Evie didn't have that luxury. She brushed her hands brusquely down her skirt, backing into Gray and Brenna, pushing them back with every step.

"If you feel there's a debt owed, you can take it up with Gray's father. I'm sure Clint would be more than happy to discuss the issue with you."

"I do not need my father to fight my battles."

"Oh for heaven's sake," she snapped over her shoulder. "Be quiet."

"Listen to your momma, little boy."

Gray predictably bristled. "She is not my mother."

Before Bull could retort, Evie stepped in. "I'm as close as you've got right now, and I say you need to be more respectful to the adults around you."

"You've got that right."

Nidia huffed. "I grow weary of this arguing with children."

The way Nidia rubbed her ample bosom against Bull's arm and side was so blatantly erotic that Evie couldn't look away or prevent her blush. Bull apparently wasn't immune either, because he reached over and pinched the plump flesh. "You just hold on to your horses, woman, and I'll be right with you."

Nidia stomped her foot. "I have waited long enough!"

Bull snarled. "The boy cut me."

She tossed her head, sending her curls tumbling about her face, and trailed her nail down his chest. "What is a little blood to a stallion like you?"

"It's the principle."

Oh good grief! Spreading her arms wide, shielding Gray and Brenna the best she could, Evie scoffed, "You are not seriously saying that you worry that not killing a child will ruin your reputation?"

Nidia snorted. "Of course he does not say something so silly, woman. Bull is a powerful man. If he lets the obnoxious child live, it is only because he is also a generous man." Walking her fingers up his chest, brushing them over his lips, she breathed, "Especially with the woman who shares his bed, eh, my stallion?"

Evie had to suppress the urge to vomit. Bull, however, seemed to be succumbing to the distraction. The muzzle wavered as he leaned down and kissed Nidia's pouting mouth. That being the case, she played her last card.

"I'm sure Clint would be more than happy to compensate you for your injury, Mr. Braeger. The McKinnelys are very honorable."

They were also viciously protective when it came to their own. Tonight would not be the end of this.

"It would be wise to have the McKinnelys in your debt," Nidia added, curving her hand around Bull's beefy neck.

The gun lowered.

Nidia snuggled against his chest. The back of her gown plunged all the way to her waist. Bull slipped the muzzle of the gun between the dress and her skin, pressing it downward. Evie could only stare as Nidia at first flinched and then relaxed, as if having a loaded gun so intimately pressed against her was a normal thing.

"Are we all done here, *mi amado*? Can we get to what's really important tonight?"

"Yeah. We're done." Bull yanked her close with the hand holding the gun. The sound Nidia made was not one of pleasure. "You tell McKinnely he owes me."

"I'll tell him." She'd tell him all of it.

Behind her, Gray made a sound that resembled a growl. After just getting the situation settled down, she did not need him starting it up again. Glaring a warning at him over her shoulder, she snapped, "The other thing I'll tell Mr. McKinnely is that the boy needs a trip to the woodshed."

"More than one if you ask me."

She hadn't asked Bull.

"He lacks respect for his betters," Nidia added.

He lacked common sense. "I'll pass that along, too."

"Good."

She took a full breath when Bull picked Nidia up in a bear hug. "Now, honey, let's you and me head on upstairs and see about getting to that important stuff."

"This I look forward to."

To Evie's ear, Nidia's voice sounded strained, maybe from the bear hug, maybe from something more. Though she kept telling herself that Nidia was a prostitute and one of the more notorious ones at that, Evie couldn't imagine that she looked forward to the evening.

The door shut behind the unlikely couple, plunging the alley into darkness.

Brenna's voice came, small and weak, out of the gloom. "Gray?"

"I'm right here."

"You can't do that again."

"You took the words from my mouth," Evie interjected, knees almost buckling with relief.

"There won't be any need. You won't be going back there."

No, she wouldn't. Evie was in agreement with that. She ushered them toward the street by way of the slivers of light pouring out between the rough slats of the saloon. "We'll take her to her mother."

Gray rolled his eyes toward the saloon. "Her mother is working."

"Her mother's a—"

"Working," Gray finished for her.

"No, she's not," Brenna interjected in a wispy voice. "She said her face hurt too much."

Evie exchanged a glance with Gray. He shrugged. Evie sighed. She would never understand why women chose prostitution for a livelihood.

"Well, then we'll take you to where she is," Evie said brightly.

"The door's locked."

"Your momma will unlock it for you."

Brenna shook her head. Her shadow swayed. "She doesn't have the key."

Which meant Brenna's mom was trapped on the wrong side of the lock. Dear God. This was more than she was equipped to handle.

"Well then, we'll find another place for you to stay tonight."

The little girl stumbled and moved closer to Gray. "I don't feel good."

Gray caught her before she could fall. Her head lolled lifelessly over his arm. Evie remembered her tiny body flying through the air and hitting the wall, the way she'd lain so still. "We've got to get her to Doc."

"He's having dinner at my house."

Clint and Jenna lived a mile out of town. Evie spun on her heel and headed for home. "Then we need to get him here."

Eighteen

THE STREETS WERE dark. Light from homes and businesses flowed onto the sidewalks, forming a checkered path to follow. Evie hid the now loaded gun in the folds of her skirt. Beside her, Gray carried Brenna, his moccasined feet making no noise despite the girl's weight, leaving only Evie's footsteps to mark their passing. A few men glanced their way. A couple strolling home cast them a look, but no one approached. A block from the house, Evie saw a familiar silhouette striding toward them.

"The Reverend comes," Gray observed.

"Well, shoot." She'd been hoping to get home and send for Doc before having to explain.

"What will you tell him?"

That it was too soon for him to be doing as much as he was. "That we went out for a stroll."

"He won't believe you."

"He won't care." Because no matter what excuse she gave him, it wasn't going to cut it with him.

Gray shook his head. "The Reverend is a very possessive man. Of his town, his people." He cast her a wry glance. "His wife."

The thrill that went through her was totally unwarranted. Women were not possessions, but watching Brad approach, shoulders back, those long legs of his eating up the distance with masculine grace and aggression, knowing that only she had the right to touch him, it didn't seem to matter. He was hers. She was his, and it was good to know.

She went to smooth her hair and remembered the gun. Darn it. She was afraid to put it into her pocket loaded, for fear it would misfire. Afraid to hold it, for dread of having to explain. Gritting her teeth she chose the lesser of two evils. Though she managed to wedge the gun in her pocket, she couldn't get her hand back out.

Wonderful. She only had time for three tugs before Brad got close enough that she had to stop trying. "Hi."

Beneath the angled brim of his hat, his gaze cut between Gray and her. "What the hell happened?"

"Gray and I ran into a little trouble."

"That I already guessed. Who's the girl?"

"A friend," Gray, standing in the fringe of shadow, answered, a clear challenge in his words.

Beyond the cock of an eyebrow in the boy's direction, Brad didn't take his gaze off her. His hand came around her waist as natural as breathing, whether out of anger or possessiveness she couldn't tell. Her body didn't care. Her heart did its usual funny hop at his presence and that sense of safety and comfort rolled over her.

"I think her mother works at the Emporium," Evie explained.

"Is she hurt?"

Evie nodded, halting the progression of his hand to her hip—where the gun lay tucked—with a press of her elbow.

"I'm assuming Doc's not in his office since you're not heading that way?"

"He's having dinner at my house," Gray offered.

"Did you come in on that wild horse of yours?"

Gray nodded in the direction they were headed. "Freedom is hitched at the livery."

Sliding his arm free, Brad reached for the girl. "Then give the child to me and ride out and get Doc."

Gray hesitated. Evie suspected why, and it wasn't because Brad had been so recently injured. The boy had a hard time trusting and the girl was important to him.

As if he understood, Brad's voice softened. "I'll keep her safe."

That low-pitched assurance didn't have the desired effect on Gray. Instead of handing Brenna over, he seemed to melt back into the shadows, the darkness welcoming him too easily. Evie had the strangest urge to grab him and pull him forward. To hug him.

"She can be foolish."

Brad just held out his hands. "So can my wife, and she's no worse for wear."

Gray stood there, indecision and responsibility warring for dominance, finally looking like the eleven-year-old he was.

"She needs help, Gray," Evie whispered, hoping to tip the scales.

Finally, with a nod, he handed over Brenna, his hand falling to the knife at his hip. "Know I will kill you if you hurt her."

Instead of laughing, Brad nodded. "Fair enough. Now ride and get Doc."

After a brief hesitation and a glance at Brenna, Gray sprinted past them toward the livery.

Brad watched him go. "The boy can run."

"Yes he can." Evie adjusted the little girl's ragged skirts over her calves. "It was nice of you not to laugh."

"At what?"

"His threat."

Moving the little girl up onto his shoulder, Brad cut her a look. "There wasn't anything to laugh at. The kid meant it."

"He's only eleven."

"A very wild, deadly eleven. I have no doubt, if I should hurt this child, Gray would find a way to end my life."

Evie remembered how Gray had battled Bull, especially the last maneuver in which he'd freed Brenna. And then she remembered how he had been with her, those moments of wisdom interrupted with moments of youth. "He's still a child."

"I know." Brad started walking. "And he's got a sense of honor bone deep, but that doesn't mitigate his skills."

She huffed. "He has skills, but me you call *foolish*."

"What do you call leaving the house without an escort?"

"Fortuitous, considering what I walked into."

She sensed that he was looking at her, but as they'd stepped out of the light she couldn't tell. "And what exactly was that?"

"It was kind of sweet, actually."

"Evie . . ."

She ignored the warning. "Gray was bringing little Brenna food. I think he watches out for her."

Brad grunted and hitched the dead weight of the little girl higher in his arms. "And how did you get involved?"

"I was curious as to what Gray was up to."

"You left the house to check on Gray?"

"No. I left the house to let Millie know I was coming back to finish my lessons."

"Hey, I thought this morning's eggs were almost recognizable."

She sighed. "I'm getting tired of 'almost.' Not to mention hungry for good food."

"The same way you're tired of being in the house?"

Surprised, she looked up to find him studying her. "How'd you know?"

"Your smiles have been absent."

They stepped into another patch of light. "I like the sunshine."

His fingers slid down her arm, curled around her wrist, touched the butt of the revolver.

Guilt made her jump. "What are you doing?"

The hat hid his expression, but she didn't need to see his face to know he was watching her with his eyebrow cocked and an expectation of answers. "I was going to hold your hand."

"Oh."

Brenna slipped to the side. He let go to shift her back up. "Why the gun?"

"You told me to keep it with me."

"I don't recall telling you to keep it loaded and in your pocket."

She decided not to tell him it wasn't loaded. "I improvised."

Another glance at the unconscious Brenna.

"I don't believe you."

"Well, why not? It was a good evasion."

He shook his head, a smile tugging his lips, pretty much against his will, she was sure. "I know when you're upset, Evie."

That was going to complicate things in the future. "I was heading over to Millie's when I got sidetracked by Gray ducking into the alley by the saloon."

"That distracted you?"

"Eleven-year-old boys have no business hanging around the alley of a saloon."

This time he did smile. "I've got news for you, darling, there's nothing more exciting to an eleven-year-old boy than a saloon."

"I take it you're an authority on the subject?"

"I did my share of doorjamb peeking."

"Is that where you learned all your tricks?"

"Between the sheets you mean?"

"Brad!" She glanced pointedly at the child.

"Can't say that wasn't a good beginning. It definitely whetted my appetite for more in-depth exploration."

She had to skip to keep up with his long strides. "It's so hard to think of you as a preacher."

"When it comes to me, sweetheart, you ought to just think of me as a man first."

Truth be told, she had a hard time thinking of him as anything else. "And forget your position in the community?"

He cocked an eyebrow at her. "Would that make you wilder?"

She could feel the blush creeping over her cheeks. "I don't think it's possible."

His hat brim shaded his eyes. That short-brimmed black hat, that on any other man would look respectable, just enhanced Brad's overt sexuality. "Now that, I'm going to take as a challenge."

She tried to look upset. "Are you trying to shock me?"

"Excitement was more my aim."

She licked her lips, and plunged forward. "Well, you're succeeding."

Her honesty got that half grin that so tickled her sense of adventure. "Dangerous territory, Evie darling, tempting a man after you've been holding him off for two weeks."

"You were injured!"

"Doesn't mean I wasn't hungry." They reached their house. He stopped her with a hand on her skirt as she got her foot on the first stair. Her eyes were level with the mischief and heat in his. The combination poured over her desire like a living flame. "Doesn't mean I'm not fair to starving now."

"I'm hungry, too," a little voice added.

Brenna was awake.

"Are you now, darling?" Brad asked in that low drawl he used with all women. With the child, it didn't hold the seductive undertones she noticed he used with women, but that didn't reduce its mesmerizing effect on Brenna. She stared up at Brad with the same rapt fascination of all females. Still trapped under his spell, she nodded.

"Then, as soon as we get Doc to check out why you took such a long nap, we'll see about filling up that tummy."

"I want biscuits."

"You'll need something else, too."

"I like biscuits," she informed him in a tone that clearly said she could like him, too, if he brought her biscuits.

Brad chuckled and climbed the steps. "Is that a fact?"

Brenna nodded. "They're my favorites in the whole world."

"Better than apple pie?"

"I've never had that."

"Apple pie is very good."

"Better than sugar cookies?" Evie asked as she held open the front door.

Brenna perked at the word *cookies*. Brad gave Evie an amused look. "Hey, no fair siccing her on my sugar cookies."

"You like sugar cookies?" Brenna asked.

"Almost as much as I like my wife."

The glance Brenna sent her questioned Evie's worth compared to a sugar cookie, but obviously a trend of loving all things Brad was starting, because she nodded. "I'll like them, too. Do you like sugar cookies?" the little girl asked Evie.

Evie wished she could be as open as Brad. "Not as much as my husband does."

Brad shook his head as he passed by. "You are a hard woman, Evie Swanson."

Was she? Evie didn't want to think so, but it wasn't as easy for her to be as affectionate as Brad, so maybe she was. Maybe she'd spent so many years fighting that she didn't know how to stop. Maybe she was as hard and crusty as a hermit.

"I don't mean to be."

Brad straightened, eyeing her with an expression she couldn't interpret. Had she said the wrong thing? "Now that will be an interesting topic of conversation for later."

Meaning they didn't have time for it, but now that she'd brought the subject up, she found she was itching to discuss it. So much so that she felt as if she was coming out of her skin. "I'll look forward to it."

That got her another strange glance from Brad, and another complaint from Brenna. "I'm hungry."

"I can't get you something to eat until Doc clears you."

Her face crumpled. "But I'm hungry now!"

For the first time, Evie saw Brad look helpless. It was both endearing and disturbing. She'd rather enjoyed thinking of him as invulnerable. Reaching over, she grabbed her sketchbook off the table by the couch. "Maybe we can have some fun to take your mind off your empty stomach."

"What kind of fun?"

"I thought maybe I'd draw a picture of you to take to your momma."

Her lips trembled. "They locked her up."

Evie started sketching. "I know, but the Reverend will get her out."

"He will?

"I will?"

She didn't look up from her drawing, working fast, adding detail to the bolder outline. "Yes, he will."

Brenna's lips kept trembling. That wasn't the expression Evie wanted to capture. Evie worked on the girl's hair, wishing she had paints to capture the vibrant red.

"Bull is very mean and very big," Brenna said.

"The Reverend has God on his side. There's no one bigger and meaner."

Brenna didn't look convinced.

Brad grunted and sat on the arm of Evie's chair. "How about I call the McKinnelys to come with me?"

"Gray, too?"

Obviously, the child thought the boy could walk on water. "I was thinking I'd assign him to guard you."

That got a smile. A big one, complete with a missing tooth. Evie sketched like a mad woman, wanting to catch the essence of the child for her mother. Brenna's mother might be a prostitute, but she'd taken a lot of care with her daughter, teaching her manners and diction. Enough so that it was clear she truly loved her. Any mother who could instill manners under those circumstances deserved to see her daughter shine. And Brenna did shine when she grinned. Her rather ordinary features took on a gamine charm when she smiled, giving a glimpse of the woman she was going to be. An unconventional beauty, but a beauty for sure.

"Are you almost done?"

"Almost."

"Will my momma like it?"

"Your momma will smile for sure when she sees it."

Adding a last bit of shading, Evie studied the work. "Not bad."

Brad took the pad from her.

"Hey."

She couldn't believe how long the seconds stretched before he offered his opinion. "Better than not bad. I'd say it's perfect." He turned the pad around. "What do you think?"

Brenna didn't say anything for the longest time. She reached out and touched the portrait. "Is that really how I look?"

It was moments like this when Evie loved her talent. "I only draw what I see."

"And I look like that?"

It was Brad who answered. "Exactly like that."

Brenna pulled her free hand back and tucked it against her stomach. "Not an ugly, freckled whore's get?"

Brad stilled. The glance he cut Evie contained a question.

"Some children were teasing Brenna about her freckles," Evie offered.

"Those must have been some very jealous children."

Brenna's chin came up defensively, as if she heard the undertone and suspected the cause had to do with her. "Gray thinks I'm beautiful."

Brad removed the page from the pad and handed it to Brenna, his voice too soft, his moves too controlled.

"Gray has excellent taste."

THE MCKINNELYS ARRIVED with a flourish. Two buggies and three horses pulled up to the house, making enough noise to wake the dead. Brad opened the door. Jenna rushed past, carrying little Bri. Dorothy and Doc were not far behind.

"Where is she?" Doc snapped, all business.

"She's upstairs with Evie."

"She's awake?"

"And hungry."

"That's a good sign, right?" Jenna asked, gripping the railing at the bottom of the stairs.

"I'd say so."

Doc couldn't get past. "Jenna, you need to move."

She looked over Doc's head to where Clint was coming in the door. With her chin she motioned to Bri.

"I need help up the stairs."

"Why didn't you say so?" Brad took a step forward.

Clint shouldered past. "Because she knows I'd have trouble with a good-looking bastard such as yourself getting near her."

"Clint!"

"What?" Clint grumbled, slipping his arm around Jenna's waist. "It's the truth."

Doc shooed them with rapid motions of his hands. "I have a patient waiting."

"No one's keeping you from her," Brad argued.

"Jenna is."

Jenna's square chin set in a stubborn line. "I promised Gray I'd be there."

"What does the boy think I'm going to do to her?" Doc growled in his gravelly voice.

"Nothing. I just promised."

Cougar came through the door carrying Mara. Shit. More trouble.

"Doc!"

Doc didn't bother looking over his shoulder. "Cougar still being a fool?"

"He's carrying Mara."

"Call me when he stops being a fool."

Brad turned. On closer inspection, Mara looked more furious than sick. "Exactly how foolish are you being?"

Cougar headed for the parlor. "She's carrying my baby."

"So you have to carry her?"

Mara, arms folded over her chest, glared at Cougar before blowing her bangs off her forehead.

"To him, it makes sense."

"I'm not losing you."

"But you're not worried about driving me away?"

He set her on the horsehair sofa with infinite care, before squatting before her. "If you run, you know I'll come after you."

"For all the good it will do you."

He sat back on his heels. "You planning on hiding?"

"You're making it sound awfully good. At least until the baby's born."

He frowned. "You're not having that baby without me."

Mara frowned right back. "Keep it up, and just watch me."

"Goddamn it, Mara."

Mara ignored him and asked Brad, "How is Gray's friend?"

"Hungry for biscuits."

"Do you have any?" Dorothy asked.

"No." Why did he feel he was remiss?

"Then I'd better get on making some," Dorothy offered with her usual cheer.

"I'll help," Mara chimed in, scooting out from under Cougar's arm. Cougar caught her when she would have skipped past. "Walk."

When she spun around and glared at him, he used her momentum to pull her into his arms. The kiss he pressed on her lips was hard and fraught with the emotion simmering under the surface. His "I worry" was gruff.

Mara melted like butter. Patting his chest, she stepped back. "I know, but you have to stop."

"Coming?" Dorothy asked.

"Yes."

Cougar watched her go.

"She's right, you know," Brad said.

"What the hell do you know about it?"

"Enough to know when someone's had enough."

"Worry about your own wife."

He did, every day. This was getting very ugly, very fast, and he was living on borrowed time. "I've got her under control."

Cougar snorted. "That why she's spending her evenings facing down Bull in the saloon alley with nothing more than bravado and an empty gun?"

Shit. The gun wasn't loaded? He and Evie were definitely going to have to talk. "She knew what she was doing."

"Sounds to me like she was winging it."

"Something for which I'm grateful," Clint interjected, coming down the stairs. "From the parts Gray glossed over, he had himself in way over his head."

"You need to get that boy under control."

"He's touchy about things he cares about."

Brad ran his hand through his hair. "And he cares about Brenna?"

"Enough to knife Bull."

First Casey coming back, and now Bull bent on revenge. Life was complicating fast. "Bull will be out for his blood."

"I'll handle it."

"Not alone, you won't," Brad muttered.

"Cougar and I can handle it."

"The bastard pulled a gun on my wife. Threatened her."

"I've never dragged a preacher to a hanging before."

"Just think of it as saving time. Brenna is Brenda's daughter."

It only took Cougar a second to put the picture together. "That would make Casey—"

"Brenna's father," Brad finished for him.

"Why didn't she recognize you?" Cougar asked.

"She was tiny last time I saw her."

"At least that's one bit of luck." Clint ran his fingers through his long hair. "You do like to complicate things, don't you?"

Apparently to the point of keeping the inevitable explosion contained. "Lately, I seem to have developed a knack."

The front door opened, and Asa and Jackson strolled in. "For finding trouble?" Asa asked.

"I didn't go looking for it."

"Got to disagree there," Jackson interrupted. "It's clear you have a soft spot for women; otherwise, they wouldn't always see you as their savior."

Brad glared at Jackson. With his long blond hair, ever-present smile, and skill at turning a joke, a person could be misled into thinking there wasn't any substance to the man. But Jackson was as practical as the day was long and his sense of fair play had caused more than one outlaw to find his life cut short because he didn't understand the skill that backed that smile. Or else underestimated the practicality that said the most efficient means to an end was to kill the son of a bitch standing between Jackson and right.

"You implying you have better things to do with your time?"

Jackson leaned against the wall just inside the door. "Absolutely. With you out of the running, there are lots of broken hearts that need consoling and I'd much prefer lounging in a soft bed to digging a grave."

"Who the hell said we were burying the son of a bitch?" Asa growled.

"I did," Dorothy called from the kitchen. "It's indecent to leave dead bodies hanging about."

"Heck, Dorothy, you ever seen Bull?" Brad called. "It'd take two days just to dig a hole big enough."

"If you're too lazy to dig a grave then I guess you'll have to settle this without killing anyone."

Which had been the point she wanted delivered. Asa sighed. "You're a hard woman, Dorothy."

"Just keeping you boys on the straight and narrow. I'm going to make some coffee. It'll be ready shortly."

Cougar shook his head. "The woman's worse than a conscience."

"So if we can't kill him, what are we going to do with him?" Jackson asked.

"Make him wish he was dead."

That wasn't going to be enough for Brad, and he suspected not enough for Gray. Speaking of which . . . "Where's Gray?"

"Repairing his pride after a trip to the woodshed," Clint answered.

Brad went cold inside. He'd had more than a few of those in his youth. "How badly is he hurt?"

Clint snapped straight. "What the hell kind of question is that?"

He was stepping in it every way he turned, but Brad couldn't let it go. "The kid stepped between Evie and a bullet. I'd be more than a bit put out if you hurt him."

"You'd be even more put out if he got himself killed," Jackson interjected.

"Shut up, Jackson."

"No need to get upset, Rev." Cougar sighed, casting a worried glance at the kitchen. "Clint doesn't have it in him to lay a hand on the kid."

Brad had seen Clint gut men without batting an eye. "Uh-huh."

"The kid's had enough trouble," Clint offered. "Beating him wouldn't make any difference."

"See," Cougar waved his hand. "Gone soft."

"So what did you do?"

Clint glared.

Jackson laughed. "Damn near talked his ear off. It's a wonder the kid didn't beg for a beating just to get out from under all the guilt Clint piled on."

"He could have gotten Brenna and Evie killed. He's not as strong as he thinks he is."

"Not to mention risking himself," Dorothy said, bringing in a tray with six coffee mugs.

Brad rose and took the tray from her.

"Thank you."

"Where do you want it?"

"The parlor's fine. You need to rein that boy in. He needs to learn it's not only him against the world. He's got family to depend on now."

"Why are you putting this on me? I'm not his father."

"Because, not being his father, your opinion will hold weight. And"—she paused to wipe her hands on her apron— "because it's your responsibility."

"How so?"

She snapped her apron straight, glaring at him as if he'd just insulted her intelligence. "Because you're family, too."

He could only stare as she headed back to the kitchen.

Asa took the tray from Brad and led the few steps to the parlor. "Didn't you know?"

He shook his head, the words flowing through him, sinking past his horror to the longing he'd never managed to kill off. *Family.* Dorothy thought he was family?

Putting the coffee on the parlor table, Asa sighed. "I probably should have warned you, having firsthand experience and all with their sneaky, claiming ways—"

Brad turned to Cougar, anger burning a cold hole in his gut. The likes of him could never be family. "You told Dorothy you claimed me?"

Cougar shrugged and picked up one of the cups. "You pretty much sealed your fate the day you turned against your gang and saved our asses."

"I would have done that for anyone given the same circumstances." He didn't hold with murder.

"But you did it for us," Clint said, helping himself to a cup.

"What the hell is she going to do when the truth about what I am comes out?"

It was Jackson who answered. "Whatever she feels is right."

Shit. "You had no right."

No right to make him vulnerable, no right to set Dorothy up for hurt. No right to create that shimmer in his long-dead dream.

"We feel differently."

"And all that matters is what you feel?"

Cougar smiled, eying Brad's clenched fists with something akin to anticipation. "In this case, Rev, pretty much."

"You two can discuss your differences later," Asa interrupted. "Right now, we have bigger fish to fry."

Brad not only planned on discussing it, he intended on finishing it, his plan to simply walk away when this was over was now dead in the water. Cougar had efficiently nipped that in the bud.

He glanced out the window to the night beyond.

Happy now? Are enough people going to be hurt by this yet to satisfy you?

As usual, there was no answer.

"What's the plan for the evening?" Jackson asked, shaking his head when Asa offered him a cup. "Are we letting Bull live or not?"

Brad grabbed the cup out of his hand, not wincing when the hot liquid splashed over his fingers, taking the small punishment for what it was, an incremental prelude to the hell the rest of his life was going to be when the events that had been brewing the last few months came to a head. "I don't know what the rest of you have planned, but I'm going to kill that worthless son of a bitch Bull, and then I'm going to get Brenda."

BRENNA WENT STIFF as a board in Evie's arms when Doc and Jenna entered the room. Evie pretended not to notice, just smiled at them from where she sat on the bed. "Thank goodness you're here, Doc. Brenna is about to expire from hunger."

"Well, it would be a real shame to lose such a fine young lady for want of such a simple cure."

Brenna frowned at him as if there was an insult couched in the compliment. "Gray says I'm pretty."

As a shield, it was a pitiful one, but Brenna threw it out like it was made of granite. Everyone had to believe someone, and Brenna obviously believed Gray.

"Yes. He does." Jenna limped in, patting a fussing Bri's back. "He told me you were beautiful."

"You're his mother."

"Yes, I am."

Her frown deepened. "He loves you."

Jenna smiled gently. "Thank you for telling me. Sometimes, I'm not sure."

Brenna folded her arms across her chest, her lips pressing flat. "He can't love me."

"Why not?" Doc asked, opening his bag.

"My father doesn't like anyone to love me."

It was the second time she'd said that. Hearing it twice didn't make it any more comfortable. "I'm sure that's not true," Evie interjected.

Brenna watched Doc with growing apprehension. Evie could feel it spread through her small body. Over Doc's flyaway hair, she looked helplessly to Jenna. Jenna knew children, knew how to deal with them. Evie didn't. Doc approached the bed.

"Now, let's see what we have here."

Brenna shrieked and tried to climb Evie's shoulder. Jenna laid her hand on Doc's arm. As if he needed any more incentive to stop.

"Brenna," she coaxed. "Look at me."

With obvious fear, the little girl did so. "Gray sent me to make sure you were safe, and to make sure no one hurt you. He said you'd know you could trust me."

Because Gray trusted her. Evie watched, feeling as if an important something she'd missed out on her entire life was finally taking shape, making sense.

Her lower lip trembled. "Why didn't he come himself?"

"He got in trouble for fighting."

Brenna's little fists bunched on Evie's shoulder. "Did his daddy hurt him bad?"

Jenna handed Bri to Doc before sitting down on the side of the bed, creating a haven for Brenna between them. "Oh no, pumpkin. There's nothing in this world that could make Clint hurt Gray. He loves him as much as he loves me."

Clearly Brenna didn't believe that, exposing the why in a harsh truth. "My Daddy hurts my momma."

Jenna's eyes filled with tears. She reached, as if to touch the little girl, and then pulled her hand back. "I'm sorry. He shouldn't do that."

Brenna's chin quivered. "We had to run away."

And for her bravery, Brenna's mother had landed locked in a saloon with Bull as her client. Evie's soul burned at the unfairness.

I won't stand by and watch our weakest members suffer.

She'd been sheltered from the reality that made Brad so passionate about women, but she understood now.

"That was very brave of your momma to take you away."

Brenna slipped away from Evie. Hugging her knees, she rocked back and forth. "Yes, it was."

With a slow, careful motion, Jenna smoothed Brenna's hair back off her pale face. "Where's your mother now?"

"In a room."

"Do you know where this room is?" Doc asked, nudging Jenna aside.

Brenna's eyes went wide as he leaned over and probed the back of her head.

She nodded.

"Good. Then I want you to whisper it to Jenna real quiet-like, while I check out the lump you have here."

She licked her lips and winced when he hit a sensitive spot.

"Sorry."

"Why?"

"Why what?" he asked.

"Why do I have to whisper it?"

"Because as soon as we're done here, Jenna is going to whisper it to Clint, Cougar, Asa, Reverend Brad, and Jackson."

"Oh."

"They're big men with mean tempers and they don't like people who hurt women and children."

"Will they help my mother?"

"Yes."

"Even if she's a bad woman?"

Evie gasped. She hadn't thought the little girl knew. Doc tipped Brenna's face up, his gaze skimming the bruise before meeting her gaze. "There's no such thing."

"That's not what people say."

"People say a lot of stupid things. It doesn't make them true."

Clearly Brenna didn't know what to believe, as clearly as she didn't know who to cling to. Her father was a bastard, her mother imprisoned, and all she had were strangers around her. Her face crumpled. "I want Gray."

"Why?" Jenna asked, her voice incredibly soft.

She shook her head, dislodging the tears filling her eyes. "He promised he'd be here."

For a moment, Evie thought Brenna would bolt.

Jenna didn't give her the opportunity. With a sob that mirrored the pain the little girl held inside, she gathered Brenna in her arms, cradling her against her chest. Her cheek dropped to the little girl's bright hair, tears ran down her face, and she promised, "Then we'll get him just as soon as Doc is done."

Brenna didn't fight, just accepted Jenna's hug with a tense expectancy. "Why?"

"McKinnelys don't break their word."

Soft as a sigh, Brenna offered up her last defense. "He claimed me."

Just as softly, Jenna whispered back, "Thank God."

And for Evie—watching Jenna hold Brenna as though she would never let her go, accepting the child's boundaries and offering her love anyway—that elusive truth that always evaded her and left her feeling like an outsider always looking in shone just as brightly as the light reflecting off Jenna's blonde hair. It didn't matter what the world said, it only mattered what those close to you thought, and she'd always been surrounded by people who'd accepted her for who she was. She just hadn't allowed herself to see it. The way she hadn't allowed herself to see the truth in her marriage. Because she was afraid if she gave her trust along with her love, it would go away, the way her father's love had, for reasons she couldn't understand. And all she'd be left holding in the aftermath would be that horrible debilitating ache of failure.

"Evie, you okay?"

She wiped the tears from her eyes and managed a smile for Doc. "Yes. I think I am."

Nineteen

HE CAME TO her in the dark, hungry and wanting, back from his hunt for Bull, his plan to save Brenda. The dip of the mattress preceded the urgency of his embrace. Still groggy from sleep, Evie snuggled into Brad's chest. "What happened?"

"Bull's dead."

She could only think of one thing that would have him holding her this tightly, as if he wanted to pull her into his skin. "You killed him?"

His fingers went to work on the buttons of her nightgown. "No, somebody else beat me to it." The first button opened without a qualm, but the second put up a fight. "Why do you wear these things?"

"To keep me decent."

"Who wants you decent?"

Smiling, she pushed his hair off his face. "Certainly not you."

The grin that greeted her quip was strained. Something was wrong. There was only one thing she could think of. And it made her uneasy. "What about Brenda?"

"She's safe."

"Out of the Pleasure Emporium?"

"Yes."

"Where?"

"The less you know, the better."

"For your information, ignorance is not bliss."

The rest of the buttons gave up the battle without a fight. Cool air breezed over her abdomen.

"Save convincing me of that for tomorrow."

"Count on it." The breeze was followed by the gentleness of his touch. "So what are you going to do now?"

He rolled them both over until he was looming above her, a

dark shadow in the darker night. "I don't know what the rest of the world is going to do, but I'm going to make love to my wife."

The lighthearted statement betrayed a thread of strain. Flattening her palms over his chest, Evie felt the beat of Brad's heart, the warmth of his skin, the tension that shouldn't be there. Was it because he regretted being married now that Brenda was back in his life? She swallowed hard and the tears that always seemed so close to the surface the last few days perked again. She wanted to be more to him than one more undeserved punishment in his life. "If you want her, we can probably still end the marriage."

As soon as the words left her mouth, she wished them back. She didn't care how he felt. She didn't want to lose him.

"That's generous of you."

She sniffed. "Well, take me up on it quick because I'm changing my mind as we speak.

He chuckled. Actually chuckled while she was lying there so exposed she didn't know how much longer she could bear it. Balling her hand up in a fist, she swung. As always, he was faster, stronger. He caught the blow, wrapped his much bigger hand around it, and pushed back until his hand pressed hers over her heart, following it down until his forehead touched hers and their breaths blended one into the other. "I already have all I could I want."

She wanted to believe that, she just couldn't. "You loved her."

"As a boy and as a sister."

She bit her lip and pressed on, driven by the devil that couldn't stand the nag of doubt. "And me?"

"I'll never let you go unless you want to leave."

It wasn't a declaration of love, but for Brad, she got the feeling it was very close. For sure her heart didn't hear a difference. "So I don't have to worry about her?"

"You don't have to worry about anyone."

Except him. She worried about him. Worried about his reckless streak, worried about the qualification he put on his declaration. She'd had a glimpse into his childhood. A man growing up like that would bear as many scars on the inside as he wore on the outside. Maybe need more reassurance than others.

"I won't leave you."

"I don't need promises, sweetheart."

He needed promises more than any man she'd ever met. Deserved them more. She couldn't find the words to say what she wanted and the moment passed, fading under the distraction of his kiss. She loved his kiss.

"Now, come here. We're running out of time."

"It's still dark out. How much time do you need?"

"A hell of a lot more than I've got."

His thigh insinuated its way between hers, the coarse hair catching on her sensitive skin. Little sparks of delight danced over her flesh. There was a roughness to his moves, an earthy sensuality to his touch on the inside of her thigh as he made a place for himself that spoke of purpose. Whatever was bothering him, he wanted to forget it. With her. She slid her hands up over his shoulders, glorying in the strength she found there. She could give him that. "I like the sound of that."

"Good."

His hand fisted in her hair, pulling her head back, arching her neck to the press of his lips. This wasn't the considerate caress he normally gave her. This wasn't the controlled lover she was used to receiving. This was a man indulging his wild side, a husband expressing his need for his wife. She arched her neck into his kiss, taking the hard press of his lips with a feeling of exultation, the nip of his teeth with a wild excitement, meeting his growl of satisfaction with a whimper of desire as everything elemental inside her responded to his primitive call. Hooking her ankles over the backs of his calves she dragged them up, taking her nightgown up with the same smooth motion, exposing herself, making herself vulnerable to him. Brad accepted the gift with a sigh and a shift that pressed his cock into her soft flesh.

"Oh, yes." She arched up, encouraging more of the same. Nothing was ever as good as the feel of Brad against her—hard, male, potent. She dug her fingers into the back of his neck, her leg around his hips, pulling him to her so she could whisper in his ear, "Have I ever mentioned I like you wild?"

"No, but I've noticed a tendency in that direction."

"Want to encourage it?"

This time his laugh was genuine and she relished it as much as she relished her ability to give it to him.

"Absolutely."

It was her turn to say "good." Reaching down, she gathered up the hem of her gown, dragging it over her head with a smile she wasn't sure he could see. She tossed it aside. "Because I don't feel like holding back either."

For a brief instant his chest pressed against her breasts, the rough mat of hair abrading her nipples deliciously as he absorbed her new brazenness. Then he exhaled and she felt his smile against her cheek. "Let's light the lamp then, and do it right."

Right. Yes, she wanted to do this right.

His chest slid across hers as he reached for the bed stand. There was wood whispering against wood, the rasp of a sulfur, and then a flare of wavering light that cast his expression in dancing shadow. If she had any sense, the passion carving his features in stone would scare her. Instead a wild burst of excitement flooded through her.

"Lift up the mantle."

Reaching over with her left hand, she did, holding his gaze the whole time, not flinching away when his eyes darkened further and narrowed in purely primitive male response. This was Brad, her husband, the man who accepted her as she was. The one man with whom she could be herself. More than ever, she wanted to see just who she could be within the freedom of his care.

The oil lamp flickered, the flame starting out hesitant before growing bolder, a visual echo of her own determination. She'd waited her whole life for this moment with this man, for him to come to her with no barriers between them, no expectations, no rules, nothing but elemental desire. The moment was here now. She wasn't going to waste it, didn't want to forget a moment of it. She memorized his face, the way it looked right now, knowing even as she did that she wouldn't re-create it. Some things were too private to be shared, too private to risk exposing to others.

Brad blew out the match, kneeling above her like a pagan god, muscles thrown into sharp relief, his shoulders looking impossibly broad, the smile on his face wicked. This was the man she'd known lurked beneath the facade. The man she'd always wanted to see.

"I love you." The words just slipped out. Brad froze above her. For an awful moment she thought she'd been too honest. "I'm sorry, I shouldn't have—"

His hand covered her mouth. The hunger in his gaze burned hotter, the edge to the emotion surrounding them grew sharper. "Don't take it back."

She'd been going to say that she shouldn't have just blurted that out. Kissing his palm, she pushed his hand away, holding his gaze, feeling as though she were dangling off the tip of a very skinny branch. "I don't want to take it back."

She just wanted him to say it back.

"Not many would say I'm lovable."

She would have thought it a strange response—a strange thing to say—if she hadn't had that glimpse into his childhood, but now that she understood, it just made her want to hold him tighter.

"Then I'm unique," she breathed as his big hand closed around her breast.

"Very unique."

Because she needed something to hold on to, she asked, "Good unique?"

His smile was positively wicked as he thumbed her nipples, keeping her pinned with his hips when she would have arched up, teasing her with another pass, and then another, pinching the engorged tips into bright red little berries that begged for more. This was everything she needed, everything she wanted. Her heart melted as he answered in his low drawl, "The best."

It still wasn't enough. "The only one for you?"

Again that curious stillness, and then he leaned down, his lips brushing her nose, her lips, kissing her eyes closed. "The only one I'll have for the rest of my life."

She opened her eyes, finding him looking back, his gaze as solemn as his voice. "You promise?"

"I promise."

It wasn't a declaration of love, but it was brutally honest and it came from the heart. And for now, it was enough.

She placed her palms on his knees and slid them up his heavily muscled thighs, stretching her thumbs inward until they touched the sides of his penis, pressing in with her nails the tiniest bit, holding him hostage.

His head cocked to the side. "Not even a little bit scared?"

Of him? Never. She gave him her most seductive smile. "No, but I'm feeling a whole lot wild."

The right side of his mouth hitched up. "Lucky me."

"Yes, I think you are."

It was just a slight adjustment to capture his cock between her palms, the slightest pressure to bring a catch to his breath.

"Feeling confident?"

"Yes, but I could use some instruction."

"In what?"

The time for hiding had long since passed. "I want to please you tonight. Will you let me?"

His right eyebrow cocked up. Her pussy clenched in want. The man was too sexy for words when he looked at her like that. "Do I have a choice?"

Squeezing gently she admitted, "You could easily overpower me."

"Do you want me to?"

A tingle went down her spine, imagining the possibilities. "Not tonight." Tonight she needed to show him how she felt, what he meant to her.

"Then we'll save that for another time."

She squeezed his cock again, enjoying the way it jumped at her touch, swelled, hardened. A drop of pre-come beaded the tip.

"Now stroke it slowly, evenly."

As she did, he watched every movement, every nuance of her expression. Every flicker of hunger as she drew his shaft down toward her mouth. And she watched back, his passion feeding hers.

"Do you want my cock, Evie?"

She nodded, fascinated, as gravity pulled that bead into a droplet. She caught it on her thumb, bringing it to her mouth, holding his gaze as she curled her tongue around her finger, savoring his essence. "I want it all."

He skimmed his cock up her body, his balls sliding in a satin caress up her stomach. From this angle his cock looked huge, the veins engorged, the flesh tinted with his hunger. The hunger she inspired. The hunger he promised to hold only for her. He hitched up a little farther, his knees bumping her arms, his balls snuggling into the valley between her breasts. A warm, soft, potent weight. It was natural to kiss the base of his cock, natural that he moaned as she tasted him, once, twice, three times.

His palms slammed flat against the wall above her head, the echo driving her smile as he knelt there, letting her pleasure him with her mouth for a few minutes, in a limited way, before he reached down and circled his cock with his fist, filling her vision with an impression of strength on strength. He backed up just a little, just enough that the fat crown brushed her lips. She opened her mouth, curling her tongue around the tip, taking in his essence, encouraging him with rapid darts of her tongue to give her more.

He accepted the invitation with a soft groan, making love to her mouth the way he made love to her body, gently at first, letting her get used to the feel, his size, his need.

"Damn, that's good."

It was, intoxicatingly so—her pleasure connected to his, her desire to his. He transferred his grip to her hair, tipping her head back as he slid in and out in shallow thrusts, only giving her so much control, dominating her body with his. "Suck me, Evie, just like that, soft and sweet. Make us both feel good."

It was thrilling—a natural give-and-take—and she loved him for it. His cock slid deeper. She sucked harder, working her tongue along the surface, arching up to take more of his cock, reaching up to capture his nipples. Remembering what he did to her, she started out slowly, pinching and rubbing, taking her cue from the way his cock slid in and out of her mouth as to how much pressure to apply. His cock grew rock hard. Her caresses grew more deliberate as his hips pumped faster.

"Evie, I can't hold back."

She didn't want him to. She wanted to please him the way he pleased her—to the bone.

"Evie . . ."

Shaking her head, she switched her grip to his buttocks, holding him closer as she took him that tiny bit deeper.

"Ah hell." Brad cupped her face in his hands, binding them together as he came, his fingers stroking her cheeks tenderly as his pleasure washed over her in erotic pulses. Taking all he gave her, suckling him gently after the last throb of his climax faded, a different kind of satisfaction smoothed over the restlessness of her own unfulfilled desire. He shuddered one last time. Still cradling her face in his hands, Brad eased his cock from her mouth.

"You all right?"

She nodded. His thumbs pressed gently. He frowned, his lips parting. She held her breath, waiting for the words she craved. With a shake of his head, he lay down beside her and pulled her against him. The kiss he placed on her temple was gentle. His hands brushed her cheek, her side, stroking her as if he didn't want the moment to end. As if for him, too, the interlude had been more than sex. He smoothed his finger over the corner of her mouth, catching the moisture there, spreading it along the inside of her lips, branding her again, the way he always did, almost as if he didn't believe a wedding ring was enough to keep her with him.

Catching his hand, she brought it to her lips, driven by instinct to repeat the vow. "I love you."

And still he kept touching her until, finally, he rolled onto his back, dragging her with him with a hand curved around her neck and her hip.

"Come here."

"Here" was draped over his chest in a wanton sprawl. Desire ground through her in a slow roll as all that hard muscle flexed beneath her. Frustration drove her to bite him. He laughed and threaded his fingers through her hair, holding her to his chest.

"Hungry, Evie darling?"

She didn't bother to prevaricate. Pleasing him had aroused her to the point that she was one big, empty ache. "Starving."

With a laugh and a small stinging swat to her rear that somehow only made her hotter, Brad tugged her lower, down over his rippling, hard abdomen. She placed a kiss on his recently healed wound and stole a taste of his navel before he pushed her lower still.

"Take me in your mouth and make me hard again."

It was a surprise, taking him in her mouth like this. Before when she'd touched him he'd been hard, but like this he felt softer, more vulnerable, as if another side to his personality was revealed, one he normally kept hidden. She looked up. He smiled ruefully.

"You're going to have to give me a minute."

She could do that. It was enough to lie here connected to him, knowing she'd given the ease he sought, anticipating the delight to come, relaxing into the sweetness of the moment, where there was only him holding her and her holding him in a soft prelude.

It didn't last though. His cock twitched and stirred, and where before she could hold all of him, as he began to grow, hardening and thickening, he tested the boundaries until she gagged.

Brad held her to him for a second before letting her pull back. "Next time you feel the urge to gag, swallow until you can take it down, just a little at a time."

He pressed back in, slowly, gently, letting her take that little bit more.

"That's good," he murmured, his voice blending with the seduction of the hot summer night. "Just like that. Now, hold it there. Swallow, swallow . . ."

Following his directions, she discovered she could take more of his cock than she'd thought possible. He groaned, the sound a seductive lure tempting her on until she was unable to stop, unable to breathe, unable to look away from the wicked magic in his eyes. Brad backed off and she took a breath, and then another. When he pushed in again, she knew what to do. It didn't make it much easier, but she loved to see that wild flair of his nostrils and the way his eyes dilated. Loved the power of knowing she could reduce him to such complete, helpless need. His hips bucked in helpless reaction. His fingers pressed with that same desperate need, encouraging her to take just a little more. She felt his inner struggle as he worked not to push deeper, to not give her more than she could take. Except she wanted it all. Taking a deep breath, she kissed the tip of his cock. "Don't hold back, Brad. I don't want that between us."

In a drawl rough around the edges he said, "Much more and there won't be anything between us."

"Yes."

"You don't know what you're asking for."

She had a good idea. "I'm asking you to show me."

"Don't."

Too late. This time it was she who had the power, she who took him, her lips sliding down his cock inch by inch until he bumped the back of her throat.

"Damn!"

The instinct to gag almost won.

"Easy."

She took him a fraction more, her throat working against the head of his cock. A glance up revealed his face racked with pleasure. Looking down, he smiled tightly. A smile that had nothing to do with pleasure and everything to do with emotion.

If she'd had the ability, she would have smiled back, because the words she wanted to hear were written in his eyes.

"Once more, Evie. Take me like that one more time."

She did, holding him longer than was comfortable, holding him because she didn't want to break that vital, fragile connection.

"Damn, so sweet. I could spend my life tucked here and die a happy man."

His fingers traced the stretch of her lips around his cock, grazed her jawline down to where she held him so tightly. A strange tension entered his expression as he asked, "And you'd let me, wouldn't you?"

Her agreement was a calming stroke of her hands down his thighs. As if all he needed was that acceptance, Brad pulled his cock free of her mouth, his gaze locked on hers. "Was that a yes?"

"I like pleasing you like that."

He closed his eyes and shook his head. "You don't leave a man much control."

His cock tapped against her lip. Immediately, she opened her mouth, and when he hesitated, she ran her tongue over her lips. "I wasn't trying to."

"So I gather."

He might know, but he wasn't actively resisting. Pursing her lips, she kissed his penis.

"So why are we stopping?"

"Because any more and you will find me pumping down your throat rather than just your mouth."

The words were almost as exciting as the act. Her womb clenched. Brad didn't miss one of the betraying signs. On a hoarse curse, he slid his cock back into her mouth, once, twice, three times in fast jabs that didn't allow her participation, going deeper each time until she pressed her hand on his thighs. Not because she didn't want the pleasure, but because she needed to breathe. With a regretful pop, she released his cock.

Cupping her face in his hands, he kissed her cheek, her forehead, holding her tightly as she struggled for breath.

"Shit, I'm sorry."

"I'm not."

Another curse, another kiss, and then he was angling his cock down her body, marking her right breast and then her left, rubbing the pout of her nipples before trailing a path downward, marking her until he got to her pussy, rubbing the broad head of his shaft against her soaked clit.

"Damn, you're wet."

"Why are you surprised? You get excited when you do that to me."

"So I do, but that's because you're all soft and sweet and pretty, whereas I'm all hard and ugly."

He talked such nonsense. "Not to me." Arching into the press of his cock, she whispered, "Make love to me, Brad."

"You're not ready."

She squeezed her thighs together. "I'm so ready, I'm going to come, and if you don't want it to happen without you, you need to hurry up."

His eyes narrowed and his nostrils flared. His hand pressed between them, testing her readiness with one finger. The first ripples of her climax stroked over her as his cock slid the length of her clit.

Grabbing his shoulders, she anchored herself with her nails. "Hurry, I want you in me when I come."

"I don't have the sponge."

"I don't care. I want you in me now, with nothing between us. Just you and me. Please, Brad."

For a split second he hesitated, and she thought he was going to refuse, but then his cock was there—pressing, pushing, stretching the sensitive tissue, overcoming that resistance that always met him at first, coaxing compliance until, with a smooth glide, he slid in those first few inches.

Oh God, he felt so good.

With a lift of her hips she took him deeper, desire and pleasure piercing her anew. "Oh yes."

With a harsh laugh, he braced himself over her, his forehead touching hers. "I'm trying to go slow."

She slapped his back, just needing the slightest push, another inch, a bit more of that delicious abrasion to put her over that edge. "Who asked you to?"

"Not a damn soul."

With a hard thrust, he buried his cock in her tight channel, the vibrant flares of sensation too much to withstand. Tension whipped through her, arching her back under its lash. Another thrust, another lash, the second wave built on the first until she came in a searing crescendo, raking her nails down his back, holding him tightly with a clench of her thighs, pierced by his cock, his desire. Shuddering, the reality crashed through her again.

I love you.

When the cataclysmic moment was over, he was still there, his cock a hard, hot brand within her, accepting the rippling caress of her pussy and all that she had to give. He kissed her softly at first, gently, easing her back into reality before the kiss changed, betraying a hunger he couldn't disguise.

She moaned as he withdrew. Immediately, she missed that overwhelming sense of fullness, the completion that came from his body being joined to hers. As she relaxed, he reached for the bedside table, opened the drawer, and pulled out a simple glass jar filled with white cream.

"What is that?"

He didn't look away, didn't prevaricate. "I told you last time that I'd be taking you here."

His cock dropped lower, catching on the rosebud of her anus, lingering as a bolt of the darkest lust burned through her, stealing her breath as it snagged on the remnants of her orgasm, gathering the embers and fanning them into tiny flames. She should be more afraid than eager, but the truth was, she wanted him that way. She didn't know if it was proper, or appropriate, but she trusted Brad and the promise of pleasure that rippled around the press of his cock.

"Will it hurt?"

Brad popped the lid off the jar and scooped the cream onto his fingers. "You're not going to care."

She believed him. Brad was the one man who could make her not care about a lot of things.

"Put your legs over my shoulders."

She did, feeling more vulnerable, more open, more exposed than she ever had as he pushed her knees back toward her shoulders. She was encouraging her own deflowering, preparing herself, submitting to his demand by opening herself to the press of his greased fingers, the seduction of his words.

"Can you feel it, Evie? Can you feel how it's going to be when your body opens to take mine when you give yourself to me like this?"

God help her, she could. "Yes."

His fingers slipped down, slick with grease. They didn't meet an impediment, from her body or her will. Evie hadn't lied. She wanted this, had thought she could imagine how it would feel until his finger touched her in a delicate swirl. Nothing could have prepared her for the erotic bite as his finger parted her, entered . . .

"Brad!"

"Easy, just relax for me."

She had nothing to grab but the sheets, nothing to do but accept what he gave her. Pleasure or pain, she'd asked for it, but as he scooped more of the cream onto his fingers, she couldn't help the burst of nervousness.

"What happens if I can't?"

"Then we don't."

"But you want it."

The harshness of his expression softened. His fingers stroked instead of probed. He kissed the inside of her thigh, her knee. "I want you, Evie."

She arched her hips, changing the caress, biting her lip as his finger pierced her that first inch. "Like this?"

He didn't look away, a haunting sadness in his eyes that sent a bolt of fear to her core. "However I can have you, for however long it lasts, and to hell with the consequences."

He wasn't talking about sex. "What consequences?"

A second finger joined the first, a slow burning stretch that had her twisting in his embrace, searching for more of the fiery, blissful torment. Brad leaned forward between her thighs, bracing his weight on his forearm, opening her more as his lips bit at hers, taking her groaning acceptance as his breath as she blindly sought more of his kiss. In a low drawl layered with a resignation she didn't understand, he warned, "There are always consequences."

Twenty

THERE ARE ALWAYS *consequences.*

Evie couldn't get the thought out of her mind any more than she could stop the memory of last night from pouring over her in a sultry wash of heat. Her womb clenched on remembered bliss as she relived that moment she'd surrendered to Brad's erotic demands, her muscles parting, slowly, steadily, beckoning . . . accepting. The lingering aches in her body were reminders of not only how wild her husband could be but also a form of erotic speculation as to how much wilder he might be tonight. She couldn't wait.

There are always consequences.

The warning slipped through her sensual memories, darker this time, grounding her in the here and now. As much as she couldn't forget last night for the way it ended, she also couldn't forget the way it began—with Nidia stepping between Bull and the unleashing of his temper. She stood in front of the saloon, a bowl of soup from Millie's in her hand. She'd spent the morning learning to cook soup, wondering and worrying about Nidia as she chopped and stirred until she couldn't stand it anymore. With a call to Millie that she was taking a break, she'd spooned soup into a bowl, placed a plate on top and added some cheese biscuits, topped it all with a napkin, and headed to the saloon. Nobody had looked twice or even cared that she was taking her break seven doors down.

In the morning light, the saloon didn't look any different from the other buildings in town—clapboard siding, dusty windows. It certainly didn't look like a house of ill repute. However, if it was any other building in town, she wouldn't be standing out here in the hot sun debating the appropriate entrance for a non-paying visitor to use. She'd just stroll in, ask for Nidia, express her thanks for last night's intervention, and skip back to Millie's before she was missed. Unfortunately, her mother's frequent lectures on propriety did not cover the etiquette for a social call on a prostitute in her place of business. Which was a shame, because Evie could really use some guidance this morning.

Down the alley she saw a woman come out the side door, adjusting her bonnet. That settled that. If the women of the establishment didn't go out the front door for fear of being detained, then she wasn't going in it. For sure, word of this was going to get back to Brad, and for sure, to her mother when she came back from her buying trip. Likely both would be mad. But this was her debt, and she wasn't going to ignore it for propriety. The memory of Nidia's face as Bull had taken her arm—the pain, the fear, but mostly the resignation—haunted her. She had to know that Nidia was all right. Had to know why she had done as she had. Adjusting her grip on the soup, she moved forward, feeling the censure like a lash, shrugging it off with absolute logic. Nidia was a parishioner. Checking on the welfare of parishioners was required of ministers' wives. Granted, Nidia was a parishioner who had to sit to the side in the back behind a screen to spare the sensibilities of others, but Nidia still came to church every Sunday like clockwork. She was still human. And she'd saved Evie's rear.

Evie strolled down the alley as if she did it every day. When she came abreast of the woman, she nodded. "Good morning."

The woman stared at her, her expression shifting between shock, disbelief, and wariness. And the one thing that stood out in Evie's mind, through all the shifts, was that she didn't look at all as Evie had thought a prostitute would look. There was no paint on her face, no rouge on her lips. She looked like every other woman in town. Except for her eyes. She had pretty grey eyes, but they were haunted and resentful. Probably because Evie was standing here in the middle of the alley, blocking her way, staring at her as if she had two heads. "Would you happen to know if Nidia is receiving callers this morning?"

Another blink. "You came to see Nidia?"

Evie made her smile brighter just in case it would influence the answer. "Yes."

"You're the Reverend's wife."

It wasn't a question. "Yes, I am. And you would be?"

"Cissy."

It was a child's name. A name that implied innocence and vulnerability. "It's nice to meet you, Cissy."

Cissy's eyes narrowed. "Why do you want to see Nidia?"

She was obviously a woman who got straight to the point. "I'm just paying her a social visit."

Cissy's gaze narrowed further as she took a step forward. The shadow of the building cut across her face, dividing her expression into an intriguing dichotomy—a baby face with ancient eyes, a sense of vulnerability wrapped in aggression. As if all the factors of the woman's life were summed up in that one moment. Evie's fingers twitched around the bowl. The question just popped out. "Would you mind very much sitting for me?"

Cissy blinked, surprise erasing the moment as if it had never been. "Here in the dirt?"

Evie shook her head, mentally storing every tidbit of the image until she was sure she could re-create it with a reflector and Cissy sitting as a model. "No, I mean I would like to paint your portrait."

"Why?"

Such a suspicious question. "You have a very interesting face."

"You just want a picture of a whore to make fun of with all your proper friends."

"No."

Her eyes narrowed and the softness within her was eradicated. "What are you going to do with it then?"

"I don't know." She never knew what to do with her paintings when she was done. For her, the passion was in the creation. "I thought maybe you'd like it."

"You paint pictures to just give them away?"

Evie borrowed one of Brad's expressions. "Pretty much."

Cissy's fingers curled within the folds of her serviceable brown skirt. "Do you want me all gussied up?"

In her whore's outfit she meant. "I'd like to paint you just like this."

Cissy blinked. "No face paint or anything?"

"No paint or anything. Just you."

"I suppose if you're any good, I could send it home to my ma."

So she'd paint two portraits, Evie decided. One that reflected the havoc of Cissy's life and another that would make a mother smile. "I'm very good."

Cissy smiled, revealing a chipped tooth and an infectious charm. "Not too confident, are you?"

Evie shrugged. "It wouldn't make much sense to pick a profession I'm not good at."

"I've heard you're an odd one."

That seemed to be the one thing everyone heard about her. "So I'm told."

"The Reverend likes you fair enough though."

"Yes, he does."

"Confident there, too."

Evie shrugged again. "As you said, I'm odd."

"In a good way, I'm thinking. Are you really here to pay a social call on Nidia?"

"She helped me out last night. I'd like to thank her."

"You could have sent the Reverend."

So she was sure she'd be told multiple times when word of this visit got out. "It was me she helped."

Cissy shook her head. "Very odd."

"So is Nidia receiving?"

"Oh yeah," Cissy said with a wry smile. "I'm sure she wouldn't want to miss your visit. Just go through that door, up the stairs, and it's the first door on your right."

"Thank you."

Before Cissy could walk away, Evie called, "So you'll sit for me?"

Cissy turned and called back, "Sure. Why not?"

Evie practically skipped through the door. At last, the kind of excitement she enjoyed.

THE DOOR OPENED to the kitchen. It was nothing like Evie had expected. She'd expected opulence, gaudy colors, broken glasses, filth, visible signs of debauchery. Instead what she found was a clean, orderly kitchen with a stove; a dark wood cupboard with cups hanging from hooks, plates stacked behind glass doors; and a big table around which sat four women in various forms of dress, some still wearing paint from the night before, others as clean faced as Cissy. From the way they stared at her though, Evie would have thought a two-headed snake had just entered the room. She forced a smile and a nod.

"Good morning, everyone."

A couple of the women nodded back. The others glared. "I'm just going up to see Nidia."

A blonde with hair so stiff it stood out in chunks grunted. Evie took it as permission and with a "thank you" headed up the narrow stairs to the right. Upon reaching the top, she found she was at the end of an equally narrow hallway. A little of the opulence she'd expected lay on the floor in a well-worn carpet in shades of faded red and gold. There was no name on the door, just the number one. This had to be it.

She knocked. There was a murmur of voices from inside. At least one of them male. Was Nidia entertaining at this hour? The last thing she needed was to be confronted with a customer. Maybe she should just leave. As soon as the thought entered her head, the turning of the doorknob rendered it moot. Evie's first impulse was to close her eyes. The second to peek. She so rarely got to see anything truly risqué. The door opened. She sighed. Apparently she still wouldn't, because it was only Elijah who stood there in his shirtsleeves, frowning at her. "What do you want?"

An angry, rude Elijah. She lifted her chin and matched him glare for glare. "Nothing to do with you, certainly. I came to see Nidia."

He leaned his shoulder against the doorjamb. "Well now, once again you've got the wrong end of the stick. Anything to do with Nidia has to do with me."

In her nicest, sweetest, softest voice she asked, "Are you her husband?"

She knew he wasn't. Everybody knew he wasn't, just as everybody knew Elijah was still somehow an integral part of Nidia's life.

"No."

"Then I don't think I have to give you the time of day."

Folding his arms across his chest, he said, "I'm her bodyguard."

"Well, I haven't poisoned the soup."

He reached for it. She tucked it closer to her side and took a step forward. "It's not for you."

His arm slammed into the jamb in front of her face. She'd never realized just how muscular a man Elijah was. "Nidia's not up to seeing company."

Did he honestly expect her to believe he would hurt her? He

was Brad's friend. Had been Amy's husband. Evie ducked under Elijah's arm. "I'm not company, I'm her friend."

From behind her, she heard Elijah's "Since when?" It didn't really register, because she was looking at Nidia, who lay on the bed, her natural beauty buried beneath layers of bruises. Staring at the woman, knowing who had done this, guessing why, she couldn't think of anything to say except, "I brought you soup."

She thought the other woman blinked. It was hard to tell as her eyes were both black-and-blue and swollen to slits.

"*Gracias.*"

Evie approached the bed, placing one foot in front of the other, trying to get past the horror. With every step, Nidia seemed to get more and more tense. "Bull did this, didn't he?"

"I didn't plan appropriately."

From the doorway came a distinct "Fuck."

That gained Elijah a look from Nidia. Evie was pretty sure it was a glare. "Your opinion is not asked for."

"It damn well should have been, before you went outside and took on Bull."

Evie had the impression they were picking up an argument she'd interrupted. "There was not time to fetch you."

"What the hell is the point of having a bodyguard, if you're not going to let him handle the dangerous stuff?"

"I don't know. I never wanted a bodyguard."

Well, that explained the strange relationship between Elijah and Nidia. And also what had likely happened to Bull.

"That doesn't change the fact that you need one."

"But maybe not you," Nidia shot back, the words not losing their heat for being pushed through her swollen lips.

"You find someone else to take over the job, and I'm out of here."

The exchange had the rhythm of an old argument. The kind one listened to between married couples. It was interesting speculation—Nidia and Elijah.

"Why do you not leave now?"

"Because you're hurt."

"The Reverend's wife is here. She can care for me while you drown your sorrows."

"Damn it, Nidia. One of these days I'm going to stop humoring you—"

"Today is not that day. Go."

With a hard glare that had Evie stepping back—and it wasn't even directed at her—Elijah jammed his hat on his head and left, slamming the door shut. For a second, silence reigned. Evie opened her mouth. Nidia held up her hand. There was a sharp rap on the door, followed by an equally sharp "Lock it."

Nidia tossed up her hands as if that order was the cap on a bad day. Evie did as ordered. Only after testing the door did Elijah walk away and then it was just Nidia and her. And the bowl of soup.

Evie brought it over and placed it on the utilitarian bed stand. For some reason, she had always thought Nidia's bedroom would be a place of opulence, decadence. This sparsely furnished, functional space didn't mesh with her image of the woman. But neither did that moment of self-sacrifice last night. Looking Nidia in the eye, she asked, "Why did you do it?"

Nidia did not pretend to misunderstand. "The Reverend's wife getting killed in my alley would be bad for business."

She was familiar enough with the give-them-the-truth-they-want-so-they-won't-see-what-is-hidden technique to recognize it when it was played on her.

"That's probably true." She took the plate of biscuits off the soup, and placed the napkin in Nidia's lap. "But I don't believe it any more than I believe my husband slept with you on my wedding night."

Shaking out the napkin, Nidia sighed. "Young brides often have false illusions."

"I don't. When it comes to people, I tend to see things very clearly." And what Evie saw when she looked at Nidia was the same thing she saw when she looked at Brad. Someone hiding behind a mask. "Thank you for stepping in last night. I'm sorry you were hurt because of it."

"So sorry you brought me soup?"

She grinned wryly. "So sorry that I didn't bring you any from the batch *I* made."

That did get a twitch of a smile from Nidia. "I heard what you did to the Simmons boy."

"You don't sound like you disapprove."

"He is a frequent visitor here, not well liked."

"I knew I didn't like him for a reason."

Nidia smiled and then grabbed her face as the muscles pulled. "If visiting my establishment was a reason to not like a man, then you would not be on speaking terms with most of the town."

"That math sounds about right."

Nidia waited a moment before she said, "Including your husband?"

The dart hit home and for a second, insecurity flashed through her. But then she thought back to everything she knew about Brad, everything she knew about how he perceived women, and she found her smile. "Nice try, but if Brad came here, it was because somebody needed help."

"You do not think your husband needs my kind of 'help' sometimes?"

"I have no doubt he's often needed help, but I also know he would never take advantage of someone to do it." And he would never avail himself of that help where he lived. It would make him too vulnerable.

"Either you've grown up, or you're bluffing."

Evie held out the bowl of soup. "Does it matter?"

"No." Nidia considered while adjusting the bowl. "I do not think it does. And as long as you keep the Reverend happy, you will not have a problem with me."

"And why does his happiness matter to you?"

She took a sip of the soup, tipping it into her mouth. It obviously hurt too much to move her lips. "We are friends."

"Then I guess we're going to have to find a way to be friends, too."

Nidia laughed and grabbed her face again, tipping the bowl. "Are you planning to invite me over for Sunday dinner?"

Evie steadied the bowl. This woman had used her body as a shield between the children and danger, had employed her wiles to save Evie. She'd done so knowing the kind of man Bull was. She'd done it without hesitating. "It would be a shocking thing to do."

"So, for this reason you will invite me?"

"No." For a whole lot of other ones. Beneath the amusement, beneath the bruises, Evie saw the one thing that Nidia probably didn't want her to see. Something she'd never seen in all the years they'd grown up together in the same town. Longing. Nidia, daughter of a whore, once a whore, and now a madam, longed for respectability. "But if I did invite you, would you come?"

"Probably." Nidia took another sip of soup, that vulnerability gone as if it had never existed, buried under a layer of cold. "If only to hear all the proper ladies of town squawk."

"Then I'll invite you."

Nidia stared at her for a few seconds, studying the level of her sincerity, and upon ascertaining it, said one thing, "Don't."

And Evie understood something else about Nidia. She was protective of her friends. While the idea of rubbing society's face in its own rules appealed, she considered Brad her friend, and she wouldn't embarrass him. Evie's respect for the woman grew.

"The McKinnelys have an interesting custom."

There was an infinitesimal break in the return of the spoon to the bowl at the mention of the McKinnelys. It didn't take much to figure out why. Nidia's attempt to seduce Cougar away from Mara at the start of their marriage had been grist for the gossip mill for months.

"They tend to claim people they want as family. To them it's a bond as strong as blood."

Nidia took another very careful sip of her soup. "For sure, Mara wants my blood."

Because Nidia had tried to take what was hers. "Why did you do it?"

She thought Nidia would pretend to misunderstand or simply not answer, but then, with a small shrug, she said, "Because I'm a whore and he was a man abandoned by his wife. Fair game. I couldn't help myself."

That was such a load of bull. Evie folded her arms across her chest. "Besides that, I mean."

"You don't believe me?"

As if anyone with half a brain would. "No. I always thought there was more to it than that."

They'd grown up together, and even though she hadn't been allowed to play with her, Evie had never gotten the impression that Nidia was stupid.

"You think too much of me." She dipped the spoon in the soup and gave it a stir, watching the move with far more concentration that it deserved. Hiding. "My mother had died. I didn't want to always be the whore as she had been, but there was no other way to feed my belly, except marriage. Cougar would have been a good provider."

Brad was right. There were too few choices for women. "Why specifically Cougar?"

This time there was a longer pause and on a sigh that told Evie this was the truth, she confessed, "I thought he would understand. He was not white, had never known acceptance, and he hurt as I did."

In other words, she'd thought they had a lot in common. Since Evie had hung the hope for her marriage on the same foundation, she understood.

Nidia pushed a noodle around with the spoon, before scooping it up. For a second she looked so young, alone. Looking up, Nidia caught her staring. Her lips twisted in a mocking smile. "Believe it or not, I intended to be a good wife to him."

And in return Cougar would have provided protection a woman who had always been a victim needed. If Cougar hadn't been falling in love with Mara, it would have been a good plan. "There will never be anybody for Cougar but Mara."

"Too late, I realized that"—her shrug was fatalistically small—"but at the time, it was a battle to prove who could serve his needs better. By the time I realized his heart was involved"—she shrugged again—"the damage was done."

Not once had Nidia's voice broken. She'd just recited the facts of her life and her choices as if they were normal, everyday things. Which they were . . . for her. Brad's words in the church came back to her again. Whatever he had planned, she was going to back it. No one's life should be reduced to such horrible choices. "I'm so sorry."

Nidia's head snapped up. "I do not need the pity of such a woman as you. A woman who depends on a man, who lives at his discretion. I've made my own way in the world. I have my own money, my own life. No longer do I serve men. Now, it is I who pity you."

More bull, and Evie wasn't in the mood to humor her. "No, you envy me, and I do feel sorry for you. I feel sorry that you never had the chance to do what you wanted, that no one gave you a chance, but I'm glad you got to stop being a prostitute."

Nidia tossed her head and then winced. "They say you're odd."

"They say you're a whore," Evie shot back.

"But you don't believe it?"

Evie shrugged. "I pretty much don't care how you make your money."

"Why did you come here, Evie Swanson?"

"I came to thank you and, I think, to see if we could be friends."

"You are as odd as they say. A misfit."

"So I've been told often enough." She stood. "I've got to get back. Millie's going to start missing me."

Nidia held out the bowl. "You don't want to land on the wrong side of the wooden spoon."

She took it. "No, I don't." There wasn't anything else to say.

As Evie unlocked the door, Nidia added, "The Reverend is a misfit, too."

With a shake of her head, Evie sighed, "If what you're trying to say is that we're good together, just say it. The world won't end because of a bit of honesty."

"I have not made up my mind."

"Well, unfortunately, I have." And the truth was, Evie liked Nidia. Darn it.

EVIE DIDN'T LIKE the man coming toward her. There was absolutely no reason for her dislike. He wasn't even looking at her, just climbing the stairs with slow, steady steps. The brown-stained hat on his head blocked his face. She only had an impression of broad shoulders, lean muscle, and purpose. It didn't matter. Everything in her went on alert. She retraced her steps, the carpeting muffling her footsteps. Keeping her eye on the man, she reached back for the latch to Nidia's room. It lifted silently. With a quick step, she backed into the room, grabbing her skirts as they swirled forward and yanking them clear before quietly closing the door.

"What is it?"

"There's a man in the hall," she whispered, dropping the lock back into place.

"This is not so strange a thing in a whorehouse."

Evie glanced over her shoulder. Nidia looked very small in the big bed. She definitely wasn't going to be much help if the stranger turned out to be trouble. "Do you have a gun?"

"Of course. Don't you?"

"I used to." Before Brad took it last night, claiming she needed more lessons before he'd trust her with it again. She backed up a step, then another. "Where is it?"

The footsteps stopped. The door latch lifted soundlessly, hit the barrier of the lock, and stopped. Evie cast a glance at Nidia. She held her finger to her lips and motioned to the vanity. Eyes glued to the door, Evie made her way quietly backward as Nidia threw the covers back. She caught a glimpse of slim thighs bearing more bruises. What had Bull done to her? The latch rattled harder this time. Evie slid the drawer open as quietly as possible. It was empty. She looked up at Nidia and shook her head.

"Elijah!" Nidia whispered his name like a curse. "Once I shot at him by accident, and he takes offense."

Evie couldn't blame him, but right now she could really hate him. They needed that gun. The door crashed opened, slammed against the opposite wall. Nidia screamed for help. Evie just screamed and threw the bowl. It missed. Her gaze fell on the vanity stool.

"What do you want, Casey?" Nidia demanded.

Casey stepped into the room, his green eyes locked unnervingly on Evie. There was something familiar in his coloring and features.

She swung the stool. He grabbed her arm, spinning her around, yanking her back against his chest. The odors of sweat and horse filled her lungs in a sharp inhalation. The man's arm locked around her throat like a vise, trapping her within. Something cold, hard, and circular jabbed under her chin. A gun. A cold sweat sprang up along her skin. If she could've taken another breath she would've screamed again as he said as calmly as if he were ordering dinner, "Her."

Twenty-one

HOMER BURST INTO the church. The front door crashed against the opposite wall.

"Reverend!"

Brad stopped on his way out the back door, sighed, and headed for the front. Homer had a flair for the dramatic. Someone's horse throwing a shoe was as much a call to panic as a man being gunned down in the street.

"Back here, Homer."

The man ran down the aisle, bumping the pews, spinning around, stumbling, getting back up, and running straight at him, his slicked-back hair falling in lank chunks about his face. Brad got the first chill down his spine.

"Reverend, they've got your wife!"

The second chill fanned outward, spreading along his nerves, freezing out emotion. Brad glanced out the window. The streets were inordinately quiet for a Tuesday afternoon. Homer skidded to a stop in front of him, breathing hard, sweat dripping from beneath his hat into his scraggly beard.

God could do what he wanted with him, but Evie was off-limits.

I won't forgive this.

He let the promise linger before asking Homer, "Who has my wife?"

"I'm supposed to give you this." Homer shoved a wrinkled-up piece of paper at him.

Brad took the missive, the sense of inevitability that had been haunting him for the last few months settling in with a strange calm.

"Doc sent for Cougar and Clint."

Cougar, Clint, and Asa were miles away, hunting a lead on

Casey. They wouldn't get back in time for anything but arranging the funeral.

Homer watched avidly as Brad unfolded the note. No doubt, if he could read, he would be blurting out the contents. There was only one sentence.

My family for yours.

That was a lie. Casey believed in the ten times rule: whatever offense that was committed against him, he believed in repaying ten times over. Casey believed Brad had stolen his wife and child. That would be a blood debt. There was no way he intended Brad, Evie, or about eighteen townspeople to survive.

"What's it say?"

Brad refolded the note. "He wants a trade."

"For what?"

"Something he's not going to get."

"You seem awfully calm."

"I'm a minister."

Homer frowned. "That mean you believe God will provide?"

God or devil, it didn't make any never mind to Brad. The bastard had his Evie. "Something like that."

"What do you want me to do?"

Homer was all foolish heart but no skill. "I want you to warn everyone to stay inside and then I want you to get inside."

Where it was safe.

"That's it?"

Brad clapped him on the shoulder and forced a smile. "Someone's got to be around to tell the tale when this is done."

Knocking his hand aside, Homer drew himself up to his full height. "I ain't no coward to be hiding out when some crazy son of a bitch comes to town picking on a God-fearing preacher man."

Except Casey wasn't crazy, and he hadn't come alone. On that Brad would bet money. "Never said you were, but this is old business."

"So?"

So I'll handle it."

"How?"

"I'll come up with something."

Homer narrowed his eyes and stepped back. "You're going to get yourself killed."

"That's not part of my plan."

Forgetting where he was, Homer spat. Spittle splattered on the polished floor. Homer, who normally worried excessively about such offenses, didn't even glance at it. "A lot of people don't plan to end up dead."

"True, and as I don't want any of them being my congregation, I need you to get to warning them."

"It ain't right—"

Brad let a little of his facade slip, let the anger and determination out. "Now, Homer."

Homer opened his mouth, closed it, and on a curse that made no allowances for where he was, stormed back down the aisle, muttering "It ain't right" the whole way.

Brad waited until the door shut, throwing the room into cool shadows. He turned and headed for the altar. The box would be where he'd left it. No one stole from the church. Outlaws tended to be a superstitious lot. They might kill in a church, but steal from God? Even the hardest bandit considered that a plague of bad luck not worth inviting in.

The plain wooden box was heavy, and settled on the altar table with a soft thud. Inside, metal jostled against metal. Brad fished the key from his pocket then hesitated, his finger on the lid. Once he opened the box there was no going back. Evie's face flashed in his mind, the imp in her grin, the fire of her anger, and now . . . He shook his head, pulled up cold. Hell, he didn't know what her face looked like in fear, and she had to be so afraid, but he couldn't picture it. Because until he'd come into her life, there'd been no reason for her to fear.

This was unnecessary.

He opened the box. The scent of gun oil and leather welcomed him back. His red-and-gold-embroidered leather vest lay on top. He picked it up, memories of his old life pouring over him—disjointed and violent, racing through his mind in an incoherent rush—almost as if he was recalling somebody else's life, borrowing their experiences. He set it aside. The gun gleamed a dull charcoal color. He curled his fingers around the butt. The grip was warm and familiar.

"So what are you going to do, Shadow?"

So Jackson knew who he was. He'd suspected as much. Brad didn't turn around, just lifted the gun belt clear and wrapped it around his hips. It didn't matter that the others knew who he was. Not anymore. "I'm going to get my wife back."

"Casey didn't come alone."

Brad turned. Jackson leaned against the wall with his familiar hip-shot nonchalance. His long blond hair flowed about the ammo strapped across his chest. In his arms he cradled a shotgun. Brad buckled the belt. "I didn't figure he would."

"He's got eight men up on the roofs, three tucked in the alley around the saloon, and four in with Evie."

Brad checked the revolver's action. The cylinders spun as smoothly as ever. The hammer tripped at the slightest touch of the trigger. "Thanks."

"He seems pretty serious about killing you."

He glanced up. "That'll work out well, then, since I aim to kill him."

"Ask me to help."

Brad snapped the loaded chamber closed. "No."

He wasn't having any more deaths on his conscience.

This is between you and me. Keep them out of it.

Jackson swore. "Taking them on by yourself is suicide."

"Someone's got to be around to make sure they spell my name right on the tombstone."

"Assuming there's going to be enough left to bury."

"There'll be enough." Elijah's deep baritone filled the church.

"Turn around and head back where you came from, Elijah," Brad ordered as Elijah approached the pulpit. "You're not part of this anymore."

Elijah just planted his feet shoulder width and angled the barrels of the rifles he held in each hand back over his shoulders. "Not going to happen, Rev."

Rev . . . when he used to be Shadow. The shift between past and present gaped and then narrowed.

"They've got Nidia, too."

Brad slid the revolver out of the right holster. "Where?"

"The saloon."

Opening the chamber, he loaded the bullets. "What the hell was Evie doing at the saloon?"

"Paying a social call on Nidia."

Shit. He snapped the chamber closed, returning the Colt to the holster before repeating the procedure with the other. "Why?"

"According to Evie, because it was her debt," Jackson interjected, coming forward.

"How do *you* know?"

"Overheard it while walking down the hall."

"You were eavesdropping at Nidia's door?" Elijah asked, a growl in his drawl.

Jackson raised an eyebrow. "That would be underhanded."

"And we all know you wouldn't do anything underhanded," Brad murmured, his eyes drawn to the vest again.

"Unless it was the quickest way to get to his goal," Elijah countered.

"I'm hurt."

Jackson didn't look hurt; he looked relaxed, if one discounted the rhythmic tapping of his fingers on the rifle stock.

"More likely upset at being found out," Elijah scoffed, before calmly asking, "So what's the plan, Rev?"

"Haven't gotten much past killing Casey and getting Evie back."

"Straightforward and to the point." Jackson nodded. "I like it."

"Would that be sarcasm?"

Jackson shrugged. "Yes. You need a better plan."

"I'll work on it on the way." Brad picked up the leather vest. The last time he'd worn this he'd been a desperate man, no home, no family, a posse on his tail, and his only future a hangman's noose. He'd "died" at the hands of the McKinnelys and been reborn—risen from the grave to create the illusion of belonging, adding to it until it was the illusion that had substance and his old life that wavered with dreamlike inconsistency.

God's little joke.

He glanced at the cross on the back wall. *Don't know how you've kept that mean streak so secret for so long.*

Brad looked around the small church with its polished pews, smooth floors, and the one stained-glass pane in the arched window above the front door. The pane that had been presented to him last Christmas from the parishioners. An outrageous expense for this small town. Given to him because they thought the simple things he did mattered. Because they were grateful. Because they thought, with him, they could build something. His fingers clenched on the wooden lid, wanting to throw the box and shatter the mockery he'd made of their belief. Evie's belief. Son of a bitch, Evie's belief.

You were born nothing, and you'll die nothing.

His father's voice. His father's curse. Every Sunday, week after week, from his earliest memory he'd stood before the pulpit and, week after week, he'd been made to apologize for his existence before his father's congregation. Made to atone for the circumstances of his birth with his blood and his humiliation until the thought of church and God put puke in his throat. Yet this pulpit had been his the last eighteen months. This town his home. These people his family. And Evie . . . he closed his eyes and took a breath. With all her outrageous ways, she was this town's smile. And though he'd never seen it coming, she had also become his.

Can you deliver?

His lips tugged in wry remembrance at the challenge. Yeah. He could. He picked up the vest. He might not be good for much, but there was one thing at which he was damn near expert. He could steal anything. He could steal back his smile.

"No." Elijah took the distinctive garment out of his hands and put it back in the box. His forest green gaze didn't flinch from the challenge in Brad's. "Shadow is dead."

Jackson came up on his other side and handed him his black preacher's coat, his gaze just as calm, just as resolved. It was easy to see why the McKinnelys depended on him in a fight. "But the Reverend's got some ass to kick."

BRAD WASN'T CRAWLING. If Casey'd hoped to break Brad with threats, he was doomed to disappointment. Evie stood with her face shoved against the window overlooking the street and felt a leap of hope, a trill of dread. Brad was a far cry from crawling. He walked down the street like he owned it, each long stride the flowing, measured approach of a predator intent on the kill. She wished she could see his face, find the man she'd married amidst this horror, but she couldn't. His black hat was angled over his face, hiding his expression from view, his black coat blowing back from the black cotton of his pants. The late morning sun reflected off the belt strapped low on his lean hips. Off the guns tied low on his powerful thighs. Off the guns he wore so naturally.

I wasn't always a preacher.

Oh damn. She could believe that now. It all made sense. The

predatory grace in his walk. His skill with cards. His ease with guns. His scars. He'd just failed to mention what he *had* been before. Whatever it had been, it had been violent. And, from the level of tension escalating in the room, he'd been good at it.

The gun under her chin pushed her face up as the man holding her called over his shoulder. "Shadow's coming."

Shadow, not Brad. There was only one Shadow. Evie blinked the tears from her eyes. He was dead.

Brad stopped just short of the saloon. As if he felt her presence, he looked up. To a stranger, his expression might have been impassive, but to anyone who knew him, the set of his shoulders signaled anger. Evie knew him. So did the man holding her.

"And he looks pissed, Bart."

Casey came over, his chest pressing against her shoulder.

"More than pissed, Bart. I'd even say he was downright desperate."

They didn't know Brad at all. Evie smiled, the twist of muscles feeling grotesquely awkward as it occurred against the window. Brad didn't get desperate. He planned, he arranged, and he made things happen. The way he wanted. A bit more hope seeped past her panic. Reverend or Shadow, she knew the man behind the names. And he was one to believe in. Wedging her bound hands up between her body and the glass, she pressed one flat, first finger and thumb drawn into a circle, just wanting Brad to know she was all right.

At first there was no response, but then he smiled that beautiful smile that always made her heart skip a beat. "You're not where I left you, Evie darling."

The words were muffled and distorted through the glass and she had to read his lips to fill in the gaps left by distance, but she understood. And, no she wasn't, but she wished she were.

"What the hell did he say?" Bart growled.

"Open the window and find out," Casey ordered, yanking her out of Bart's hold and against him as he stepped back.

The window stuck. Bart pounded it open. Evie winced with every blow. Brad waited in the street, watching. From where she sat on the bed, Nidia watched with the same tense anticipation.

"Nice of you to stop by, Reverend," Casey called.

"It's a nice day for a walk. It was no never mind to stop by and pay a visit."

"I was expecting you to bring company."

"Your would-be guests weren't feeling sociable."

"The point was for you to make them want to be."

Brad pulled his coat back from his gun and rested his right hand on his hip. He looked so incredibly masculine right then, so dangerous, so deadly, and so absolutely exposed, standing to the side of the street.

"My positive wasn't able to overcome your negative." He pulled his coat back from his other gun, resting that hand on his hip as well, in a blatant challenge. "Truth is, Casey, you're a damn unlikable sort."

"Isn't that a bit of the pot calling the kettle black?"

"Why don't you come down and we'll discuss it?"

"Just the two of us?"

"Man to man."

From behind someone muttered, "Hot damn. We're finally going to find out who's faster, Casey or Shadow."

Casey pushed Evie forward until her face once again was pressed up against the window. Shielding him from any possible shot from below, while Brad just stood there exposed. Evie wanted to swat him and order him to get under cover.

"It's a date," Casey hollered down.

Brad tipped his hat back; his eyes caught the sun and reflected bright blue. "You hold on, Evie darling, and I'll be right with you."

What was she supposed to do with that? She tried to nod but Casey twisted his hand deeper in her hair. She drove her elbow back into his side. He didn't even grunt, just mashed her check harder against the window.

"Don't worry, she'll be right here waiting for you."

Over his shoulder, he ordered the men in the room, "As soon as I get down there and give the signal, shoot her. Make it messy."

"Can't get messier than a head shot," offered one of the men whose name she didn't know.

"Then make it a head shot," Casey snapped before adding, "As soon as she's dead, people are going to start filling the street. Signal the men to take out twenty and then we'll move on."

"That's going to have every marshal in the state on our ass."

"As the only people who really know who we are will be dead, they'll be chasing ghosts."

Bart laughed. Actually laughed.

"They know your name," Evie pointed out desperately. He couldn't seriously plan on killing all those innocent people.

Casey laughed. "They know a name, but it's not mine."

Evie exchanged a horrified look with Nidia. This wasn't good.

With a small jerk of her chin Nidia indicated the mattress. Two downward stabs with her fingers and Evie got the message. She had a knife under the mattress—for all the good that was going to do them. Her hands were tied as tightly as Nidia's. Maybe more so. They were outnumbered, outgunned, and in no position to do anything.

"What the hell are you two making eyes about?" Casey asked.

"We're conspiring against you," Evie answered.

He dismissed the threat with a snort.

"I'm waiting, Casey," Brad called from the street.

Casey looked around. "You all know what to do?"

The men nodded. "We know."

He stopped by Nidia's side and caught her chin on his hand, yanking her face up. "If you want your death painless, you might consider telling me where my wife is."

Nidia spat in his face. He backhanded her again. This time she didn't bounce back. She just lay on the mattress unconscious.

"Oh God," Evie groaned.

Bart hauled her over to the window. "Too late for prayers."

Brad—Shadow. She closed her eyes and took a breath, the confusion of to whom she was married momentarily overwhelming her. She took a breath and started again with the only point that mattered. Her husband stood in the street, watching the door Casey would be coming through. She didn't know what he was doing. He was a sitting duck. She wanted to kick his butt. She wanted to kiss him. She wanted to slap him. There was only one thing she wanted to do more than all of that. As if he felt her need, Brad looked up. Her lips shaped the words. His eyes narrowed and he shook his head. He hadn't understood.

Bart put the gun to her head. She swallowed, panic welling until she realized that, if she couldn't see Casey, neither could Bart. He wasn't going to pull the trigger yet.

She put her hands against the sill, tears burning her eyes. What did it matter now what Brad called himself? Who he'd been before? What name he called himself had nothing to do with how she felt about him. In a few minutes she'd be dead, and while there were some things she'd willingly take to the grave, this wasn't one of them.

She caught his gaze, held it. She meant to yell a warning. "I love you" was all that came out. Taking another breath she tried again. "He's going to—"

Bart clapped his hand over her mouth, cutting off the warning she was going to give. She struggled, biting and kicking. A door banged shut below and Casey shouted, "Reverend!"

No! Eyes wide, Evie braced her feet against the wall and heaved, sending Bart stumbling backward. Tangling her feet with his, tripping him in a last-ditch effort to delay the inevitable, she accepted the reality. They were out of time.

SHE LOVED HIM. She went and fucking told him again that she loved him while some bastard had a gun to her head. As soon as Brad got done paddling her ass for not staying safely where he'd put her, he was going to talk to her about the importance of timing.

He turned. Casey stood just outside the saloon door, staring at him, an amused smile on his lips.

"I confess, I was a little disappointed to find you alive."

"Sorry."

"No, you're not."

Brad smiled. "I'm not, but I am curious. Why didn't you tell anyone who I am?"

"Why do you think?"

Brad grunted. "Didn't figure it had much to do with goodwill."

"I rather like the thought of you dying as a nobody." He motioned to Brad's attire as he stepped off the walkway. "Seems fitting, since you went back to religion after all."

"A man can't outrun his past."

"No." Casey smiled. "He can't."

Brad bared his teeth and smiled as well. "You're not my past, Casey. You're just an annoying pest that I didn't have the sense to squash when I should have."

"Because you let Brenda talk you out of it. It's always a mistake to listen to a woman."

As he shrugged, Brad noticed the flash of a rifle barrel on the roof to the left, two doors down. "I'm a slow learner."

"Yes, you are." Casey glanced at the flutter of the curtains at Millie's. "Where's my family?"

"Safe."

He laughed and smiled that smile that made him popular with the ladies in any town they'd ridden into. "From me?"

"Yes."

"You risked everything for nothing, Reverend. We both know Brenda will come back to me. She always does."

"Not this time. You hurt her daughter."

Anger flashed across Casey's handsome face, erasing the charmingly friendly facade no one seemed inclined to look beyond. "*My* daughter."

"Not anymore."

"How do you figure that?" Casey moved to the center of the street. Brad didn't follow. Any farther out and the snipers on the right would have a shot at him, too. His odds were bad enough as it was.

He had to keep Casey talking until such time as Jackson and Elijah got their shots. Then, his fingers flexed, then he'd end it.

"The McKinnelys have some interesting customs."

"So?" Casey kept edging out. Brad turned with him, the hairs on the back of his neck prickling as he put his back to the buildings.

"There's one of which I'm particularly fond. They hold kinship by claim as strong as kinship by blood."

"What the fuck does that mean?"

"It means I've taken that custom as my own. It means I've claimed Brenna."

Casey actually snarled. He pushed his coat away from his gun, fingers twitching. "I'm going to enjoy killing you."

Brad remembered Evie's scared face smashed against the window, her brave signal that she was okay, her desperate declaration of love. The cold fury that swept over him only centered his focus. He wasn't taking his last breath until Casey was dead. "Funny, I had the same thought about you."

You hear that? This doesn't end until Evie is safe.

Casey raised his hand. As if that were a signal, everything happened at once. A woman screamed. Eight rifle shots exploded almost simultaneously. Bullets peppered the dirt around him. Brad dove for cover, rolling across the ground to the minimal shelter of the saloon steps.

A shot rang out from above. "Evie!"

The only answer came in a hail of bullets that kept him pinned. Son of a bitch! "Evie!"

Jackson and Elijah had better not have missed. The men in the room with Evie had better be dead.

He barely got his gun clear of his holster before he was pinned down by fire again.

Casey stood in the middle of the street, that charming grin on his face spreading as a bullet kicked up dirt between Brad's thighs.

"That was a close one, Reverend."

Too damn close. A scream came from inside the saloon. The front door burst open. "Brad!"

In the split second Casey smiled and turned, Brad knew what he'd planned.

"No." He sprang to his feet, throwing himself into Casey's line of fire as he lunged for Evie.

"Get out of the way," Evie screamed, whipping up her hand and pointing the gun over his shoulder.

Bullets hit the ground around him, creased his side, punched into his shoulder. He couldn't see anything except Evie standing there on the porch, blood spattered across her face and clothes, all hell breaking loose around her, pistol in her hand, ready to take on all comers.

"You damn fool." Grabbing her arm, he hauled her down, throwing his body over hers as a shotgun exploded nearby, tucking as much of her as he could under him, expecting to feel Casey's bullet in his back any second.

For the first time in twenty-five years, he asked rather than demanded.

Please, don't let her be hit.

The sound of battle changed. Intensifying rather than dying off. The reports changed in nature; there were revolvers, rifles, shotguns, and . . . derringers?

Brad lifted his head, putting his hand over Evie's skull, keeping her as protected as he could. What greeted his eyes made him blink. Townsmen lined the street, armed to the teeth with whatever they had. And from the bodies lying in the dirt, damn successfully. Across the way, he saw Casey lying dead, a bloody hole in his chest. Only one thing made a wound like that. Shotgun at close range. Patrick, Homer, and Cyrus stepped off the walk and stood in front of him, using their bodies as shields and their guns as protection.

"You just keep yourself down there with your pretty wife, Reverend," Patrick instructed in his rolling brogue. "Soon enough we'll be having the riffraff moved along."

Brad blinked at the novelty of being seen as helpless and in need of protection.

"Moved along, hell," Cyrus grunted. "I thought we were putting their sorry asses in the ground."

Homer spat toward Casey's corpse, hitching his shotgun up. "Told 'em it ain't right to think they can come into our town and pick on a God-fearin' preacher man."

As Brad absorbed the reality that the town had risen to his defense, the battle died down to sporadic shots. Beneath him Evie shifted.

He leaned aside. She took a breath, shuddered.

"Shit!" Was she hurt? "Are you hurt, darling?" Damn it, she'd better not be hurt.

He turned her over and ran his hands along her torso, checking for wounds. She caught his hand, moving it away from her side, bringing it to her face. His gaze naturally followed. The blood staining her skin was an assault to his senses. He wiped at it with his sleeve. She had the shell-shocked expression of someone in their first gun battle, but, ah God, she was alive. Blessedly alive.

Around them he could hear the shouts of the townspeople as they checked on each other, checked on him. They blended into a cacophony that echoed outside the beauty of this moment. A blur in the periphery of his awareness. All he cared about, all he wanted to see, was before him. Evie, alive and well.

"The Rev and his missus are just fine," Cyrus called.

"I'd say the good Lord was working hard to keep all those bullets from finding their mark," Herschel called from across the way, holding his derringer high.

Yes, he had. As Brad knelt there in the dirt, his wounds burning, looking at everything right in his world, he felt something that had been broken for too long gently click back into place. Subtly without the fanfare with which it had shattered.

Maybe because it hadn't been broken at all. The years he'd spent waiting on an answer to his demands—no, challenges—had been for nothing. The answer had been in front of him all along. He'd just been too angry to listen.

This time when Brad glanced heavenward, it felt right, natural, the way it should, the way it had before he let his father convince him God wasn't for him. The prayer he offered was simple, straightforward. From his heart.

Thank you.

Evie groaned, drawing his attention. Pale and shaken. He remembered her bursting out of the building, gun drawn, risking everything, intent on saving his ass. She was a hell of a woman and he'd deceived her, used her, enjoyed her. The last of the blood came off. Loved her. She deserved better.

"Ah, Evie, I've been a very stubborn man, but I'll do right by you."

Still dazed, she stared at him uncomprehendingly. Brad stopped wiping and started kissing, reaching for her in the most elemental way he could. Still needing to pretend a little longer. Evie's lips stirred under his, opened, invited. Her other hand came around his neck. The revolver bumped the back of his head. Through the whole tumble, she hadn't let it go. He removed it from her hand. She blinked, glanced at him, then at the gun, and then back at him.

"I didn't even get off a shot."

Well, hell. Neither had he.

Twenty-two

"THE MAN HAS the devil's own luck," Doc said, snapping his medical satchel closed. "All he got was creased."

"What does that mean?" Evie asked, gripping her arms in a desperate hold. Ever since they had gotten back to the house the reality of the situation had been sinking in. She had almost died. Brad had almost died. All because of a past she couldn't reconcile with the man she now knew.

Doc gave her a grin. "Well, if you were worried you were going to have to hold back celebrating that you're alive tonight? Don't. He's healthy enough for relations."

She couldn't find a smile to give back to him. When he left, she was going to have to deal with all that had been revealed today, and she wasn't sure how to do that. Or even if she could. "Thank you."

He made it to the front door before he stopped, his hand on the knob. He didn't look back as he said, "It's not so important, Evie, what a man's been, so much as what it is he's become."

"And what has Brad become?"

Letting go of the knob he turned to face her, his bushy brows snapping down over his eyes. "A damn decent human being."

Was he? How could *she* know that? She didn't even know his real name. But Doc had. And he'd kept it from her. "How long have you known who Brad was?"

"From the beginning."

That hurt. "Why didn't you tell me?"

His expression softened. "For multiple reasons. The first being that Brad's reputation as an outlaw was as much for the good deeds he did as the bad."

That was true. Along with being legendary for pulling off the most impossible robberies, Shadow Svensen had been seen by many as a Robin Hood of hope, often distributing money to those who needed it, interrupting robberies, stopping rapes, beatings.

"What he didn't have the reputation for, was untoward violence," Doc continued.

That was true also. But it wasn't enough. She needed more. She needed to know why everyone had believed in Brad to the point they had been willing to fool her. "What was another reason?"

He glared at her as if those he'd given her should be enough. It wasn't. Her world could be ending. She needed to know the details of the destruction.

"For the same reason I didn't tell your folks you were following him around like he was your private party."

"And why was that?"

"Sometimes people who are lost need time to find themselves."

"And Brad was lost?" She wanted to believe he'd been lost. It was so much better than believing he'd used her, and she'd been fool enough to allow it.

"Not wholly. He knew what he wanted. He'd just been taught it wasn't for him."

"Because of his father?"

"You know about his father?"

"Some."

"Now is not the time to clam up."

"It's not my business to tell."

"You kept it from me. You owe me. I want to know."

Doc settled his hat on his head and headed for the door, and for an instant she thought she'd lost, then he paused.

Turn around. Talk to me.

As if he heard, he stopped just before the door. His right hand clenched in a fist. "I met the Elder Swanson once, and Brad, too, though he doesn't remember."

"You did?"

"About twenty years ago."

Brad would have been about ten. "And?"

Doc shook his head. "And if you'd seen him then, you'd wonder how the boy survived to be the man he is today."

"I know his father was harsh."

Doc snorted and his mouth thinned to a flat line. "It's not my place to reveal what the Rev likely wants forgotten, but the only time I ever came close to shooting a man in cold blood was in Elder Swanson's church." His gaze grew distant, sad, and then he shook his head. "To this day it's my biggest regret that I didn't. No one should have to grow up like that, be treated like that."

She licked her lips and gathered her courage. She couldn't hide from this anymore. If Brad had lived it, she could hear it. "He had a dream after he was sick. His father used to beat him."

"Every Sunday like clockwork."

"In front of the congregation?"

Doc nodded.

The part of her that had been hoping delirium had exaggerated his suffering withered and died. "Why? What did he do?"

"Not a damn thing except be born."

"I don't understand . . ."

"Hell, it doesn't make sense. The man was loco, but in his craziness he was convinced the devil lived in Brad. And he made war on that devil."

As a child, Brad would have been helpless against a grown man's attack. "Dear God."

No wonder he fought so hard for the weak. He knew what it was to be powerless.

"That's why he cares so much. Takes so many risks."

"I guess if someone spends enough time telling you you're nothing, somewhere along the line you begin to believe it." Doc sighed.

"He's not nothing."

With a grunt, Doc jerked his chin toward the second floor. "Remember that when you go up there."

"Why?"

"Because your husband is the overly responsible type."

"Meaning?"

"Meaning his first instinct is always to protect you."

And what happened today wasn't going to sit well with that. She hadn't thought of that. "Thank you."

Doc dropped his hand from the knob. His fingers clenched in a fist. Opened. Blowing out a breath, he turned and met her gaze. He had old eyes, wise eyes. The kind that made everyone who met him trust him. Usually they held the light of humor. Right now, they were deadly serious. "Don't take this wrong, Evie, but if you decide to go up those stairs, do it for the right reasons or don't do it at all."

"And what would they be?"

"Because you're playing for keeps."

The door closed softly behind him, leaving Evie alone with her thoughts and two options—stay or leave.

Rubbing her hands up and down her arms, she shied away from the latter. Leaving wasn't an option. She didn't know if she should stay, or even could stay, but she was absolutely sure she couldn't leave. Not now. No with things like this. Not without seeing him.

She remembered how Brad had stepped between her and the bullets, thrown her down, and covered her. The sickening impact as the bullet had hit his flesh, and how he'd refused to move, just laid his big body over hers in the ultimate sacrifice.

He was always making sacrifices. All too willing to trade his life for others.

I guess if someone spends enough time telling you you're nothing, somewhere along the line you begin to believe it.

That had to stop. He was her husband, her source of laughter, her strength, and her support. The man she loved and trusted. He was this town's uniting force. The man everyone looked to for guidance, laughter, solace. They didn't need him sacrificing himself. They needed him around to do what he did so well.

Climbing the stairs, she heard the sounds of drawers opening and closing. There would only be one reason for that. Brad was packing. It was ten steps from the top of the stairs to her bedroom. By the time she got there, Brad was shrugging into his shirt. A black satchel sat on the floor at his feet. The bandages on his abdomen were stark white against the tan of his skin. Looking at him now like this, she couldn't understand how she'd ever believed he was merely a preacher. Everything about him spoke of an active, violent life. Just like everything about him spoke of integrity, strength, and reliability.

Sometimes people who are lost need time to find themselves.

Brad had never given her anything but time and patience. And room to grow, she realized as he flicked his collar straight.

He caught her staring. His expression closed up tight. "I'll be out of here by sundown."

She folded her arms across her chest and leaned against the doorjamb the way she'd seen him do so many times. "If I can't cut and run, neither can you."

He shot his cuffs and then paused as what she'd said sank in. With deliberate nonchalance that didn't fool her for an instant, he buttoned the right cuff. "What do you mean?"

"We're married. Until death do us part, remember?"

"You can't want to stay married. I'm a goddamn outlaw."

"Shadow Svensen is dead." And he was, she realized. Brad might have come here to hide, but somewhere along the line, he'd become what he'd pretended to be. A minister to the people.

"Only until such time as somebody decides he's not."

"Who's going to tell? All of Casey's people are dead, and unless you know something I don't, they didn't tell anybody who you were."

Brad fastened the button on the other cuff with the same care. "You could."

"You don't think much of me if you think I'll fall for a dare like that."

"It would be the easiest way out of our dilemma. An annulment would be simple. Within a year you could be on your way to Paris."

"Or I could just stay here."

"What's for you here?"

He stood there, his hair falling over his forehead in that sexy way, half naked, wearing bandages over wounds he'd received while saving her life, daring her to betray him. Taking a step into the room, she smiled. "You."

"Hell." He fastened the cuff. "Walk out on the street and grab the first man you see, and you'd be doing better."

"Would you like that, Brad. Me with another, taking his kiss, his touch, his c—"

He yanked her toward him with a viselike grip on her wrist. "Hell no, I don't want that. I want to kill any man who gets near you, but what I want isn't important."

"I disagree."

His teeth snapped together. "I lied to you."

She stood very still in his grip. Some things she did need to know. "Is your real name Brad Swanson?"

"Yes."

"Are you a preacher?"

"Yes, but—"

She didn't let him finish, needed to make her points before his conscience got its chance to make his. "Then it doesn't matter."

"The hell it doesn't." Grabbing her chin, he tipped her face to his. "You can do better."

"Nobody else sees me the way you do."

"They would, if you let them."

She wrapped her fingers around his wrist, the rightness of holding him, of being held by him flowing through her. "What if I won't let them?"

"Don't be a fool."

She smiled. "I think this is where we started."

And it was. They'd come full circle, back to the point of decisions regarding their marriage, but this time there were no secrets, no fears, no one standing at the altar with a shotgun. It was just Brad and her and what they wanted. And he wanted her. She could see it in every line of his body. He just had to reach out and take it.

"A smart woman would walk away."

"Where would the fun be in that?"

His fingers left her chin, skimmed down her neck, skated inward from her shoulder to curve around her nape. "It would be safer."

He was weakening. Closing her eyes, wallowing in the knowledge that she had a second chance, Evie leaned into his hand. "I don't need safe, Brad. I don't even particularly like it."

"I can't guarantee you that what happened here today won't happen again, baby."

The way he said *baby* about broke her heart. He said it with the slow catch in the syllables of one letting go of a dream. He wasn't losing any more dreams. Not if she had anything to say about it. And she intended to have a lot of say in his future.

Opening her eyes, she declared, "We'll start over."

"I'm an outlaw."

The truth lay between them, delivered with uncompromising bluntness. The reality he didn't think she could get around. "You were a preacher first."

"I took the vows to escape a beating."

She rolled her eyes. He had all his walls up, braced for the reality he'd always dreaded. "But you took them." And knowing what she knew about his personality, he'd meant them.

He backed away. "And promptly broke every one."

To whom did he think he was talking? He'd stood for her, for Erica, for Gray, for Jenna. While bleeding to death he'd thought of Cougar first; when his position in the community had been shaken, he'd still taken on Bull and laid down an ultimatum that challenged everyone to do right. Brad had protected this town and its inhabitants in a hundred different ways while guiding them. He was a preacher to his core, the kind too rarely found. It was time he accepted that. "You were a lousy outlaw, Brad."

His chin jerked up. "The hell I was."

She waved away his indignation. "Outlaws are selfish, deadly men who prey on the weak. You spent your entire nefarious carer supporting those in need."

That earned her a glare. "I stole."

"And feel free to ask forgiveness for that."

"I killed."

"Only in self-defense."

"I'm not some fucking saint."

No, he wasn't. She took a step closer, watching his eyes. "Cattle Crossing would eat a saint alive."

His jaw set. "The town won't want an ex-outlaw for their preacher."

"Your past is none of their business."

He blinked. "What the hell are you doing, Evie?"

Another step. "You have a lot of courage, Brad. You have done a lot of things. I'm only asking you to do one more."

His lids flickered. He knew it was a trap. She took strength from the fact he responded anyway. "What?"

"I need you to love me."

"Loving you is not the problem."

Closing the distance between them again, stepping in until her skirts wrapped around his legs and her breasts flattened into his chest, she placed her hand over his heart, feeling its steady beat, holding his gaze, aching for the pain she could see deepening his eyes. So many years of believing the worst of himself. "Then what is?"

Beneath her palm she felt the leap of Brad's heart that was

hope. His hand covered hers, his fingers tucking beneath. "Keeping you safe. The things I love tend to get hurt."

If she could go back in time, Evie would shoot his father. Maybe not dead. Not at first, but she'd start low, likely with his foot and work her way up until she got his attention. "Bullshit."

His smile was gentle. Sad. Final.

"You'll meet someone else. Someone better suited. And when you do, you'll be glad I didn't take you up on your offer."

She was getting sick of this.

Grabbing his shirt front, Evie tried to shake him. It was like trying to shake a tree. Damn, he was stubborn. "I won't give you a divorce."

"You won't have a choice."

Planting her feet, she met the steel in his gaze with every bit of conviction inside. "You have no idea how much choice I can create when I set my mind to it."

His expression grew harder if possible. "No amount of stubborn's going to change my mind about this. What happened today could happen again. Next week, next month, next year." Letting go of her hand, he grazed the back of his fingers down her cheek. "I couldn't live with anything happening to you because of me."

Evie pushed the growing softness away. Brad was very good at playing emotions to get his way. But not this time. This time he wasn't doing the right thing for them, and she wasn't going to allow it. However much time they had, no matter how it ended, she wanted him. "Then just imagine how harrowing it's going to be with me tailing behind you all over the country."

"You wouldn't."

She could tell from the way the words trailed off that he knew she would.

"Without breaking a sweat." She folded her arms across her chest. "I might even consider it an adventure."

"Hell, Evie . . ."

He didn't know the half of it. Hell would be a picnic if he put her through chasing him down. "If you run, I'll follow you. Make no mistake about it."

"I'm an outlaw. I've got a past."

"You've also got a future. People come West to start over every day. There's no reason you can't be one of them."

"It's not the same. I'm Shadow Svensen."

He was using that as a shield. This time when she took a step forward, he didn't step back, but he also didn't reach out, didn't take her hand, didn't smile. Didn't do one of a hundred things he could have done to let her know she was welcome. "I have it on very good authority that Shadow Svensen is dead."

"Which would be good if you could count on him staying buried."

He was determined to make this as difficult as possible. Slipping her hand under his shirt she opened her palm over his chest, feeling the strength, the warmth, the beat of his heart.

Without opening her eyes, she said, "Tell me something."

"What?" There was nothing in that curt syllable to feed her belief and everything to sustain her doubt. The query caught. She cleared her throat.

"Besides being Shadow Svensen, do you have any more skeletons in your closet? A child you haven't claimed? A wife you left behind?"

"No."

Feeling like she was running in the dark with obstacles all around, she played her hand. "So the only thing standing between you and me is . . . you?"

Beneath her palm, she felt that leap of his heart again. She was afraid to read too much into it. Afraid to read too little.

His hand closed over hers, but he didn't immediately break the contact, and against her stomach she felt the hardness of his erection. A thing like that could give a woman ideas. After all, how often had he used the passion between them to influence her?

"There's a hell of a lot more than that."

She decided that he could tell her in bed.

Taking his hand, the calluses abrading her palm, reminding her how good that roughness felt against her skin, she backed toward the bed, tugging him along. She got to be in charge for three steps before he pulled her up against him, anchoring her with a hand at the small of her back.

"What are you doing?"

Reaching up, making sure to arch her back so he could enjoy the thrust of her breasts, she started pulling the pins from her hair. "You're not much of a teacher if you don't recognize when you're being seduced."

His grip loosened. She danced back the remaining four steps. Scared, exilherated, sick to her stomach with the possibility of rejection, she challenged him, tempted him, lured him into taking the last two steps to the bed before falling backward. He caught her with those lightning reflexes, holding her by the hands, keeping her arched and suspended just above the mattress. Her bun unraveled under the weight of gravity. She shook her head and let her hair tumble around her the way he liked.

He tugged her up just a bit and his gaze met hers. Beneath the cold facade she could see the fear of a boy who'd been taught nothing good was ever meant for him. "Be sure, Evie."

She didn't flinch. "I love you, Brad Swanson, probably since the first moment I laid eyes on you. I've never been more sure of anything in my life. How you feel about me is what seems to be in doubt."

He let her go. There was a momentary sensation of tumbling before the mattress cushioned her fall. Brad followed her down. Catching his weight on his forearms, he lowered his forehead to hers. "You know damn well I love you."

"Actually, I don't."

When he looked at her as if she'd lost her mind, she shrugged. "It shouldn't shock you that I've never considered myself particularly lovable."

"That's because you're a nut."

"But you love me anyway."

With every damn breath in his body, and it was never going to stop, Brad knew. And it scared him. Because it was good. Gently, carefully, she slid her hands around his neck and stroked lightly, holding him to her. "Want proof?"

She cuddled her hips to his in blatant invitation. "Yes."

The laughter caught him by surprise, though it shouldn't have. He had in his hands the one miracle of his life—the only woman he could ever love. He might never get over the miracle of her loving him back. Not the man he showed the world, but the man behind the mask. Not only that, she loved him enough to give him a second chance. From here on out, every morning was going to start with a prayer of thanks. For bringing him here, for sparing her life. He kissed her temple, relishing the pulse that beat against his lips before moving on to gently kiss the bruise on her jaw. "Fair warning, it's going to take me a hell of a long time to forget the sight of you running headlong into a hail of bullets."

"If you hadn't been standing in the open like a sitting duck, I wouldn't have had to come rescue you."

She called that a rescue? "I was the distraction, so Elijah and Jackson could pick off the men holding you and Nidia hostage."

"What would've happened if they'd missed?"

"They never miss."

"It was still a terrible risk you took."

"It was a calculated one."

She slapped his shoulder and said, "Well, don't do it again."

"Then stay where I put you."

She huffed, and that tantalizing mouth of hers drew up in a pout. He could easily imagine her lips moving over his torso and lower in soft presses of flame while he unbuttoned her blouse and exposed her equally tantalizing breasts.

"Then you'll need to make it worth my while."

The challenge caught on the edge of his desire, taunting it. "I'll work on it. Anything else?"

As if reading his thoughts, her attention turned to the first button. It slipped free of its slot.

"Actually there is." The second button put up no more fight than the first. "I need you to tell me you want me."

Before he could tell her she was crazy, she placed her palm over his mouth. "Not physically, but the forever kind. The kind that means you'd marry me again, not because you had to, but because you wanted to."

The whole length of the speech, her other hand was busy working those buttons free of their holes, revealing intriguing bits of lace and then a hint of cleavage. Heaven.

"There is no penalty if you don't want that," she continued, her speech picking up speed. "I'll never tell anyone who you are, so you can walk way with no consequences."

Just leave the other half of his soul behind. Cupping his hand around hers, Brad pressed her palm into his kiss. "I don't want to walk away."

She blinked. A tear rolled down her cheek. He caught it on his fingertip, interrupting its journey. How could she doubt how much he wanted her? If he could, he'd bind her to his side so she'd never be out of his sight, always be under his protection, always be safe.

Parting the lapels of her shirt with one finger, he traced the edge of her camisole. "I love you, baby. More than I could ever convey."

"Good, because I do have a couple more terms."

He watched the flush color her torso.

"Name them."

"I don't want to live here. I realize we might not be able to afford to live elsewhere for a while, but I need to know we'll have a home of our own that suits us."

He already had that covered. He'd started arrangements the day after Evie had said how much she hated the house. "Agreed."

She eyed him suspiciously. "You agreed to that awfully quick."

Since she seemed to have forgotten about the buttons, he took over for her. "I'm inspired. Next."

"You can't leave me at night without telling me where you're going, no matter how pretty you think I am when I'm sleeping."

He smiled. "Done."

"You have to keep your promise to help those weaker. Especially women like Nidia."

He spread her shirt off her shoulders, revealing the pink of her corset and the white of her camisole beneath. Pink and white were fast becoming his favorite colors. "Nidia won't take help, even if you offer it to her."

Evie ducked his gaze.

He sighed and pulled the ribbon free of the camisole, sliding it across Evie's chest, smiling at the rise of her blush. "What?"

"I kind of made her promise."

"What kind of promise?"

"She saved my life in that alley. In return I told her at any time she could come to you and me and ask for anything and it would be granted."

He didn't have a problem with that. Evie was his world. Nidia could have anything she wanted whenever she wanted it. "Done."

The ribbon spilled down her chest and over her nipple. Even though there was no way she could feel the contact through her camisole, Evie shivered and her nipple puckered. His cock jerked with the same enthusiasm. She had very pretty breasts, sensitive, perfect for loving. "What else?"

"I want to live in Cattle Crossing."

Now that was a surprise. He looked up. "I was thinking of taking you to Paris."

She was shaking her head before he finished. "Maybe for a vacation, but this is home. I want our children to live here. *I* want to live here."

It was his home, too. At first *home* had been a hard concept to wrap his mind around, but he was rather attached to it now. "Done."

"Which brings me to the next thing. And this is a big one." Her flush deepened. "I don't want you to . . . keep yourself from me anymore."

He had to think on her meaning and when he did, his balls pulled up tight. "You want me to come in you?"

Her breath caught, and she licked her lips. For a second, her gaze became unfocused, as if she were imagining it. "Is it really bad of me to say . . . a lot?"

After this, she'd be lucky if he didn't keep her constantly full. Skimming his fingertips up her side, he smiled ruefully. "Not from where I'm sitting."

She turned her breast into his palm, teasing him the way she always did with that smile and bold spirit of adventure. "Good."

He flicked her nipple with his thumb, taking advantage of her subsequent arch to slide his hand beneath her shoulder blades and pull her up into his kiss. "Anything else?"

"No."

He kissed the corner of her mouth, nibbled the bow of her upper lip. "Then open your mouth, Evie darling. Take me, my kiss, my promise, my love."

Tears dripped down her cheeks, but Brad wasn't worried. Those were what Jenna called happy tears.

"For how long?" she breathed, pulling him closer.

The petal-soft silk of her sheath closed around him, accepting him, welcoming him, inviting him deeper. Into her body, into her love, into her life. This was his woman, the gift he never thought would be his. The woman that understood him, fit him, was perfect for him. The woman who could have anyone she wanted, but who'd chosen him. He could never be close enough. "Forever, Evie. I'll love you forever."

Epilogue

THREE MONTHS LATER, Evie stood on the porch of her new home waiting for Brad to come in from settling the horses. They'd bought Elijah and Amy's old place with Elijah's blessing. Though Elijah had said to burn the belongings, Evie had packed them away. All except the hope for the future. Evie liked to think that stayed. Their old house was now a home for women in need. Ruth had moved in, helping the women settle, giving them a motherly figure to look up to and stories about her grand love to give them hope. She seemed to enjoy the job.

Dorothy, Pearl, and Millicent taught the women skills they'd need to survive—cooking, sewing, nursing. Elijah provided protection. Which was a good thing, because a lot of men refused to believe they weren't welcome to come sneaking around the back door.

The barn door swung open and Brad stepped out, dressed in his usual black. She waved. He smiled and nodded. He smiled a lot more lately. Genuine smiles. The only issue left over from his childhood was Brad's worry about what kind of father he'd be. Evie shook her head. He would be wonderful, but that was something Brad was going to have to prove to himself, and she could let him. Just like he'd let her prove to herself that she was lovable.

A wind kicked up. She pulled her wrap about her, warding off the chill of fall. She'd finally talked to her mother about her father. It hadn't been a comfortable conversation, and in the end, the explanation for her father's withdrawal was so simple. Thanks to a rough spot in their marriage during which her father had worried her mother had been unfaithful, he'd started doubting everything, including whether Evie was his. Unfortunately, since he couldn't look at her and not think that she might not be his, he'd just stopped looking at her. Pearl was convinced he would've come around if he had had the time. Evie wanted to believe that, too, so she was trying. Sometimes the way to make things happen was just to believe that they would.

"I waited for you."

Brad climbed the porch steps, his gaze shadowed by the brim of his hat. As he scooped her up in his arms, she plucked the hat off his head. She wanted to see the love in his eyes.

"So you did."

She looped her arms around his neck. "What do I get for my reward?"

He stepped over the threshold into the house. "Me."

"Perfect." Pulling herself up, she kissed his chin. "I've got something for you, too."

"What is it?"

"Carry me to the bedroom and see."

His hair fell over his forehead and he smiled that rakish smile. "I can already tell I'm going to like this present."

Yes, he was. When he put her down just inside the bedroom, she pointed to the floor. "Stay right there."

Reaching around behind the door, she pulled out a sheet-draped painting. "Open it."

He did, with the efficiency that marked everything he did. He stared at the painting of himself naked, rendered just as precisely as before but with one . . . *big* difference. When another few seconds passed and he didn't speak, she wondered if she'd gone too far.

And then he laughed—a real laugh. The kind he was indulging in more and more often. He hooked his arm around her shoulder, pulling her into his side. "I don't even want to know where you got that idea."

"The barn can be a wonderful source of inspiration."

"The hell you say. Now I've got to wonder about the competition."

"You could do that or . . ." Stepping away, she unbuttoned her dress and let it fall to the floor. She was only wearing a sheer camisole and stockings beneath. She climbed into the middle of the big bed while he watched her with an intensity that stroked over her nerves with the tease of a touch. "Or you could make me forget all about it."

His boots came off, first the right and then the left. "Did you forget your mother's coming over, expecting stew and biscuits in a couple of hours?"

She leaned back on the bed, drawing her leg up while easing her camisole strap down. "Then I guess you'll have to be quick as well as thorough."

Buttons flew as he ripped his shirt off, exposing all that delicious muscle she loved to feel moving against her. "Is that a dare?"

"Absolutely."

THEY WERE COMING.

Sarah Anne stared down the hillside, her night vision casting the trees and rocks in contrasting black and white touched with glimmers of silver. Through the shifting mist, she watched bits of deeper darkness weave through the natural shadows. Wolves. Their hiding place had been discovered. There was nowhere left to run. She and the other women would have to make their stand here. Beside her, her five-year-old son, Josiah, a wolf to the core, snarled. His small canines flashed white in the night. Sarah Anne dropped her hand to his head, desperation pulsing through her like a living nightmare. She had to keep him safe.

Her two-year-old daughter, Meg, as human as her father, was tiny, delicate, ever so vulnerable. She clung to her brother's hand and gave name to the emotion scenting the interior of the cave. "Mommy, I'm scared."

So was Sarah Anne. "There's no need to be afraid. We've prepared."

Three women. Two werewolf, one human. All armed with a few guns, ammo, and a mother's drive to protect. They were going to hold off ten were-soldiers. They didn't have a prayer.

"Are they the McGowans?" Teri asked from behind her.

"No." The promise of help from the Boudine pack had just been another shimmering illusion. Sarah Anne was on her own the way she'd always been, ever since the day it became evident that her tainted genetics had left a mark. She'd come to the human world to avoid persecution. It had found her anyway. And now endangered her children.

Teri spun on her heel. "I'll get the guns."

Sarah Anne exchanged a glance with Rachel. Teri had no

idea what they faced. The guns would delay, but not prevent, the inevitable.

"We should probably tell her."

Sarah Anne shrugged. "She already thinks werewolves are monsters. No sense proving it and removing all doubt. Not when we have to fight."

"She wouldn't be here at all except for her pregnancy."

"She wouldn't be pregnant at all except for them." With a wave of her hand, Sarah Anne encompassed the encroaching scum. She wouldn't call them soldiers. Wolf soldiers didn't rape. Wolf soldiers had honor. Integrity. They protected women. They didn't abuse them.

Behind them a shotgun cocked.

"I told you before what happened isn't your fault." Teri stood with her feet apart, the rifle and a shotgun looking awkward in her small hands. Dark red rows of newly healed scars peeked out from beneath her light green mock turtleneck. Shame flooded Sara Anne anew. Right behind it came guilt.

"They wouldn't have found you if not for me."

"That's ridiculous."

Teri handed the rifle to Sara Anne. Being human, there was no way Teri could understand the sense of unity and responsibility that was part of werewolf culture. What one member of the pack did, all did. What wrong one committed reflected on them all.

"I still feel guilty."

"Well, don't. I wouldn't trade our friendship for the world."

The lie was in her scent. If Teri could, she'd go back in time and erase the friendship that had exposed her to the wolves who'd breathed her scent, recognized her as a potential breeder, and raped her, responding to instinct rather than logic. Half-blood children had no worth. Sarah Anne couldn't blame her any more than she could bring herself to dispute Teri's claim. The woman had just regained her emotional feet. And strangely, the pregnancy had provided the vehicle.

"So what's our plan?" Rachel asked.

"Same as before. Shoot as many as we can."

Teri smiled a cold smile. "That works for me."

Sarah Anne cast Teri a glance. If she was terrified, she was hiding it well. "Remember, shoot for the organs and the brain.

Do as much damage as possible on each individual. Wolves don't go down easily."

Only a catastrophic series of injuries could bypass a werewolf's ability to heal.

Teri smiled. "I'm good with that."

The scars were the tip of the iceberg when it came to the injuries Teri had sustained. Sarah Anne could easily believe she was fine with anything that had to do with taking out a male wolf. The shadows glided closer. Still only ten as far was she could tell. It might as well be one hundred.

"Rachel."

"I know."

She needed to say it anyway. "Don't let them get my son."

Rachel placed her hand on Sarah Anne's arm. Her scent, her energy, all radiating comfort. Sarah Anne didn't know how Rachel held on to hope. "Things aren't going to be that bad."

They already were. "Take Josiah, shift, go out the side entrance, and then run like hell."

Rachel grabbed Josiah's hand. "Maybe I can carry—"

Sarah Anne shook her head. "We already discussed it. You can't carry Meg, and she can't change." Like her mother. "She'll never be able to keep up."

Meg hearing her name, sensing the tension, puckered up and stamped her foot. "I want 'Siah!"

Every instinct in Sarah Anne echoed Meg's cry. She wanted to keep her son with her, within reach, where she would have a hand in his fate. Sarah Anne pulled Meg against her thigh, rubbing her hands up and down her daughter's tiny ribs. How was she supposed to make this choice? She stared at the figures getting closer, the wind carrying the taint of their scent, and she knew. She just did. "Josiah's going with Aunt Rachel."

"No."

She met Josiah's stare. Someday he'd be an Alpha, maybe a Protector, but right now he was a baby and staring down his mother was beyond his capacity. But not by much. "You go with Rachel, Josiah. You do everything she tells you and you make your father proud."

His little feet planted shoulder width apart. A snarl rumbled in his chest as his nostrils flared, scenting the warning of danger riding the wind. "I'm not leaving you."

Sarah Anne blinked at the flash-forward to the man he'd someday be. His father would have been so proud. Smoothing her hand over his rich, chocolate-colored hair, she blinked again, this time in an effort to hold back the tears. "You have to go. Rachel needs protection, too, and I don't have anyone else to send with her."

His chin set. "She can stay here."

He also had his mother's stubbornness. "No, she can't. She has to take an important message to Pack Boudine."

"I do need you, Josiah," Rachel interjected.

His chin trembled. He suddenly became her little boy again. Her little boy who was trying so hard not to be scared as she asked the impossible of him. Meg hugged her leg and looked up, blue eyes big with the belief that her mother could work miracles. "Please, Mommy?"

Sarah Anne heard the faint swish of brush against clothing as the soldiers approached. They were out of time. She grabbed Josiah, bending to hold her son and daughter close in her arms one last time—her life, her future—breathing in their familiar scents, playing over in her mind every good memory she could find, bonding them together in that moment, just in case there wasn't another. "Remember who you are, Josiah."

He nodded against her leg, the tear he wouldn't let her see seeping through the thin denim of her jeans. "I'm Protector."

"And Stone. Don't ever forget that or think it's not a valuable part of you."

Another nod.

"We have to leave, Sarah Anne," Rachel interjected quietly.

With one last squeeze she let Josiah go. "Be careful"

Rachel put her hands protectively on Josiah's shoulder as she met Sarah Anne's gaze, a small, strained smile on her face. "I'm the careful one, remember?"

Sarah Anne did remember, along with many other things.

Teri looked out the entrance. "It's now or never, guys."

A bolt of pure fear stabbed through Sarah Anne. Josiah's escape out the side entrance had to be perfectly time so he wouldn't be seen or scented, and even with perfect timing they only had a scant chance of success. Sarah Anne felt so empty without the sturdy body of her son. She wrapped her arms around Meg, the weight of impossibility straining her voice, as she lifted her daughter up. "Run very fast, Josiah."

He nodded, looking like a little boy again as he asked, "And you'll meet us at the south ridge come morning?"

Nothing short of death would keep her away. "That's the plan."

It was enough for him. She caught Rachel's hand as she turned away, tugging her around. She had to say it. "Thank you."

The words were so paltry compared to the emotion backing them. If they got out of this alive, Rachel could ask anything of Sarah Anne that she wanted and Sarah Anne would grant it.

Rachel inclined her head. "Anything for the Alpha female."

"I'm not Pack." Even after seven years, it still hurt to say that.

Rachel, grimaced. Teri looked at them both and shook her head. "If Pack means family, then I think we're it." She hefted the shotgun. "Now, if nobody objects, I've got some damage to do."

"You can't fault them for courage," Garrett murmured as a woman and a boy slipped out the side entrance of the cave, shifted, and then started to run perpendicular to the hillside, blending into the night, the female shielding the cub. The gunfire from the interior picked up in a rapid spate, no doubt in a hope to keep the main group pinned down.

Beside him, Cur snarled as two bigger shadows slid into the night behind the woman an child, "Can't fault them for a damn thing, but I've got a hell of a bone to pick with those SOBs hunting them." He touched his hand to the transceiver attached to his ear.

"Daire, you've got two friendlies in fur heading your way."

Daire's distinctive gravely voice rumbled over the connection that linked all five Protectors on this mission. "I've got them."

"They've got company following."

Daire's satisfied growl proceeded his, "Good."

"Nice to know his reputation isn't inflated," Cur grunted over Garret's private frequency, swinging wide to cut off two soldiers heading up toward the side entrance.

Garret supposed it was. He moved to the left, flanking the two soldiers who comprised his targets. The scum didn't know it yet but they were surrounded. He switched to Cur's frequency.

"I'm just glad he's on our side," Daire was a big son of a bitch, even for a were, and he wore the violence of his history in the scars on his body. It took a hell of a lot to scar a were.

"Thought when he went freelance he went rogue?"

"I'm not sure he hasn't."

He wasn't sure of anything when it came to this new Pack, least of all Daire's reasons for joining this mission. His and Cur's motivations were easy to see. Neither had chosen to become part of the packless lost, and when the McGowans had approached them in the bar they ran and offered them Pack status, they hadn't hesitated. The McGowans were legend. Fierce fighters. Old school Protectors that put pack and honor first. It would have been an honor for any Protector to be asked to join forces with the McGowans. For outlawed rogues like he and Cur, it was a prize without equal.

Below, there was movement. Garret sighted his rifle on one of the soldiers closing in on Kelon McGowan, just in case. He switched his transceiver back to all frequencies. "You've got trouble on your tail, Kelon."

Through the sight, he could clearly see the smile flash across Kelon's face. "Thanks."

The enemy leapt straight for Kelon's seemingly unprotected back. The rogue might be a soldier but Kelon was a Protector and that much faster, that much stronger, and that much more pissed. He spun and caught the wolf mid leap, evaded the swipe of the soldiers claws through the simple expedience of breaking his arm, and then in the spit second while the man hung helpless, gutted him with lethal efficiency. Justice delivered with a graceful simplicity Garrett admired. And when the call came, he'd do the same to the two men marked as his. These men hunted the women and children of his new Pack. They would not survive the night.

The sense of rightness strengthened as Garrett slid the rifle into the scabbard on his back and moved forward, ears tuned for the call to battle, adrenaline pumping through his body in a familiar rush, enhancing the drive of muscle, the acuteness of his senses, as for the first time he entered battle not to defend himself, or an ideal, but in defense of his Pack. Satisfaction and pride blended with cold calculation as he crouched and waited, his marks in sight, one moving up the slide of rock to the cave entrance, the other tucked behind a tree ten feet away, gun aimed at the cave mouth. Garret smiled, claws extending. He'd never get that shot off.

"Everyone in position?"

Donovan McGowan's question whispered through his earpiece.

Four echoes of "Go" whispered back.

He looked up toward the entrance. His second target had reached it, fanatically dedicated to his mission, clearly confident he could take the women inside. He didn't have much more time.

Gun fire flashed from the mouth of the cave.

A second later the McGowan war cry split the night, reverberating across the valley. Garrett leapt for the sniper, the element of surprise making the kill simple. Too simple for the rage pumping through him. Without hesitating, he picked up the battle cry echoing around him and raced up the hill. A hint of a woman's fear blew down on the wind, catching on some instinctive recognition inside. Pulling it forward, centering his rage, his focus. A baby screamed.

He sent his promise ahead on another howl.

Touch them and die.

SARAH McCARTY has traveled extensively throughout her life, living in other cultures—sometimes in areas where electricity was a concept awaiting fruition and a book was an extreme luxury. While she could easily adjust to the lack of electricity, living without the comfort of a good book was intolerable. To fill the void, she bought pencil and paper, and sketched out her own story. In the process, Sarah discovered the job of writing.

Sarah writes what she loves to read: fast-paced stories with vivid dialogue, intense emotion, and well-developed characters. Her attention to detail in her stories has earned her multiple awards and reserved her novels a spot on keeper shelves everywhere.

For more information on Sarah and her books,
visit www.sarahmccarty.net